Debbie Macomber is a #1 *New York Times* bestselling author and a leading voice in women's fiction worldwide. Her work has appeared on every major bestseller list, with more than 170 million copies in print, and she is a multiple award winner. The Hallmark Channel based a television series on Debbie's popular Cedar Cove books. For more information, visit her website, www.debbiemacomber.com.

After thirty-five years as a nurse, **Patricia Davids** hung up her stethoscope to become a full-time writer. She enjoys spending her free time visiting her grandchildren, doing some long-overdue yard work and traveling to research her story locations. She resides in Wichita, Kansas. Patricia always enjoys hearing from her readers. You can visit her online at patriciadavids.com.

#1 *New York Times* Bestselling Author

DEBBIE MACOMBER

ANY SUNDAY

HARLEQUIN
BESTSELLING
AUTHOR
COLLECTION

**HARLEQUIN®
BESTSELLING
AUTHOR
COLLECTION**

Recycling programs
for this product may
not exist in your area.

ISBN-13: 978-1-335-40629-3

Any Sunday
First published in 1988. This edition published in 2022.
Copyright © 1988 by Debbie Macomber

A Home for Hannah
First published in 2012. This edition published in 2022.
Copyright © 2012 by Patricia MacDonald

For questions and comments about the quality of this book, please contact us at CustomerService@Harlequin.com.

Harlequin Enterprises ULC
22 Adelaide St. West, 41st Floor
Toronto, Ontario M5H 4E3, Canada
www.Harlequin.com

Printed in U.S.A.

CONTENTS

ANY SUNDAY   7
Debbie Macomber

A HOME FOR HANNAH   173
Patricia Davids

Also by Debbie Macomber

MIRA

Blossom Street

The Shop on Blossom Street
A Good Yarn
Susannah's Garden
Back on Blossom Street
Twenty Wishes
Summer on Blossom Street
Hannah's List
"The Twenty-First Wish" (in *The Knitting Diaries*)
A Turn in the Road

Cedar Cove

16 Lighthouse Road
204 Rosewood Lane
311 Pelican Court
44 Cranberry Point
50 Harbor Street
6 Rainier Drive
74 Seaside Avenue
8 Sandpiper Way
92 Pacific Boulevard
1022 Evergreen Place
Christmas in Cedar Cove (*5-B Poppy Lane*
and *A Cedar Cove Christmas*)
1105 Yakima Street
1225 Christmas Tree Lane

Visit her Author Profile page on Harlequin.com,
or debbiemacomber.com, for more titles.

ANY SUNDAY

Debbie Macomber

In memory of Darlene Layman.
My treasured friend through the years.

Chapter 1

Marjorie Majors's deep brown eyes widened as a flash of burning pain shot through her side. Feeling hot and flushed again, she guessed she was running a fever. Her smile was decidedly forced as she walked across the showroom floor, weaving her way around the shiny new Mercedes while lightly pressing her hand against her hipbone. She'd thought that if she ignored the throbbing ache, this unexplained malady would vanish on its own. So far her reasoning hadn't worked, though, and the mysterious discomfort had persisted for days.

"Is your side hurting you again?" Lydia Mason, the title and license clerk for Dixon Motors, called from behind the front counter.

"A little." Now that had to be the understatement of the week, Marjorie mused. The shooting pain had been coming and going all day with no real rhyme or reason.

She should have known she wasn't going to be able to fool Lydia. Her friend had a nose for news. Little transpired at Dixon Motors without Lydia knowing about it.

"Honestly, Marjorie, why don't you just see a doctor?"

"I'm fine," she protested. "Besides, I don't have a doctor."

Lydia, who stood barely five feet tall and wore heels that increased her height an additional two inches, moved around the counter. Her mouth was pinched into a tight line of determination. "But you haven't been feeling good all week."

"Has it been that long?"

"Longer, I suspect," Lydia murmured, shaking her head. "Listen, no one is going to think less of you for needing a doctor, for heaven's sake. Just because you're one of only three female salespeople here, that doesn't mean you have to behave like Joan of Arc."

"But it's just a little stomachache."

"What did you have for lunch?"

Marjorie shrugged noncommittally, preferring not to lie. A wry smile lifted the corners of her full mouth as she pretended to survey the parking lot, hoping a prospective buyer would magically appear so she would have an excuse to drop the conversation. She didn't want to admit that with her stomach acting up, she hadn't bothered to eat lunch. And now that she thought about it, breakfast hadn't appealed to her, either.

"You didn't have any lunch, did you?" Lydia challenged.

"I didn't have time since…"

"That's it, Marjorie—that's the final straw. I'm making you an appointment with my gynecologist."

"You're what?"

"You heard me." Lydia didn't wait for an argument. With her manicured fingernails, she flipped the hair that had fallen across her cheek to the back of her shoulder and marched around the counter with the authority of a marine drill sergeant.

"Don't call a gynecologist! That's crazy. I don't need a woman's doctor—an internist maybe…"

Ignoring Marjorie's protest, Lydia pressed the telephone receiver to her ear and turned her back to her friend. "What's crazy," she said, twisting her head around, her eyes sparking with impatience, "is suffering for days because you're afraid to see a doctor."

"I am not afraid! And a gynecologist is the last person I want to see." Marjorie couldn't seem to get it through her friend's thick skull that a queasy stomach was unworthy of all this fuss. From the way Lydia was behaving, Marjorie fully expected her friend to dial 911 to report a minor pain that came and went without warning. She'd lived with it for the last few days—a little longer wasn't going to matter. More than likely it would disappear as quickly and unexpectedly as it had come. Or so she continued to hope.

"Today, if possible." Lydia spoke firmly into the telephone. She placed her hand over the receiver and turned to Marjorie. "Listen, I had a friend once with similar symptoms, and it ended up being female problems and—" She broke off abruptly. "Five o'clock would be fine. Thanks, Mary."

Although Marjorie knew it wouldn't do any good, she tried again. "Lydia…"

The telephone was replaced in its cradle before Lydia turned around. "And something else. Dr. Sam isn't your

run-of-the-mill doctor. He's wonderful! If you need to
see someone else, he'll refer you, so stop looking so
worried."

"But I'm sure this pain is nothing."

"Then checking it out won't be any big deal. Right?"
Marjorie shrugged.

"He has an opening this afternoon at five."

"His name is Dr. Sam?" Now Marjorie had heard
everything. "Will Nurse Jane be there, too?"

"He's really terrific," Lydia announced with a loud
sigh, obviously choosing to ignore Marjorie's sarcasm.
"I think I fell in love with him in the delivery room just
before Jimmy was born. He was so gentle and understanding when I was in labor. He made me feel like I
was the most noble, heroic woman in the world for en-
during the pain of childbirth."

"Hey, I've got a stomachache. I'm not looking to find
Prince Charming."

"But he's handsome, too."

"Does Dr. Sam have a last name?" She wasn't bothered by the thought of seeing a physician, exactly, but
the simple truth was that Marjorie hated relying on
anyone else. She could take care of herself very well,
and relying on another person went against her fiercely
independent nature.

"His name is really Sam Bretton, but everyone calls
him Dr. Sam."

Marjorie rolled her eyes toward the ceiling. "I don't
know if I can trust a man who sounds like he keeps an
office on Sesame Street."

"Wait and see," Lydia claimed, writing out directions
to the medical center on a piece of paper and ripping

it free of the tablet before handing it over to Marjorie. "He's marvelous—trust me."

Marjorie folded the paper in half and stuck it inside her purse. If nothing else, it would be interesting to meet the guy. Lydia wasn't generally free with her praise, yet she hadn't been able to say enough good things about this guy.

"You'll like him, I promise," Lydia added.

Marjorie made a barely perceptible movement of her head, as if to say it made no difference to her how she felt about him. She didn't care what he looked like as long as he could give her something for this blasted pain.

At precisely ten minutes to five, Marjorie pulled into the parking lot of the large medical complex north of Tacoma General Hospital. The ache that had troubled her most of the day had vanished, just as she'd known it would, and she felt better generally. If she'd had a fever earlier, she was convinced it was gone now. Briefly she toyed with the idea of heading back to her apartment and forgetting the whole thing, but that would be irresponsible, and if Marjorie knew anything, it was the meaning of responsibility. Besides, her friend would be furious with her for canceling at the last moment.

Two other women were seated in the waiting room. Both were in the advanced stages of pregnancy. One sat with her hands resting on her protruding belly, looking content, while the other was knitting. The thick needles, encased in a pastel shade of yarn, moved furiously. Their smiles were friendly as Marjorie stepped up to the reception desk to announce her arrival. An older, gray-haired woman asked Marjorie to fill out several forms and handed her a clipboard.

Marjorie took it and located a seat in the corner beside a dying houseplant. The yellowish leaves did little to boost her confidence in this unknown physician.

"Is this the first time you've seen Dr. Sam?" one of the soon-to-be-mothers asked.

Marjorie nodded. "My friend recommended him."

"He's absolutely wonderful."

"And good-looking to boot," the knitter added.

"Real good-looking!"

The two pregnant women eyed each other and shared a smile.

"I suppose all women fall in love with their doctors," the woman with the knitting needles commented, "but I've never known a man who's as caring as Dr. Sam is."

"I'm not pregnant." Marjorie didn't know why she felt it was necessary to tell them that. This physician might do wonders with mothers-to-be, but all Marjorie cared about was his expertise with sharp, persistent pains.

"You don't have to be pregnant," the two were quick to assure her.

"Good." Marjorie completed the information sheets and returned them to the receptionist, then subtly glanced at her watch. She hadn't experienced any real discomfort in hours and was beginning to feel like a phony. Again, the thought of skipping out of the appointment sprang to mind. Sheer stupidity, of course. If nothing else, it would be interesting to stick around and meet this doctor who seemed to be a paragon of virtue. From what Lydia and the two patients in the waiting room had said, Dr. Sam Bretton was a cross between Brad Pitt and Mother Teresa.

"It'll only be a few minutes," the receptionist told her.

"No problem," Marjorie answered softly, wondering if the woman had read her mind.

A few minutes turned out to be fifteen. Marjorie was escorted into a small cubicle by a nurse who was dressed as though she were shooting a scene from a day-time soap opera. Her gray hair was perfectly styled in a bouffant, and even after a full day in the office, not a single strand was out of place.

Marjorie stopped just inside the room, her mind whirling. She'd been in her teens when she'd last seen a physician. Over the years there'd been minor bouts with the flu and a bad cold now and again, but overall she'd been incredibly healthy. There might have been times when she should have seen a physician and hadn't, mainly because she wasn't particularly fond of anyone poking around her body, but usually she could take care of herself just fine.

"Go ahead and have a seat," the nurse instructed, gesturing toward the upholstered examination table.

Reluctantly Marjorie walked into the room and pressed her backside against the oblong examining table, her elbows resting on top of the padded cover. She crossed her ankles as though she posed this way regularly, hoping to give the picture of utter nonchalance. Chagrined, she realized she'd failed miserably.

Thankfully the nurse didn't seem to notice. "What seems to be the problem?"

Marjorie shrugged. "A little pain in my side. I'm sure it's nothing."

"We'll let Dr. Sam decide that." The woman pulled out a digital thermometer and, before Marjorie could protest, stuck it under her tongue. Motioning with her hand, the nurse told Marjorie to sit on the end of the table and skillfully took her blood pressure.

"Go ahead and get undressed," the nurse said afterward. She leaned over and pulled a paper gown from a cupboard. "When you've finished, put this on. The doctor will be with you in a couple of minutes." She left, quietly closing the door.

Marjorie mumbled grumpily to herself as she pulled the paper gown over her head and sighed with disgust when the opening for her arm hung far wider than necessary. Keeping her arms tucked close to her side for fear the gown would reveal the sides of her breasts, she wrapped the tissue sheet around her waist and sat on the end of the paper-lined examination table. The whole idea of introducing herself to a man when she was nude felt ridiculous. All right, so he was a physician, but all that stood between her body and this stranger was a piece of tissue that felt as though a big sneeze would destroy it.

Her bare feet dangled, and she kicked at the air aimlessly. Her brilliant red toenails looked funny, and she absently decided to change the color. Next time she would use a more subdued shade.

Just when she had convinced herself she was wasting her time, a polite knock sounded at the door. The knob twisted, and Marjorie painted a welcoming smile on her lips, doing her best to swallow the panic that unexpectedly gripped her.

Dr. Sam Bretton entered the examination room, reading Marjorie's chart, his wide brow furrowed as he took in the information.

The first thing Marjorie noticed was his stature. Five foot seven in her stocking feet, she'd never considered herself short, but this man dwarfed her. His shoulders were broad and fit his height. His chest was deep. He wore his hair short, and his sideburns were clipped neatly around his ears. A few strands of gray at his temple provided a distinguished, sophisticated touch. He was good-looking-not strikingly handsome, but attractive enough to give credence to Lydia and the other women's claims. His eyes were a deep, dark shade of brown and the gentlest Marjorie had ever seen in a man. For an instant they mesmerized her into speechlessness. A stethoscope hung from his neck and rested against his broad, muscled chest.

"Ms. Majors." Sam smiled at his newest patient. Mary, his receptionist, had come to him earlier and asked about fitting this young woman into his already-tight schedule. A friend of Lydia Mason's, Mary had said, and Sam had agreed because he was fond of Lydia. Later he'd regretted the impulse. His day had started early, and he was tired, but with one look at the wide, frightened eyes of the woman sitting on the examination table he realized he'd made the right decision. Rarely had he seen a more expressive pair of brown eyes. Marjorie Majors was as nervous as a young mother and struggling valiantly to disguise it. Her chin trembled slightly, yet she met his gaze with pride and more mettle than he'd seen in years. She resembled a lost kitten he'd once found in a rainstorm; her wide eyes were round and appealing, and she looked as though she might turn and bolt at any moment.

"Doctor." The return of her voice brought with it the reappearance of her poise and aplomb. Her chin came up with the forced determination not to let him know how nervous she was. She handed him her business card.

"I realized I forgot to put my work number on the form," she said by way of explanation.

He removed the card from her stiff fingers, read it casually and nodded before sticking it inside the folder. "Your chart states that the last time you saw a physician was at age fourteen." He grimaced; whatever was bothering her now must be traumatic for her to seek medical help. In the last ten years he'd seen everything, and now a list of possibilities ran through his mind, most of them unpleasant.

"I had an ear infection." Marjorie pointed to her right ear while her heart beat at double time. She was literally shaking. She couldn't understand why she was reacting this way. Certainly this doctor didn't frighten her. His demeanor inspired confidence, not fear.

"You're experiencing pain in your right side?"

"That's correct," Marjorie said, and her voice wobbled as she jabbered on witlessly. "I don't think it's anything to be concerned about…probably one of those common female problems. No doubt it will go away in a couple of days."

"How long has it been bothering you?"

"A few days…maybe longer," she admitted reluctantly.

His thick brows contracted into a single, dark line. "Fever?"

Marjorie nodded. "But not high. It seems to be worse at night."

"Nausea? Dizziness?"

Again Marjorie answered with a nod.

"How has your back felt?"

"Sore." She wondered how he knew that. "Is that bad?" she asked hurriedly. "I mean, I can suffer with the best of them... In fact, I have a high tolerance for pain, and if you tell me it'll simply go away, I'm sure I can get through it."

"There's no need for you to do any suffering. Go ahead and lie back." He gave her his hand to guide her into a reclining position.

His hand curved around her fingers, and Marjorie's grip was surprisingly tight. What the others had said was true: Dr. Sam did inspire faith. She only wished he would stop looking at her as though she were a pathetic, scared doe caught in a hunter's sights.

"There's no need to be nervous," he said softly. "I promise not to bite."

"It's not your teeth that bother me."

He smiled again and stepped closer to the table to stand at her side. "Are you always such a wit?"

"Only when I'm forced to introduce myself to a strange man when I'm in the nude."

"Does this happen often?" Sam couldn't believe he'd asked her that. He clamped his jaw tightly. As a physician, he had taken an oath to treat all patients equally, but this one struck a chord, and the danger of looking upon her as a warm, desirable woman was strong.

"Meet men when I'm nude? No!"

He laughed outright at that, relieved. "I guessed as much." Carefully he lifted up the tissue sheet at her waist and placed his fingers on her abdomen, suspecting he would find rigidity and tenderness at McBurney's point, halfway between the navel and the crest of the hipbone.

"Actually, I've been feeling better the last couple of hours," Marjorie said hurriedly, hoping to suggest that whatever was wrong was curing itself. His hand felt cool and soothing against her heated flesh, and she closed her eyes. However, the instant he glided his fingers to her side and pressed down, her eyes shot open at the excruciating pain searing through her like red-hot needles.

She swore loudly and jumped from the examination table. "What do you think you're doing?" she shouted, her hands crossed protectively over her stomach. The agony lingered, and she nearly doubled over with the force of it.

"Miss Majors…"

"And what were all those platitudes about not needing to suffer?"

"Miss Majors, if you'd kindly return to the table…"

"Are you crazy? So you can do that again? Forget it, buddy."

"I may be able to forget it," he said solemnly, with a hint of chastisement, "but you won't. The pain isn't going to go away. In fact, it will get worse. Much worse. You should have seen a doctor days ago."

"It's already worse, thanks to you."

"Miss Majors…"

"For heaven's sake, call me Marjorie."

"Marjorie, then. Running out of here like a terrified rabbit isn't going to make everything all right."

So he'd noticed the way she was eyeing the neat pile of her folded clothes. She wouldn't run, because that would be silly and stupid, but she couldn't keep from looking at the door longingly.

"You have an inflamed appendix."

She swallowed past the tightness in her throat. The shooting pain hadn't ebbed; if anything, it had gotten steadily worse from the moment he had touched her tender abdomen. Oh, dear heaven, her appendix. She didn't need a fortune-teller to explain what would happen next. Surgery. The sound of the word was as ominous as that of a trumpet in a funeral march.

"Your temperature is rising, and my guess is that your white cell count is sky-high," he continued. "A blood test will confirm that easily enough."

A weak smile wobbled at the corners of her mouth. "My appendix," she repeated.

Sam nodded. "Go ahead and get dressed. When you've finished, I'll have my nurse draw some blood and escort you into my office. That'll give me a few minutes to make the necessary arrangements. We'll talk, and I'll explain where we go from here."

"Okay." Her voice sounded scratchy and thin, like an ailing frog's.

He eyed her again, his gaze tender and concerned. He regretted having hurt her. The look of suppressed pain in her eyes bothered him more than he'd expected, and he tried to lend her some of his own confidence. "Don't look so worried—everything's going to be fine."

"Everything's going to be fine?" Marjorie echoed, unable to disguise her sarcasm. "Sure it is." The minute he left the room, she snapped her teeth over her bottom lip and bit down unmercifully. Her hand trembled as she brushed a thick strand of hair away from her face, and the room appeared to sway slightly. The last time she'd felt this shaky had been at her parents' funeral.

As if on cue, the nurse reappeared the minute Marjorie had completed dressing and led her into another room, where she drew blood from her arm.

While he waited for Marjorie, Sam contacted Cal Johnson, a surgeon and good friend. His instincts told him the sooner they had her in the hospital, the better. When he explained her symptoms to Cal, his friend concurred and agreed to take the case. His second telephone conversation was with a member of the staff at Tacoma General.

When Marjorie appeared in the doorway of his office, Sam saw her from the corner of his eye. She hesitated, and he motioned for her to come inside and take a seat.

"I don't think we should wait any longer," he said into the receiver. "Good. Good. Yes, I can have her over there in a half hour. I'll assist."

In an effort to keep from looking as though she were listening in on his conversation, Marjorie scanned the walls. Certificates, diplomas and service awards decorated every available spot. His desk was neat and orderly. The sure sign of a twisted mind, she mused darkly. She glanced his way again and sighed. Heavens, she hoped he wasn't discussing her! He must have been. If he felt surgery was necessary, then she would at least like a couple of days to mentally prepare herself. A week would be even better.

Marjorie's soft, expressive eyes pleaded with him, but Sam's gaze just missed meeting hers, and she realized that, although he hadn't mentioned her name, he wasn't likely to be talking about another patient.

"Sorry to keep you waiting," he said, when he'd hung up.

"No problem." She smiled, and her fingers curved around her purse in her lap.

"I was just talking to Tacoma General."

Marjorie pointed her finger over her shoulder. "Did you know that you have a dying houseplant in your waiting room?" she asked in an effort to delay the bad news she knew was coming.

"I wasn't aware of that."

"You want to operate on me, don't you?"

"We don't have a lot of options here, Marjorie. I've contacted a friend of mine. He'll be doing the actual surgery, but I'll be there, as well. Your appendix is at a dangerous stage and could burst at any time."

He said her name in a soft, caressing way that she knew would have made another woman's knees turn to tapioca pudding. Not Marjorie's. Not now. Panic was overwhelming her, dominating her thoughts and actions.

"Where's your family?" he asked in a low, reassuring voice.

"I don't have one."

The memory of the orphaned kitten returned to Sam's mind. Cold. Lost. Frightened. And vulnerable.

At his look of surprise, Marjorie hurried to explain. "No parents, that is… One sister, but she doesn't live in Washington State. Jody's attending the University of Portland."

"What about a boyfriend?"

With effort she held her head high, her chin jutting out proudly. "I've only been in Washington a few months." She was about to add that she didn't have time to date much, not when she had to earn enough money to support herself and keep her sister in school. She managed to stop in the nick of time. This man was almost a complete stranger, yet she had been about to spill her guts to him. He had a strange effect on her, and Marjorie found that oddly intimidating.

"Is there anyone you can call?"

"No." No one she felt she could trouble. She'd made it on her own this far; she could get through the operation and a lot more if necessary. "When do you want to do the surgery?"

"Soon. Cal Johnson will make that decision."

A lump worked its way up her throat. The battle to hold back the fear was nearly overwhelming. Even breathing normally had become a difficult task as she labored to appear unaffected and calm.

"So *you* won't be doing the surgery?" This was a man she could trust. Like the others, she had known that instinctively. Now he was pawning her off on another physician, and the thought was almost as terrifying as the actual operation.

"Do you think you should trust a doctor with a dying houseplant?"

"I...don't know." Marjorie realized he was attempting to help her relax, and she appreciated the effort. He really was a nice man. Lydia and the others were right about that. She envisioned him with other women, offering security and assurance. He'd chosen his profession well.

"The truth is, I may not have a green thumb, but when it comes to surgery you don't have any worries."

"Then why won't you operate on me?"

"The appendix isn't my area of expertise. Dr. Johnson has done countless appendectomies, whereas I've only done a few. I'll assist."

"But I know you." As soon as the words ran over her tongue, Marjorie realized how ridiculous they sounded. They'd met less than a half hour earlier.

"You'll do fine with Dr. Johnson."

"I suppose I will," she said without much confidence.

"I can honestly say that you're the first woman who's jumped off the examination table, ready to swing at me." His smiling eyes studied her.

"Hey, that poke hurt."

"I know, and I apologize," he answered sincerely. "I don't want you to worry about this surgery. I'll be there with you. Cal Johnson's an excellent surgeon, and there shouldn't be any problems, since we've caught this in time."

Marjorie nodded.

"I'm not going to let you down."

"You say that to all your patients, don't you?"

His eyes widened briefly. "No." He opened the top drawer and took out a single sheet of paper. "Here. Let me show you what we're going to do."

Marjorie wasn't sure she wanted to know. He must have read the doubt in her eyes, because he added, "I learned long ago that my patients aren't nearly as nervous if they have an idea of what's going to happen."

She nodded and cocked her head so that she could see the picture he had started drawing.

"As you're probably aware, the appendix is a small pocket, from one to six inches in size." He illustrated it, dexterously moving his pencil across the sheet of paper.

Marjorie understood only a little about what he was telling her, but she nodded as though she had recently graduated from medical school and knew it all.

He talked for several minutes more, explaining where Dr. Johnson would be making the incision and what he would be doing. "Once you're admitted to the hospital, you'll undergo a series of tests, including several X rays."

"X rays? Why?"

"We want to be sure that your lungs aren't congested. No need to borrow trouble."

"I see," Marjorie commented, although she didn't really. Whatever he and the other doctors thought was fine with her.

"You'll only be in the hospital a couple of days, depending on how you feel, and you'll be back to work within three weeks."

"Three weeks," Marjorie echoed. "I can't take off that much time!"

"You don't have any choice."

"Wanna bet?" Defiantly, she slapped the challenge at him. "In case you don't realize it, a car salesperson works solely on commission. If I don't sell cars, I don't eat."

His mouth tightened momentarily. "Let's play that part by ear. No doubt you'll surprise me."

"No doubt," she echoed.

Sam rubbed the pencil between his palms. "How'd you get into car sales?"

Marjorie shrugged. "The usual way, I suppose. I started out working in a computer store four or five years back. We worked on commission, and I did well."

"That figures. So where did you go from there?"

"Boats."

"Do you know a lot about them?"

She crossed her knees, winced in an effort to hide the pain, then grinned sheepishly. Naturally he noticed, but he was kind enough not to comment. "At the time I didn't know a thing, but before long I learned everything there was to know."

"And from there it was a natural progression to cars?"

"More or less. I like selling a top-of-the-line product, so selling Mercedes sedans and sports cars was a natural next step."

He continued working the pencil back and forth across his palms. He didn't normally spend this much time with a patient, but he wanted her to feel comfortable with him. She was alone and scared to death, and it was his job to do what he could to reassure her. Success in health care had a lot to do with attitude, and he wanted Marjorie Majors to feel confident and secure about whatever lay ahead.

"I've always wanted a Mercedes," he said.

Marjorie realized he was doing everything he could to ease her fears and help her relax. It was working; the tense terror that had gripped her only moments before was slipping away.

He placed his hands against the edge of the desk and rolled back his chair. "I'll see you at Tacoma General," he said, his gaze holding hers.

"I wasn't planning to run away."

"I didn't honestly think you were."

The smile that curved his mouth did funny things to

her heart rate, but Marjorie quickly dismissed the effect as having anything to do with attraction. She was grateful, that was all. Grateful—nothing less, nothing more.

Chapter 2

Marjorie felt strange. She lay on her back, staring above her as the dotted white tile loomed closer and closer, then gradually faded back into place. Her eyes narrowed, and she tried to tell herself that the ceiling wasn't actually closing in on her. This phenomenon was the result of the shot the nurse had given her a few minutes earlier to help her relax before they came to roll her into the operating room.

"How are you feeling?" Sam Bretton moved beside her gurney and placed his hand over hers.

Again Marjorie was struck by how gentle his dark eyes were. A man shouldn't possess sensitive eyes like that. In her drugged condition her imagination was running away with her, suggesting thoughts she had no right to think. She stared back at him, then blinked twice, because it seemed as though she could see straight into his heart. It was large and full, and his capacity to care and love seemed boundless.

"Marjorie?"

She pulled her gaze past the I.V. drip to Sam and lightly shook her head in a futile effort to clear her befuddled mind. "You wouldn't believe the treatment I got," she said, trying to disregard the strange effect of the medication.

"You met Cal Johnson?"

She nodded. He wasn't another Sam Bretton, but he would do, especially if Sam felt he was the right man for the job.

"So they put you through the mill?"

His smile dazzled Marjorie, and she reminded herself anew that at the moment her senses couldn't be trusted. "Your call must have done the trick, because there was a whole crew just waiting to get their hands on me the minute I walked in the door."

"You can thank Cal for that."

"Oh sure! If you think I believe that, then there's some swampland in Nevada that might interest me, right?"

"Are you saying you don't trust me?" Sam's eyes widened with feigned outrage. He liked Marjorie. Even now, when she was dopey from the effects of medication, he found her sense of humor stimulating. Her ready smile had wrapped itself around him the moment he'd walked into the room. She was fresh and alive; her mind was active, her wit lively, and her courage in difficult circumstances was admirable.

"I'll have you know that in the last hour I've been poked, pinched, prodded and a bunch of other disgusting things I don't even want to discuss."

His lips trembled with suppressed mirth, and he squeezed her fingers reassuringly. "Is there anything I can get you?"

Marjorie tried to smile, but her mouth refused to cooperate. "That sounds suspiciously like a last request."

The dark eyes that studied her crinkled at the corners as he revealed his amusement. "It wasn't."

"You mean I don't need to ask for a priest?"

"Not this time around. Anything else?"

The inside of her mouth felt thick and dry. "Something to drink. Please."

He reached behind him and took a chip of ice from a water jug. Again the urge to reassure her, to stay with her, was strong. Her hair spilled out across the pillow, and the red highlights suggested that her temper would be as quick as her smile. "This will have to do for now. Suck on it and make it last."

Obediently she opened her mouth, and he slipped the ice chip inside, then paused to wipe a drop of moisture from her chin. It wasn't until then that Marjorie noticed he was dressed entirely in green. A cap covered his head, and a surgical mask hung free around his neck.

"Green surgical gowns?" she asked, holding the ice chip against the back side of her mouth so she could speak clearly. "Is that because red stains are so difficult to remove from white fabric?" She sucked in her breath and closed her eyes. "Don't answer that—I don't want to know."

"Don't let your courage fail you now, Marjorie, you're doing fine."

Her eyes shot open. "It's not you who's going under the knife. I'll be scared if I want, and I don't mind telling you, I'd rather be anyplace else in the world but right here." Shot or no shot, sedative or no sedative, she'd never been more unsure about anything. More than that, she was astonished that she had admitted how afraid she was to Sam. It wasn't like her. That shot must have contained a truth serum.

"Everything's going to work out," he said in that calm, confident voice of his.

Without much effort Marjorie could envision him talking someone out of jumping off the Tacoma Narrows Bridge. He had the kind of voice a salesman would kill for—low-pitched, confident, effortless, sincere.

"Don't worry," she said with feigned composure, seeing herself standing on the edge of the steel precipice, looking into the swirling waters far below. "I'm not going to jump."

He gave her a funny look but made no comment.

"That didn't make any sense, did it?" She tossed her head from side to side in an effort to clear her thoughts. It didn't work. Everything scrambled together until she wasn't sure of anything.

He patted her hand. "Don't worry about it. The medication has that effect."

Marjorie wondered if it actually was the shot. No, she was convinced his silk-edged voice and kind eyes were the cause of all this, mesmerizing her. Her eyes drifted closed, and she moistened her lips as she imagined Sam Bretton leaning over her and whispering words of love in her ear, then taking her in his arms and kissing her with such tenderness, such passion, that her thoughts forcefully collided inside her head. A fireworks display that rivaled a Fourth-of-July celebration exploded, and she forced her eyes open and felt the blood rush through her veins.

"Go ahead and sleep," he said softly. "I'll be here when you wake up."

"Please don't leave me." Her eyes rounded, and her mouth filled with the bitter taste of panic. She needed this man she barely knew more than she'd ever needed anyone. The terror that gripped her as she stared ahead at the wide double doors that led to the operating room was intense and nearly overwhelming.

"I'm not going anywhere," Sam assured her, continuing to hold her hand, his fingers firmly entwined with hers.

Somehow it seemed vitally important that he be there every minute. Still, she hated needing anyone. People had always let her down. She was a stronger person than this, and Dr. Sam Bretton was little more than a stranger. Yet she trusted him enough to place her life in his capable hands.

"Don't worry, I'll be fine," she said, and realized her voice was barely audible. "You...you don't need to stay with me. I'm a big girl. I'll get through this...really... Don't tell Jody, she'll only worry... Must call Lydia."

"That's all taken care of," he said, and his voice seemed to come from a great distance.

"Thank you, Sam," Marjorie mumbled, and started slipping into a light sleep.

A female voice made its way through to her fading consciousness. "Dr. Johnson is ready, doctor."

An invisible force pushed the gurney forward, and Marjorie struggled to open her eyes. Someone lifted her head and placed her hair inside a confining cap.

She managed to open one eye and was greeted by blinding lights. Sam was at her side, and Cal Johnson, who she'd briefly met earlier, stood on the opposite side of the room, examining her X rays. Sam leaned over her and explained that the anesthesiologist would be there any minute. Marjorie nodded, even managed a weak smile, then decided that it was better not to look around. She settled back down and tightly shut her eyes.

Soon other voices met over her head, some deep, others crisp, and a few soft. In her drug-induced drowsiness Marjorie sorted through them and tried to assimilate only Sam's words. The nurses joked and flirted with him like a longtime friend. She sighed with the realization that if his patients fell in love with him, then the women on the hospital staff must be equally vulnerable to his charms. Maybe he was already married. Of course, that was it! Sam Bretton had a wife. Her disappointment was keen. He was married. He had to be. Rats! All the good ones were already taken.

Finally it got too difficult to concentrate, and she gave up trying. When she woke, this troublesome episode would all be over, and she could get on with her life and forget that any of this had ever happened.

Impatiently, Marjorie waded through huge billows of thick, black fog. She shivered with cold and sighed when Sam's familiar voice asked for a heated blanket. She felt the weight of a quilt on top of her, and she sighed contentedly. The fog parted as warmth seeped into her bones, and for the first time she could decipher a path that led through the haze. She tried to speak, but her lips seemed glued together, and no amount of trying could pry them apart.

"Marjorie?"

Getting her eyes to open required an equal amount of effort, but when she managed that task, she was blinded by a flash of high-intensity light. She groaned and lowered her lashes.

"Am I in the morgue?" she mumbled, having difficulty getting the words over her uncooperative tongue.

"Not yet," Sam answered.

"That's reassuring."

"You're in the recovery room. Everything went without a hitch. We're lucky we got the appendix when we did. From the look of things, it was ready to burst, and then there could have been some unpleasant complications."

"Close, but no cigar, huh?"

"In this case you don't want a cigar."

"So I'll live and love again?"

Sam brushed the hair from her temple. "You're good for at least another fifty years."

For some inexplicable reason it seemed easier to concentrate with her eyes closed. Her lids fluttered shut even though she strained to keep them open.

"Go ahead and sleep," Sam told her softly. "I'm here, like I promised."

Marjorie wanted to thank him; she searched for some way to let him know how grateful she was that she hadn't woken up alone. The hospital might seem a warm, congenial place to him, but he was there every day. To her, it was a disinfected torture chamber, and she was scared witless. It seemed so important to tell him that his presence comforted her that she wrestled to keep awake even as she felt herself slipping back into the thick, dark fog.

Pain woke Marjorie up the second time—a dull, throbbing ache in her side, quite different from what she'd experienced before meeting Sam. She raised her hand, rubbed her eyes and yawned. The room wasn't as brilliant as before. The light appeared muted, and she was grateful. She rolled her head and realized she was in a small room. The drapes were closed, but a ribbon of light entered between them. A noise distracted her, and she turned her head in the opposite direction and discovered Sam Bretton sitting at her bedside, reading the latest Scandinavian thriller.

"Sam?"

He closed the book, turned to face her and smiled. "Hello again."

"What time is it?"

He rotated his wrist. "Almost six."

"In the morning?"

He nodded and stood, setting his novel aside. He took her wrist and pressed his fingers over her pulse while he stared at the face of his watch.

"Have you been here all night?" It seemed incredible that he would have stayed with her ever since her surgery. She noticed then that the blood-pressure cuff was wrapped around her upper arm, and fear renewed itself within her. There had been problems! Big problems! She swallowed around the tightness in her throat. All night she'd teetered on the brink of death, and Sam had stayed with her and fought for her very life. For hours her fate had hung by a delicate thread, and this man had valiantly battled to save her.

"What happened?" Her question was hoarse, revealing a hundred doubts.

"Nothing," he answered crisply. "All surgeries should be such a breeze."

"Nothing went wrong?"

He frowned, puzzled. "Nothing."

"But…the blood-pressure cuff… And you stayed with me all night. Why?"

His frown deepened, marring his smooth brow with three nearly straight lines. "Because I said I would. You needed someone."

Guilt fell heavily upon her shoulders. She certainly hadn't meant for him to do this. He must have gone without sleep the entire night, and all because of a few silly words she'd uttered in the throes of panic. "But, I didn't—"

"Hey, don't worry about me," he interrupted quickly. "I've got the day off."

"I suppose you golf on Wednesdays?" she asked.

"I don't play golf."

Marjorie feigned shock. "You don't golf? Just what kind of doctor are you? No one told me that before I made my first appointment with you."

"Count your blessings, Majors."

"Oh?"

"I could charge by the hour."

The effort to smile was painful, but holding back her amusement would have been impossible. "Hey, don't make me laugh—it hurts." She groaned and placed her hand over her abdomen. "How soon will the pain go away."

"In a few days."

"A whole lot of good that's doing me now."

"Stop being so impatient."

He spoke with just enough of a challenge for her to quit arguing. She would grin and bear it.

"I'll get the nurse," Sam informed her, smiling. "Cal left instructions for you to sit upright once you woke."

Marjorie snapped her mouth closed and pressed her

lips together to smother a protest. Dr. Johnson didn't actually expect her to move, did he? She couldn't—not yet. If breathing hurt this much, she could only imagine the agony that sitting up would cause. Great! Sam and his friend had grabbed her from the jaws of death, only to let her die a slow, torturous death from pain.

From the moment she'd met Dr. Sam, Marjorie had been looking for some imperfection. Anything. He was much too wonderful to be real. Now the flaw stood out like a fake diamond under a jeweler's eyepiece. Clearly, she decided in her still-drugged state, Sam Bretton enjoyed watching people suffer.

Again Sam proved her wrong. The nurse who came to her room came alone. Her name tag was pinned to her uniform: Bertha Powell, R.N.

"Dr. Sam sent me," Bertha announced.

Marjorie studied the older woman, who looked as though her previous profession had been mud wrestling. She was built as solid as a rock, and from the glinting light in her eyes, she was just waiting for Marjorie to start something.

"Where's Sam?"

"*Doctor* Sam asked me to tell you that he'll be back later this afternoon."

"Wonderful," Marjorie muttered, and wiggled her big toe as an experiment. The pain wasn't debilitating, but she wasn't exactly up to swinging from jungle vines, either.

Bertha pulled back the sheet. "Are you ready?"

Marjorie wondered what the other woman would do if she announced that she refused to move. Briefly she toyed with the idea, then decided against it. Her teeth gritted, she cautiously did what had been requested of her.

Exhausted afterward, Marjorie slept for six hours. Someone moving inside her room woke her. When she stirred and opened her eyes, she found Lydia standing at the foot of her bed with a small bouquet of flowers in her hand.

"Hi, Marjorie," Lydia said in a soft voice.

"I had my appendix out," Marjorie grumbled. "I stopped your friend in the nick of time from doing a lobotomy."

Lydia looked relieved and set the flowers on the bedside table. "Same ol' Marjorie."

"I didn't mean to snap at you."

"Hey, no problem. I'm used to it, remember?"

Marjorie tried to wipe the tiredness from her eyes. "I bet you're waiting for me to tell you how right you were."

"It'd feel good, but I can wait." Obviously she couldn't, because she added, "Didn't I tell you it had to be more than a queasy stomach? I figured it out long before you, didn't I?"

"Yup, you did," Marjorie returned, with more than a hint of amused sarcasm. "Where would I be without you?" That much wasn't in jest. She was sincerely grateful her friend had made the appointment when she did, especially after what Sam had told her.

Lydia pulled a chair close to the hospital bed and plunked herself down. Without so much as pausing to inhale, she started off with a long series of questions. "How do you like Dr. Sam? Isn't he wonderful? Didn't I tell you he was a marvel? Now that you've met him, you'll probably be like everyone else and fall madly in love with him."

"No doubt."

Lydia's face blossomed into a wide grin. "I knew you'd like him."

Just managing to avoid her friend's gaze, Marjorie asked, "What's his wife like?"

"His wife?" That stopped Lydia cold. She opened and closed her mouth twice. "I didn't know he was married."

"You mean he isn't?" Hope flared. Naw, he had to be married—and probably had a passel of kids to boot. All in diapers, no doubt. Knowing the type of doctor he was convinced Marjorie that Sam Bretton would be a devoted husband and father. She, on the other hand, was definitely not the mother type.

"I don't know anything about a wife," Lydia answered thoughtfully, chewing on the corner of her bottom lip. "I really don't think he's married. I can't remember seeing a wedding band, can you?"

"It doesn't matter," Marjorie muttered. He'd been wonderful...more than wonderful, but she had far more important matters to deal with that didn't involve risking her heart over a physician whose second job entailed throwing women's equilibriums off balance.

In order to change the subject Marjorie scooted her gaze past Lydia to the bouquet of carnations and roses on the bedside table. "Thanks for the flowers."

"Hey, no problem. They're from all the salespeople at Dixon's."

"All?" Marjorie cocked one delicately shaped brow suspiciously. "Even Al Swanson?"

Lydia grinned sheepishly. "He tossed in a buck and suggested I buy a cactus."

That Marjorie could believe. Al had made it clear that he didn't approve of women in the car business. That was tough, she mused, since she was at Dixon Motors for the long haul, no matter what Al or anyone else thought. It wasn't that Al had taken a dislike to her and her alone. He had a problem with everyone. He had yet to learn that sales work was often a team effort. Marjorie's gut feeling was that Al Swanson wouldn't be around Dixon much longer.

"Oh!" Lydia exclaimed. "I nearly forgot. Dr. Sam phoned and told me to get the key to your apartment so I could pick up some personal items you're going to need."

Once again the man had amazed Marjorie with his thoughtfulness. "I hate to put you to all the trouble."

"It's no trouble. Honest. You'd do the same thing for me."

Marjorie smiled her thanks. Accepting anyone's assistance was difficult for her—more than it should have been, she realized. She'd practically raised Jody with little or no help from any state agencies. With a limited college education she'd forged her own way in the world, designed her career, and earned enough to support herself and pay for her sister's college tuition. Sam Bretton had the wrong impression of her, and to Marjorie's utter embarrassment, she had to admit she'd been the one to give it to him.

"The key," Lydia reminded her.

"Oh, it's in my purse." Guessing where it would be stored, she nodded toward the closet door.

Lydia stood and moved in that direction. "Dr. Sam gave me a list, but you might want to read it over."

"I'm sure he thought of everything," Marjorie responded distractedly. She had to set Sam straight. She wasn't a helpless clinging vine, although he had good reason to believe she was. The memory of how she'd pleaded with him not to leave her was a keen source of her present chagrin.

Triumphantly Lydia held up Marjorie's key chain. "I'll run over to your place and get your things now."

Marjorie could do little more than nod. Her thoughts were light-years away, spinning out of control. She would talk to Sam the next time he stopped in to see her. She would explain everything. Yawning, she placed her hand over her mouth and determinedly tried to suppress the exhaustion that gripped her. How strange it felt to become so weary so easily. Of their own accord, her eyes drifted closed.

Sam was there when she woke. He smiled down on her before noting something on her chart. "How's the patient feeling?"

"I don't know yet. Give me a minute to sort through the various pains." To her surprise she noticed that her purple velvet housecoat was neatly folded across the bottom of her bed. Lydia must have returned with her things, and Marjorie realized she had somehow managed to sleep through her friend's second visit.

"Dr. Johnson wants you up and walking before dinner."

The protest that sprang automatically to her lips died a quick death. Sitting up in bed earlier had been difficult enough! Sam had to be out of his mind if he believed she was going to traipse around this room or down these halls, dragging an I.V. pole with her, and all because some man she barely knew had ordered her to. She, of all people, should know when she was ready to risk life and limb by walking again.

Sam glanced up from his notations, his eyes studying her. "What, no argument?"

"When can I get out of here?"

"Soon, but that's up to Cal," he answered noncommittally. "Listen, before you think about leaving the hospital, focus your energy on getting out of bed and moving."

He sounded so reasonable, so calm and confident, that the brick walls of her rebellion crumbled before she had them completely raised. Marjorie cautiously moved the sheet aside and struggled a little higher against her pillows.

"Careful, Marjorie. Don't try to move on your own." Sam closed her chart and hung it at the end of the bed.

"No," she said through gritted teeth. "I'll do it myself." One foot freed itself from the tangled sheet, and she raised herself up onto one elbow.

Disregarding her words, Sam placed his arm around her shoulders and helped her into an upright position. Flushed and embarrassed by how incredibly weak she was, Marjorie reached for her housecoat, astonished that the simple task of sitting could tire her so much that she was practically panting.

Sam draped her robe over her shoulders, then located her slippers and slipped them onto her feet. "Okay, let's take this nice and easy."

"Trust me, I'm not exactly ready to jump off this bed and race down the corridor." The spinning room gradually circled into place and came to a stop. "I think I'd feel better about this in the morning."

"Now, Marjorie."

She wanted to argue with him but hadn't the strength. "I'm not normally like this," she said, with as much force as she could muster. "I'm sorry I asked you to stay with me... I realize now I shouldn't have...."

"Marjorie, I stayed because I wanted to, not out of any obligation." He stepped around the bed and stood directly in front of her, leaning down only slightly. Because the hospital bed was so high, their eyes met. His were warm and sincere, while hers flashed with frustration and regret.

Although his words had filled her with an absurd amount of pleasure, Marjorie still felt compelled to explain herself. "But I'm not like that...really."

"Like what?"

"Weak and sniveling."

"I never once thought that."

"Oh, you're impossible!"

Sam's thick brows shot upward. "I'm what?"

Marjorie lightly tossed her head. "Nothing."

"Do you doubt my word?"

"Not exactly. It's just that I feel I've given you the wrong impression of me. I'm a capable, responsible adult. I even figured out my own taxes last year."

"I'm impressed." He pushed a small stool across the floor so she could use that as a step to climb off the bed.

"You're actually going to make me do this?" Marjorie couldn't seem to get her body to cooperate. One foot eased itself downward as she cautiously scooted to the edge of the mattress.

Sam placed a supporting arm under her elbow to help her down. She felt small and incredibly fragile in his embrace. Once again she reminded him of the rain-drenched kitten he'd discovered all those years ago. And like the half-drowned feline, Marjorie Majors required love and attention, too. Only Sam wasn't in any position to give those things to her. She was his patient, not a potential girlfriend. The two didn't mix. Couldn't mix.

With both feet firmly planted on the floor, Marjorie paused, half expecting to keel over. When she didn't, she felt a glowing sense of triumph. She'd made it, actually made it.

"Good job," Sam said, and reluctantly dropped his arm. "Now take a few steps."

"You don't really mean for me to walk, do you?" She was only hours from having been under the knife. Hours from the most frightening experience of her life.

"I certainly do want you to walk. You know, one foot in front of the other in a forward direction."

She flashed him a look of irritation.

"And soon, if you're good, I'll take you upstairs."

"Upstairs? Is there something up there that would interest me? Like food?"

"You're hungry?"

"Famished! I haven't eaten in two days." That was entirely true. Marjorie liked her food and seldom skipped a meal. Luckily, gaining weight had never been a problem. She guessed she was fortunate in that department, but it seemed she would quickly melt away if this hospital had anything to say about it. She hadn't been offered a single meal so far.

Sam knew her digestive system couldn't handle anything solid for a few days, but he decided against telling her so. He would leave as many unpleasant tasks as possible for Cal Johnson. After all, Cal was the physician of record.

While guiding the I.V. pole beside her, Sam manipulated them through the doorway and into the broad hallway.

"This afternoon, while you were sleeping, I delivered a set of twins," Sam boasted proudly. Birth, even after countless deliveries, had never ceased to humble him, and twins were always special. "They're upstairs," he continued. "I'll take you to see them later, if you want."

Marjorie looked at him and blinked. She didn't know how to explain that babies frightened her. All right, they terrified her. Some women took to motherhood and dirty diapers like hogs to mud. But, unfortunately, that would never be the case with her. The only times she'd ever been around babies, they'd cried. Within ten minutes she'd been ready to wail herself. After several embarrassing episodes in her youth, she had decided that anyone under two was allergic to her.

"I... I think I'd better wait until I've got more strength," she said.

"Of course," Sam agreed. "I wouldn't dream of dragging you upstairs your first time out. Tomorrow, maybe, or the next day."

"Sure. Anytime," Marjorie answered, but the words nearly stuck in her throat.

Chapter 3

Marjorie stared at the orange tray and grimaced in pure disgust. If she so much as looked at another bowl of plain gelatin, she was going to start screaming and say something unladylike that would shock the entire hospital staff. Everything they'd brought to her so far only vaguely resembled food.

"Good morning," the nurse's aide greeted her, as she strolled into the room. "And how was your breakfast?"

"You don't want to know."

The young girl glanced at the untouched tray. "You didn't eat a thing."

"I couldn't," Marjorie muttered. It wasn't this poor woman's fault that the hospital had chosen to starve her.

"Aren't you feeling better? Usually my patients are more than ready to eat by this time. Are you in a lot of pain? Perhaps I should notify Dr. Johnson."

"Contacting the doctor isn't going to convince me to eat…this. I'd rather die," Marjorie said dramatically. "I refuse to swallow anything that slithers down my throat."

The aide chuckled. "Let me see what I can do." She left, and Marjorie stared after her with visions of cheesy pizza, crisp fried chicken and a thick, juicy steak playing havoc with her imagination. Marjorie was convinced she smelled bacon frying in the distance, the odor wafting toward her and tormenting her with delicious dreams.

"Problems?" Sam sauntered into the room, looking sympathetic.

"Sam," Marjorie said, and brightened instantly. She hadn't seen him in nearly twenty hours and had rarely been more pleased to lay eyes on anyone. Sam Bretton could be trusted. She wasn't so sure about anyone else in this antiseptic place, but Sam would help straighten out this mealtime mess.

"You didn't eat your breakfast." His voice was only lightly accusing.

"I couldn't," she said, her eyes softly pleading with his. "The oatmeal had more lumps than a camel, and heaven only knows what flavor of gelatin they wanted me to eat… Liver, I think, and even with whipped topping, it looked disgusting. As for the tea and toast, could they be any more boring? Why can't I have a mushroom omelet, with home fries on the side? Something…anything, but gelatin and oatmeal."

"Soon."

Marjorie's face mirrored her reaction. Obviously *soon* wasn't going to be this morning, and she needed nourishment *now*, if not earlier. Disappointment consumed her. She'd thought of Sam as her ally, her friend. The amazing part was that he seemed to look better to her every time he walked in the room. When he was with her, even the pain lessened. He filled her room with an assurance of well-being and safekeeping. He lent her confidence, stamina and the conviction that this, too, would pass, and when it did, he would be there for her.

Sam reached for her hand, and his eyes gentled. "Marjorie, listen." He did understand her position, but she had to realize that stronger foods had to be reintroduced gradually into her digestive system. "You're not being a very good patient."

"Oh, spare me," she snapped, quickly losing a grip on her fragile patience. Her temper was always quick to fire when she was hungry. "No one told me I had to pretend I was on the good ship Lollipop."

"All we're asking is that you do as we say."

"And die of starvation in the process."

"Don't be so dramatic. You're a long way from that. Most women look forward to dropping a few pounds during their hospital stay." The moment the words slipped from Sam's mouth, he recognized his terrible mistake. It was too late to retract his statement; his only hope was that she would let it slide. He tried smiling, praying the action would take any sting from his words. It didn't.

Marjorie's face grew as red as a California pepper, and her anger was just as hot. "Are you insinuating Tacoma General is a fat farm and that I'm overweight?"

"No, you misunderstood—"

"Your meaning was more than clear," she said coldly, and reached for the buzzer to call the nurse. Immediately the red light above her bed flashed on.

"Marjorie… I didn't mean to be so tactless. You're not the least bit plump… I'm doing a poor job of this." Sam wiped a hand around the back of his neck and sighed. He regretted getting trapped in this no-win conversation. When it came to dealing with his patients, he usually had more finesse than this.

She ignored him and tossed aside the sheet, sticking her bare leg out in an ungraceful effort to climb down from the high hospital bed. "Nurse," she cried, but her voice was weak and wobbly.

"Marjorie, you have to stay where you are and eat your breakfast," Sam said.

Their eyes met and clashed. Marjorie was hurting and hungry, a lethal combination that resulted in the most embarrassing reaction. Tears. Embarrassed, she turned her face away from him and motioned toward the door, wordlessly asking him to leave.

Sam hesitated. Once again his heart went out to her, and he had to force himself to walk out of the room. In the few days since he'd met Marjorie, she'd touched him in ways few women ever had. He had been a silent witness to her courage and realized that she possessed a rare personal strength. Her laughter was a sweet melody, her movements innately graceful. Several times over the past twenty-four hours he'd found his thoughts drifting to her, and he smiled at the memory of her waking from the operation to ask if she was in the morgue. At each meeting he realized all the more how proud she was. Proud. Fiery. Straightforward. He found it utterly astonishing that she wasn't married. And he was grateful. He wanted to get to know her better—a whole lot better.

Sam knew he'd made a mess of this and was angry

with himself. He patted her shoulder and turned to leave the room.

The nurse's aide met him outside her door and raised questioning eyes to him. "Doctor?"

"I believe she'll eat her breakfast now," Sam answered, his thoughts distracted.

"Very good." The younger woman beamed him a warm smile impressed, he imagined, with his ability to deal with a difficult situation.

Sam did his best to return the friendly gesture. He had a reputation for working well with unreasonable patients, but Marjorie wasn't that, only confused and miserable.

And he'd made a mess of things.

Marjorie heard Sam tell the nurse's aide that she would be eating her meal and glared after him, half tempted to toss the liver gelatin at his arrogant backside. She didn't, though, because he was right. Once again she'd made an idiot of herself in front of him and the hospital staff. She didn't like herself when she behaved this way, yet she seemed powerless to change.

The moisture on her cheeks felt like burning acid, and she brushed the tears aside, thoroughly embarrassed by their appearance. She wasn't a crybaby—at least she hadn't been until Sam Bretton walked into her life. Then everything had quickly fallen to pieces. Whatever it was about that insufferable, wonderful man that reduced her to this state should be outlawed.

The tea was only lukewarm, but at least it was strong enough to satisfy Marjorie's need for caffeine. The dry wheat toast was surprisingly filling, and the oatmeal

passable as long as she dumped three sugar packets over
the top. The gelatin she ignored.

In order to avoid the triumphant look on the nurse's
aide's face, Marjorie pretended to be asleep when the
woman returned for the tray. To her surprise, she actually did fall into a restful sleep and woke midmorn-
ing with a game show blaring from the TV positioned
against the wall.

"I see you're awake." The mud-wrestling star was
back. Bertha Powell, R.N., looked stiff in her starched
white uniform. "Dr. Johnson wants you up and walking today. Ten laps."

"Laps?" Marjorie repeated, still caught in the last
dregs of sleep. Did the hospital provide a running track
for surgery patients?

"The corridor," the muscular woman informed her
primly. "Ten times up and back. That's your goal for
today. But don't do too much at once. Two or three
round trips at a time. No more."

Marjorie resisted the urge to salute. Bertha Powell
seemed to be looking for a few good men—or women—
to gleefully whip into shape. Marjorie didn't doubt that
the nurse would count every single lap.

To her credit, the nurse aided Marjorie into an upright position and helped her on with her robe. There
was some confusion with the I.V., but Bertha figured
it out, and after only a few minutes, Marjorie was on
her way.

Steadier on her feet than she'd been before, she was
pleased with her slow but sure progress. Although it
was hours until noon, the hospital was a hive of ac-
tivity. If she'd been in a grumbling mood, she would
have pointed out that Dr. Johnson had suggested she get

plenty of rest, but the hospital staff had awakened her before the sun was anywhere close to the horizon. The only people up at that time of the morning were mass murderers, teenagers and nurses' aides.

The woman who had brought in her breakfast tray grinned as Marjorie passed the nurses' station.

"Hey, you're doing great."

Marjorie smiled back. "Yes, I think I'll donate my body to science."

"Science fiction might appreciate it more," said a deep male voice from behind her.

"Sam?" Marjorie laughed and turned her head, pleased to see him again.

"To your room," he instructed.

Marjorie was more than happy to comply and glanced with wide-eyed curiosity toward the brown paper sack in his hand. "What's that?"

"You'll see."

"I thought you had appointments all day," she said once they were back in her room, not that she was disappointed to see him. Nothing could have been further from the truth; she was overjoyed.

"I just finished my rounds."

"Oh." Once again Marjorie couldn't take her eyes from his dazzling smile. "How are the twins?"

"As cute as a bug's ear. I'll take you to see them this evening, if you want."

It was all Marjorie could do to nod. She'd brought up the subject of the babies because she knew they were close to Sam's heart. She was interested, but not to the point of overcoming her instinctive apprehension. When the time came that she couldn't avoid it any longer, she would look through the glass and ooh and aah with ap-

propriate enthusiasm, and Sam would never guess she
was frightened to death.

"I brought you something to tide you over until
lunch," he said, holding out the sack to her.

Marjorie took it and eagerly peeked inside. The choc-
olate-coated ice-cream bar produced a small squeal of
delight. If they'd been anyplace but the middle of a hospital, she would have thrown her arms around his neck
and smudged his face with kisses to thank him properly.

"Thank you, Sam. Really."

"It's my pleasure."

Those gorgeous eyes of his seemed to look straight
into her heart. "I felt terrible about the scene I made
earlier," Marjorie admitted, centering her greedy gaze
on the melting Dove Bar. Her mouth started to water.
This man was special. Really special.

"There's no need to apologize," he said. "I wasn't
exactly helpful."

"But you tried." She didn't understand why he was
so good to her, but she wasn't willing to question it.
From the moment she'd walked into his office, he'd be-
friended her, then seen her through the most difficult
days of her life, all the while hardly leaving her side.
No wonder his patients were so willing to admit they
fell in love with him.

Sam's heart throbbed painfully with desire. Marjorie's wide eyes regarded him with such sweet gratitude
that it seemed the most natural thing in the world to
lean forward and press his mouth to hers. He didn't, of
course, but that didn't stop his imagination from running rampant. He could all but taste her honey-sweet
lips. He could all but feel her mouth shaping and fitting to his own, and her ripe body pressing against him.

Inhaling deeply to discipline his thoughts, Sam took a step back. Marjorie Majors had caught him completely off guard. Over the years he'd been subjected to every female ploy imaginable, but the majority of women who were interested in him were mostly concerned with the money he was making and the social position that would go with becoming his wife. They hadn't soured him on marriage, but they *had* made him extra cautious. He didn't succumb easily to a woman's charms, and he wasn't about to start now. He was looking for a special woman to become his wife. A partner and a friend.

And now there was Marjorie. Her candor had caught him unaware. She was a natural beauty. Even without makeup and with her dark hair tied lifelessly away from her face, he couldn't help being attracted to her. From the moment she'd angrily jumped off his examining table, Sam had been enraptured with her. Everything about her acted as a powerful aphrodisiac, but nothing could come of this attraction until after she was released from the hospital.

Sam left abruptly, but Marjorie was too busy eating her ice-cream bar to pay much attention. She sucked on the wooden stick until the last bit of chocolate had long since melted on her tongue, then carefully set the stick aside.

Dragging the I.V. stand with her, she walked slowly and carefully down the corridor until she reached the nurses' station. There wasn't any way to be tactful about what she needed to know, but she was in dangerous territory here, feeling the way she did about Sam Bretton.

"Ms. Powell?" she said as sweetly as she could.

"Yes?" Bertha Powell glanced up from the chart she was updating, and her eyes narrowed with displeasure.

"I've done five laps."

"That leaves five more for this afternoon."

"Right."

The woman returned her attention to her work.

"Ms. Powell?"

"Yes." Once again the older woman's voice revealed her lack of patience. She gripped the pen tightly and glanced up at Marjorie before slowly exhaling one long breath.

"Dr. Bretton was in earlier. I was wondering if I could ask about..."

"His wife?" the older woman finished for her.

The room swayed, and the floor felt as if had buckled under Marjorie's unsteady feet. She gripped the edge of the counter until she regained her balance and the hospital had righted itself once more. But she had to ask, and surely the hospital staff would know for sure, while Lydia had only been guessing.

"That *is* what you wanted to know, isn't it?" the woman pressed.

It was all Marjorie could do to nod and say, "He's married, then?"

"Not as far as I know," Bertha answered almost kindly. "But I swear that man breaks more hearts than George Clooney. There isn't a woman on this floor who wouldn't give her eyeteeth to be married to him. He's the type we're all looking for."

"But..."

"Be smart, Ms. Majors. Listen to the voice of experience and learn from it. All Dr. Sam's patients fall in love with him. It's gratitude, I suppose. Heaven knows he's hunk enough to melt anyone's heart—even mine."

Marjorie clenched her jaw to hide her reaction.

"Now I don't want you to feel bad about this. It's common enough, believe me."

The heat that exploded into Marjorie's cheeks was hot enough to fry eggs. She hadn't realized her feelings were so obvious. Under normal conditions she didn't fluster easily, but when it came to Sam, she lost all her poise.

"He's a wonderful person," Marjorie managed to say with some semblance of calm.

"Honey, you don't know the half of it. I saw that man sit for hours with a young couple after their baby died. More than once I've been a witness to his tenderness— that's why I'm telling you what I am. Believe me, if I were twenty years younger, I'd be in love with the man myself. Truthfully, I *am* in love with him. We all are."

"Thank you." Already Marjorie was walking away, trying to disguise her embarrassment. She'd tried to be subtle, tried to find out what she could without making a total idiot of herself. And she'd failed.

After a few moments to think the nurse's words over, Marjorie relaxed. An odd reassurance replaced her chagrin. It was good to know she was merely one of the masses. Bertha Powell was right. Women tended to fall in love with their doctors. It was a common enough malady, and one she should have anticipated.

The sooner she was released from the hospital, the better, Marjorie decided. With a determination that drove her to the brink of exhaustion, she did five more laps up and down the long corridor, then fell into a deep sleep the minute the dinner tray was removed from her room.

"Morning, doctor," Marjorie said casually when Cal Johnson paid his morning visit. He was a bald, grandfatherly type who certainly hadn't affected her the way Sam had.

"I see you've made considerable progress," he said, reading over her chart.

"I hope so."

"You're walking?"

"Every minute I can."

"Good." He nodded approvingly.

"When can I be discharged?" The question had been on her mind from the moment she talked to Bertha Powell. "I feel great—I want to go home."

"I'm pleased to hear that. However..."

"Doctor, please, I need to get home."

The grandfatherly brows molded into a tight frown. "I want to keep you until I'm sure you're a little stronger. A couple of days—maybe."

"Two days!" Marjorie would never last that long. For the sake of her sanity, she had to get out of this place. Heaven only knew what would happen when she saw Sam next. The way matters were progressing, she would profess her love for him the moment he walked in the door. That was just the kind of crazy, foolish thing she might do.

"We'll see how things progress today," Dr. Johnson said on his way out the door.

A half hour after Dr. Johnson had left her room, Sam appeared.

"How are you feeling?"

"Fine," Marjorie responded in a flat, emotionless tone. She did her utmost to pretend she was looking straight at him when in reality her gaze rested on the wall behind him. Even looking in Sam Bretton's direction was dangerous to her equilibrium. She should be reassured that she was like every one of his other patients, but she wasn't. Such strong emotions were strangers to her and best avoided.

"Marjorie, what's wrong?"

"I want out of here!"

"You aren't alone in that, you know. Everyone who ever stays in the hospital is eager to get home."

"But I feel terrific." That wasn't entirely true. "I'm as strong as an ox."

"Why don't you leave it in Dr. Johnson's hands?" he offered gently. "He knows what he's doing."

"But two days is an eternity," Marjorie insisted.

Sam's cajoling smile vanished. "Cal suggested you could leave then?"

"Yes."

"I'm sure he's mistaken."

"What do you mean?" Marjorie grumbled.

"Dr. Johnson's obviously forgotten that there isn't anyone at your apartment to watch over you when you're released."

"In case you hadn't noticed, I'm a big girl. I've been taking care of myself for a long time now. I'm not going to keel over because someone isn't there to hold my hand and place wet washcloths over my forehead every ten minutes."

"That's not the issue, Marjorie."

"Then what exactly is?"

"You've gone through a life-threatening episode. Take advantage of this time to be waited on and pampered."

"Take advantage of it?" She laughed sharply. "You've got to be kidding. What's with you doctors? Do you get a kickback for every additional day a patient stays in the hospital?"

Marjorie's ability to attract him paled beside her capacity to anger him. He knotted his hands into tight fists, and clenched his jaw to keep from saying something he would regret. Her suggestion was so outrageous and so unfair that it offended him beyond anything he'd felt in years.

"I think it would be best if I left."

"By all means go, Doctor."

Sam retreated, shoving the door with such rage that it nearly slammed against the wall. A kickback? She couldn't actually believe that, could she?

Marjorie watched him go and swallowed down a mouthful of remorse, nearly choking on the aftertaste. She hadn't meant to suggest such a ridiculous thing, hadn't planned to say the words. But she was desperate to escape. How ironic it was that a man—a doctor who had dedicated his life to saving lives—could be responsible for breaking so many hearts.

All Marjorie wanted to do was to put this unfortunate episode behind her and get on with her life. Every day she spent in the hospital was another day without income. She hadn't been joking when she told Sam that if she didn't sell cars, she didn't eat. Most of her customers tended to glamorize her job, but it wasn't anything like they imagined. She was in a cutthroat business.

In her frustration, she walked the halls until she was convinced her feet had made imprints in the polished linoleum squares. When Lydia arrived at five-thirty, she was so pleased to see her friend that she nearly threw her arms around the other woman and wept for joy.

"You look great. I don't believe it! Your color's almost back." Lydia slid the lone chair closer to Marjorie's bed and took a seat. "Dixon's doesn't seem the same without you."

Despite her bad mood, Marjorie laughed, then sucked in a pain-filled breath and pressed her hand against her side. She hadn't healed as much as she thought.

"Are you resting enough?"

Just the mention of sleep produced a yawn that Marjorie hid with the back of her hand. "You wouldn't believe it. I haven't slept this much since I was a newborn."

"What about Dr. Sam? Have you seen much of him?"

"He's been in a few times," Marjorie said in a flat tone. The scene from that morning played back in her mind, along with the awful accusation she'd thrown at him. Once again, Marjorie was struck by her own foolishness.

Lydia paused and closely studied her friend. "What's the matter? You said that as though you don't want anything to do with the man."

"Oh, Sam Bretton is everything you said he was... and more. But to be frank, he simply doesn't interest me."

The perfectly shaped eyebrows above Lydia's dark eyes drew together sharply. "He doesn't interest you?"

"Not really." Marjorie studied her fingernails with feigned interest.

"Do you have a raging fever, girl? Are you stupid? He's wonderful... He's handsome enough to tempt any red-blooded American woman."

"Not me," Marjorie claimed, her voice gaining conviction. "Nice guy, but not my type."

"He's every woman's type!"

"Maybe." That was as much as Marjorie was willing to concede.

The way Lydia was regarding her, Marjorie had the feeling her friend was considering having her arrested for treason. If she didn't watch it, she would be dragged before a firing squad at dawn.

"I don't understand you," Lydia said in a low, curious tone. "The last time I came to visit, the scent of a good old-fashioned romance was so thick in this room that I walked away intoxicated. I was convinced you were hooked and would be head over heels in love with him within a week."

"I'm sorry to disappoint you."

"What went wrong?" Lydia crossed her arms and glared at Marjorie as though she'd let a million dollars' worth of gold slip through her fingers. "When Dr. Sam phoned before the surgery, he sounded… I don't know… interested, I guess. We must have talked for a half hour. He asked a hundred questions about you."

"He did?" Marjorie wasn't sure she wanted to hear that.

"I don't know what happened between then and now, but obviously something did."

"I'm his patient," Marjorie insisted, because to do anything else would be ludicrous. That relationship was not to be tampered with. All afternoon she'd forced herself to view it as something like the relationship between a woman and her priest. It was much safer that way.

"That's too bad," Lydia said with an exaggerated sigh. "I was really hoping things would work out between you two."

"Why?"

"Why?" Lydia repeated, astonished. "Because I think Dr. Sam is the most amazing man I know, and because you're my best friend. That's why. The two of you are perfect together."

"You've got to be kidding!" Marjorie cried. Her words resounded throughout the room; the echo taunted her for long hours afterward.

Chapter 4

Marjorie paused just inside the Mercedes showroom and drew a deep breath. It felt wonderful to be back. Wonderful and right. Three weeks recovery time was what Sam had told her she would need, and she had used every minute of those twenty-one days to recuperate. Even now she felt weak and a little shaky, but the thought of another day holed up in her tiny apartment was enough to make even the most sane person go stir-crazy.

With a sense of appreciation that never waned, Marjorie ran her hand over the trunk of an SLK roadster. Rarely had she been more eager to get to work. Bit by bit she had regained her strength, and now she would quietly resume her life.

"Welcome back," Lydia called eagerly from behind the customer-service counter. "How are you feeling?"

"Terrific, thanks." Marjorie realized her clothes were a little loose and her complexion a bit chalky, but all in all, she felt great.

"Has your sister gone back to Oregon?"

Marjorie nodded. Her sister had left a few days before, and it had not been a minute too soon. When Jody had learned about the surgery, there had been no stopping the twenty-year-old from coming to her sister's aid. Despite Marjorie's protests, Jody had dropped her studies and immediately driven to Tacoma to play the role of the indulgent nurse. Marjorie loved her sister, but after one entire week of Jody giving an Academy Award-level imitation of Clara Barton, Marjorie had been on the brink of madness.

Within the first hour of her return to Dixon Motors, two of the salesmen stopped by her desk to welcome her back. At ten Lydia delivered a cup of coffee, closed the door and pulled out a chair. "Well?" she asked, as she plunked herself down and leaned forward intently, propping her elbows on the corner of Marjorie's desk. Her eyes were both wide and curious.

Marjorie blinked back her surprise. "Well, what?"

"Did you hear from Dr. Sam?"

"Of course not." With jerky movements she tore off three weeks, a day at a time, from her desktop calendar.

"Dr. Sam didn't contact you?" Lydia's voice rose dramatically in disbelief.

"I just told you he didn't." Marjorie had seen Sam exactly twice since that heated episode when she'd accused him of getting a kickback from the hospital. Both times had been strained, as she battled her very strong and very real attraction toward him. Again and again she was forced to remind herself that women patients tend to fall in love with their doctors and that she wasn't any more immune to his charms than the rest. Keeping her perspective had been difficult, especially when Sam returned the following day and behaved as though nothing had happened. He had chatted easily with her, but she noted regretfully that he stayed only a few minutes. His second visit had been even shorter.

"That depresses me," Lydia lamented, as she gracefully rose from her chair. "I was convinced he really liked you."

It depressed Marjorie, too, but it didn't surprise her. Overall, she was grateful to have met Sam Bretton. He'd taught her several surprising lessons about herself-mainly that she wasn't as invincible as she would like to think. And secondly, as much as she strove to avoid relationships that were more than casual, her heart was vulnerable. He'd proved beyond a doubt that plenty of red-hot blood flowed through her veins.

Painful experience had taught her that most men liked their women soft and clinging. A woman who could change her own oil, balance a checkbook and build a bookshelf seemed to intimidate them. That left the strong, independent types, like herself, out in the cold.

Sam Bretton sat in his office and chewed on the end of a pen. His thoughts were dark and heavy. He hadn't seen Marjorie in more than two weeks, but still she kept popping into his mind when he least expected it. He had seen her smile on a new patient's face as he entered the room to introduce himself. His coffee cup had made it halfway to his lips when he thought he heard Marjorie's laugh. Last week he'd been convinced he'd seen her in the parking lot. Even his dreams had been affected. A couple of times he'd caught himself staring into space, remembering something witty she'd said or the way her eyes narrowed when she was angry. Friends had begun to comment that he seemed preoccupied.

Preoccupied? That wasn't the half of it. Forcefully he opened his desk drawer and tossed the pen inside. He'd been thinking about her for days—all right, weeks—and still he wasn't convinced anything between them would work. She was so proud, so headstrong, and he wasn't entirely persuaded she was interested in him. Without being egotistical about it, Sam realized that there were plenty of women who found him attractive. Unfortunately, Marjorie didn't appear to be one of them.

Well, he was a big boy; he could deal with that. What was difficult to handle was the fact that he wasn't convinced that a future for them was out of the question. Her streak of independence was a mile wide; she didn't want or need anyone. At least that was what she wanted to think. He wasn't so sure, but so long as she stuck to her guns, he was stymied. He just wished he could put her out of his mind.

Marjorie looked at Lydia sitting across the table from her in the deli opposite Dixon Motors. She watched as her friend checked suspiciously between the thick slices of rye bread for the mustard she'd ordered with her pastrami sandwich. "I've been thinking," Lydia muttered under her breath.

"Careful," Marjorie warned, hiding a smile. "That could be dangerous."

"No, I'm serious." Her look gave credibility to her words.

"About what?" Marjorie continued to study her friend while she wrapped the second half of her own turkey sandwich in a paper napkin to take back to the office for a snack later.

"Didn't you tell me Dr. Sam was interested in buying a Mercedes?"

"I… Yes, now that you mention it, he did say something along those lines."

The edges of Lydia's mouth lifted with unsuppressed delight. "Then get moving, girl! I've never known you to look a gift horse in the mouth."

"I…" Marjorie's tongue felt glued to the roof of her mouth.

"If you don't move on this, then you know Al Swanson will."

The arrow hit its mark. Al Swanson was her nemesis, and he wouldn't think twice about robbing his own mother of a sale. "I'll think about it," Marjorie said, and gave her friend a bright smile.

Lydia pushed her plate aside and stood, looking pleased with herself. Marjorie thought she looked determined to get her together with Sam even if she had to lock them in a room herself.

Marjorie checked her watch and was grateful to note that she was free to leave in fifteen minutes. After her second day back at work she was eager to get home and relax. Her afternoon hadn't gone well. She'd crossed swords with Al Swanson when he'd attempted to steal a sale. One of her clients had taken out a sedan for a test drive, and when he'd returned, Al had explained that Marjorie was out to lunch and had asked him to wrap up the deal. Luckily, she had overheard him, and quickly inserted that she was back and would take over for him.

Incidents like this had happened in the past, and she refused to stand for it. She didn't like tattling to the manager, but she wasn't about to let Al cheat her out of her commission.

The bell chimed as the large double doors opened, indicating that a customer had entered the showroom. The salespeople took turns dealing with the influx of prospective buyers. She'd only recently finished helping a young executive, so she left the field open to Jim Preston, the senior salesman.

"Marjorie," Jim called, and stuck his head in the door. "Someone's here to see you."

Once again, she glanced at her watch. Staying late hadn't been a problem before, but she tired easily now and was eager to head back to her apartment. "Thanks, Jim," she muttered, and pushed herself away from her desk with both hands.

Out in the showroom, she paused in midstep and nearly faltered in an effort to disguise her surprise.

"Sam." His name came out in a rush of confusion and delight.

Sam turned away from the light blue convertible he'd been examining. He liked the sleek lines and the classic style of the SLK, but fifty-five thousand dollars for a car, any car, was more than he cared to spend.

"Hi." Some of Marjorie's composure had returned, and she greeted him with a careful smile. She didn't want to appear overjoyed to see him, although her heart felt as if it were doing somersaults inside her chest.

Sam couldn't take his eyes off her. She looked wonderful. If he'd found her attractive before, it was nothing compared to the way she appeared to him now. To think he'd once pictured this woman as a lost kitten trapped in a storm. This kitten wasn't an ordinary, run-of-the-mill stray. She was of the highest pedigree.

Without even realizing what he was doing, Sam gave a low wolf whistle. He couldn't stop looking at her and finally managed to say, "I see you've recovered."

"You promised I'd live and love again."

Sam grinned and, still a little bemused, rubbed the side of his jaw, unable to carry on the conversation.

Marjorie knew that men found her attractive, but what amused her was the shocked look on Sam's face. "I didn't think the brochure had time to reach you," she said, her gaze holding his.

"Brochure? What brochure?" He suspected he was beginning to sound like an echo.

"I mailed one off to you yesterday afternoon," she said, and casually crossed her arms over her double-breasted tweed jacket. "You'd mentioned something about wanting a Mercedes, and I extended an invitation for you to come in and take a test drive."

"I'd enjoy that," Sam murmured, glancing toward the sticker on the side window of the car he'd been inspecting.

"Perhaps it would be best if I explained the different models," Marjorie continued, her gaze following his. "Our cars start in the range of fifty thousand dollars," she said in an even, smooth voice, "depending, of course, on the options you decide on."

"Naturally."

Leading the way into her office, she turned back and asked, "Would you care for a cup of coffee?"

"Please."

Marjorie's thoughts were racing as she directed him toward a chair. From the corner of her eye she happened to catch a glimpse of Lydia, who flashed her a triumphant grin and the universal signal for okay.

Once Sam was comfortably seated, she poured him a mug of coffee. Although she remained outwardly poised, her heart was pumping so fast that she felt dizzy and a little shaky. She knew her face was flushed.

When Marjorie was dealing with a prospective buyer, she usually approached them with an angle. This involved asking a few subtle but pertinent questions and discovering their individual concerns. Some potential buyers were looking at a Mercedes for performance— the German-made automobile was built to cruise at twice the speed of U.S. freeways. Marjorie realized, though, that Sam wasn't interested in traveling over a hundred miles an hour. From what she knew about him, he wasn't the type who cared a great deal about prestige, either. The safety issue would evoke a response in him.

"The Mercedes-Benz is one of the safest cars in the world." She handed him a brochure from her desk drawer and took her seat.

As a saleswoman, she was as slick as frost on mossy rocks, Sam thought. Yes, she was a beautiful woman, but once she had a customer's attention, it was cars she was there to sell.

"I like to tell prospective buyers that purchasing a Mercedes-Benz is another form of life insurance," she continued. "As a physician, I'm sure you can appreciate our cars' many safety features."

Sam flipped through the pages of the glossy pamphlet and nodded. She knew her stuff, he had to give her credit for that. "You're very good."

Marjorie paused. "How do you mean?"

"As a salesman."

"Salesperson," she corrected with a smile.

"I don't think many men would be able to turn you down."

A couple of the salesmen had protested that very point when Marjorie was first hired, claiming she had an unfair advantage over the rest of them. They claimed that, sitting across the table from a good-looking female, a man would have a difficult time negotiating a price. The men might have convinced a few of the others they had a point, but Bud, the manager, was behind Marjorie. Her sales record spoke for itself. She sold cars, and that was the purpose of the dealership. If she possessed an unfair advantage, the manager didn't care as long as cars moved off the lot. But Marjorie knew that she didn't need to use her feminine wiles; the cars sold because she was a good salesperson.

"I get turned down plenty of times," she responded, her smile fading.

Sam turned the page of the brochure and read over the information on the E350. "I'll take this one."

"Pardon." Marjorie wasn't completely sure she had heard him right.

"This sedan—in a light blue, if you have it."

"You mean you want to buy one now?"

"Is that a problem?" He withdrew his checkbook from inside his coat pocket.

Marjorie had sold plenty of cars, but never any quite this way. "Don't you want to drive one? Negotiate the price?"

"Not particularly. I know you aren't going to cheat me."

"But…" Experience told her to shut up. She didn't

need to kill a sale by arguing with him. She clamped
her mouth closed and swallowed her questions. Sam
was an adult; he knew what he wanted. Far be it from
her to stand in his way.

"I trust you to be fair," he continued, adding the pertinent details to the blank check. "How much should I
fill in for the amount?"

Hours later Marjorie was still completely bemused.
She wandered around her apartment, moving from room
to room, listless and bored and, at the same time, excited. She'd seen Sam again, and even if he had come
into the showroom to buy a car and not just to see her,
she was thrilled. At the same time, she regretted the
encounter. Knowing that other patients fell in love
with him had been reassuring, but to her dismay she'd
learned that the attraction she'd experienced toward
Sam hadn't lessened with time. It had been weeks since
she'd last seen him, and he looked better to her than
ever. All the emotions she'd struggled so valiantly to
bury had surfaced the minute she'd walked into the
showroom to discover him standing there. All the pleasure of seeing him again had returned to remind her
how strongly Sam Bretton appealed to her.

When Sam walked back into Dixon Motors late the
following morning, every word that Marjorie had re-
hearsed so carefully, every scenario she'd spent hours
plotting, fell by the wayside. All she could see was the
gentle man who had sat at her bedside and held her hand.

"Hello, Sam." It was amazing that she'd been able
to utter those few words. She was trembling inside. No
longer was she an inept hospital patient but a woman

who knew what she liked—and Sam Bretton was it. The thought terrified her.

"Hello again."

"Everything's ready." She straightened the French cuffs of her sleeves, bemoaning the fact that virtually everything she owned was either blue, black or gray. It wasn't any wonder dates were few and far between. Marjorie swallowed her self-doubts and gestured toward the customer-service counter. "Lydia will need you to fill out a few forms."

Sam looked mildly surprised, but he followed Marjorie into the other office. Lydia greeted him with a wide smile, and Sam was left with the impression that he'd done something very right to have gained her undying gratitude.

Surely buying the Mercedes couldn't have been any more obvious, even to Marjorie. Against his better judgment, he'd decided he wanted to see her again. He'd planned on getting a luxury car someday, and now seemed as good a time as any. Besides, he wanted her to have this sale. He remembered her telling him once how she lived on commissions alone. This was his way of helping her through what was sure to be a difficult month, since the first three weeks had been spent recuperating from surgery. Because of that, he had even decided against negotiating the price.

While Sam was with Lydia, Marjorie stood on the showroom floor, pacing back and forth while she waited for him to finish. Her hands felt damp, her throat dry, and yet to all outward appearances she was as cool as a pumpkin on a frosty October morning.

When Sam was finished, she approached him with a grin and handed him the keys to his shiny new E350 sedan, which she'd arranged to have waiting for him in front of the dealership.

"That didn't take long," she said as if surprised, but it was just a means of starting a conversation. From experience, she knew the paperwork didn't take more than ten or fifteen minutes.

"Have you got time to take a spin with me?" Sam invited.

She nodded, hoping she didn't appear as eager as she felt. "Of course."

Like the true gentleman he was, Sam held open the passenger door for her, and she gracefully slipped inside. He joined her a moment later, inserted the key into the ignition, and paused to inhale the fresh scent of new leather and study the dials in front of him.

It was on the tip of Marjorie's tongue to give him another sales pitch and quote what *Car and Driver* had to say about the E350. She knew her stuff, but the sale had already been made, and he only had to drive the vehicle to be impressed.

Wordlessly Sam eased the sedan into the busy Tacoma traffic, quickly acquainting himself with the mechanics of the car. They rode past the digital signboard above the Puget Sound Bank.

"Actually, you being able to pick up the car this morning works rather well," Marjorie said.

"How's that?" Sam looked away from traffic long enough to glance in her direction.

"I can treat you to lunch." As soon as the words slipped from her lips, she was flabbergasted. She didn't know where the invitation had come from.

"Marjorie…"

"That is unless you can't… I mean, if you're due

back at the office… The reason I asked is that I always treat new customers to lunch. It's my way of showing my appreciation for your business." She was convinced her lies would someday return to haunt her.

"But *I* was thinking of taking *you* out."

"I owe you this one," she insisted. "For the car, yes, and everything else."

"You're a difficult woman to refuse."

How Marjorie wished that were true. "How do you like Mexican food?"

"Love it. But I really would prefer it if you allowed *me* to buy lunch."

"You'd break tradition." She was convinced her nose would start growing at any minute.

Sam grinned. The more he came to know this woman, the more he learned about pride. "Are you always so stubborn?"

"Always," she answered evenly, and pointed to the left-hand side of the street. "The restaurant is about a block farther on. There's parking on the street and a small lot around back."

Sam parked easily. Once inside, they were forced to put their name on a list, but Marjorie assured him the food was well worth the wait. They were seated within ten minutes; the waitress seemed to know Marjorie.

"Do you come here often?"

She nodded and finished munching on a warm tortilla chip before answering. "At least once a week. I'm worthless in the kitchen, and it's easier for me to eat out."

Sam's insides tightened. He should have guessed that she would be a terrible cook, and he felt almost guilty because it bothered him. He'd always thought the woman he was looking to build his life with should possess at least the rudimentary culinary skills.

"The last time I experimented with a recipe," Marjorie continued, "I set off the fire alarm and cleared the entire apartment complex. Under direct orders of the building manager and the Tacoma Fire Department, I've been asked to refrain from any kitchen activities," she joked.

The sound of Sam's strained chuckle mingled with the chatter in the small restaurant.

"My sister swears that I'll make someone a wonderful husband." In many ways what Jody claimed was true; Marjorie could fix just about anything. But cooking and sewing were lost arts to her.

Sam found the food to be as good as Marjorie had claimed. He watched her eat with undisguised gusto and then pause, obviously embarrassed, to explain that she was only now regaining her appetite.

As she dabbed a drop of hot sauce from the corner of her mouth with a paper napkin, Marjorie's gaze fell to her empty plate. No doubt most women Sam dated were dainty things who ate like sparrows and wore a size two. She downed the remainder of her Mexican beer, equally sure she'd done the wrong thing by ordering it. Sam's women probably drank tea diluted with milk. For once in her life she wished she could be different. She wanted Sam to like her even with her healthy appetite and appreciation of good beer.

The waitress returned for their plates and served two cups of coffee. Sam noted the sudden lag in the conversation that followed and picked it up easily, entertaining Marjorie with anecdotes from his youth.

She was so engrossed in his stories that when she

finally checked her watch, she saw that it was one-forty-five.

"Oh, Sam, I've got an appointment at two." A stockbroker was coming in to test-drive a S600 sedan, and she couldn't be late.

They hurried out of the restaurant, and Sam had her back at the dealership with minutes to spare. Even though her customer was due to arrive at any time, Marjorie was reluctant to get out of the car. She turned to face him, her hand on the door handle, wanting to tell him so many things and not knowing where to start.

"Thank you, Sam," she said softly. That seemed so inadequate. "It seems I'm always having to thank you for one reason or another. Have you noticed that?"

"No," he answered evenly. "Besides, I should be the one thanking you."

"It was only lunch." And she owed him so much more than a simple meal. He'd given her another argument when the tab arrived, but she'd won. She realized now that it probably would have been better if she'd let him pay, male pride being what it is.

"Next time it's my turn."

Marjorie was outside the car before his words registered. "Right," she answered, and her smile broadened.

He waved. "Bye, Marjorie."

"Bye, Sam." She waited until he'd driven away and was out of sight before she entered the dealership.

No sooner had she stepped onto the showroom floor than Lydia appeared. "Where in heaven's name did the two of you take off to? You've been gone for hours! Where'd you go? Did he ask you out again? I told you he was interested. Remember what I said?"

"We went to lunch."

Lydia nodded approvingly. "I bet he took you to a fancy place on the waterfront for lobster."

Marjorie had a difficult time containing her amusement. "Actually, I treated him at The Lindo."

"That Mexican place you're always bragging about?"

"The food's wonderful."

"And you paid?"

"I… I told him I do that with all first-time car buyers."

Lydia's frown relaxed into a soft, encouraging smile. "Hey, not a bad idea."

"He said he'd treat next time." Marjorie cast her gaze longingly toward the street. "Do you think he'll phone?" She hated feeling so insecure, but more than anything else, she wanted to see Sam again.

"I bet you ten dollars he calls by tomorrow."

Lydia lost the bet.

Two days later Marjorie had chewed off two fingernails and was quickly becoming a nervous wreck. She'd never been a patient person, and waiting for Sam to contact her was slowly but surely driving her crazy.

"You aren't going to sit still for this, are you?" Lydia said over lunch.

"What other choice do I have?"

"Oh, come on, Marjorie!" Lydia declared, crumpling her napkin and tossing it atop her empty plate. "I've watched you chase after a sale when anyone else would have given it up. You have a reputation for putting deals together when others would have thrown their hands in the air."

"Yes, but selling cars and dealing with a man are two entirely different matters."

"No they're not," Lydia disagreed sharply.

"You think I should phone him?" The idea didn't appeal to her. Sam had left her with the impression that he'd contact her.

"No…" Lydia gazed thoughtfully at the ceiling fixture. "You need a more subtle approach."

"I suppose I could do what *he* did," Marjorie murmured thoughtfully.

Lydia's stare was blank. "What do you mean?"

"Meet him on his own ground. I could call for an appointment, claim I was having problems with the insurance company or something."

Lydia nearly tipped back the chair in her enthusiasm. "That's perfect, and there wouldn't be anything out of the ordinary in you showing up with the forms."

Even though it sounded easy, it took Marjorie nearly all afternoon to work up the courage to contact Sam's office. Since she feared the receptionist would probably handle any insurance work, she asked for an actual appointment and was given one later the following week. Now that she'd taken some positive action, she felt a hundred times better—until she saw Lydia's shocked face later that afternoon.

"What's the matter?"

"Dr. Sam's office just called."

"And?"

"And, well…apparently Dr. Sam looked over his schedule and saw your name."

"So?"

"Marjorie, I'm sure there's a logical explanation."

"Lydia, for heaven's sake, will you stop beating around the bush and tell me what's going on?"

"You know Mary and I are good friends, don't you?"

From what she remembered, Mary was Sam's receptionist. "Yes, what did she say?"

"Mary told me that when Dr. Sam saw your name, he got upset, swore under his breath, and asked Mary to call you and suggest you make an appointment with another doctor."

Chapter 5

Marjorie turned on the television, and plunked herself down on the overstuffed sofa, crossing her arms in a defiant gesture. Five minutes later she dug through the sofa cushions to find the remote and switched channels, not that it helped any. She was too furious for coherent thought, and the possibility of a mere television movie salving her injured ego was nil.

Men! Sam Bretton in particular! None of them were worth all this aggravation. She had behaved like a fool over Sam, and knowing it made her lack of savoir faire all the more difficult to swallow.

Hindsight nearly always proved to be twenty-twenty, but she should have known not to trust a man who preferred mild salsa on his enchiladas. If he couldn't eat a jalapeño straight from the jar, he wasn't her type. She liked her food *and* her men spicy and pungent. Sam was too…too wonderful. That was it, much too wonderful.

Depression settled over her shoulders like a dark mantle, and she rubbed her forearms to ward off a late-evening chill that had little to do with the mild Puget Sound weather. Sam and she were simply too different. Sam no doubt liked moonlight walks and a glass of wine in front of the fireplace, and she liked…moonlight walks and a glass of wine in front of the fireplace. Well, going over every detail a hundred times wasn't going to settle anything. He didn't want to see her again, and that was that.

She was an adult; she should be able to handle disappointments. Obviously Sam was interested in meek, mild women who knew their place. She was neither, and it was far easier to face that truth now than later, when her heart was completely infected and the prognosis for recovery would be against her.

Once Marjorie had sorted through her myriad thoughts, she felt better, even good enough to put this unpleasantness behind her and think about fixing herself something to eat. She left the television on and wandered into the kitchen. The freezer contained a wide assortment of prepackaged meals, but none of them appealed to her. Popcorn suited her mood—something crunchy and salty would help to vent her frustration. Microwave popcorn, naturally. What she'd told Sam about her lack of expertise in the kitchen had been true. She could manage spreadsheets and calculators in her sleep, but recipes baffled her. Having her anywhere in the vicinity of hot grease was like putting a submachine gun in the hands of a raw recruit. In fact, she didn't even own a complete set of cookware. The less she involved herself with a stove top, the better.

Marjorie inserted the popcorn bag, set the timer and

waited. Soon the sounds and smells of the butter-flavored kernels filled the small apartment.

She had just opened the bag and munched down the first handful when the doorbell chimed. A glance at the wall clock told her it was after nine. She certainly wasn't expecting anyone. The hope that it might be Sam caused her to hurry. It wouldn't be him, of course—she knew that—but she so wanted to see him again that her mind tormented her with the possibility.

With an eagerness that was difficult to explain, she opened her front door. Sam was standing on the other side. It was as though her wishful thinking had conjured him up.

"Hello, Sam." She greeted him as though she'd been expecting him all along, revealing no surprise.

He looked terrible. Exhausted, overworked and not himself. She would have thought he would never allow a strand of hair to fall out of place, but his hair wasn't the only thing rumpled; everything about him looked unkempt. His clothes hung on him, and the top two buttons of his shirt were unfastened. He hadn't shaved in a couple of days, or so it appeared.

"I have had the most exhausting day of my life," he announced, walking past her and into the apartment.

Bemused, Marjorie remained at the entrance, her hand on the doorknob. She'd expected contrition, guilt, grief, but not this out-and-out appeal for sympathy.

"It's been one thing after another," he continued undaunted. Without invitation, he picked up her remote and cued up the guide at the bottom of the screen.

"Would you like something to drink?" she offered, choosing to ignore his opening statement.

"Please." He sank onto her sofa and leaned forward

to wipe the tiredness from his eyes. He'd planned on calling her hours earlier and inviting her to dinner. Before he could get to a phone, Nancy Brightfield had gone into labor, and he'd spent the next five hours at the hospital with her. The delivery had been difficult, and he hadn't been able to get away until now. The unexpected trip to the delivery room and the arrival of Baby Brightfield had been a climax to a long, tedious day.

Sam realized that arriving unannounced on Marjorie's doorstep probably hadn't been one of his most brilliant ideas, but he wanted to straighten out a few things between them, and delaying the discussion was potentially unwise. He was beginning to know Marjorie Majors, and the message she was bound to read into the canceled appointment would be all wrong.

Marjorie went into her kitchen to survey her meager supply of refreshments. All she could find was a two-liter bottle of flat cola in the back of her refrigerator, a can of tomato juice with a rusty crust over the aluminum top, and a carton of milk she'd been meaning to toss for the past week.

"Is instant coffee all right?"

"Fine, fine." He really didn't care. All he really wanted was the chance for a long talk with her. He leaned back and inhaled deeply, paused, then asked, "Do I smell popcorn?"

Grinning, Marjorie stuck her head around the corner of her kitchen. Nothing smelled better than freshly popped popcorn. "Want some?"

Sam shook his head. "No, thanks. I haven't had any dinner."

"This is my dinner."

His face twisted into a mock scowl that revealed his

amusement. She had to be joking with him. "You're kidding, right?"

"No."

Sam jumped up from the couch with a reserve of energy he hadn't realized he possessed. "You can't eat that for dinner...it's unhealthy."

"I disagree." Everything she'd read contradicted Sam. The kernels were reported to be a good source of fiber, and since she ate her main meal at noon, it made sense to have something light in the evenings.

"Don't you know you're not supposed to argue with a doctor?" Actually, Sam wasn't as concerned about the nutritional value of popcorn as he was that her choice for her evening meal gave him an excellent excuse to invite her out.

"Sam, it isn't any big deal...."

"Come on, I'll take you to dinner."

Marjorie hedged. "But you just said today's been the most exhausting day of your life. What you need is to put up your feet and enjoy a good home-cooked meal." Oh, heavens, why had she suggested that? Sam would assume she planned to do the cooking, and then there would be real trouble. She might be able to bluff her way through some things, but a complete meal was out of the question.

The idea of Marjorie preparing a meal for him appealed to Sam, but he studied her carefully. Maybe he'd misunderstood her earlier. "You told me you don't cook."

At that moment she would gladly have surrendered three commissions to Al Swanson in exchange for the ability to whip together a three-egg cheese-and-mushroom omelet, but she knew better than to offer. Still, the temptation was so strong. She opened her mouth and closed it again. "I make excellent microwave popcorn," she offered weakly, and gestured toward the open bag sitting on the counter behind her.

"Then popcorn it is," Sam said, lowering himself back onto the couch. While he waited, he glanced back at the television and recognized an old-fashioned romance from the late fifties. He wouldn't have thought Marjorie would appreciate anything so sentimental. But then, she'd surprised him before.

"Here's your coffee and dinner. It's the specialty of the house." She brought in a steaming cup and handed it to him, along with a breadbasket filled with hot popcorn. "I'll be back in a minute."

"I owe you a dinner, you know."

"As I recall, it's a lunch, and if you're counting that, you might as well add a movie and popcorn to the list." He didn't owe her anything. Not really. She was the one in debt to him. Sam had given her so much more than she could ever hope to repay.

He relaxed against the thick cushions and felt his body release a silent sigh of relief. He'd missed Marjorie over the past couple of days. Missed her wit. Missed her warmth. Missed her smile. He'd wanted to see her again despite his reservations. For two days he'd been trying to find the time to call her, but there were never more than those odd five minutes here or ten minutes there. Besides, what he had to say would be better said in person. There was too much room for misunderstanding over the phone. But letting another day pass without seeing her would only add to his mounting frustration, so he'd headed over here tonight despite the late hour.

She joined him a minute later, stretched her legs on

top of the coffee table and crossed them at the ankles. Judging exactly where she should sit had been a problem. If she sat too close, he might read something into that. On the other hand, if she positioned herself as far away as possible, he might think she didn't want him around, and nothing could be further from the truth.

They sat quietly and watched the movie for a moment, then she ventured into conversation. "So. Tell me about your day."

"It was nonstop busy, and then, just as I was getting ready to leave, a woman came in, ready to have her first baby. And then, as sometimes happens, I had a difficult delivery."

Even as she tried not to, Marjorie started laughing. "*You* had a difficult delivery? How's the poor mother doing?"

"Better than me, I think. She got her girl."

"And what did you get?"

The same reward that came with every new life he brought into the world: pride and a deep sense of satisfaction.

"Plenty," he answered, in a gentle way that assured her that no matter what problems he faced, he was content with his life.

The unexpected vision of Marjorie with a baby, their baby, in her arms produced such an intense longing that his breath jammed in his lungs. He shook his head to dispel the image, but it remained, clearer than before. For years Sam had brought children into the world. He'd spent countless hours encouraging new mothers and an almost equal amount of time soothing soon-to-be fathers, but only rarely had he thought about the woman who would give *him* children one day.

Their eyes met, and Sam's smile embraced her. She didn't know what he was thinking, but if she'd been holding her coffee cup, it would have slipped from her fingers. Sam had the most sensuous smile of any man she'd ever known.

"So how have *you* been?"

"Good." She nodded once, then swallowed and headed for the deep end. "About that appointment..."

"Yes, I wanted to talk to you about that."

"I got the insurance papers straightened out—no problem."

"Insurance papers? You made the appointment to go over some papers?" Sam felt like a heel now. He'd thought she'd wanted a physical or something else equally impossible.

Her excuse to see him sounded so flimsy now that a deep flush crept up her neck and over her ears.

"It would be best if you got another physician," Sam said, and cleared his throat. "I'd be more than happy to recommend one if you want."

Marjorie couldn't believe what she was hearing. He said it so calmly, without so much as a hint of regret, as though they were discussing the weather or something equally trivial. With those few words he was telling her that he wanted her out of his life.

Unable to trust her voice, she nodded.

"It's important for everyone to have a regular physician," Sam insisted. "Cal Johnson will be doing the follow-up after your appendectomy, but he's a surgeon, and you need a general practitioner."

Marjorie's throat closed up on her, the tightness making it difficult to breathe evenly.

The wounded look in her eyes tore at Sam's heart. It

was apparent that she still didn't understand. He would have to spell it out for her.

"I think you're wonderful, Marjorie."

Sure he did. Enough to dump her right when she needed him.

"I'd like to see a lot more of you," Sam continued, "and I can't do that if you continue to be my patient."

Marjorie jerked her head around. What had he said? He wanted to see her? As in date her? Spend time with her? Be with her? She blinked and pointed her index finger at her chest. "You want to see more of me?"

"Don't look so surprised."

"I'm not… It's just that…"

"It shouldn't seem all that sudden. You must have known in the hospital I was interested. Believe me, I don't spend that much time with all my patients."

"I know, but… I don't know…" She was unsure, confused. Her gaze narrowed as she studied him. It would be best to clear away any misconceptions up front. "It's not gratitude, you know."

"It's not?" He didn't quite follow her meaning.

"Of course I'm grateful for everything you've done, but if we'd met on the street, I'd have felt the same things I do now."

"Which are?" he prompted, scooting closer to her. His dark eyes surveyed her with renewed interest.

"Never mind," she said with a small laugh. She could see no reason to inflate his ego any higher than it was already.

With his eyes steadily holding hers, Sam tucked a finger beneath her chin and slowly raised her mouth to his. Marjorie's eyelids fluttered closed as she awaited the warm sensation of his lips settling over hers. He didn't keep her waiting long. His arms encircled her, drawing her gently against his hard chest.

Their lips met in an unrushed exploration, as though they had all the time in the world and there wasn't any reason to hurry anything. His mouth was moist and pliant against her own, moving with such gentleness, such care that a tiny shudder worked its way through Marjorie, and with it came a helpless moan.

After torturous seconds Sam's lips reluctantly left hers. He buried his face in the curve of her shoulder and inhaled a calming breath. He'd felt physically drained when he'd arrived. Now he was alive, more alive than he could ever remember being. Holding Marjorie, touching her, energized him, filled him with purpose, exhilarated him, eased the ache of loneliness that followed whenever he returned to an empty house after a delivery.

The wealth of sensation took Marjorie by surprise. A simple kiss—their first—had left her with a hunger as deep as the sea. Emotion clogged her throat, and she held him to her, her fingers weaving through the thick strands of his dark hair.

"Marjorie?"

"Hmm?"

"Do you always smell this good?"

Her eyes remained closed, and she grinned. "I think it's the popcorn."

"Not this. It's roses, I think."

"My perfume."

"And sunshine."

"I showered when I got home."

He shook his head, declining her explanation. "And something more, something I can't define."

"*That's* probably the popcorn."

Sam shook his head. "Not this," he countered softly. "Not this."

The reluctance with which he loosened his hold thrilled her. They straightened and went back to watching the movie. He tucked his arm around her, and she rested her head against his shoulder. The warmth of his nearness convinced her that the man beside her was indeed real and not the product of a fanciful imagination or some delayed anesthesia-induced illusion.

A multitude of unanswered questions ran through her mind. It was on the tip of her tongue to blurt out everything she felt for him, but she feared ruining this special evening.

"So you enjoy old movies," he said, the thought pleasing him.

"Especially the classics. They did romances so well in those days."

"You like romance?"

Marjorie nodded and hid a smile. "I'm liking it more all the time."

"I am, too," Sam agreed, and turned her toward him. He wanted to kiss her again, taste her sweetness and experience once again that special power she possessed that filled him with such energy.

It was a long time before Marjorie saw any more of the movie. Or cared.

Chapter 6

"You aren't going to let Al get away with it, are you?" Lydia cried in outrage, indignation flushing her cheeks.

Marjorie didn't need to be angry about Al Swanson's latest attempt to steal a customer from her; Lydia was furious enough for the both of them. "Bud will be the one to decide."

"But you know Al is lying."

"It's my word against his, and unfortunately Bud's only the manager, not Solomon."

"But it's so unfair."

"Tell me about it," Marjorie grumbled.

Once again Al had tried to horn in on her deal. Only this time he'd succeeded. Marjorie had spoken to a couple about a E63 AMG sedan, worked with them, called twice to keep them interested, and even rode with them as they went on four different test drives in order to answer their numerous questions. The last time, the couple had gone home to sleep on the decision and returned the following day with a deposit. Al had met them at the door, claimed Marjorie had stepped out of the office, and they had accepted his offer to write up the deal on her behalf. This was the same trick he'd used once before, only this time it worked. Once the paperwork was firmly clenched in his hand, Marjorie didn't have a leg to stand on. She had complained to the manager, insisted she had been at the dealership and not out, as Al had alleged. Since Bud had been gone and there wasn't anyone to verify her story, things didn't look good for her. But she knew the manager wasn't completely naive when it came to Al. She was certain he'd heard complaints from several of the other salespeople. Bud's fair assessment of the situation was Marjorie's only real hope. Unfortunately, Al's name was on the paperwork.

The commission scale was based on how much profit the dealership made on the sale of each new car. Marjorie collected thirty percent of the capital gain. In this case she'd worked hard to give the couple the best deal possible. Her share was meager enough. If forced to split her commission with Al, she would have worked long, hard hours for practically nothing. Everything rested on Bud's decision.

"But Bud doesn't know Al the way we do," Lydia continued insistently.

Marjorie studied her friend and was hard-pressed to hold back her own indignation. Al might think he was getting away with something, but if she had anything to do with it, the cheating salesman would spend the next fifty years regretting his underhandedness. Given enough rope, Al Swanson was bound to hang himself sooner or later, and she intended to be around to see it happen.

"If he's tried those things with me, you know he's done it with the others," she said thoughtfully after a while. Yes, she was furious, but losing her cool wouldn't solve anything.

"It's the meantime that I'm worried about," Lydia mumbled, crossing her arms and righteously over her chest. "When's Bud going to let you know?"

Marjorie glanced at her watch. "As soon as he gets in."

The low hum of the intercom caught their attention. "Marjorie, call on line three. Marjorie—line three."

"I better get that," Marjorie mumbled, and sighed. "It could mean another sale."

"Not if Al can get his greedy hands on it," Lydia responded sourly, and returned to her place behind the customer-service counter.

With her friend's words ringing in her ears, Marjorie walked over to her office and reached for the phone. "Marjorie Majors," she said in a cordial, businesslike tone.

"Dr. Sam Bretton here," Sam returned.

She sat down and propped her elbows on the desktop. A rush of pleasure washed over her, taking with it some of the bitter aftertaste of Al's trickery. "Hello."

"I was just thinking about you."

"Oh?" She knew that she sounded about as intelligent as mold, but he'd taken her by surprise.

"I just returned from the hospital, and my first appointment isn't scheduled for another five minutes, so I thought I'd give you a call. You don't mind, do you?"

"No…it's a pleasant surprise."

"How's your day going?"

"Fair." It would have been much better if things were settled between her and Al, but none of this mess was Sam's problem. "How about your morning?"

"Hectic, as always." Actually, he'd been preoccupied, thinking about Marjorie and angry with himself for not setting a date for their next…well, date. He'd left her apartment feeling exhilarated and excited. They'd sat and talked long after the movie had finished, easily drifting from one subject to another. She was well-read and knowledgeable about current affairs. He'd found her opinions insightful and intelligent, and marveled that he'd found a woman who stirred his heart as well as his mind. So she didn't cook; he could deal with that. He enjoyed her company, relished their time together and longed to see her again soon. Unfortunately, his head had been in the clouds, and he hadn't thought to make plans. He'd tried calling her apartment, but she'd already left for work. He knew she worked long hours and decided his best chance of catching her was at Dixon's. He didn't want to wait another two days to see her again.

"I suppose I should apologize for last night," she said softly.

"Why?" Something was wrong. Sam could detect the subtle difference in her voice. Whatever it was, he hoped she would share it with him.

"I feel bad about not being able to offer you anything more appetizing than microwave popcorn."

"I can't remember when I've enjoyed a meal more."

Marjorie was sure that couldn't be true. No doubt there were a thousand nurses out there who longed to lure him into their arms with hot chocolate-chip cookies straight from the oven. Her microwave couldn't hope to compete with all the talented, domestically inclined women who wanted him.

"Are you free tonight?" he asked, thinking about taking her to the waterfront for a lobster dinner. He wanted to wine and dine her, and give her an evening she would remember the rest of her life. He thought about bringing her to his home and showing her his view of Commencement Bay. He wanted to sit by the fireplace with her and watch the flickering light dance over her face.

"Tonight?" she asked, confused by the unexpected invitation.

Sooner, if possible, Sam thought, but he knew his schedule wouldn't allow it.

"Actually, I'm working late, so maybe..."

"What time do you get off?"

She wished he wasn't so insistent. With Bud's decision hanging over her head, she needed some time alone to clear her thoughts. When she was with Sam, she wanted to look and feel her best. "Would it be all right if I called you next week sometime?"

Sam's breath caught at the implication. There wasn't a woman alive who threw him off course with as much ease as Marjorie. Just when he was prepared to overlook her flaws and lay his heart at her feet, she made it sound as though going to dinner with him was an inconvenience.

"Sure," he returned flippantly. "You call me. That won't be any problem."

But it was, and Marjorie recognized it from his stiff tone. She had just opened her mouth to explain when he spoke again.

"Listen, I've got to get back to my patients. We'll talk soon." He was eager to get off the phone. The entire conversation had left a bad taste in his mouth. He'd read Marjorie wrong, read everything wrong. It wasn't the first time she'd led him astray. The stock market was more predictable than Marjorie Majors.

"Right." But her voice was barely audible. "Goodbye, Sam. Thanks for calling."

He didn't answer, and she bit her bottom lip to keep from shouting that she would love to see him any night, any time, if only she didn't have this mess with Al to settle first. The phone went dead, and Marjorie felt physically ill. She'd ruined everything.

The polite knock outside her office lifted her from the pit of despair.

"It's only me," Lydia said, opening the door and peeking inside. "Hey, you look like you just lost your best friend. What happened? Another deal fall through?"

The words congealed in Marjorie's throat, and it took a few moments for her to unscramble her thoughts. "That was Sam."

"Dr. Sam?"

It was all Marjorie could do to nod. "I blew it."

"Oh, good grief," Lydia said. "Not again."

Marjorie dropped her gaze to the floor. "I'm afraid so."

"What did you do?"

"He suggested we get together tonight, and I said I was busy and that it would be better if I contacted him next week."

A moment of stunned silence followed.

"You didn't! Tell me you didn't say that!" Lydia marched into the room and pressed both hands on top of Marjorie's desk, leaning forward so that their faces were scant inches apart. "If the two of you ever get together, I swear it will be a miracle. Good grief, what made you put him off that way?"

"I don't know. This thing with Al's really got me down, and I wanted Sam to see me at my best, not my worst."

Lydia closed her eyes and slowly shook her head. "I've got more bad news for you."

"What's that?"

"Bud's here," Lydia announced starkly. "And he's in one hell of a bad mood. He wants to see you right away."

Even before Marjorie left the dealership at a quarter after nine, she knew she wasn't heading home. Sam's Brown's Point address was tucked safely away in her purse, and she had every intention of talking to him before she did anything else. Maybe she could undo some of the damage.

She located the house without a problem, pulled into the wide driveway and turned off her engine. Sam's home was a magnificent sprawling ranch house made of used brick. Huge picture windows faced the street.

Her heart was pounding like a locomotive chugging uphill. Now she understood what courage it had taken for him to arrive unannounced at her apartment. She didn't often do this sort of thing, and the need to swallow her pride made it all the more difficult.

While her conviction held, she climbed out of the car and marched up to his front door like a soldier making his way to the front of a firing squad. Her hand faltered as she rang the bell.

She heard Sam's footsteps long before the door was opened.

"Marjorie." He blinked, certain she was a figment of his imagination.

"I know I should have called, but…"

"No," he said, and smiled that slow, sexy smile of his as he stepped aside. "Come in, please."

Relieved by his warm welcome, she entered his home. The first thing that she noticed when he led her into the huge, tiled entryway was the large, unobstructed view of Commencement Bay from the floor-to-ceiling living-room windows. The twinkling lights of barges and ferryboats lit up the inky black night and reflected off the water.

"Oh, Sam," she said, her voice low in wonder. "This is so beautiful…it's marvelous." Words failed her, and she simply stared into the night.

"I love it, too." He didn't know what had brought her here, and he didn't care. She'd been on his mind all day. He regretted the abrupt way in which he'd ended their telephone conversation, and all because his fragile ego had been pricked. Most of the evening had been spent trying to come up with a way to see her again and preserve both his pride as well as hers.

"Sam," she said, tearing her gaze from the water and turning to face him. Her features were strained with an expression of practiced poise. "I've come to apologize for this morning."

"No," he countered quickly, sensing her apprehension. "I should be the one to do that." The appeal in her gaze cut a path straight to his heart, but he kept his own features tightly controlled.

"You?" she said, and laughed shortly. "I was the one who was rude."

"Something was troubling you. I knew it the minute

you spoke." He longed to ease whatever was bothering her and kicked himself more than once for having been such a fool.

Her eyes narrowed as she studied him. If Sam found her so readable, it would be difficult to hide anything from him.

"Come in and relax," he offered, leading her into the living room. The white leather couch was L-shaped, and decorated with several huge pillows in brilliant shades of blue to complement the plush carpet.

Marjorie sat, and her gaze drifted once more to the panoramic view of Commencement Bay. Just being here with Sam soothed her. All day she'd been battling her resentment toward Al and what the loss of this commission would mean to her already strained budget.

"Do you want to tell me about it?" Sam asked, taking a seat beside her.

Marjorie nodded. "I owe you that much, at least." For the next half hour she explained what had happened with Al—though she was careful not to name names— and how his devious methods had cheated her out of half the commission. By the time she'd finished, Sam was pacing in front of the coffee table with barely restrained anger. The corners of his mouth were pinched and white, his hands knotted in tight fists.

"What's being done about this?" he demanded.

"Nothing."

"Nothing?" Sam repeated incredulously.

"The decision's already been made."

"But he lied."

"I know that, and so does nearly everyone else, but it's his name on the contract, so he's entitled to a commission no matter how much time I spent with those

people. At least my protest to the manager earned me
half of it. That's the way things are done in sales."

It had been a long time since Sam had felt this angry.
He wanted to find Marjorie's coworker in a dark alley
some night and teach him a lesson. The intensity of
his fury shocked him; he hated unnecessary violence.

"I'll take care of this for you," Sam said without
any real plan in mind. He knew how hard Marjorie
worked—the long hours with few free weekends. She'd
climbed her way up the sales ladder and deserved to be
a success. The last thing she needed was someone sab-
otaging her efforts. The burning desire to protect her
seared through him like a surgical laser beam.

"Sam, please. I'm a big girl, I'll find a solution my
own way."

"No." He shook his head once, hard. "I want to handle this."

"Sam." His reaction wasn't a joke, she realized. If
she'd known this was the way he was going to be, then
she wouldn't have told him about Al. As it was, she
was glad she'd been careful not to mention Al's name.
"Listen to me. I appreciate your concern, but I don't
involve myself in your business, so I'm asking you not
to interfere in mine. Things have a way of working
themselves out."

"But this heel deserves—"

"Everything he's going to get." She stood and placed
her hand on his forearm. "I don't need anyone to rescue me. I've been on my own for a long time now. This
guy hasn't made many friends at Dixon's. He won't
last long."

"You're sure?" At her nod, Sam relaxed a bit. "Have
you eaten yet?"

"No," she answered with a smile, surprised to realize how hungry she was. "Are you offering to feed me?"

"Better than that," he answered with a slow, sensuous grin that edged his strong, well-shaped mouth upward. "I'm willing to cook for you."

Just looking at Sam made Marjorie feel light-headed. She could drown in those appealing eyes of his, dark, deep, penetrating.

"Follow me," he instructed, taking her hand and leading her into his kitchen. He was a good cook and thought he might be able to teach her a thing or two.

Sam's kitchen was huge and equipped with every modern convenience. An island with restaurant quality gas burners was set up in the middle of the expansive floor. A wide assortment of copper pots, pans and skillets was suspended from the ceiling above the island.

"Wow," Marjorie said, and released a slow, wondering breath. "You must be some chef."

"I try." He pulled out a stool for her to sit on. "First things first." With that he opened the wine refrigerator and, with little hesitation, drew out a bottle, then chose two tall wineglasses from a cabinet.

Expertly he removed the cork and poured them each a glass, pausing to taste his first. He gave his approval before handing the second glass to Marjorie.

While she sipped her Chablis, Sam set to work with a huge wok, a large supply of fresh vegetables and a sharp cleaver.

It had been hours since she'd last eaten, and the first glass of wine went straight to her head. "Here, let me help," she offered, slipping off the stool.

"No, you don't. You're my guest," Sam insisted, noting the way her cheeks were reddening. She was already a little tipsy.

He refilled her glass, and she sat down again and took another sip. "So you don't want my help. Have you been talking to the fire department?"

"No." Sam chuckled and set about slicing the vegetables in neat, even sections. "This is a recipe a friend of mine from Hong Kong taught me several years back. It's authentic and delicious."

"Is there anything you can't do?" she asked, only a little intimidated.

"A few things."

She sighed, crossed her legs and sipped some more wine. "My grandmother used to do all the cooking."

"Your grandmother?" he prompted. She rarely talked about her childhood, he'd noticed.

"Jody and I went to live with her after Mom and Dad were killed in an automobile accident."

"How old were you?"

"Twelve going on twenty. Grandma loved us, don't get me wrong. She tried to make a decent home for the two of us, but she was old, and her health wasn't good. The main problem was money. Grandma took care of Jody and the house, and I found work to bring in extra income."

Sam reached for the wine bottle and replenished her glass. The Chablis was loosening her tongue.

"So your grandmother raised the two of you?"

She nodded, holding the stem of the glass with both hands. "Right. This room feels awfully warm?" she said, and fanned her face.

Suppressing a smile, he gazed at her, trying not to laugh outright. "I think I'd better feed you, and the sooner the better."

"I'd rather you kissed me," she told him, then blinked and covered her mouth with her hand. "Oops, I didn't mean to say that."

Sam pushed the vegetables aside. "Did you mean it?"

Sheepishly, she nodded. "I think the wine's gone to my head."

"I think so, too." He walked around to stand directly in front of her. His smile was filled with confident amusement.

Her dark eyes followed his movements and innocently pleaded with him for a kiss. Unable to resist her, he leaned forward and gently covered her mouth with his own. His intention had been to appease her until he'd finished stir-frying their dinner, but the instant his lips met hers, he was lost. He deepened the kiss, his lips playing over hers as though she were a rare musical instrument.

His kiss burned through Marjorie like fire raging through dry brush. When he reluctantly lifted his head from hers, she swayed, and his hands on her shoulders were all that kept her from tumbling to the floor.

"I think you're right," she admitted. "I need something to eat…quick."

Sam's eyes burned into hers, and his strong, steady voice shook slightly. "I was just thinking that we should forget about dinner and continue with the kissing."

She tilted her head up to look into his eyes, resisting the urge to reach out and cling to him. "You were?"

"But you're right."

"I am?" At the moment she didn't think so as she watched him turn back to the stove. After a while she stood on shaky feet, unfastened her jacket and removed it. By the time she'd finished loosening the top buttons of her shirt, Sam had their meal ready.

He handed her a plate and pulled another stool up beside hers. The tantalizing scent of hot oil and ginger wafted toward her, and her stomach reacted with a loud growl. She placed her hand over her abdomen and smiled sheepishly. "Sorry."

"When was the last time you had anything to eat?"

"Noon." Soup. She'd been too upset to down anything else, so now she was famished.

Sam used chopsticks, holding the plate with one hand while dexterously using the wooden sticks with the other. She tried the same thing and nearly dumped her dinner on her lap.

"You'd better use a fork," he advised, humor lurking in his eyes.

She nodded meekly. Once she had a fork in her hand, she discovered the food was both hot and spicy. Closing her eyes, she savored each mouthful as though she hadn't eaten in weeks instead of hours.

"Oh, Sam, this is really good."

"I do my best," he answered, but his interest wasn't in the dinner. Marjorie, the woman who had tormented his dreams for weeks, was sitting across from him. Part angel, part temptress. Complicated, vital and ripe, an opulent beauty. He'd dreamed of having her with him in his home, envisioned carrying her into his room and laying her across his king-size bed. He wanted to love her, ease the ache of loneliness he read in her eyes and make up to her for the childhood she'd lost.

Following the meal, Sam made a fresh pot of coffee. Marjorie, feeling sober and steady on her feet after the delicious dinner, poured them each a cup and carried them into the living room. They sat close to each other, and she tucked her feet up under her and placed her head on his sturdy shoulder.

"You're not going to drift off on me, are you?" he asked gently. His hand curved around her nape, and his fingers stroked the slope of her neck and shoulder.

"If you keep doing that, I will." She felt him smile against her hair. "I'm sorry to be such poor company," she said, uttering the words through a loud yawn.

"You're not."

She half lifted her head. "I don't know what it is, but every time I'm around you all I do is sleep."

"I often have that effect on women," Sam said, and chuckled. The rich sound of his amusement echoed around the room. He was thinking of going to bed, too, but not in the same sense she was. Holding her close was a tough temptation to handle.

She tried unsuccessfully to stifle another yawn. "Believe me, I know how women react to you."

"I'd better get you home, Kitten."

"Kitten?" No one had ever called her anything but her name, at least not to her face.

"You remind me of one," he explained softly. "You're all soft and cuddly."

"I have claws."

Again he smiled. "Now that's something I can personally attest to."

Marjorie was smiling when she unfolded her legs from beneath her and stood. She collected her jacket and purse, and paused in the entryway. "It seems I'm always in your debt."

Sam's brow furrowed as he rose. "How's that?"

"First you rescue me from the jaws of death…"

"That's a slight exaggeration."

"Then you buy a car from me…"

"One I intended to purchase anyway."

"Next you feed me."

There was a lot more Sam was interested in doing for her, and if she didn't hurry up and leave, he was going to have more problems refusing her.

"Thank you, Sam, once again."

"Thank *you*."

They paused in front of the door, and Sam turned her in his arms. His hands locked at the small of her back, pulling her closer against the solid wall of his chest. His hips and thighs pressed against hers, and still they weren't close enough.

Marjorie had no intention of refusing his kiss, not when she craved it herself. His mouth closed possessively over hers, searing his name onto her heart. Again and again he kissed her with a fierce tenderness, shaping and fitting her lips with his own.

Sam's arms circled her protectively while his tongue explored the soft recesses of her mouth until she shook with a sensation she had never known.

"Sam…"

"Kitten," he murmured.

Wildly consuming kisses followed, and Marjorie felt as though she were on fire. Never had she felt so willing, so sensuous. There'd been little time for puppy love when she was young. Later, the men she'd dated had resented her streak of independence. When it came to lovemaking and men, she was shockingly innocent. The sensations Sam had awakened in her had been dormant far too long. Now that she'd discovered love, she wasn't going to let go lightly.

An insistent beeping surrounded them, and Sam's impatient groan told her the noise wasn't the bells on the hill tolling their love.

"What is it?" she whispered, hardly able to find her voice.

"Not what, but who."

She blinked, not understanding.

"That's my pager. I'm needed at the hospital."

Chapter 7

The phone pealed loudly in the darkened bedroom. At first Marjorie incorporated the irritating sound into her dream. By the third ear-shattering ring she realized it was her telephone.

Without lifting her head from the pillow, she stretched out her arm and groped for the receiver, locating it in time to cut off the fourth ring.

"Yes," she mumbled, and brushed the wild confusion of hair from her face.

"Kitten?"

Her eyes flew open, and she struggled into a sitting position and reached for the small clock on her nightstand. "Sam?"

"I'm sorry to wake you, but I wanted to be sure you got home safely."

She blinked and focused her gaze on the illuminated

clock dial. It was a few minutes after four. "I didn't have any problems. How did things go at the hospital?"

"Great. Wonderful, in fact."

She relaxed and leaned against the thick goose-down pillow, savoring the warmth that never failed to infuse her whenever Sam called. "Did you deliver another baby?"

"Two, actually, or I would have been back hours ago."

"Girls? Boys?"

"One of each." He felt like a fool, calling her at this ungodly hour, but he'd walked into his empty house, and everywhere he looked, he thought of Marjorie. The memory of her presence swirled around him like the soft scent of summer. Often the stark loneliness of his lifestyle had hit him after a nighttime delivery, but never more than it had this time. He would have given anything in the world to have found her curled up and sleeping in his bed, waiting for him. Hearing her voice was a poor substitute, but one he couldn't deny himself.

"I realized when I got back to the house," he continued, "that I hadn't asked to see you again." Even to his own ears, the explanation sounded lame.

"No, we both had other things on our minds."

"Dinner tonight, then?" he asked.

Marjorie wasn't thinking clearly; her mind was clouded with the last dregs of sleep. "What day is this?"

"Friday."

Her disappointment was potent enough to produce a bout of aching frustration. "I can't," she moaned. "My sister is driving up from Portland, and I'm working late both days this weekend."

"I'll take both you and your sister to dinner, then." That was an easy enough solution.

"But, Sam…"

"No arguing. Your sister, and anyone else you want, is welcome to join us." He didn't care if he had to buy dinner for every employee at Dixon Motors as long as he could spend time with Marjorie.

"You're sure?"

"Absolutely. And while we're on the subject of dinners and dates, I know it's next week and you might be busy, but do you have plans for July Fourth?"

"No."

"You don't have to work?"

"No," she murmured, and smiled. "That would be un-American. What makes you ask…about the Fourth, I mean?"

"Another doctor and his wife, Bernie and Betty Miller, have a cabin on Hood Canal, and they invited me up. Would you spend the day with me?"

Marjorie closed her eyes to hold back the tears of joy. "I'd be thrilled."

"I'll let the Millers know, then."

They must have talked for another half hour before Marjorie realized that Sam's slow responses revealed his exhaustion.

"Oh, Sam, I'm sorry. You must be dead on your feet, and I'm talking your head off."

His grin was both lazy and content. "No. Listening to you relaxes me. Normally when I get back from the hospital, especially this late, I'm too tense to sleep— too keyed up. Now I feel like I could easily drift off."

"Good night, then," she murmured softly, regretfully. She was falling head over heels for Sam Bretton. She knew the pitfalls and still wanted to love him.

* * *

"A doctor?" Jody squealed with unrestrained delight. At twenty she was a younger version of Marjorie, the only difference being her hair, which was cut fashionably short, and her sportier and more colorful clothes.

"You behave yourself," Marjorie warned. Now that her health was back and she didn't have to submit to Jody's orders, she could more fully appreciate her sibling.

Jody looked her sister full in the eye. "You mean I can't tell Sam about the time you snuck out of the house to kiss Freddy Fletcher behind the toolshed?"

"You do, and I'll smack you upside the head."

The light, musical sound of Jody's laughter filled the cozy apartment. "I have to admit, though, you look a hundred times better than the last time I was here. I wonder if your doctor friend has anything to do with that?"

"I look better because I haven't been forced to eat your cooking, which is even worse than my own."

Jody pretended the remark had greatly offended her, but neither of them had been blessed with talent in the kitchen, and they enjoyed teasing each other about that fact.

"So Sam was your doctor," Jody said, as she slumped on the couch and crossed her legs Indian style beneath her. "How come you didn't mention him before now?"

"I… He… Well, what really happened is…"

"Oh honestly, Marjie, look at your face. You're actually blushing. I can't believe it. My big sister is in love. Well, good grief, it took you long enough."

Marjorie's hands flew to her cheeks in embarrassment. They did feel hot and were no doubt as flushed as her sister claimed.

"You're in love with him, aren't you?" Jody asked, pretending to study her nails, but actually aiming her gaze toward her older sister.

"Yes," Marjorie answered honestly.

"Have you gone to bed with him yet?"

"Jody!"

"Well, have you?"

The heat in Marjorie's face intensified a hundred-fold. "Of course not! What kind of question is that?"

Jody's eyebrows rose suggestively. "But you'd like to, wouldn't you."

"I can't believe we're having this conversation." With as much composure as she could muster, which wasn't much, Marjorie reached for her glass of iced tea and took a large swallow.

Amused, Jody pinched her lips together in mock disapproval. "Come on, Marjie, would you stop being my mother long enough to talk to me like a big sister? Tell me everything. I want to know the most intimate desires of your heart."

Despite the subject matter, Marjorie relaxed. "My desires? That's easy."

"Sam?" Jody coaxed.

"Sam," Marjorie repeated. "I can't believe this is happening to me after all these years of being so sensible about men. With Sam, everything's different." She paused and then continued, telling her sister how Sam Bretton had stayed with her in the hours following her surgery. "I didn't know any man so wonderful existed. I feel giddy every time I'm with him."

Jody nodded knowingly and smiled through a haze of tears.

"Honey, what's wrong?" Marjorie asked quickly.

Jody wiped the moisture off the high arch of her cheekbones. "This is the first time I can remember when you've talked to me like a...sister. You never shared anything with me before—at least not like this. I'm happy for you, really happy."

Marjorie blinked back her surprise, ready to argue the point. Then she thought about how right her sister was. She had never felt she could share with Jody; her sister was so much younger that it hadn't seemed right to burden Jody with her problems. Jody had to be protected, and because of that their relationship had to be part parent, part sibling. She'd had to be Jody's mother and sister both.

"You know something," Jody said, her voice unsteady. "I love Sam already."

"Wait until you meet him," Marjorie answered, her own voice wavering. "He's been so good to me."

"You deserve him, and he deserves you."

They wrapped their arms around each other and squeezed tightly, neither willing to let the other go. They had reached a deeper understanding of what it meant to be sisters, and for that Marjorie would always be grateful.

Sam arrived about fifteen minutes later, amazed at Jody's warm welcome. He liked her immediately but wished he could have had time alone with Marjorie. It seemed a hundred years since he'd last talked to her, and a thousand since he'd held her sweet warmth against him and relished the special feel of her in his arms.

The evening proved to be a fun one. He treated the two women to a delicious seafood dinner in a four-star restaurant that overlooked Commencement Bay. Following the meal, the three of them walked along the dock outside the Lobster Shop and gazed at the bright lights that sparkled like shiny stars from the opposite shore.

"I can't remember the last time I ate this well," Jody said, holding her stomach and exhaling a deep, contented sigh. "I'm stuffed."

Marjorie's worried gaze instantly flew to her younger sister. "I knew it! You're not eating right."

"I'm in perfect health."

Sam's arm around Marjorie's waist tightened, and she managed to hold back any further argument.

Jody looked at the two of them, and with a smile lifting the corners of her full mouth, she feigned a loud yawn. "I can't believe how tired I am all of a sudden. That drive from Portland can really wear a person out."

Sam and Marjorie shared a secret look and struggled to hide their amusement. Jody couldn't have been any less subtle had she tried.

"I think she's offering us some time alone," Sam whispered close to Marjorie's ear. He was hard-pressed not to flick his tongue over her lobe, knowing her instant response. "Are we going to accept?"

Marjorie's nod was eager.

"Just drop me off at the apartment, and you two can escape," Jody announced, looking pleased with herself. "Far be it from me to block the path of true love."

"Far be it from me to let you," Sam joked, as they headed toward the restaurant parking lot.

Sam drove directly back to Marjorie's apartment, and Jody hurriedly scooted out of the car, winked and reached for Marjorie's keys. "Don't hurry back on my account."

"We won't," Sam assured her. He appreciated what Jody was doing, but he wouldn't keep Marjorie out long. It was obvious the two sisters were close. He'd seen for himself the various roles Marjorie played in Jody's life, slipping from one to the other with hardly a breath in between.

Marjorie remained in Sam's car while Jody let herself into the apartment. Then he reached for her hand, squeezing gently. "I like your sister."

"She's impressed with you, too." That was a gross understatement, Marjorie thought to herself. Jody had been giving her signals all night that showed her whole-hearted approval of Sam. In the ladies' room she had gone so far as to suggest that if Marjorie didn't want Sam, she'd take him.

But Marjorie wanted Sam Bretton even more than before. She couldn't look in his direction without her eyes revealing everything that was stored in her heart. She couldn't hide her love for him any longer.

"I have to stop off at the hospital for a minute," he said, as he pulled out of the parking lot of the apartment complex. "Is that a problem?"

"No, of course not. If you want, I'll stay in the car."

"There's no need for you to do that," Sam came back quickly. "I want to introduce you to a couple of my friends. And this will give you a chance to see the two babies I delivered the other night."

Marjorie's heart shot to her throat. Babies. Sam was as comfortable with them as she was with interest rates and electromechanically fuel-injected engines. Anyone under the age of two terrorized her; babies made her nervous and served to remind her of how inadequate she was in the traditional female role. Her biggest fear was that Sam would bring her into the hospital and expect her to go inside the nursery. He might even expect her to hold an infant, and then he would learn that not only were babies allergic to her, she was allergic to them.

"How does that sound?" Sam asked, cutting into her troubled thoughts.

"About the babies?" she hedged.

"Yes, they're—"

"Sam, listen," she said, rushing her words. "Maybe it would be better if I went back to the apartment with Jody."

He shot her a puzzled frown. The disappointment that welled up in him was strong. He couldn't understand her sudden objection. Sure, she hadn't especially enjoyed her hospital stay, and he could understand why. But her hesitation now puzzled him. "Go back to the apartment? Whatever for?"

Marjorie made the pretense of glancing at her watch. "It's late and…"

"It's barely after nine," he countered, studying her. She was growing paler by the minute.

Marjorie couldn't look into Sam's eyes and refuse him anything. "You're right," she said, determination squaring her shoulders. "I'm being silly. Of course I'll go with you and meet your friends and see the babies. Everything will be wonderful."

She knew her tone was falsely cheerful, but she decided it was far better for her to confront her fears than leave them unconquered. He would be with her— nothing would go wrong.

He helped her out of the car, and led her through a

side entrance and to the elevator beyond. When the door shut, he punched the floor number and pulled her into his arms for a brief, ardent kiss.

She tried to respond, but her heart was beating as hard and loud as a drum, and her insides were quivering with apprehension. She wanted to do everything right with Sam, and her fear of babies was sure to ruin her chances.

He pulled her close to his side and stared at the closed doors. Marjorie was perfect, with her soft skin, her wide, soulful eyes, and a heart he longed to fill with his love.

The elevator doors smoothly glided open, and Marjorie braced herself for the inevitable. Sam meant so much to her, and it was vital that she be the kind of woman he needed. Without meaning to, she pressed her flattened palms together and rubbed them back and forth several times. When he looked her way, he frowned, so she smiled tightly and freed her hands, letting her arms drop lifelessly to her sides.

With his hand at the base of her spine, Sam directed Marjorie over to the nurses' station and introduced her to three of the staff members he worked with regularly. The purpose of this visit was more social than anything else. He'd partially fabricated the need to stop in, in an effort to casually introduce her to his peers. It seemed as though she'd been a natural part of his life forever.

"Is Bernie around?" Sam asked the oldest of the nurses, who reminded Marjorie of Bertha Powell. The two could have been sisters.

"Dr. Miller's in the lounge."

Sam reached for Marjorie's hand, lacing his fingers through his as he led her down the wide hallway.

"Nice to have met you," Marjorie said brightly over her shoulder.

"A pleasure," the oldest nurse returned. The other two said nothing. Their wide-eyed stares told her that both of them were convinced she wasn't good enough for their beloved Dr. Sam. The feeling of being watched persisted long after the staff members were out of sight.

Bernie Miller was sitting at the round table in the middle of the doctors' lounge, holding a cup of coffee. He was leaning over the table and holding his head up with one hand. When Sam and Marjorie entered the room, he raised his head, his gaze brightening. His fatigued features relaxed into a slow grin.

"Bernie, I'd like you to meet Marjorie Majors."

Slowly Dr. Miller rose to his feet, but his gaze didn't waver from Marjorie's. "Hello there."

"Hi." She stepped forward and offered him her hand.

"So this is her?" Bernie's gaze shot from Marjorie back to Sam as they ended the brief handshake.

"In the flesh." Sam draped his arm across Marjorie's shoulder as he smiled down on her, his gaze filled with warmth. He hadn't told many of his friends about Marjorie, but hiding the news of how he felt from his best buddy had been impossible. Bernie had known he'd met someone important the minute Sam casually mentioned her a few days earlier. Bernie had wanted to know all about her, but Sam had hesitated. He hadn't been sure of his own feelings then. Marjorie appealed to him more than anyone in a long time, but she wasn't exactly the happy homemaker, and that realization had pulled him up short. Until he'd met Marjorie, the woman he'd pictured in his life had been able to both seduce him in the bedroom and whip up a five-course dinner.

"I understand that you're joining us for our picnic on Wednesday."

"Yes," Marjorie said, and nodded for emphasis. "Thank you for including me."

Sam poured two more cups of coffee while she sat down and talked to Bernie, then joined them at the table. Marjorie mused to herself that things were going well. If only they could stop here. She had no trouble relating to adults; it was infants and children who caused her to break out in hives.

"I'm going to take Marjorie to the nursery," Sam was saying.

Doing her utmost not to choke on her coffee, she pushed her cup aside and stood. If she thought her heart had been pounding in the elevator, now it was crashing like a Chinese gong as she followed Sam out of the doctors' lounge. No doubt the three nurses she'd met earlier never had this problem. Most likely any one of them would gladly surrender her eyeteeth to have Dr. Sam Bretton.

He led her down the wide corridor and into the nursery. Rows of bassinets were lined up in uniform fashion. Some of the infants were blanketed in pink, others in blue. Their surnames were written in bold letters in front of their mock cribs. Two of the nurses that Marjorie had just met now sat in rocking chairs, soothing crying infants.

Sam donned a surgical robe and handed Marjorie one.

"Sam," she whispered, barely able to speak. "There's something you should know."

"Just a minute," he murmured, grinning boyishly. With a gentleness she'd witnessed several times in the last month, Sam lifted a small pink bundle from a crib and looked up at Marjorie, beaming proudly.

"What do you think?" he asked, scooting sideways so she could more easily view the squirming infant in his wide embrace.

Her eyes dropped to the scrunched-up face and minute fists as the baby struggled to get free of her bindings. She forced a smile, unable to think of anything to say.

"Would you care to hold her?"

Her dark eyes widened with alarm, and she forcefully shook her head. "No…thanks." By the time she'd finished speaking, she'd backed herself out the door.

"Marjorie, are you feeling all right?"

"I'm a little… I'm fine," she managed somehow. "Really."

As carefully as he'd lifted the infant, Sam replaced her in her bassinet. By the time he'd finished, Marjorie was leaning against the wall in the corridor outside the nursery.

"What's wrong?" he asked softly, coming to stand beside her.

"I…it's no big thing."

"You look like you're about to faint."

"Don't worry, I'm not the type," she said. "I'm not the kind of woman who goes all mushy at the sight of a baby, either. In case you hadn't noticed, not all of us are alike. There are some of us who cook and crochet and get pregnant at the drop of a hat. And then there are others, like me, who are allergic to baby powder and dirty diapers, and content to eat TV dinners the rest of our miserable lives."

Sam's eyes were incredulous. "Are you trying to tell me you don't like babies?"

"Sure, I do," she said. "In somebody else's arms."

Sam blinked, hardly able to believe his ears. He felt as if the world were crashing in around him. He'd decided not to worry about Marjorie's lack of culinary skills, deciding that her strength and independence were more important than any domestic qualities. But when it came to having children, he wouldn't—couldn't—compromise.

"Babies are fine for the right kind of woman," she said. Her voice had gained in volume with the strength of her convictions. "Unfortunately, I'm not one of them."

"You don't mean that." His words were sharp.

By now their heated exchange had attracted the attention of the hospital staff. If Sam's nursing friends had disapproved of her earlier, it was nothing to the censure she felt being aimed at her now. They thought Sam deserved someone far better than she would ever be, and every accusing glare said as much.

Without thought for the wisdom of her actions, she turned and half ran, half walked, down the polished corridor to the elevator, fighting back tears all the way.

"Marjorie, wait!" Sam cried.

Since the elevator wasn't there yet anyway, she didn't have much choice if she wanted to maintain her dignity. They descended in tense silence. Even when they left the hospital building and headed toward Sam's car, neither of them spoke. By that time her throat was so clogged that it felt as though someone had a stranglehold on her. With everything that was in her, she yearned to be all Sam wanted in a woman, yet she'd failed miserably.

Sam opened her door for her. His feet felt heavy as he walked around the car and let himself in. He didn't know what to say or how to say it. He wanted a family, longed for children, and he yearned for Marjorie to give them to him.

She watched him with despair. The tears that had been so close to the surface ran down her cheeks like water over a dam after an early spring thaw, and she turned her head away so he couldn't see. At that moment she would have sold her soul to be different. She took a deep, shuddering breath. "You want children, don't you?"

Her heart cracked when he was silent, and she realized he couldn't deny it. Sam Bretton would make a wonderf   father; he was a natural.

"Yes," he answered finally. He couldn't deny his desire for a family. Almost from the beginning, he'd pictured Marjorie with a child in her arms—their child. For years he'd been seeking a woman who was strong enough to stand on her own, and tender enough to need and love him. These last weeks with Marjorie had led him to believe he'd found that special woman…until tonight.

"I'm no good with babies, and I'm even worse with children," she whispered in a choked voice. "That's not going to change."

Chapter 8

For the second time that morning, Marjorie checked the picnic basket. Her nerves were shot. She hadn't heard from Sam, nor had she contacted him. For three days she'd done nothing but think about him and how wrong they were for each other. The realization didn't do any good, though; she still loved him, still wanted him, still yearned for them to build a life together. She would give anything to be the right person for him, but she couldn't change what she was, couldn't become someone different.

Now it was the Fourth of July, and she wasn't even sure he would show up to take her to the picnic and wouldn't blame him if he didn't.

She paused to take a calming breath and rubbed her hands down the thighs of her new jeans. They had been Jody's idea. Marjorie hadn't told her sister what happened between her and Sam, but Jody had guessed something was drastically wrong. The following morning she had insisted they go shopping, claiming there wasn't any ailment a department store couldn't cure. The jeans, Jody claimed, did great things for Marjorie's legs. For all Marjorie cared, they could have been made from sackcloth.

The weather outside wasn't promising; thick gray clouds had formed overhead. As an afterthought, she tucked a thick sweater inside the basket.

The doorbell chimed, and her heart lurched. She swallowed and opened the door. Sam, dressed in jeans and a T-shirt, stood on the other side. He didn't look any better than she felt. Although he was outwardly composed, turmoil and regret were evident in his eyes and the hard set of his mouth.

He stepped inside her living room and hesitated, then smiled. The movement transformed his face.

"What's wrong?" she asked, convinced she should have worn anything but jeans. Denim might help her legs, but it didn't do a thing for her hips.

"The jeans," Sam managed.

"They're all wrong, aren't they?" Silently she blamed her sister. Marjorie knew better than to listen to the advice of a college student who was toying with the idea of tinting her hair blue.

"No," he murmured.

"I can change, don't worry," she went on brightly. "It'll only take a minute."

"Don't," he said, and smiled briefly. "You look fantastic." His gaze was warm and sincere.

Marjorie thought she would cry. She'd been as taut as a violin bow, as well as nervous and worried. Until the minute he spoke, she'd had no idea what he was thinking. Apparently he'd decided to put the incident in the hospital behind them—at least for today. She knew that they should talk and try to settle this problem, but in three days she hadn't been able to come up with a solution, and from his haggard look, she suspected that Sam hadn't, either. Today they would put their troubles aside and enjoy the holiday. She was grateful.

"Every woman should look so good in Levi's," he said.

A smile curved her mouth. "You honestly like them?"

"Yes, Kitten, I do."

Sam longed to take her in his arms and hold her, but he didn't dare. These last days without her had been a self-imposed nightmare. After years of searching for a woman he could love, respect and admire, he'd been convinced he'd found her in Marjorie. No, she wasn't exactly the woman he'd pictured, but he'd discovered he could accept her quirks, loved her all the more because of them. They were part and parcel of who she was. But children... He'd dedicated his life to reproduction and childbirth. To him, children were as essential as food and water. He needed a woman who wanted to give him a family. He could find no way to compromise on an issue so basic to his happiness.

After that night at the hospital, Sam had decided to make a clean break from her. There didn't seem to be any purpose in prolonging the agony. But he'd learned it wasn't that simple. He thought about her constantly, longed to talk to her. After two torturous days he'd known that forgetting about her would be impossible. He would have to think of something to help him solve this problem.

"I've missed you," he murmured, as his eyes held hers.

"I've missed you, too," she answered, and her voice was filled with regret. "Sam," she whispered, "I'm so sorry."

"I am, too, Kitten." He drew a deep breath, then exhaled slowly. She couldn't change what she was, and he couldn't help loving her. He prayed they could find a solution to this, because now that he had found Marjorie, he couldn't let her go.

"Betty," Sam said, his arm loosely draped over Marjorie's shoulder. "This is Marjorie Majors. Marjorie, Betty."

"Hi," Betty Miller said cordially, her blue eyes twinkling. She was bouncing a toddler on her hip, and the shy little boy hid his face against his mother's shoulder. "I'm so pleased you could make it. Can you believe this weather? Only on Puget Sound would we have a fireplace going on the Fourth of July."

"Thank you for inviting me."

Betty was slender and pretty, exactly the type Marjorie had always pictured as a doctor's wife. Her deep blue eyes were warm and gentle, and Marjorie doubted that Betty Miller had an enemy in this world.

"The ruffian on my hip is Kevin. He's three," Betty added, and encouraged her son to look up long enough to greet their company. Kevin, however, held his fists over his eyes and refused to acknowledge Marjorie *or* Sam.

"Hi, Kevin," Marjorie offered stiffly but to no avail.

The little boy buried his face deeper into his mother's shoulder. "He's a little bit shy," Betty explained, her face flushed with embarrassment.

"That's all right," Marjorie said, in an effort to reassure her. She understood far better than Betty could realize. Kids instinctively knew she was rotten mother material. She didn't know how they knew, but they did.

"Kevin, do you want to show Uncle Sam where your daddy is?" Betty asked, and there was a hopeful note in her voice.

To everyone's surprise, Kevin nodded eagerly and climbed off his mother's hip. Without looking in Marjorie's direction, the three-year-old held out his hand in order to lead Sam away.

Sam must have noted the distress in Marjorie's eyes, because he murmured something about being right back.

"Take your time," Betty returned. Once Sam and Kevin were out of sight, she let out a soft sigh and changed the topic as she led the way toward the cabin, which was located on the fertile bank of Hood Canal and was surprisingly modern. She gestured expansively. "You'd think Bernie had constructed the Empire State Building for the amount of time and effort that's gone into this infamous deck."

"Bernie built the deck himself?" Marjorie had to admit she was impressed with the wraparound structure, as she followed her hostess into the kitchen. A series of stairs led down onto the sandy, smooth beach below.

"Don't encourage him," Betty warned with a short laugh. "In his former life Bernie claims to have been a carpenter. He thinks he missed his calling." Still grinning, she poured them each a tall glass of iced tea and led Marjorie into the living room. A small fire gave the room a cozy feeling.

Marjorie sat in the overstuffed chair opposite her hostess.

Betty's chest rose with a deep breath, and she smiled at Marjorie. "You don't know how relieved I am to finally meet you."

"Me?"

"Sam's hardly talked about anything else from the day you went in for surgery."

"He told you about me?" Amazed, Marjorie flattened her hand over her heart.

"In elaborate detail. Does that surprise you?"

"It shocks me." And pleased her. And excited her. Then she remembered there could be no future for them.

"Bernie and I have been waiting years for Sam to finally meet the right woman. We'd almost given up hope. He's so dedicated to his patients. The one thing that's suffered most over the last few years has been his personal life."

"He *is* a wonderful doctor."

"You won't get any arguments out of me. I should know—Sam delivered both Kevin and Shelley."

"Shelley?" She was going to have to deal with more than one child?

"Shelley's sleeping, like all good four-month-olds. You'll see her later."

Marjorie only nodded. She liked Betty and didn't want to disillusion her with her own lack of anything approaching the maternal instinct.

"You know, I knew Sam before I even met Bernie," Betty explained, gazing into her iced tea. Her face took on a solemn look.

"Are you a nurse?"

Betty nodded. "I know that sounds old hat, but the

path of romance was anything but smooth for Bernie and me. It isn't like we saw each other from across a crowded room and instantly heard fate calling."

"No?"

Betty crossed her legs and grinned sheepishly. "Well, to be honest, I was dating Sam when I met Bernie. Later Bernie was assigned to the ward where I was working."

"So it was being in close proximity that ignited the fires between you?"

Laughing, Betty shook her head. "Hardly. If there were any fires ignited, they were from the arguments we had. Bernie and I couldn't agree on anything, and I found him impossible to work with. Once he even went so far as to warn Sam that I was a meddling busybody and he'd do well not to see me again."

Marjorie found all this a little difficult to believe. She'd met Bernie and seen for herself the way his gaze softened when he mentioned his wife's name.

"I know it sounds unbelievable now, but we had serious problems." Betty paused and ran the tips of her fingers over the chair's armrest, caught up in her memories. "It seemed that no matter what I did or how careful I was, I couldn't please the demanding Dr. Miller. Every time he and I were together, we ended up in a shouting match. There wasn't a staff member on the entire floor who would come within twenty feet of us when we got going."

"What happened to change all that?"

Betty shrugged, then a lazy smile began to grow until it practically lit up her round face. "Bernie came to my apartment one night after work. I'll admit he looked terrible, but we'd had another one of our confrontations that day, and I wasn't in any mood to be friendly."

"What did he say?" Marjorie couldn't help being curious.

"He wanted to talk." Betty paused and grinned. "I told him to take a flying leap into the nearest cow pasture."

Marjorie laughed outright. The idea of tiny Betty standing up to a stern-faced Bernie made for a comical picture. "I don't imagine he was any too pleased with that suggestion."

"No. I could tell he was struggling not to tell me where I should fly. But he didn't. Instead he asked me how serious I was about Sam."

Marjorie suspected that Bernie had been attracted to Betty from the first, but he was decent enough not to get involved with his best friend's girlfriend.

"Sam was a friend," Betty continued. "A good one. We'd dated off and on for years, but there was never anything serious between us. Fun stuff. You know—a baseball game, hikes now and again, that sort of thing. Neither one of us ever thought it was a romance for the ages."

"But you let Bernie think otherwise."

"Why not? He'd been a pill from the first. Besides, what was happening between Sam and me wasn't any of his business. I told him that, too."

"I suppose he left then."

"Yeah, how'd you know?"

"Lucky guess," Marjorie said, holding in a knowing smile.

"We didn't argue after that. Not once. Bernie treated me like every other nurse on the ward, and within a week I was so bored I wanted to cry. Until that moment I didn't realize how much I looked forward to sparring with him." She smiled as she remembered. "That was when Sam invited me to have coffee with him in the cafeteria after work one day. When I sat down, the first thing he did was ask about Bernie. I said I didn't have any idea what he was talking about. Sam looked surprised at that. He claimed Bernie had gotten drunk one night and stormed at him to hurry up and marry me before he   Bernie—did something stupid."

"I can imagine Sam's reaction to that."

Betty grinned and continued. "Sam told him he liked me fine, but he couldn't see the two of us ever getting married."

"What did Bernie say to that?"

Betty rolled her eyes toward the ceiling. "Apparently he tried to swing on Sam. You have to understand how out of character that is for Bernie to fully appreciate him doing something like that."

"I think I can understand," Marjorie said. Any person who would dedicate his life to the care and well-being of his fellow man would naturally deplore violence. "How did the two of you ever manage to get together?"

"It was easy once I sorted through my feelings. I figured that since he'd come to me once, I'd have to be the one to approach him. Not right away, mind you. It took some thinking on my part. The most difficult part was realizing I was in love with Bernie Miller and had been for weeks. The hardest thing I've ever done was invite him over for dinner. Funny thing, though, once we stopped arguing, we discovered how much we had in common. Within a month of our first dinner date we were engaged, and you can guess the rest of the story."

Marjorie took a sip of her tea. "The two of you are

perfect together. It's obvious talking to either one of you that you and Bernie are in love."

"We work on it." Betty slapped the armrest. "Enough about me. I want to know about you."

"There really isn't much to tell." A bit uneasy, Marjorie spoke in general terms about her job and her sister. The whole time she was talking, she was aware that there was nothing that made her any different than the other women Sam had dated in the past ten years.

"He's crazy about you," Betty commented. "You know that, don't you?"

Marjorie could feel the other woman studying her. Sam might have been crazy for her at one time, but she had ruined that.

"To be honest, I wondered what made you different. But ten minutes with you and I can understand it. You're exactly the type of woman Sam needs."

Marjorie's look must have revealed her disbelief.

"A doctor needs a woman in his life who has a strong and independent nature. So many other people are constantly making demands on his time and his energy that sometimes there's not much left for anyone else. Above anything else, Sam needs a respite from the demands of work. For men like Sam and Bernie, death is the enemy, and they'll fight for a life with little or no thought to the physical or emotional cost to themselves."

Marjorie nibbled on her lower lip. "I hadn't thought about it like that." Betty had far more insight into Sam and Bernie's needs than she'd considered. All she herself knew was that she loved Sam Bretton and that she would consider herself the most fortunate woman in the world to be his wife.

"I know Bernie so well that I recognize the signs

now. He doesn't need to say a word," Betty went on. "There's a look about him, a tiredness in his eyes and in the way he walks. All of those things tell me the kind of day he's had. He'll snap at me every now and again, but I forgive him because I know that he's probably had to tell someone's son or daughter that their mother won't be coming home from the hospital, or he's had to tell someone that their test results show they have cancer."

The thought of having to give someone such bad news tightened a knot of compassion in Marjorie's stomach.

"The last thing Bernie needs when he gets home is a list of demands from me. I wouldn't do that to him, and you wouldn't do that to Sam. He knows that, just the way I did as soon as we met."

A cool sip of her drink helped alleviate the tightness in Marjorie's throat. "I'm not the right woman for him. I don't deserve him."

Betty settled back in her chair and grinned. "He said almost exactly those same words to Bernie about you."

Marjorie blinked back her surprise and lowered her gaze. Her heart was filled with such misery that it was impossible to hold it all inside. She felt as though she would burst into tears in another minute.

"In fact, Bernie got so sick of hearing about you that he threatened to cancel their poker night if Sam didn't bring you around and introduce you."

"He must have taken him seriously, because we made a trip to the hospital Friday night."

"Bernie mentioned that, too. He told me that one look at the two of you together and he knew Sam had finally found the right woman. By the way, what is it about Sundays with you?"

"Sundays?"

"Yes. Sam phoned the other day and said the only time he can play poker from now on is Sunday afternoons."

Marjorie set the tall glass aside. "I work weekends. Hopefully someday I'll have Sundays free, but unfortunately, that probably won't be for some time yet."

Slowly Betty shook her head. "Believe me, when a man puts a woman before a long-standing poker game, he's serious about her."

Marjorie dropped her gaze and felt obliged to add, "We aren't serious. There are...problems."

"Wait and see, you'll settle them," Betty returned with unshakable confidence. "Sam's never been more ready for a wife than he is now."

Betty looked as if there were more she wanted to say, but before she could speak the sliding-glass door opened, and the two men, plus Kevin, walked into the house.

"Have you shown Marjorie my deck yet?" Bernie asked, beaming proudly.

Betty tried not to smile and failed. "It was the first thing I mentioned."

"I've been thinking that since this project went so well, I might try my hand at something a little more complicated."

Betty eyed her husband speculatively. "Like what?"

"An addition to the house," he said enthusiastically. "I could add on to the master bedroom. You've told me more than once that we need more closet space."

"Men," Betty groaned under her breath to Marjorie. Sam walked over to Marjorie and sat beside her on the cushioned arm of the chair. He slipped his arm around her and cupped her shoulder.

A warm sensation filled her, and when she glanced up, she discovered Sam studying her. The love that filled her eyes was as unexpected as it was embarrassing.

His fingers bit into her shoulder as his gaze held hers. "I love you," he whispered. "We'll work this out."

"But, Sam…"

He bent down and kissed the top of her head. "Listen, we'll adopt kids. Older kids. Okay?"

Biting her bottom lip, Marjorie nodded.

Sam reached for her hand, lacing their fingers together, as though bonding them. She loved this man more than she ever thought it was possible to care about another human being. Whatever problems they faced in the future could be conquered with Sam at her side. She was sure of it.

"When are we going to eat?" Kevin demanded, placing his hands on his hips. "I'm hungry." The little boy still wouldn't look directly at Marjorie, but that was an improvement from hiding his face in his mother's shoulder.

"The barbecue's already hot," Bernie told his wife. "I'll put the steaks on now, if everything else is ready."

"I want a hamburger," Kevin insisted.

"And you will get one," his father promised. "Come along, big boy, and you can help your dear ol' dad and Uncle Sam with the cooking."

"I'll start setting the table out on the deck," Betty said.

"Is there anything I can do?" Marjorie volunteered, quickly rising to her feet. "I brought some chips and dip, and some potato salad and sliced pickles." Sam caught her eye and revealed his surprise. "Deli made," she whispered, and he grinned back.

"Why don't you unpack those while I set the picnic table?" Betty suggested.

The others left to take care of things, and Marjorie found herself alone in the kitchen. She went over to the wicker basket and lifted the top. The potato salad was nestled between the pickle jar and the dip. As she was drawing it out, she heard a faint cry coming from the back of the house. She paused, then remembered Betty mentioning that the baby was napping. Marjorie went to the cabinet and proceeded to take out a couple of bowls and fill them with the potato salad and dip. To her chagrin, the infant's crying grew louder.

A quick check outside told her that Kevin had managed to distract his mother from the job of setting the table. The two of them were down on the beach. Betty was bent over, examining something Kevin was pointing to in the sand. The men were across the yard, busy chatting while Bernie stuck T-bone steaks onto the hot grill.

Before Marjorie could call out to anyone, the baby's cry split the air.

Alarmed, she ran into the back bedroom. The infant's cries died to a soft gurgle once she arrived.

"Hi," she said stiffly, standing a good three feet from the crib. "Your mother's on the beach. Would you like me to do something before she gets here?"

The baby's fists flailed in the air.

"Don't cry, okay? I'm sure she'll be back any minute."

The infant whimpered softly, and that alone was

enough to cause Marjorie to take two steps in retreat. Once four-month-old Shelley realized she was losing her audience, she let go with another loud, earnest cry. She paused then, and inserted her fist into her mouth, sucking on it greedily.

"Oh, I get it," Marjorie murmured, retracing her steps. "You're hungry." She dropped her gaze to her own full breasts. "Sorry, I can't help you in that department." She smiled at her own joke.

The baby gurgled again, seemingly amused by Marjorie's attempt at humor.

"I suppose you've got a wet diaper, as well."

Shelley made a chuckling sound that cut straight through Marjorie's heart. "I don't think I'm going to be much help in that area, either. You see, babies and I don't get along."

Shelley giggled at that. Two arms and legs punched the air as she smiled up at Marjorie, who found she had somehow ended up leaning over the crib.

Sam came into the house and took a Pepsi from the refrigerator. He looked around for Marjorie, and when he didn't find her, he opened the front door, thinking she might have forgotten something in the car. She wasn't there, either. Concerned now, he started for the deck to find Betty.

A faint noise stopped him. It was almost indiscernible at first, so faint that he didn't recognize it until he paused and listened intently. It was a baby cooing happily. He turned into the narrow hallway that led to Shelley Miller's bedroom and found Marjorie at last.

She was sitting in a rocking chair, cuddling Shelley in her arms as though she never intended to let the baby go. Tear tracks streaked her face, creating a bright sheen on her flushed cheeks. She sniffled loudly and wasn't able to keep her chin from trembling.

"Marjorie," he murmured, falling to his knees in front of her, hardly able to believe his eyes.

Chapter 9

"Sam," Marjorie whimpered softly. "I'm holding a baby."

"I see that, Kitten."

"She's so beautiful." A teardrop rolled down her face and landed ingloriously on Shelley's cotton jumpsuit. Cooing, the baby reached out to catch the next drop.

With the gentleness she had come to expect from him, Sam tenderly brushed his hand over her face, wiping away the tears. "I've never seen a woman as beautiful as you are right this minute."

"Sam, I didn't think I could get close to a baby. I didn't dare dream I'd feel this way—ever."

"I suspected as much," he countered, resisting the urge to wrap her and the baby in his arms and hold them both for eternity. "I prayed it would only be a matter of time until you recognized the mothering instincts were there. They have been all along."

"They're here, all right," she whispered, smiling and crying at once. "I feel so tender inside—I don't know how to describe it. Sam," she said, raising her eyes to meet his, "if I feel this strongly about a baby I barely know, I can't imagine how much love I'd have for one of my own."

"We'll discover that together, Kitten."

The tightness that jammed her throat made it impossible to speak. He was talking about them having children together, and although the thought frightened her, it thrilled her far more. She yearned to ask him if he meant it and to tell him she was willing, but every time she opened her mouth, all that came out were soft, strangled sounds. She managed to free one hand from beneath Shelley to caress the rugged line of Sam's jaw. Closing her eyes, she pressed her cheek against the side of his head.

He edged away from her, and their gazes met and held. The promise between them was more potent than anything she had ever known. She didn't need words to recognize what was in his heart; his feelings were all there for her to read in his eyes.

Sam bent toward her, and her dark eyes shimmered with an aching need for his love, a need that was echoed in his own heart. Her parted lips offered him an invitation he couldn't ignore.

This was the man she loved, the man who had filled her life with purpose and realized her dreams. He'd helped her to conquer her fears, laying the groundwork to destroy one after another with unlimited patience. He had gently proved to her that there wasn't anything they couldn't face together, nothing the force of their love couldn't overcome.

"Oh, Sam," she murmured, not wanting him to stop but knowing he had to. "The baby..."

He nodded and straightened, although his hands continued to grip her shoulders. The sight of Marjorie holding Shelley, knowing that someday she would be cradling their own baby, burned through him with the effectiveness of a hot knife. He felt weak with desire, weak and yet so powerful.

"Was that Shelley I heard?" Betty asked as she came into the small bedroom. If she noticed Marjorie's tears, or the fact that Sam was on the floor beside her and the baby, she didn't comment. "Thanks for getting her up for me," she said smoothly, and reached for her daughter.

With some reluctance, Marjorie surrendered the infant. "She's a wonderful baby."

"I'm convinced she gets that easygoing disposition from her mother," Betty said with a cheerful smile.

Bernie coughed in the background. "What about her old man?"

"*And* her father," Betty amended, and shared a secret smile, a wordless disclaimer, with Marjorie.

Marjorie managed to smother a laugh. When she stood, Sam slipped his arm around her waist and gently hugged her. "Do you think it'd be considered impolite to eat and run?" he whispered, so she alone could hear.

"Not if we're not too obvious," she said after a moment. As much as she liked Bernie and Betty, there were so many things she wanted to tell Sam, so much she yearned to share.

"It's selfish, I know, but I want to be alone with you," he added, after their hosts had taken the baby and headed into the other room.

Marjorie wanted it, too, and her gaze told him so.

"Soon," he promised.

"Soon," she agreed.

By the time they returned to the living room, Bernie had finished barbecuing the steaks. They all worked together, and within a few minutes the picnic table on the Millers' newly finished deck was set. The salads, potato chips and other dishes were brought out.

Sam sat beside Marjorie, and the four of them talked and joked throughout the meal. When they'd finished, Marjorie sat on the lounge chair and cradled Shelley as though she'd been handling babies all her life. Every now and again she felt Sam's loving gaze, and they shared a special look that said more than mere words.

"I can't get over the way Shelley's taken to you," Betty commented, joining her. The weather had cleared as the lazy afternoon sun burned off the clouds.

"Marjorie's a natural with children," Sam said proudly. "I don't suppose she told you, but she nearly raised her sister."

"Sam!" she cried, embarrassed. "I'm not a natural at all."

A sharp shake of his head discounted that notion. "She's been around children most of her life," he added. Studying her, his mouth curved into a faint smile. He had prayed that, given time, she would recognize most of her fears as unfounded. The mothering instinct was as strong in her as it was in any woman, only Marjorie had failed to recognize it.

She held out her hand to him, and he gripped it firmly. In many ways he understood her better than she did herself. Sometime, somewhere, she'd done something very good in her life to deserve this man.

* * *

Late Saturday afternoon Marjorie had changed her outfit twice, unable to decide what to wear. Sam wanted her to meet his parents. Although she had readily agreed to dinner with his family, she was a nervous wreck. She'd been in and out of clothes faster than a quick-change artist. Worse, she was convinced that his mother was bound to disapprove of her lack of domestic skills, though Sam himself had dismissed that fear.

Five minutes before he was due to arrive, she chose a soft knit dress Jody had suggested when she made a frantic call to Portland. It was more casual than anything she wore to work, and she was doubtful. This meeting was so important, and she longed to make a good impression so as not to embarrass Sam.

She needn't have worried. His parents stepped onto the front porch when he pulled into the driveway, and they looked as anxious as she felt.

"Don't be so nervous," Sam said, reaching over to squeeze her clenched fist. "They're going to love you."

"Oh, Sam, I hope so." She forced herself to relax, uncoiling her fingers and flexing them a couple of times to restore the blood flow. Normally she was able to disguise any uneasiness, but the prospect of meeting his family had completely unnerved her.

"Mom and Dad have been waiting years to meet you."

"I only hope I'm not a disappointment."

"You won't be, Kitten, I promise."

Sam's mother came down the front steps and walked toward the car. Marjorie studied the streaks of silver in the older woman's dark hair, then shifted her gaze to the classic profile. None of the other woman's features resembled Sam's. Not the faint gleam in her dark eyes, not the warm, friendly glow in her complexion. Yet if Marjorie had met her in a crowded room, she would have known instantly that this woman was his mother.

Sam helped Marjorie out of the car and slipped his arm over her shoulders.

"Mom and Dad," he said proudly, "this is Marjorie Majors. Marjorie, my parents, Roy and Irene Bretton."

"I hope you don't mind us coming out to greet you like this, but Roy and I couldn't wait another minute." Irene took both of Marjorie's hands in her own and nodded approvingly. "I can't tell you how very pleased we are to meet you—at last."

"Thank you. The pleasure is all mine." Marjorie felt stiff and awkward. The inside of her mouth was dry, yet her hands were moist. Sam's warmth was the only thing that kept the chill of anxiety from seeping all the way through her bones. She had so little to impress this family with—no real background or prestigious relatives. She could offer them nothing but her love for their son.

"Please come inside. Dinner's almost ready," Irene invited, leading the way. "I fixed your favorite, Sam— fried chicken, potatoes and gravy, with my homemade biscuits."

"Mom's a wonderful cook," Sam explained, grinning down at her. He hoped Marjorie knew that he wasn't concerned about her ability to burn water.

Marjorie's return smile was feeble at best.

"I'll give you all his favorite recipes if you want them," Irene offered Marjorie.

She nodded her thanks, knowing it would be a complete waste of time, but she hated to disillusion Sam's mother so quickly. Later she would explain that her presence in the kitchen invariably resulted in a fiasco, that when she turned on the stove, the entire Tacoma Fire Department went on standby.

"I better go check on the chicken," Sam's mother said, as soon as they entered the house.

The luscious smells that greeted them could have rivaled a four-star restaurant. It was obvious that Sam had underplayed his mother's culinary abilities.

"Let me help," Marjorie offered hurriedly.

"Nonsense, you're our guest." Irene gestured toward the sofa. "Sit down and make yourself at home. I insist."

Marjorie smiled and tried to relax. Sam's parents were exactly as she'd expected: warm and sincere.

She lowered herself onto the wide sofa. An afghan, crocheted in fall colors of gold, orange and brown, was spread across the back.

Sam claimed the seat next to her and reached for her hand. His father saw the gesture and grinned proudly, as though he were personally responsible for bringing the two of them together.

A moment later Irene Bretton returned. "Dinner will be ready in another fifteen minutes," she announced, and took the chair beside Sam's father.

Roy Bretton looked all the more pleased. "Good. We have enough time for a glass of wine first." He eyed his son intently, as though he expected Sam to make some momentous proclamation.

"Dad patronizes several local vineyards," Sam explained, ignoring his father's look.

"There are a dozen or so excellent wines bottled right here in Washington state," Roy added, filling in the conversation. "I found another superior winery recently, near Bonney Lake."

Marjorie nodded and started to relax against the back of the sofa. There wasn't anything to be nervous about, especially since Sam's parents appeared to be even more anxious to make a good impression than she was.

"Give me a hand, son," Roy said, standing.

"Sure."

The two men left the room, leaving Marjorie and Irene alone.

"Sam has spoken fondly of you on several occasions," his mother said, clearly seeking a way to start the conversation. "His father and I are very proud of him."

"You have every right to be."

"It will take a special woman to share his life."

Marjorie dropped her lashes, fearing that Sam's mother was suggesting that she wasn't the right one for their only son. Her heart pounded wildly, filled with doubts.

"I knew from the moment he mentioned your name that you were special to him." Irene smiled and smoothed her hand across her skirt in a nervous gesture. "A mother knows these things about her children. For instance, I knew long before Sam—or even his father—did that he would be a physician. Roy was sure Sam's career would involve animals. He had pets from the time he was little and was forever collecting more."

"He's the kindest, most generous man I've ever known."

"He always was," Irene said. "I swear, that boy brought home more stray dogs than the city pound ever collected. His heart would melt over things that you and I would hardly notice." She warmed to her subject and scooted forward in the chair, her face bright with love for her son. "I remember one time—he must have been around ten or twelve—anyway, he found an orphaned kitten in a rainstorm, a sickly, weak, half-drowned little thing. By the time he got her home, she was more dead than alive."

Marjorie's smile went weak. Sam called her Kitten, had for weeks now, and like the stray cat he'd found in his youth, she, too, was an orphan. Little things played back in her mind. Minor incidents came into focus. Puzzle pieces fell into place, painting a clear picture. Sam was a rescuer, always had been and always would be. He'd seen it as his duty to take care of her the night she went into surgery.

When they'd first started dating, he had tried several times to rescue her. He'd wanted to step in when Al had cheated her out of her commission. He'd bought the Mercedes more for her benefit than his own. Now that she was seeing him regularly, she knew that he had a perfectly serviceable car and had no reason to purchase another.

"What happened with the kitten?" She was almost afraid to ask.

"He nursed her back to health. You should have seen that silly cat. She was the most prickly, bad-tempered thing—wouldn't let anyone near her. You'd think she would have been more appreciative of everything he had done for her."

The knot in Marjorie's stomach tightened to a punishing level of discomfort. After her surgery she'd lashed out at Sam at every turn. She'd even accused him of getting a kickback from the hospital for every patient he forced to stay. At least she'd felt guilty later and had apologized.

"He... Sam kept the cat, though, right?" she asked, sure she already knew the answer.

"Named her Kitten and ignored her bad moods."

"Didn't he get tired of her moods and lose interest after a while?" Once again, she was certain of the answer, and her stomach sank.

Irene nodded. "It was bound to happen. Summer came, and Sam had his friends. But he kept her, and she became a regular member of the family. I remember the funniest thing about that cat. The first time Kitten became a mother, she wouldn't let anyone close to her except Sam. He was with her when she gave birth. Years later, when she died, Sam was in his first year of high school, and he was real broken up for a long time afterward. But he got over her, and he's owned several cats since."

Marjorie struggled to disguise her distress. All his talk about accepting her as she was, loving her and needing her, was a lie. Sam hadn't accepted her. He never had. To him, she was a pitiful, lost soul, helpless and in need of being rescued. From what his mother had told her and from what she'd seen herself, she was forced to admit that Sam had yet to accept how truly independent she was. And like the kitten from his youth, Sam would eventually replace her, too. His interest would wander, and his feelings for her would change.

A numb, tingling sensation spread to her arms and legs. She felt physically ill along with being emotionally distraught.

How she made it through dinner was a mystery to her, but somehow she managed to say and do what was expected of her as though nothing were wrong. She answered his parents' questions and responded appropriately to what was going on around her. Yet all the while the world was crashing down around her feet.

At one point Sam's father commented that she didn't eat enough to keep a bird alive, and Sam responded that he planned on taking care of her from now on. It had taken every ounce of composure she possessed not to inform him that she was perfectly capable of taking care of herself. She didn't need him to see to her meals or ensure that she made enough money to pay the rent or anything else.

By the time they left, she had never been so grateful to get away from anywhere in her life. The sun had set, and dusk had settled over the landscape. Grateful for the cover of impending night, she hoped that Sam wouldn't notice how pale she was or how sick to her stomach she felt.

Neither spoke as they rode back to her apartment, and when they arrived, he climbed out of the car and walked her to her door.

"Invite me inside," he said.

She felt so unsure, so unsettled. Still, she couldn't resist him, so she nodded and unlocked the front door. "I'll make coffee," she murmured, heading toward the kitchen.

Sam followed her. She'd been unusually quiet on the ride back, but then again, so had he. All evening he'd been mentally rehearsing everything he wanted to say to her. It wasn't every day a man asked a woman to be his wife, and he wanted to make this moment special.

Briefly he toyed with the idea of pulling the diamond out of his pocket and just handing it to her. But that seemed so abrupt, especially when there was so much he longed to tell her. First he planned on saying how loving her had changed his life. Since he'd met her, he felt totally alive. He loved her—that much was obvious and had been for weeks—but simply telling her that he loved her was too inadequate, especially since there was so much more to the way he felt than mere words could express.

Marjorie's hands shook as she turned on the faucet to fill the teakettle. Her back was to him as she spoke. "I like your parents."

"They like you, too, Kitten. I knew they would."

She flinched. "Why do you call me that?"

"Kitten?"

Nodding, she set the kettle on the stove.

"I'm not exactly sure," Sam responded. "I had a cat named that once."

"The one you found in a rainstorm?"

He glanced up, surprised. "Yes. How'd you know?"

"Your mother mentioned it." She swallowed tightly, still unable to turn and face him. "She told me what a prickly, ungrateful cat she was."

Sam chuckled. "She came around in time."

"Like I did," Marjorie said in a wobbly but controlled voice.

"You?" Sam asked, surprised. "I thought we were talking about Kitten."

"We are!" She whirled around to face him, her hands braced against the counter behind her. "Me. *I'm* Kitten."

Sam looked stunned. "That's ridiculous!"

"Tell me, Sam, why did you buy the Mercedes? You didn't need another car."

He shifted uncomfortably. "No, but my other one's a couple of years old now and…"

"And you wanted me to collect the commission from the sale."

"All right," he said, struggling not to respond to the anger in her voice. "That's true, but I was looking for a way to see you again, and buying the car seemed a perfect solution."

"It was an expensive one, too, don't you think?"

"I didn't care."

"This may surprise you, Sam Bretton, but *I* care. In fact, I care a great deal. I don't want your charity. The next time you want to throw money away, give it to cancer research."

"It wasn't charity!" he shouted.

Marjorie ignored him, clenching her hands into tight fists at her sides. "What was it about me that attracted you in the first place?" She didn't give him a chance to respond as she hurried on. "There's nothing that makes me any different than a thousand other women who parade through your office."

Drawing a calming breath, Sam waited a moment before answering. "This conversation isn't getting us anywhere. I suggest—"

"You can't answer me, can you, Sam?"

"I think it would be best if I left and gave you a chance to calm down."

"I don't need any time!" she shouted, and to her horror, her voice cracked.

Unable to see her cry and not do something to ease the pain, Sam took a step toward her and held out his arms. "Kitten, listen…"

"Don't call me that!" she cried, pointing at him and retreating several steps. "Or I'll… I'll…" She couldn't think of anything to threaten him with. "Or I'll scream," she said finally.

"Or worse yet, you might cook for me."

Marjorie's eyes widened with the pain his words inflicted. "Just leave, Sam. The next time I need someone to rescue me, I'll give you a call. But don't wait around for me to phone. It might astonish you to learn that I'm a capable human being."

His frustration was nearly overwhelming, and Sam paused to rub his hand along the back of his neck. "I didn't mean that wisecrack about your cooking."

Her back stiffened with resolve. "No? Well, I meant every word *I* said," she responded coolly, struggling to maintain her crumbling composure.

"No, you don't. You love me. You need me."

He was so confident, so sure of himself, that Marjorie wanted to kick herself for being so gullible. The signs had been there from the beginning, and she'd refused to see them, refused to believe them. Her love for Sam had blinded her to the truth. She was a charity case to him in the same way that kitten had been all those years ago. He might believe he felt something for her now, but time would prove him wrong. He honestly believed she couldn't get by without him.

"Marjorie, I'm not exactly sure what's going on in that wonderfully crazy mind of yours, but if you want me to tell you that I associated you with that lost kitten, then I'll admit as much—but only in the beginning."

The room swayed, and she reached out a hand in an effort to maintain her balance. Briefly she closed her eyes. "You admit it?"

"Yes. But only in the beginning," he repeated softly.

"You were so fragile, so afraid, and there was no one there for you when you were ill."

"Do I hear violin music in the background?" she taunted. It dented her considerable pride to hear Sam refer to her in those terms, though, to be fair, she remembered how she'd clung to him, begging him to stay with her. That had been a low point in her life, and now he was using it against her. Worse, he hadn't an inkling of why she was so offended, and she'd thought he knew her so well.

"Later I was attracted to your courage," he added, ignoring her gibe. "And your pride and your candor. I discovered that I spent half my time thinking about you. When you were discharged, I racked my brain for days trying to think of a way to see you again. I wanted to help you—and I finally came up with the idea of buying the car. By then I knew you were special."

"As I explained before, I don't need your charity."

"It wasn't charity, not in the way you think!" Sam shouted, losing his patience. "The only thing I did was help you, and you make it sound as if I've committed some terrible crime."

As far as Marjorie was concerned, he had.

"I was in love with you then—only I didn't know it. And now I know I love you. More than I thought it was possible to love another human being. If you don't want me to call you *kitten* again, then fine, I won't."

A tense silence wrapped itself around them. She couldn't believe that she was having the most important discussion of her life while standing in her kitchen waiting for the kettle to boil.

Sam's level gaze trapped hers from across the room. His anger had vanished as quickly as it had come, leaving his face an impassive mask of pride. Abruptly, he spun away, his impatient strides carrying him to the door. He paused and turned toward her.

"There's a diamond ring in my pocket, Marjorie. I'd planned to ask you to be my wife."

Calmly she met his gaze. She wanted Sam. The temptation to swallow her doubts and dismiss her pride nearly overwhelmed her. She would have, too, if she hadn't remembered what his mother had said about him losing interest in the kitten after a while. He had his friends, his mother had said. There was nothing to guarantee that anything would be different when it came to *her*, that within a few months he wouldn't regret having married her.

"I think you already know my answer to that," she said, looking everywhere but at the huge diamond he now held in his hand.

"You're right—I do know." With that, he slipped the ring back inside his pocket. Then he turned and walked away from her in lightning-quick strides.

The door slammed. Feeling incredibly weak, Marjorie cupped her hands over her face and sagged against the counter.

Chapter 10

Confounded, Marjorie stepped out of her manager's office and paused, her hand lingering on the doorknob. Her mind was racing with the details of her conversation with Bud.

"Well, what happened?" Lydia wanted to know. She walked around the customer-service counter and stood expectantly in front of her friend. When Marjorie didn't immediately respond, Lydia waved her hand in front of her bemused face.

The action captured Marjorie's attention. "I got a promotion," she said, shaking her head, still befuddled. Starting the first of the month, her Sundays would be free. For weeks her schedule had conflicted with Sam's. Now, when it didn't matter if she had the day off, her Sundays were open. Life was filled with such ironies.

"A promotion!" Lydia cried. "Cool!"

"I can't believe it myself," Marjorie returned, and shook her head in an attempt to dispel her pensive mood. She'd been numb for days; nothing seemed to penetrate the dull ache that had ruled her thoughts and actions since she'd last seen Sam. Not even this promotion, which would have given her plenty of reason to celebrate a week earlier, could penetrate the fog of her sadness.

"What did Bud say to Al Swanson?" Lydia asked next, her eyes wide with curiosity.

"I'm not sure…he's still in there." Marjorie had noted how disgruntled he'd looked when Bud announced her promotion. That alone had been worth the apprehension she'd suffered all morning before the meeting.

"And you thought you were going to get fired." Lydia flashed her a triumphant smile and shook her head knowingly. "What did I tell you?"

"Not to worry," Marjorie quoted back to her friend in a monotone, and rolled her eyes toward the ceiling.

Lydia was obviously pleased that her words had proven to be prophetic. "Now all I have to do is straighten out this mess between you and Dr. Sam."

Marjorie stiffened at the mention of his name. "Don't even try," she said forcefully. "As far as I'm concerned, the subject of Sam Bretton is off-limits."

"What did he do, for heaven's sake?"

"Lydia, I already told you, I refuse to discuss the matter!" Purposeful strides carried her across the showroom floor. Once again she was running away, doing anything she could to escape the emotional pain that blossomed when anyone asked her about Sam. Before she'd met him, she had prided herself on her ability to confront unpleasantness. Since her last evening with him, she found it easier to hide than deal with her feelings.

Undeterred, Lydia followed her friend. "Hey, we're talking about the man who had you waltzing around here with your head in the clouds not more than a week ago. Something happened, and I want to know what it was."

"Lydia, please, just drop it." The pain was so fresh that even hearing someone casually mention him produced an ache that came all the way from her soul.

She walked into her office and braced her hands against the side of her desk, inhaling deeply, praying the action would alleviate the surge of emotional pain. She'd done a great deal of thinking since the last time she'd seen Sam. As much as she hated to admit it, she needed him. The realization that she depended on him hadn't been easy to swallow. She loved him, but she hated to think she was nothing but the subject of his charity.

Following close on Marjorie's heels, Lydia came into the office and shut the door. "Listen, I've tried to be a good friend and—"

"I know," Marjorie said, cutting her off. "And I appreciate that, but there are some things that are better left alone." She couldn't deal with Lydia's questions *and* answer her own. She whirled around to confront her friend. "And this is one of them."

Lydia hesitated, then. "If you'd just tell me what he did that was so terrible, then I could hate him, too."

Marjorie could deal with any multitude of problems— irate customers, unreasonable loan officers, cheating salesmen—but her friend's persistent inquisitiveness had finally worn her down.

She crossed her arms over her chest and exhaled a slow, laborious breath. "He called me *kitten*."

Before she could go on, Lydia's mouth fell open in astonished disbelief. "That was it?"

"No. He asked me to marry him, too."

A pregnant pause followed as Lydia's eyes narrowed in speculative scorn. "You're right," she finally said in mock disgust. "The man should be sent before a firing squad. He wanted to marry you. Well, of all the nerve!"

All Marjorie could manage was a sharp nod.

Lydia ran her fingertips over the top of the desk, avoiding eye contact. "Marjorie…when was the last time you had a decent vacation?"

"About ten years ago. Listen, I can see what you're getting at. You think I've gone off the deep end, and maybe I have. I don't know anymore. I…turned Sam down, but my reasons are my own. Just accept that I know what I'm doing, and it's for the best, and kindly leave it at that."

"I can't believe you turned Dr. Sam down." Lydia glared at her as though Marjorie should be psychoanalyzed that very minute. "The most marvelous man I've ever known, and he wanted to marry you and…"

"And I refused him," Marjorie said flatly.

"You're not going to see him again?"

"No… I don't think so."

"And that's the way you want it?" The incredulousness was back in Lydia's voice, raising it half an octave.

Marjorie couldn't answer. Lying by saying "yes" to Lydia was one thing, but trying to fool herself was another. She was slowly shriveling up without Sam. Her days felt like empty, wasted years. The hours dragged, especially when she was home alone. The walls seemed to close in around her, suffocating her. Normally she enjoyed her own company, but since she'd been without Sam, even the everyday routines seemed useless. The happy expectancy was missing from her life, as was the excitement. Without him, her future looked astonishingly bleak.

It would have been far better, she decided, if she'd never met the man. Again and again she'd gone over the events of that last evening with his family, seeking a solution that would salvage both his pride and her own, some misunderstanding about the way he saw her. But he had made that impossible. He'd admitted openly that he pitied her, and she was scared to death of the fact that she needed him. What a mess this had turned out to be.

Lydia's steady gaze lacked any sign of sympathy. "It's your decision."

Marjorie's gaze held her friend's. "I know."

Lydia headed out of the office. "Be miserable, then. See if I care."

With Lydia gone, the emptiness inside the small office was oppressive. Dejected, Marjorie sat at her desk and read over some paperwork she'd been putting off. However, nothing held her attention for long, and within moments she was silently staring at the walls, her thoughts focused on Sam.

Suddenly Lydia burst into her office and excitedly clapped her hands. She marched around Marjorie's desk to confront her face to face.

"Lydia! What's going on?"

"You're going to love this. I certainly do."

Sam. Marjorie's heart rocketed into space. He'd come for her. He'd decided that his life would be an empty wasteland without her. He'd realized he honestly needed her.

"Sam?" Marjorie asked expectantly, half rising from her chair. "He's here?" Oh, please, God, she prayed, let him be here.

"Sam? Heavens no." Lydia gave her an odd look and shook her head. "It's Al Swanson. Bud just gave him the ax."

"Bud fired Al Swanson? You mean…he's leaving?"

"From the way he's packing up his things, I'd say he can't wait to get out of here. He'll be gone in five minutes."

"Oh." Marjorie was surprised by how little elation she felt at the news. A week ago, her behavior would have rivaled her friend's. Now all she felt was a cloying sense of disappointment that Sam hadn't come for her. Discouraged, she reclaimed her seat.

"Apparently," Lydia went on to explain, "one of Al's schemes backfired on him. Bud found out about it, and Al's out of here."

Marjorie had known from the first that Al was his own worst enemy, and that, given enough rope, he would do himself in without any help from anyone else.

Crossing her arms, a subdued Lydia paused to study her friend. "You thought Sam had come to talk to you?"

Marjorie's fingers tightened around the pencil she was holding; it was a miracle it didn't snap in two. "It wouldn't have done any good."

"Hey, he could have withdrawn his marriage proposal. That might have settled things, don't you think?"

Marjorie shook her head. "Lydia, please. I don't want to talk about him."

"Hurt too much?" her friend asked, lowering her voice into a soft, coaxing tone.

The answer was so obvious that the question didn't require a response. Marjorie was lost without Sam, but she would get over him in time. The only question that remained was how long it would take. A lifetime, her heart told her, but she refused to listen.

Two days later, a cocky smile curving her lips, Lydia sauntered into Marjorie's office, her hands clasped behind her back.

Pretending she'd been interrupted, Marjorie glanced up from the report she'd been trying to read. "You look like the cat that just swallowed the canary."

"Really?" Lydia swayed back and forth on the balls of her feet. "I have a tasty tidbit of information, if you're interested."

"About Al Swanson?" The details of what had happened between the salesman and the manager had been the favorite topic of conversation with the other staff members ever since his firing. The rumors had been flying around the dealership like combat planes, dropping bombs of speculation.

Lydia shook her head. "What I have to tell you involves a certain doctor, but according to you, I'm not supposed to mention his name."

"Sam?" Marjorie's heart stopped, then pounded frantically against her ribs.

"The one and only."

The temptation to strangle Lydia was powerful. Marjorie returned her gaze to the report. "I refuse to play your games."

"Okay," Lydia announced with typical nonchalance. "If you don't care, then far be it from me to announce that the very doctor in question happens to be in this building at this precise minute."

Marjorie's gaze froze. "Here?"

"Not more than twenty yards from this office door, if you must know."

The papers Marjorie had been holding slipped from her fingers and fell to the top of her desk. Uncaring, she left the scattered sheets there.

"But you are apparently over Dr. Sam," Lydia commented, studying the ends of her polished nails, "so it would be best if you stayed holed up in here and did your best to pretend he isn't anywhere around."

Without realizing what she was doing, Marjorie stood, her knees barely strong enough to keep her upright.

"I don't mind telling you," Lydia said, grinning, "I'm having a difficult time not giving Dr. Sam a piece of my mind. The man is obviously a pervert."

Marjorie blinked, sure she'd misunderstood her friend. "Sam's nothing of the sort."

"Imagine Dr. Sam wanting to get married," Lydia continued with a sigh. "Doesn't he realize how old-fashioned that is? A woman should live with a man fifty, maybe sixty, years before making that kind of commitment. Dr. Sam expects too much."

As best she could, Marjorie ignored her friend's sarcasm. "Sam's here?"

Smiling unabashedly, Lydia nodded. "You'll see him the minute you walk out of this office."

Nothing could have kept Marjorie where she was.

As Lydia had claimed, Sam was in the dealership, standing at the service counter. For a solid minute Marjorie was unable to breathe. He looked tired, overworked, hassled. He wasn't taking care of himself, and he looked as though he'd lost weight. As if drawn by a magnet, she walked to his side.

"Sam." His name came from her lips without her even being aware she'd spoken out loud.

He tossed a look over his shoulder and froze when his eyes met hers.

"Hello," she said in an effort to avoid calling attention to herself. "How are you?"

"Fine," he answered stiffly. "And you?"

"Okay...wonderful, actually."

"Yeah, me too."

A tense silence followed while she struggled for something more to say. Her gaze fell to the service desk. "Is something wrong with the car?"

He shook his head. "It's time for an oil change."

The tense quiet returned.

"...babies?"

"...work?"

They spoke simultaneously.

Sam gestured with his hand. "You first."

"I got a promotion." She didn't mention that her Sundays would be free from now on; she couldn't see the point.

"Congratulations."

She attempted a smile. "Thank you." In the ensuing silence, she nodded at him, indicating it was his turn. "You look like you've been busy."

He nodded. "I delivered another set of twins last week."

"Girls?"

"No, both boys. Identical."

"Oh." For the life of her, Marjorie couldn't think of another thing to say. Small talk had always been her forte, and there were a thousand things she wanted to tell him but couldn't.

Seeing him like this made her feel so unsure, so uncertain. Her mind stumbled over her thoughts. "Kitten" wasn't such a terrible name, she realized. So she'd reminded him of a pathetic cat; no doubt that was the way she'd looked when she visited his office that first time. She loved the way his pet name for her sounded on his lips, almost as though the word were a gentle caress. So she needed him. That wasn't such a terrible thing. It was time—more than time—that she faced the fact that needing someone was normal and right. It was on the tip of her tongue to tell him so when Bud strolled past.

"There's a customer here to see you."

Feeling guilty, although she didn't know why, she nodded and glanced over her shoulder. "I guess I'd better get back to work," she said, getting back to Sam.

He didn't respond. "I suppose you should."

"Goodbye, Sam."

"Goodbye, Kitten." The instant the word slipped out of his mouth, he wanted to take it back. "I apologize. I didn't mean to say that."

"Don't worry. It's not such a bad name."

"Only it's not right for you," he said, his gaze unwavering.

Marjorie wasn't in any position to argue with him; holding back tears required all the energy she could muster. "Right," she answered weakly, giving up the fight.

Without looking back, she headed outside, where the insurance salesman she'd talked to earlier in the week was waiting for her. As she walked out the door, she heard Sam ask what time he could expect his car to be finished. By the time she returned, he was gone.

Lydia seemed to be waiting for her when she got

back inside, though. Her friend came over to meet her. "Well, what did he have to say?"

"The insurance salesman?" Marjorie asked, playing stupid.

"Of course not. Sam!"

"Nothing."

"But he must have said something! You two talked for three minutes. I timed you. You must have gotten something settled in that amount of time."

"Unfortunately, we didn't."

"Marjorie, this craziness has got to stop. I talked to Mary, Dr. Sam's receptionist, and she told me he hasn't been the same from the moment you two split up. He's melancholy and moody, and everyone knows that's not the least bit like him."

"He'll get over it," Marjorie said flippantly.

"Maybe," Lydia returned with barely controlled skepticism. "But will you?"

Her friend's words echoed in her mind for the remainder of the afternoon. Lydia was right. Her world was crumbling at her feet, and she was too proud, too stubborn, to do anything about it. Just seeing Sam again had proven that. She was ruining her life over something incredibly silly. She'd overreacted and behaved stupidly, and the time had come to own up to that.

Filled with determination, she marched over to the service department.

"What time did you tell Dr. Bretton his car would be ready?"

Pete, the head mechanic, who had been with Dixon Motors for ten years, flipped the pages of the service book. "After three. As I recall, he told me he wouldn't be in to pick it up until six."

Marjorie nodded, pleased. "Have you finished with it?"

"Yeah. It seemed pointless to change the oil on a vehicle that doesn't even have a thousand miles on it. But we did it—couldn't see the point in arguing with him."

That small bit of information sent Marjorie's spirits soaring. Sam must have used the Mercedes as an excuse to see her. Her relief felt like a thirst-quenching rain after a long August drought. "Could I have his keys, please?"

The mechanic gave her an odd look. "You want Dr. Bretton's car keys?"

"Right. When he comes in, send him to my office."

The barrel-chested mechanic scratched the side of his head. "If that's the way you want it, Ms. Majors."

"I do. Thanks, Pete."

The remainder of the afternoon crept by. At precisely six, Marjorie was waiting in her office. Sam didn't keep her in suspense long.

He knocked once and stepped inside. "What's this about you having my car keys?" he demanded, his temper showing. He'd been a fool to think that coming to the car dealership would solve anything between them. She wanted blood, and he wasn't about to give it to her. The more he reviewed their earlier conversation, the angrier he became. That wounded, hurt look in her eyes had accused him of greatly wronging her. All he'd ever wanted was to marry her and make her happy, and she'd reacted as though he'd insulted her.

Marjorie blinked. "Yes, I have your keys."

He held out his open palm. "I'd like them back."

"Of course." She remained outwardly calm, but adrenaline was racing through her system as though she were running the Boston Marathon. "I have a couple of questions first, if you don't mind answering them."

He made a show of glancing at his watch. "Make it quick—I have an appointment."

"Oh, Sam, you always were such a poor liar."

He snapped his jaw closed and pulled out a chair. "As it happens, I do have to be someplace in less than an hour. But obviously my word isn't to be trusted."

"This will only take a minute."

He crossed his legs, hoping to give the impression of indifference. Nothing could be further from the truth, but anger was his only defense against Marjorie. It was either yell at her or yank her into his arms and kiss some sense into her.

Her fingers closed around the cold metal keys. "It's about that ring you offered me."

Sam shot to his feet. "Listen, Marjorie, we're talking about our lives here, not a car deal. There are no counteroffers."

"Yes, I know."

"The offer stands as it was."

"All right," she said, her voice strong and sure.

"All right, what?"

"I'll marry you."

If Sam had been flustered before, it was nothing compared to the confusion he felt now. "You will?"

"That is…if you still want me for your wife."

He ran his fingers through his hair. "What happened? Did you check around and discover that you couldn't make a better deal than me?"

"No…that's not it at all." This was going so much worse than she'd hoped.

He eyed her speculatively. "I'll call you *kitten* any time I please!"

She nodded, because speaking would have been impossible.

"We won't have a long engagement, either. I want us married before the end of the summer."

She met his fiery gaze with feigned calm, then answered him with a quick nod of her head.

He mellowed somewhat and lowered his voice. "Do you have to check this out with your manager?"

"No."

His gaze moved to the shimmering moistness of her lips. He was dying to hold her, starved for a taste of her, and just looking at her disturbed his concentration. His control was slipping fast. Walking around to her side of the desk, he reached for her. Hungrily his mouth devoured hers as he pulled her hard against the solid length of his body so she would know how desperate he'd been without her. His hand roamed possessively over her, molding her to him, uncaring that anyone outside the office might be watching.

Only partially satisfied, Sam dragged his mouth from her, his hunger sated for the moment.

The iron band of his arms held her a willing prisoner. "Sam, I love you... I'm sorry to be so insecure. I don't know what made me say those things. It's just that I've been on my own so long that it hurt my pride to think you pitied me, and I..."

"It doesn't matter, Kitten," he said, his voice husky and thick against her hair.

Overcome by a searing happiness, she laughed breathlessly. The sound was short and sweet. "I can't imagine why I objected so strongly when I love the name *kitten*."

"Good, because I meant what I said about calling you that."

Her arms circled his waist, and her heart swelled. She was home, truly home, for the first time since she'd lost her parents.

"We're getting married as soon as I can arrange it."

She grinned, more than agreeable to any terms he wanted. "Any Sunday."

He paused and looked deep into her misty, diamond-bright eyes, letting her words sink in. "You got a promotion?"

She nodded and started to say more when Lydia burst into her office.

Her friend's mouth dropped open as she stopped abruptly. "Oh…hi."

"Hi," Marjorie answered for them.

"Have you two patched things up?" Lydia asked casually.

"It's either that or we have a peculiar way of arguing," Sam answered, and chuckled softly.

"So are you two getting married or what?"

"We're getting married," Marjorie said, beaming.

It looked for a moment as though Lydia doubted them. "When?" she asked speculatively.

Sam and Marjorie shared a lingering look. "Any Sunday," they answered in unison.

* * * * *

Also by Patricia Davids

HQN

The Matchmakers of Harts Haven

The Inn at Harts Haven

The Amish of Cedar Grove

The Wish
The Hope
The Prayer

Love Inspired

Brides of Amish Country

The Inn at Hope Springs
Katie's Redemption
The Doctor's Blessing
An Amish Christmas
The Farmer Next Door
The Christmas Quilt
A Home for Hannah
A Hope Springs Christmas
Plain Admirer
Amish Christmas Joy
The Shepherd's Bride
The Amish Nanny
An Amish Family Christmas: A Plain Holiday
An Amish Christmas Journey
Amish Redemption

Visit her Author Profile page at Harlequin.com,
or patriciadavids.com, for more titles.

A HOME FOR HANNAH

Patricia Davids

In memory of Dave.

The one, the only, the love of my life.

Chapter 1

"Bella, what's wrong with you?" Miriam Kauffman pulled her arm from beneath the quilt to squint at her watch. The glow-in-the-dark numbers read one forty-five in the morning. Her dog continued scratching frantically at the door to her bedroom.

Miriam slipped her arm back under the covers. "I'm not taking you out in the middle of the night. Forget it."

Her yellow Labrador-pointer mix had other ideas. Bella began whining and yipping as she scratched with renewed vigor.

Miriam was tempted to pull her pillow over her ears, but she wasn't the only person in the house. "Be quiet. You're going to wake Mother."

Bella's whining changed to a deep-throated bark. At eighty-five pounds, what Bella wanted Bella usually got. Giving up in exasperation, Miriam threw back her quilt.

Now that Bella had her owner's attention, she plopped on her haunches and waited, tongue lolling with doggy happiness. In the silence that followed, Miriam heard a new sound, the clip-clop of hoofbeats.

Miriam moved to her second-story bedroom window. In the bright moonlight, she saw an Amish buggy disappearing down the lane.

When she was at home in Medina, such a late-night visit would mean only one thing—a new Amish runaway had come seeking her help to transition into the outside world. But how would anyone know to find her in Hope Springs? Who in the area knew of her endeavors? She hadn't told anyone, and she was positive her mother wouldn't mention the fact.

Miriam pulled a warm cotton robe over her nightgown and grabbed a flashlight from the top of her dresser. She patted Bella's head. "Good girl. Good watchdog."

Guided by the bright circle of light, she made her way downstairs in the dark farmhouse to the front door. Bella came close on her heels. The second Miriam pulled open the door, the dog was out like a shot. Bella didn't have a mean bone in her body, but her exuberance and size could scare someone who didn't know her.

"Don't be frightened—she won't hurt you," Miriam called out quickly as she opened the door farther. She expected to find a terrified Amish teenager standing on her stoop, but the porch was empty. Bella was nosing a large basket on the bottom step.

Miriam swung her light in a wide arc. The farmyard was empty. Perhaps the runaway had changed his or her mind and returned home. If so, Miriam was glad. It was one thing to aid young Amish people who wanted to leave their unsympathetic families when she'd lived in another part of the state. It was an entirely different thing now that she was living under her Amish mother's roof. The last thing she wanted to do while she was in Hope Springs was to cause her mother further distress.

Bella lay down beside the basket and began whining. Miriam descended the steps. "What have you got there?"

Pushing the big dog aside, Miriam realized the basket held a quilt. Perhaps it was meant as a gift for her mother. The middle of the night was certainly an odd time to deliver a package. She started to pick it up, but a tiny mewing sound made her stop. It sounded like a baby.

Miriam straightened. *There's no way someone left a baby on my doorstep.*

Bella licked Miriam's bare toes, sending a chill up her leg. She definitely wasn't dreaming.

She took a few steps away from the porch to carefully scan the yard with her light. "If this is someone's idea of a prank, I'm not laughing."

Silence was the only reply. She waited, hoping it was indeed a joke and someone would step forward to fess up.

The full moon hung directly overhead, bathing the landscape in pale silvery light. A cool breeze swept past Miriam's cheeks carrying the loamy scent of spring. The grass beneath her bare feet was wet with dew and her toes grew colder by the second. She rested one bare foot on top of the other. No snickering prankster stepped out of the black shadows to claim credit for such an outrageous joke.

Turning back to the porch, she lifted the edge of

the quilt and looked into the basket. Her hopes that the sounds came from a tape recorder or a kitten vanished when her light revealed the soft round face of an infant.

She gazed down the lane. The buggy was already out of sight. There was no way of knowing which direction the driver had taken when he or she reached the highway.

Why would they leave a baby with her? A chill that had nothing to do with the cold morning slipped down her spine. She didn't want to be responsible for this baby or any other infant. She refused to let her mind go to that dark place.

A simple phone call would bring a slew of people to look after this child. It was, after all, a crime to abandon a baby. As a nurse, she was required by law to report this.

But that would mean facing Sheriff Nick Bradley.

"Miriam, what are you doing out there?" Her mother's frail voice came from inside the house.

Picking up the basket, Miriam carried it into the house and gently set it in the middle of the kitchen table. "Someone left a baby on our doorstep."

Her mother, dressed in a white flannel nightgown, shuffled over, leaning heavily on her cane. "A *boppli!* Are you joking?"

"*Nee, Mamm,* I'm not. It's a baby."

Miriam's first thought had been to call 9-1-1, until she remembered who the law was in Hope Springs. She'd cut off her right arm before she asked for his help. Who could she call?

Ada Kauffman came closer to the basket. "Did you see who left the child?"

"All I saw was a buggy driving away."

Ada's eyes widened with shock. "You think this is an Amish child?"

"I don't know what else to think."

Ada shook her head. "*Nee,* an Amish family would welcome a babe even if the mother was not married."

"Maybe the mother was too afraid or ashamed to tell her parents," Miriam suggested.

"If that is so, we must forgive her sins against *Gott* and against her child."

That was the Amish way—always forgive first— even before all the details were known. It was the one part of the Amish faith that Miriam couldn't comply with. Some things were unforgivable.

Miriam examined the basket. It was made of split wood woven into an oval shape with a flat bottom and handles on both sides. The wood was stained a pale fruitwood color with a band of dark green around the top for decoration. She'd seen similar ones for sale in shops that carried Amish handmade goods. The baby started to fuss. Miriam stared at her.

Her mother said, "Pick the child up, Miriam. They don't bite."

"I know that." Miriam scooped the little girl from the folds of the quilt and softly patted her back. The poor thing didn't even have a diaper to wear. Miriam's heart went out to their tiny, unexpected guest. Not everyone was ready to be a parent, but how would it feel to be the child who grew up knowing she'd been tossed away in a laundry basket?

Stroking the infant's soft, downy cap of hair, she felt the stirrings of maternal attachment. She couldn't imagine leaving her child like this, alone in the darkness, depending on the kindness of strangers to care for it. Children were not to be discarded like unwanted trash.

Old shame and guilt flared in her heart. One child had been lost because of her inaction. This baby deserved better.

Putting aside her personal feelings, she called up the objective role she assumed when she was working. Carefully she laid the baby on the quilt again to examine it. As a nurse, her field of expertise was adult critical care, but she remembered enough of her maternal-child training to make sure the baby wasn't in distress.

Without a stethoscope to aid her, it was a cursory exam at best. The little girl had a lusty set of lungs and objected to being returned to her makeshift bed. Who could blame her?

Ada started toward the stairs. "A little sugar water may satisfy her until you can go to town when the store opens and stock up on formula and bottles. I have your baby things put away in the attic. I'll go get them. It's wonderful to have a child in the house again."

Miriam stared after her mother. "We can't keep her."

Ada turned back in surprise. "Of course we can. She was left with us."

"No! We need to find out who her mother is. She has made a terrible mistake. We need to help her see that. We need to make this right."

Ada lifted one hand. "How will you do that?"

"I… I don't know. Maybe they left a note." Miriam quickly checked inside the basket, but found nothing.

"*Vel,* until someone returns for her, this *boppli* needs a crib and diapers."

Miriam quickly tucked a corner of the quilt around the baby. "*Mamm,* come back here. You shouldn't go climbing around in the attic. You've only been out of the hospital a week."

A stormy frown creased her mother's brow but quickly vanished. "I'm stronger than you think."

That was a big part of her mother's problem. She didn't realize how sick she was. Miriam tried a different approach. "You have much more experience with babies than I do. You take her, and I'll go hunt for the stuff."

Her mother's frown changed into a smile. "*Ja,* it has been far too long since I've held such a tiny one. Why don't you bring me a clean towel to wrap her in first."

Miriam did as her mother asked. After swaddling the babe, Ada settled into the rocker in the corner of the kitchen with the infant in her arms. Softly she began humming an Amish lullaby. It was the first time in ages that Miriam had seen her mother look content, almost…happy. Miriam knew her mother longed for grandchildren. She also knew it was unlikely she would ever have any.

Ada smiled. "I remember the night you and Mark were born. Oh, what a snowstorm there was. Your *daed* took so long to come with the midwife that I was afraid she would be too late."

"But the midwife arrived in the nick of time." Miriam finished the story she'd heard dozens of times.

"*Ja.* Such a *goot,* quiet baby you were, but your brother, oh, how he hollered."

"Papa said it was because Mark wanted to be born first."

"He had no patience, that child." Ada began humming again, but her eyes glistened with unshed tears.

Miriam struggled with her own sadness whenever she spoke of her twin brother. Mark's death had changed everyone in the family, especially her, but the old story did spark an idea.

"*Mamm,* who is the local midwife?"

"Amber Bradley does most of the deliveries around Hope Springs."

"Bradley? Is she related to…him? Is he married to her?" Did he have a wife and children of his own? Thinking about him with a family caused an odd ache in her chest. Miriam had taken pains to avoid meeting him during her months in Hope Springs. She realized she knew almost nothing about his current life.

Ada said, "*Nee,* he's not wed. Amber may be a cousin. *Ja,* I'm sure I heard she was his cousin."

Nicolas Bradley was the sheriff, the man Miriam had loved with all her heart when she was eighteen and the man responsible for Mark's death. Would the midwife involve him? Miriam hesitated but quickly realized she had no choice. She didn't have any idea how to go about searching for the baby's mother. If Amber chose to notify Nick, Miriam would deal with it. She prayed for strength and wisdom to make the right decision.

"The midwife might have an idea who our mother is. She is certainly equipped to take care of a newborn. If nothing else, she will have a supply of formula and the equipment to make sure the baby is healthy."

Ada frowned at her daughter. "I have heard she is a good woman, but she is *Englisch,* an outsider. This is Amish business. We should not involve her."

"I'm no longer Amish, so it isn't strictly Amish business. Besides, she may feel like we do and want to keep this out of the courts. I'm going to call her."

"You know I don't like having that telephone in my house."

Her mother tolerated Miriam's *Englisch* ways, but she hated to allow them in her Amish home. It was a frequent source of conflict between the two women.

Irritated, but determined to remain calm, Miriam said, "I'm not giving up my cell phone. You are a diabetic who has already had two serious heart attacks. You could need an ambulance at any time. If you want me to stay, I keep the phone."

"I did not say you should leave. I said I do not like having the phone in my house. If I live or die, it is *Gottes wille* and not because you have a phone."

"It might be God's will that I carry a phone. Did you ever consider that?"

"I don't want to argue." Ada clamped her lips in a tight line signaling the end of the conversation.

Miriam crossed the room and dropped a kiss on her mother's brow. "Neither do I. I have said I'll only use the phone in an emergency and for work. I think this counts as an emergency."

When her mother didn't reply, Miriam quickly ran upstairs to her bedroom and pulled her cell phone from the pocket of her purse. A call to directory assistance yielded Amber Bradley's number.

When a sleepy woman's voice answered the phone, Miriam took a deep breath and hoped she was making the right decision. "Hi. You don't know me. My name is Miriam Kauffman, and I have a situation."

After Miriam explained what had transpired, Amber agreed to come check the baby and bring some newborn essentials. She also agreed to wait until they had discussed the situation before notifying the local law enforcement.

Miriam returned to the kitchen. Her mother was

standing beside the kitchen table. She had taken the quilt out of the basket. Miriam said, "Amber Bradley is on her way. I convinced her to wait before calling the police, but I know she will. She has to."

Ada held up an envelope. "I told you not to involve the *Englisch*. I found a note under the quilt. The child's name is Hannah and her mother is coming back for her."

The farmhouse door swung open before Sheriff Nick Bradley could knock. A woman with fiery auburn hair and green eyes stood framed in the doorway glaring at him. "There has been a mistake. We don't need you here."

The shock of seeing Miriam Kauffman standing in front of him took him aback. He was certain his heart actually stopped for a moment before chugging ahead with a painful thump. He struggled to hide his surprise. It had been eight years since he'd laid eyes on her. A lifetime ago.

He touched the brim of his trooper's hat, determined to maintain a professional demeanor no matter what it cost him. How could she be more beautiful than he remembered? "Good morning to you, too, Miriam."

After all this time, she wasn't any better at hiding her opinion of him. She looked ready to spit nails. Proof, if he needed it, that she hadn't forgiven him. A physical ache filled his chest.

"Miriam, don't be rude," her mother chided from behind her. Miriam reluctantly stepped aside. A large yellow dog pushed past her and came out to investigate Nick's arrival. It took only a second for the dog to decide he was a friend. She jumped up and planted both front feet on his chest. He welcomed the chance to regain his composure and focused his attention on the dog.

"Bella, get down," Miriam scolded.

The dog paid her no mind. The mutt's tail wagged happily as Nick rumpled her ears. He said, "That's a good girl. Now down."

The dog dropped to all fours, then sat quietly by his side. He nodded once to Miriam and entered the house. The dog stayed outside.

His cousin Amber sat at the kitchen table. "Hi, Nick. Thanks for coming. We do need your help."

Ada Kauffman sat across from her. A large woven basket sat on the table between them. The room was bathed in soft light from two kerosene lanterns hanging from hooks on the ceiling. The Amish religion forbade the use of electricity in the home.

He glanced at the three women facing him. Ada Kauffman was Amish, from the top of her white prayer bonnet on her gray hair to the tips of her bare toes poking out from beneath her plain, dark blue dress. Her daughter, Miriam, had never joined the church, choosing to leave before she was baptized. Tonight, she wore simple dark slacks and a green blouse that matched her eyes. Her arms were crossed over her chest. If looks could shrivel a man, he'd be two feet tall in about a second.

His cousin Amber wore jeans, sneakers and a blue T-shirt beneath a white lab coat. She served the Amish and non-Amish people of Hope Springs, Ohio, as a nurse midwife. Exactly what was she doing here? If Miriam's trim figure was anything to go by she didn't require the services of a midwife.

Amber wasn't normally the cloak-and-dagger type.

He was intensely curious as to why she had insisted he come in person before she'd tell him the nature of the call.

He said, "Okay, I'm here. What's so sensitive that I had to come instead of sending one of my perfectly competent deputies? Make it snappy, Amber. I'm leaving in a few hours for a much-needed, week-long fishing trip, and I've got a lot to do."

"This is why we called you." Amber gestured toward the basket. He took a step closer and saw a baby swaddled in the folds of a blue quilt.

"You called me here to see a new baby? Congratulations to whomever."

"Exactly," Miriam said.

He looked at her closely. "What am I missing?"

Amber said, "It's more about what we are missing."

"And that is?" he demanded. Somebody had better start making sense.

Ada said, "A mother to go with this baby."

He shook his head. "You've lost me."

Miriam rolled her eyes. "I'm not surprised."

Her mother scowled at her, but said, "Someone left this baby on my porch."

"Someone abandoned this infant? When? Did you see who it was?" He pulled his notebook and pen from his pocket and started laying out an investigation in his mind. So much for starting his vacation on time.

"About three hours ago," Miriam answered.

Was she serious? "And you didn't think to call my office until thirty minutes ago?"

Miriam didn't answer. She sat in a chair beside his cousin. Amber said, "Miriam called me first. We've been discussing what to do."

"There is nothing to discuss. What you *do* is call your local law enforcement and report an abandoned child. We could have had a search for the parents started hours ago. Amber, what were you thinking? I need to get my crime scene people here. We need to dust for prints, collect evidence."

Miriam said, "No one has committed a crime."

He glared at her. "I beg to differ."

Her chin came up. She never was one to back down. He'd missed their arguments as much as he'd missed the good times they shared. If only they could go back to the way it had been before.

For a second, he thought he saw a softening in her eyes. Was she thinking about those golden summer days, too? Her gaze slid away from him before he could be sure. She said, "According to the Ohio Safe Haven Law, if a baby under one month of age is left at a fire station, with a law enforcement officer or with a health care worker, there can be no prosecution of the parents who left the child."

He didn't like having the law quoted to him. "This baby wasn't left with Amber or at a hospital. It was left with you."

"I'm a nurse."

She really enjoyed one-upping him. He had to admire her spunk. "But this isn't a hospital, it's a farmhouse. I still have to report this to the child welfare people. They will take charge of the baby."

"That's why we wanted to talk to you and not to one of your deputies." Amber had that wheedling tone in her voice. The one that had gotten him in trouble any number of times when they were kids.

Ada smiled brightly. "Would you like some coffee, Sheriff? A friend brought us cinnamon rolls yesterday.

Perhaps you would enjoy a bite." She shuffled across the kitchen and began getting out plates.

The baby started to fuss. One tiny fist waved defiantly through the air. Miriam stood and lifted the child out of the basket. She sat down in the rocker beside the table. Holding and patting the baby, she ignored him.

He exhaled the frustration building inside him. The Amish dealt with things in their own fashion and in their own time. He knew that. Miriam might not have been baptized into the faith, but she had been raised in it. Intimidation wasn't going to work on her or her mother.

He crouched in front of Miriam and took hold of the infant's waving fist. The baby grasped his finger and held on tight. It was a cute little thing with round cheeks and pale blond hair. He smiled. "Is it a boy or a girl?"

Miriam wouldn't meet his gaze. "A girl."

He looked at Amber. "Is she healthy? I mean, is she okay?"

"Perfectly okay," Amber assured him.

"How old do you think she is?"

"From the look of her umbilical cord, a day at the most."

He looked around the room. "What aren't you telling me?"

Miriam finally met his gaze. Perhaps it was a trick of the lamplight, but he didn't see anger in their depths. She said, "I saw an Amish buggy driving away."

He wasn't expecting that. To the Amish, faith and family was the core around which everything was based. An abandoned Amish child was almost unheard of. It had never happened in his county.

"She's coming back for her child," Ada stated firmly.

Miriam stayed silent. She didn't take her eyes off the baby's face.

Amber laid a hand on Nick's shoulder. "The baby needs to be here when she does."

He rose to his feet and held up his hands. "Wait a minute. There are protocols in place for things like this. The child goes to the hospital to be checked out."

Miriam quickly said, "She's fine, but we'll take her into the clinic in Hope Springs for a checkup."

"Child Protective Services must place the baby with a licensed foster care provider or approved family member. I can't change that rule."

"I'm a licensed foster care provider," Miriam said and smiled for the first time. The sight did funny things to his insides. She should smile more often.

Surprised by a sudden rush of attraction, he struggled to regain his professionalism. "Good. Then you can offer your services to our child welfare people. If they agree, I don't see why you can't care for the baby. I would have brought a car seat with me if you'd told me I was coming to pick up a child. Now, I'll have to have someone bring one out. Unless you have one I can borrow, Amber?"

"I have one, but hear us out before you make a decision or call anyone else."

"I'm not breaking the law for you, cousin."

"Nor will you bend it, even if the outcome destroys a life." Miriam stood with the baby and moved away from him.

He'd been waiting for that. She knew exactly how to dig at the most painful part of their past. "Miriam, that's not fair. You know I would change things if I could."

"You can't. My brother is still dead."

"It was *Gottes wille,* Miriam. You must accept that. I forgave Nicolas long ago," her mother said quietly.

Miriam didn't reply. Nick knew a moment of pity for

her. It couldn't be easy carrying such bitterness. It had taken him a long time to forgive himself for the crash that took her brother's life. With God's help, he had found the strength to accept what could not be changed and to live a better life because of it.

He caught Amber's questioning look. She had no idea what was going on. He shook his head and mouthed the word *later*. His history with the Kauffman family had no bearing on this case.

"What is it you want me to do?" he asked.

Amber said, "The mother left a note. She's coming back in a week. We feel that technically she hasn't abandoned her child. She simply left her with neighbors."

"Why am I here at all?" he asked.

Ada withdrew the note from her pocket and handed it to him. It was written on plain notebook paper.

Please help us. I know this isn't right, but I have no choice. It isn't safe to keep my baby right now, but I'll be back for her. Meet me here a week from tonight. If I can't make it, I'll come the following week on Friday at midnight. I love my baby with all my heart. I'm begging you to take care of her until I return. I pray God moves you to care for her as you would your own. Her name is Hannah.

Amber said, "We called you because it's clear this young woman is in trouble. We want you to help us find her."

He glanced at Miriam. She was expecting him to deny their request. He could see it in her eyes and in the set of her chin. No matter what Miriam thought of him there was a woman in trouble and he couldn't ignore that. He said, "Ada, do you have a clean plastic bag?"

"Ja." She opened a cabinet door and withdrew a zip-top bag.

Nick said, "Hold it open for me." She did, and he slipped the note inside.

He glanced around at the women in the room. "What I think should happen is irrelevant. I have to uphold the law. I'm not sure if we have a crime here or not. I need to speak with the county attorney before I can let this child stay here."

Miriam glanced out the window for the umpteenth time. Dawn was spreading a blanket of rose-colored light across the eastern sky. Nick had spent the past twenty minutes sitting in his SUV. Now, he held his phone to his ear as he slowly paced back and forth on the porch. Bella sat watching him, her normal exuberance totally missing. Miriam found it hard to believe that Nick hadn't rejected their request outright and whisked Hannah into protective custody.

He owed no allegiance to the Amish. They didn't vote him into office or elect any officials. While they were a peaceful, quiet people, many *Englisch* saw them as an annoyance. Their buggies slowed traffic to a crawl and even caused accidents. Their iron horseshoes damaged the roadways for which they paid no motor vehicle taxes to maintain. They often owned the best farmland and rarely sold to anyone who wasn't Amish. Many outsiders looked down on them because they received only an eighth-grade education. They were outdated oddities in a rapidly changing, impatient world.

"What's taking him so long?" she muttered.

Amber spread a fluffy white towel on the table and laid the baby on it. From her case, she withdrew a disposable diaper and a container of baby wipes. "Nick understands what is needed. He respects the Amish in this community. He'll help us, you'll see."

Miriam found her eyes drawn to Nick once more. He made a striking figure silhouetted against the morning sky in his dark blue uniform. He'd always been handsome, but age had honed his boyish good looks into a rugged masculinity that was even more attractive. He'd gained a little bulk in the years since she'd seen him, but it looked to be all muscle. He was tall with broad shoulders and slim hips. At his waist he wore a broad belt loaded with the tools of his trade: a long black flashlight, a gun and handcuffs among other things.

As she watched, he raked his fingers through his short blond hair. She knew exactly how silky his hair felt beneath her fingertips. His hat lay on the counter beside her. She picked it up, noticing the masculine scent that clung to the felt. In an instant, she was transported back to the idyllic summer days they had enjoyed before her world crashed around her.

Thinking of all she had lost was too painful. Quickly she put the hat down and clasped her hands behind her back. "What is taking so long? Surely, he could make a decision by now. Either the baby can stay with us or she can't."

The outside door opened and Nick came in. He looked around the room until his gaze locked with Miriam's. She couldn't read the expression on his face. Was it good news or bad?

Chapter 2

"Well? What did you decide?" Amber demanded. "Do we have to involve social services?"

Nick couldn't take his eyes off Miriam. Emotions could cloud a man's judgment, and Miriam raised a whole bushel of emotions in him. She had since the first day they met when he was nineteen and she was an eighteen-year-old, fresh-faced, barefoot Amish beauty. Did she remember those wonderful summer days, or had her brother's death erased all the good memories of their past?

He brought his attention back to the present issue. "I've talked it over with the county attorney. He is willing to agree that the baby has not been abandoned, although the situation is certainly unusual. Hannah can remain in the custody of Ada and Miriam Kauffman for a period of seven days."

Miriam's eyes widened with surprise. "She can?"

"For *two* weeks," Amber said with a stubborn tilt of her chin.

Nodding curtly, Nick said, "However, if the family has not returned for her after two weeks, she becomes an abandoned infant, and I will call Child Protective Services."

"I'm sure someone will come forward before then." Amber's obvious relief eased some of his misgivings. She was more familiar with the Amish in the Hope Springs area than almost anyone. If she thought he was doing the right thing, he was willing to follow her recommendation.

Miriam didn't say another word. It was a struggle to keep from staring at her. He couldn't believe she still had such a profound effect on him. He had stopped seeing her the summer he turned twenty because he knew how strong her faith was and how important it was to her. He hadn't been willing to make her choose between her religion and his love.

The truth was he'd been afraid he would come out the loser. As it turned out, he had, only for a different reason.

He cleared his throat. "I've checked for reports of missing or abducted infants. Just because you saw an Amish buggy driving away doesn't automatically make this an Amish infant. Fortunately, there aren't any babies under one week of age that have gone missing nationwide. We'll go with your theory until there is evidence otherwise. If an infant girl is reported missing, that changes everything."

He paused. They weren't going to like the rest of what he had to say. "Now, I'm not willing to let someone who dropped a baby on your doorstep just waltz in and take her back. If they do show up, this will be immediately reported to Social Services."

Miriam glared at him. "I thought the point of us keeping the baby was to avoid that?"

"By letting you keep the baby, I'm making it easier for the mother to return or for her family to come forward when they might not do so otherwise. I'm sorry. I won't budge on this. Someone who is desperate enough to leave her child with you in the dead of night needs help—she needs counseling. I mean to see that she gets it."

The women exchanged looks. Ada and Miriam nodded. Nick breathed a mental sigh of relief. He said, "The note is too vague to open an official investigation into the mother's whereabouts. I see concern, but there is no evidence of a crime. 'It's not safe' could mean any number of things. However, I agree that we need to make an effort to find this young woman. The sooner, the better."

Amber threw her arms around him. "You're the best cousin I could ever ask for."

"That's not what you said when I wouldn't tear up your speeding ticket."

Amber blushed and cast a quick look at Miriam. "He's joking."

He rolled his eyes. "Right. Ladies, I don't want word of this baby getting out to the general public. Keep it in the Amish community and keep a lid on it."

Miriam frowned. "I would think public exposure is exactly what we want."

"When news of an abandoned baby surfaces, the nut cases come out of the woodwork. Women who desperately want children will claim it's their baby. Some are crazy enough that they will try to take legal action against you. People who want to adopt and simple do-gooders will come forward with offers to take the child. Trust me, it could become a media circus and a nightmare trying to sift fact from fiction."

"All right. Where do we start?" Amber asked.

"We can start by trying to tie the basket or the quilt to a specific family."

Ada spread the blanket open on the table so they could examine it. It was a simple quilt of patchwork blocks with a backing of blue-gray cotton. She said, "I don't see a signature or date, nor do I recognize the stitch work. It's fine work. Perhaps someone in the community will recognize it."

Nick put the basket on the quilt and snapped several pictures with his cell phone. "I'll email these photos to some of the shops that carry Amish goods. Maybe we'll get a hit that way."

Amber's cell phone rang. She opened it and walked away to speak to the caller.

"What else can we do?" Miriam asked.

"Do you recall what kind of buggy it was?"

"It was dark. I saw a shape, not much else."

"Did it have an orange triangle on the back, reflective tape or lights?"

"I couldn't tell."

"So we can't even rule out the Swartzentruber Amish families in this area. They don't use the slow-moving-vehicle signs. What about the horse? Could you recognize it again if you saw it?"

"No, I didn't see the animal, just the back of the buggy."

Amber returned to the room and said, "I'm sorry,

but I've got to go. I have a patient in labor. Miriam, I'll leave the car seat with you. Nick, can you help me get it out of my car?"

"Sure." He followed his cousin outside to her station wagon knowing she was going to grill him about his past relationship with Miriam.

Amber opened the door to the backseat. "It sounds like you have a history with the Kauffman family. Why don't I know about it?"

He leaned in to unbuckle the child safety seat. "It was years ago. You were away at school."

"Care to fill me in now?"

Lifting the seat out of the car, he set it on the roof and stared out across the fertile farmlands waiting for spring planting. He could hear cattle lowing in the distance and birds chirping in the trees. The tranquility of the scene was at odds with his memory of that long-ago night.

He closed his eyes. "The summer I turned nineteen, I started working for Mr. Kauffman as a farmhand. They lived over on the other side of Millersburg back then. It was our grandmother's idea. She thought I should learn how hard it was to work a farm the way the Amish do. She thought it would give me a better appreciation of the land."

"Grandmother is usually right," Amber said with a twinkle in her eye.

"She is. Anyway, I worked there for two summers. Miriam, her brother Mark and I became good friends."

"Why do I sense you and Miriam were more than friends?"

"We were kids. We fell in love with the idea of being in love, but she was strict, Old Order Amish. We both knew it wouldn't work. We chose to remain friends. It wasn't until a few years later that things changed."

"What happened?"

Nick took a stick of gum from his pocket using the added time to keep his emotions in check. Even now, it was hard to talk about that night. He popped the gum in his mouth, deftly folded the foil into a small star and dropped it back in his shirt pocket.

"Ten years ago I was a brand-new deputy and a bit of a hotshot back then. I didn't go looking for trouble, but I didn't mind if I found it. One night, we got a report of a stolen car. On the way to investigate, I caught sight of the vehicle and put on my lights. The driver didn't stop. Long story short, a high-speed chase ensued. A very dangerous chase."

"What else were you supposed to do?"

"Protocol leaves it up to the responding officer's discretion. What I should have done was drop back and stop pressing him when I saw the risks he was willing to take. I should have called for a roadblock to be set up ahead of us. I didn't do any of those things. I kept after the car. It was a challenge to outdrive him, and I wasn't about to back down."

"It sounds like you were doing the job you'd trained to do. I know your father was killed during a traffic stop. I'm sure that made you doubly suspicious of anyone who tried to get away."

She was right. "That did factor into my decision, but it shouldn't have. I tried to get around the car, but we slammed into each other. The other driver lost control and veered into a tree. I'll never forget the sight of that wreckage. The driver was killed instantly. It was Mark, Miriam's twin brother."

Amber laid a comforting hand on his shoulder. "I'm sorry. I didn't mean to make you relive the whole thing."

"You want to know the really ironic thing? I'm the one who taught Mark how to drive. I never understood why he didn't just stop. He'd never been in trouble. I doubt he would have spent more than one night in jail. To have his life ended by a *rumspringa* stunt, a joy ride, it wasn't right."

"The Amish believe everything that happens is God's will, Nick. They don't blame you. That would be against all that they hold sacred."

"Miriam blames me. I tried to talk to her after Mark's funeral. Even months later she wouldn't see me. As you can tell, her feelings haven't changed."

"Then she needs our prayers. Finding forgiveness is the only way to truly heal from such a tragedy."

He lifted the car seat from the roof of Amber's car. "You should get going. You don't want the stork to get there ahead of you."

Amber grinned. "You're still planning on coming to my wedding, right?"

"Rats, when was that again? I might be fishing."

She punched his arm. "A week from this coming Saturday and you'd better not stand me up for a trout."

"Ouch, that's assaulting an officer. I could arrest you for that."

"Whatever. Phillip would just break me out of jail."

"Are you sure of that?"

"Absolutely—almost sure. Tell Miriam she can bring the baby into our office anytime tomorrow morning. I happen to know Dr. White has a light schedule. If the baby begins to act sick before then, she should take her to the hospital right away. She's a nurse. She'll know what to do."

"I'll tell her."

Her expression became serious once more. "Nick, Miriam had to know when she called me that I would involve the law. She might not admit it, but I think she reached out to you."

Nick considered Amber's assertion as she drove away. What if she was right about Miriam's actions? What if she was reaching out to him? Could he risk the heartbreak all over again if she wasn't? He glanced toward the house. She had left her Amish faith. That barrier no longer stood between them, but the issue of Mark's death did.

Nick was about to start a week's vacation. If he left town now, he might never have another chance to heal the breach with Miriam. He wanted that, for both their sakes. In his heart, he knew there was a reason God had brought them together again.

He shook his head at his own foolishness. He was forgetting the most important part of this entire scenario. Somewhere there was a desperate woman who needed his help. She and her baby had to be his first priority.

Miriam decided to ignore Nick when he came into the kitchen again. He held a car seat in his hands. The kind that could easily be detached from the base and used as an infant carrier. He said, "Would you like me to put it in your car?"

"I'll get it later."

"Is there anything else you ladies need?"

"We're fine," Miriam said quickly, wanting him out of her house. She'd forgotten how he dominated a room.

Ada spoke up. "Would you mind bringing the baby bed down from the attic for us?"

His eyes softened as he smiled at Ada. "Of course not."

"I'll get it later, *Mamm,* I'm sure the sheriff has other things to do."

"I've certainly got time to fetch the crib for your mother."

His cheerful reply grated on Miriam's nerves. She felt jumpy when he was near, as if her skin were too tight.

Her mother said, "*Goot.* Miriam, I'll take Hannah."

Miriam handed over the baby. Her mother smiled happily, then looked to the sheriff. "Nicolas, if you would give me the bottle warming on the stove, I'll feed her."

He lifted the bottle from the pan at the back of the stove. To Miriam's surprise, he tested it by shaking a few drops of formula on his wrist, and then handed it over.

Did he have children? Was that how he knew to make sure a baby's formula wasn't too hot? Had he been able to find happiness with someone else, the kind of happiness that eluded her?

He caught her staring when he turned and asked, "Which way to the attic?"

She all but bolted ahead of him up the stairs to the second floor. The attic was accessed by a pull-down panel in the ceiling of her bedroom. She rushed into the room, swept up her nightgown and the lingerie hanging from the open drawer of her bureau, stuffed everything inside and slammed it shut. She whirled around to see him standing in the doorway.

Her bed wasn't made. Papers and books were scattered across her desk. A romance novel lay open on her bedside table. The heat of a blush rushed to her face. For a second, she thought she saw a grin twitch at the corner of his lips. Her chin came up. "I wasn't expecting company in my bedroom today."

The heat of a blush flooded her face. She stuttered, "You know what I mean."

Stop talking. I sound like an idiot.

Nick pointed to the ceiling. "Is that the access?"

"Yes." She worked to appear calm and composed, cool even. It was hard when his nearness sent her pulse skyrocketing and made every nerve stand on end.

He crossed the room and reached the cord that hung down without any trouble. The long panel swung open and a set of steps came partway down. He unfolded them and tested their sturdiness, then started upward. When he vanished into the darkness above her, Miriam called up, "Shall I get a flashlight?"

A bright beam of light illuminated the rafters. "I've got one."

Of course he did. She'd noticed it earlier on his tool belt. Sheriff Nick Bradley seemed to be prepared for every contingency from checking baby formula to searching cobweb-filled corners. *Strong, levelheaded, dependable,* they were some of the words she had used to describe him to her Amish girlfriends so long ago. It seemed that he hadn't changed.

Miriam jerked her mind out of the past. This had to stop. She couldn't start mooning over Nick the way she had when she was a love-struck teenager. Too much stood between them.

He leaned over the opening to look down at her. "Any idea where the baby bed is? There's a lot of stuff up here."

"No idea. If you can't find a crib in an attic, you're not much of a detective." Her words came out sounding sharper than she intended. She was angry with herself for letting him get under her skin.

The sound of a heavy object hitting the floor overhead made her jump. It was quickly followed by his voice. "Sorry. I don't think it broke."

She scowled upward. "What was that?"

"Just an old headboard."

"Great-grandmother's cherrywood headboard, hand carved by my great-grandfather?"

"Could be." His voice was a shade weaker.

Miriam started up the steps. "Let me help before you bring the house down on our heads."

"It's tight up here."

"It might be for a six-foot moose," she muttered. She reached the top of the steps to find him holding out his hand to help her. Reluctantly, she accepted it and stepped up into the narrow open space beside him. They were inches apart. She wanted to jump backward but knew there was nothing but air behind her. It was hard to draw a breath. Her pulse skipped and skittered like a wild thing. She pulled her hand from his.

He said, "It's tight even for a five-foot-three fox."

She could hear the laughter under his words. Annoyed at his familiarity, she snapped, "It's not politically correct to call a woman a fox."

He cleared his throat. "I was referring to your red

hair, Miriam. It's also not politically correct to call an officer of the law a moose."

Turning away, he banged his head on a kerosene lamp hanging from one of the rafters.

She slipped past him on the narrow aisle. "If the shoe fits… I think the baby stuff is down here."

Beneath the dim light coming through a dormer window, she spied a cradle piled high with old clothes and blankets. A wide-rimmed black hat and a straw hat sat atop the pile. She knew before she touched them that they had belonged to Mark.

Tenderly Miriam lifted the felt hat and covered her face with it. She breathed deeply, but no trace of her brother's scent remained. A band tightened around her heart until she thought it might break in two.

"Are they Mark's things?" Nick asked behind her.

She could only nod. Even after all these years, it was hard to accept that she would never see him again. He'd been her other half. She was incomplete without him. She could hear his laughter and see his face as clearly as if he were standing in front of her.

Nick lifted a stack of boxes and papers from the seat of a bentwood rocker and set them on the floor. He took the clothing and blankets from the cradle and laid them aside, leaving the flashlight on top of the pile. Picking up the cradle, he said, "I'll take this down. You can bring the baby clothes when you find them."

He didn't wait for her reply. When he was gone, she sat in the rocker and crushed her brother's hat against her chest as hot tears streamed down her face.

Nick descended the attic steps with the sound of Miriam's weeping ringing in his ears. He wanted to help, but he knew anything he offered in the way of comfort would be rejected. It hurt to know she still grieved so deeply.

After making his way down to the kitchen, he found Ada and the baby both asleep in the rocker. The bottle in Ada's slack hand dripped formula onto the floor. When he took it from her, she jerked awake, startling the baby who whimpered.

"Habe ich schlafe?" Ada peered at Nick with confusion in her eyes.

"Ja, Frau Kauffman. You fell asleep," he answered softly.

Childhood summers spent with his Amish grandmother and cousins had given him a decent understanding of the Amish language. While it was referred to as Pennsylvania Dutch, it was really Pennsylvania *Deitsh,* an old German dialect blended with English words into a language that was unique.

Ada sat up straighter and adjusted the baby in her arms. "Don't tell Miriam. She already worries about me too much."

"It will be our secret. Where shall I put the cradle?"

"Here beside me. I sleep downstairs now. Miriam insists on it. She doesn't want me climbing the stairs."

Taking a dishcloth from the sink, Nick mopped up the spilled milk. "I imagine Miriam gets her way."

Ada looked toward the stairs, then leaned closer to Nick. "Not so much. If I get well, she will leave again. I may be sickly all year."

He grinned. "That will be our secret, too."

"Goot. Where is she?"

Nick's grin faded. "She's still in the attic. She found

some of Mark's things. I don't think she was ready for that."

"My poor daughter. She cannot see the blessings God has given her. She only sees what she has lost."

"She needs more time, that's all."

"No, it is more than that. I miss my son every day. I miss my husband, God rest his soul. I mourn them, but in God's own time I will join them in heaven. Until then, He has much for me to do here on earth. It will soon be time to plant my garden. With the weather getting nicer, I must visit the sick and the elderly. I have baking to do for the socials and weddings and I must pray for my child."

"I'll pray for her, too."

"Bless you, Nicolas. I accept that Miriam will never return to our Amish ways, but my child carries a heavy burden in her heart. One she refuses to share. I pray every day that she finds peace."

Ada struggled to her feet. Nick gave her a hand. *"Danki.* Take the baby, Nicolas."

"Sure." He accepted the tiny bundle from her amazed at how light the child was and how nice it felt to hold her.

"Sit. This cradle needs a good cleaning after more than twenty years in the attic. I'm so happy it is being put to use. It has been empty much too long."

Nick sat in the rocker and gave himself over to enjoying the moment. He hoped one day to have children of his own. Finding a woman to be their mother was proving to be his stumbling block.

He remembered how badly his mother had handled being a cop's wife. Even though he'd chosen small-town law enforcement over the big-city life his father craved,

Nick wasn't eager to put a family into the kind of pressure cooker he knew his job could create. It would take a very special woman to share his life. Once, he'd hoped it would be Miriam, but that dream had died even before the wreck took her brother's life.

Chapter 3

Miriam had recovered her composure by the time she came downstairs. She saw Nick rocking Hannah while her mother was busy wiping down the dusty cradle. Miriam's eyes were drawn to the note still sitting in the plastic bag on the table. Somewhere, a young woman needed her help. She would concentrate on that and not on her tumultuous emotion.

She said, "It sounds like Hannah's mother is in an abusive relationship."

Nick said, "We're only guessing."

Miriam bit the corner of her lip. A young mother was having the worst day of her life. She'd done the unthinkable. She'd left her newborn baby on a doorstep. In her young eyes, the situation must have seemed desperate and hopeless. Miriam's heart went out to her. At least, she had chosen to give her child a chance. It was more than others had done.

Nick said, "The note raises questions in my mind about the mother's emotional state and about her situation but doesn't spell out a crime. I'll have it checked for fingerprints, but that's a long shot. If the person who wrote the note is Amish, I doubt we'll have his or her prints on file."

Miriam held up the bag to study the handwriting. "You think the father may have written this?"

"I think our mother had help. Do you believe a new mother could harness up the horse and buggy drive out here after she'd just given birth? That's one hardy woman if she did it alone."

Nodding, Miriam said, "You have a point."

Ada finished cleaning the cradle and covered the mattress with a clean quilt. "Amish women are tough. I know several who have had their child alone, and then driven to the home of a relative."

Nick handed the baby to Ada. "That may be, but I have to consider the possibility that she had help. Miriam, did you see which way the buggy turned after it reached the highway?"

"I'm sorry. I didn't." Miriam racked her memory of those few moments when the buggy had been in sight for something—anything that would help, but came up empty.

Somewhere a young woman needed help or she wouldn't have taken the drastic measure of leaving her baby on a doorstep. Miriam had spent too many hours with confused, frightened Amish teenagers not to know the signs. This was a deep cry for help. She had turned her back on one desperate mother years ago. Nothing but bitter ashes had flowed from that decision. She would not do it again. This time, she had to help.

Turning around, she grabbed her denim jacket from the peg by the door. "The lane is still muddy from the rain yesterday. We might be able to tell which way they turned."

"Good thinking." Nick pulled the door open and held it for her. Bella was waiting for them outside. She jumped up to greet Nick with muddy paws. He pushed her aside with a stern, "No." Bella complied.

Miriam glanced over her shoulder. "*Mamm,* it's time to check your blood sugar. This added stress and lack of sleep could easily throw it out of whack."

"All right, dear. I'll get the baby settled and I'll check it." She rocked the baby gently in her arms and cooed to her in Pennsylvania Dutch.

"You know what to do if it's low?"

"*Ja.* I'll have a glass of milk and recheck it in thirty minutes. The honey is in the cabinet if it is too low, but I feel fine. Stop worrying."

"I'll be back in a few minutes." Worrying was what Miriam did best these days. Her mother didn't seem to realize how precarious her health was.

Outside, Miriam walked beside Nick down the lane. He asked, "How long has your mother been ill?"

"She had her first heart attack seven months ago. That's when they discovered she was a diabetic. She had a second heart attack three weeks ago. Thankfully, it wasn't as bad as the first one. She's been doing okay, but I think she should be recovering more quickly than she has. Her energy level is so low. Everything makes her tired, and that frustrates her."

"You've been here in Hope Springs for seven months?" He seemed amazed.

"Yes." She'd taken pains to remain under his radar.

Coming face-to-face with Nick was the last thing she wanted. His presence brought back all the pain and guilt she'd worked so hard to overcome. Now, he was in her home and in her business with no signs of leaving. Why hadn't she followed her mother's advice and left the midwife out of this?

"I imagine you had to quit your job in order to stay this long." His sympathetic tone showed real compassion. It was hard to stay angry with him when he was being nice.

"I took a leave of absence from my job. My leave will be up in another month. I don't know what I'll do if I can't go back by then."

"That's got to be hard on both of you."

"She doesn't have anyone else." As soon as Miriam said it, she regretted pointing out the obvious.

A muscle in his jaw twitched, but his voice was neutral when he spoke. "We both know the Amish community will take care of Ada. She isn't alone."

"I know they will keep her fed and clothed, but she needs more than that. She needs someone to monitor her blood pressure and glucose levels and to make sure she takes her meds. She needs someone to make sure she eats the right things. If one more person drops by with a pan of cinnamon rolls or shoofly pie for her, I'm going to bar the door."

"Want to borrow my gun?" There was a hint of laughter in his tone.

"Don't tempt me," she replied, amazed that he could so easily coax a smile from her. Her anger slipped further away. They had both suffered a loss when Mark died, but their lives hadn't stopped. Nick had managed to move on. Perhaps she could, too.

He stopped and squatted on his heels to examine the ground. "My tires have erased any tracks the buggy might have left. I don't see anything distinctive about the horseshoe marks."

"Do you think the mother was coerced into leaving the baby?"

He rose and hooked his thumbs in his wide belt as he scanned the countryside. "Frankly, I don't know what to think. The whole thing doesn't fit. The Amish don't operate this way. It's so out of character."

"The Amish have flaws and secrets like everyone else." She would know. Flaws and secrets haunted her, every day and every night.

He must've heard something odd in her voice for he fixed her with an intense stare. She gazed at her feet.

He asked, "Who knows you are a nurse? Is it common knowledge?"

"I'm sure my mother has mentioned it to some of her friends."

"Did you notice the note said 'Meet me here a week from tonight.' Did that strike you as odd?"

"A little. Why?"

"I don't know. It just didn't seem to fit. What about someone from your past? An Amish friend who might know you're here with your mother."

"No, there's no one like that."

"How can you be so sure?"

"We were Swartzentruber Amish, remember? They are the strictest of the Old Order Amish. When I refused to join the faith, my parents had to shun me. My friends did the same. It wasn't until after my father died that my mother chose to become a member of a less rigid order."

"Didn't that mean she would be excommunicated by her old bishop?"

"Yes. She gave up her friends and the people she'd known all her life. It was very hard, but she did it so that she could see me again. She was accepted into Bishop Zook's congregation about a year ago. They are more progressive here. Unlike my old congregation, Bishop Zook's church believes a person has the right to choose the Amish faith. Those who don't are not punished."

He said, "Bishop Zook is not the only bishop who believes that. Amber's mother and my mother are sisters who both chose not to join the faith. They have siblings who remained Amish. My grandmother embraces all her family, Amish and English alike."

"Some districts are that way, some are more strict, some are rigid in their beliefs and don't tolerate any exceptions. People hear the word *Amish* and they think the Plain People are all the same. There are enormous differences."

Miriam cocked her head to the side. "Wait a minute. If your mothers are sisters, why do you share the same last name with Amber?"

He grinned and started walking again, scanning the ground as he went. "Our mothers are sisters who married two brothers. Got to love small-town romances. Where did you live before you moved in with your mom?"

"Medina, Ohio."

Bella left Miriam's side and went hunting through the old corn stubble of the field beside them. It would soon be time for the farmer who rented her mother's land to begin planting new crops.

"What kind of nursing do you do?" Nick asked, slanting a curious glance her way.

Was he really interested? "I work in adult critical care."

"That's a tough job."

"Overdoses, strokes, trauma, heart attacks, we see it all."

"And car accidents." He looked away, but she saw the tension that came over him.

"Yes, car accidents," she replied softly.

She expected him to drop the subject, but to her surprise, he didn't. "Do you like it? I mean, not all the outcomes can be good."

"Every patient deserves the chance to reach their full potential. I'm part of a team that works to make that happen. Sometimes, what they regain isn't as much as they had before their event, but it's not for lack of trying on our part. For every loss of life, we see a dozen recoveries." It struck her as odd to be talking about her work with Nick, but she wanted him to know she was about making a difference in people's lives and she loved her work.

"When do you find the time to foster little kids?"

"I don't. I foster teens."

"Really?"

She met his gaze. There was a new respect in his eyes that she hadn't seen before. Lifting her chin, she said, "They are mostly Amish runaways."

He stopped in his tracks. "Today has been chock full of surprises."

"You don't approve? They are kids with nothing but an eighth-grade education. They don't have driver's licenses or social security cards. They are completely ill prepared for life in the outside world."

"I know that."

"If by some stroke of luck they can find work, they have to take low-paying jobs. Most get paid under the table from employers happy to take advantage of them. Without outside help, leaving the Amish is almost impossible for some of them."

"You left."

She started walking again. "Don't think it was easy."

"When did you start hating the Amish way of life?"

Stunned, she spun to face him. "I don't hate it. It's a beautiful way to live. The Amish believe in simplicity. Their lives are focused on faith in God and in keeping close family and community ties."

Quietly, he said, "They believe in forgiveness, too, Miriam."

"It sounds easy to say you forgive someone. Actually doing it is much harder. Did they ever catch the man who shot your father?"

He looked away. "No."

"It's tough when there's no justice in life, isn't it?"

Meeting her gaze, he nodded. "Yes. That's why I trust that God will be the ultimate judge of men."

She waited for the boiling anger to engulf her, but it didn't materialize. Maybe she was just too tired. She wanted to stay angry at him, but it was easier when she couldn't see the pain in his eyes. He knew what it was to lose someone he loved.

Nick started walking again. "If you admire the Amish, why help kids leave?"

"Because there are other ways to live that are just as important and as meaningful. You can't be a doctor or

a nurse if you are Amish. You can't create new medi-
cines or go to college, build dams or explore the oceans.
You can't question the teachings of your church lead-
ers. That said, two-thirds of the teenagers who come
to me wanting a taste of *Englisch* life go back to their
Amish families. Why? Because it's what they desire in
their hearts. My job is to help them sort out what they
truly want."

"Okay, I get it. That's cool." He walked to the edge
of the highway and sank to his heels again as he examined the ground.

Did he get what she did and why? Or was he simply
trying to placate her? She stopped a few feet away from
him. Her shifting emotions made it difficult to stay focused on the task at hand.

He looked at her. "Could your efforts to help Amish
youth be the reason someone brought this baby to you?"

"I don't think so. No one here knows what I do in
Medina. My mother doesn't approve. While I'm living
under her roof, I have to respect her feelings. Most people know me only as a driver for hire. I needed some
kind of income while I'm here, and I can't spend the
long hours away from Mom that a nursing job would
require."

He gestured toward the road. "Our buggy went toward Hope Springs. See the way the impression of the
wheels turn here and carried the mud out onto the highway."

"I do." She gazed at the thin tire track disappearing down the winding roadway. She could see half a
dozen white Amish farmhouses along either side of
the road before the road vanished over the hill. How
many Amish families lived in that direction or on one

of the many roads that branched off the highway? Fifty? A hundred? Where would they start looking for one scared, desperate young woman?

"Ah, now this is useful." Nick took a step closer to the roadway. A small puddle had formed after the rain. The imprint of the buggy wheel was deep where it rolled through the mud.

"What is it?" she asked.

He pointed to the print. "The buggy we are looking for has a jagged crack in the steel rim of the left rear wheel. If it breaks all the way through, someone is going to need a new rim put on."

"It looks like a crooked *Z*. It should be easy enough to spot."

He stood and rubbed a hand over his jaw. He took another stick of gum from his pocket, unwrapped it and popped it into his mouth. Carefully he folded the silver foil into a star. He noticed her stare and said, "I quit smoking a few years ago, but I can't kick the gum habit."

He had his share of struggles like everyone else. It made him more human. Something she wasn't prepared to see.

She looked away and asked, "How do we begin searching for Hannah's mother?"

"Even if I had the manpower to launch a full-scale investigation, I couldn't check every buggy wheel in the district. Most Amish families have three or four buggies, depending on how many of their kids are old enough to drive. It could take months."

"And Hannah has only two weeks before her mother's rights are severed if she doesn't return."

"Time may not be on her side."

"That's it? You're going to give up before we've started? I'm sorry I let Amber call you. I can tell you aren't going to go out of your way to save this family. I don't know why I thought you would."

Nick studied the myriad expressions that crossed Miriam's face and wondered where such passion came from.

He said, "I'm not sure I know what you want me to do?"

"We have a letter asking for help. We can't ignore it. This young girl's life may be ruined by a rash decision. I don't think we should wait for her to come back. I think we should go find her."

"Is there something you aren't telling me?"

It was as if his question had caused a mask to fall over her face. Her expression went completely neutral. Instead of answering his question, she said meekly, "I want to help, that's all."

Miriam's abrupt switch triggered his cop radar. She was hiding something. By her own admission few people knew she was a nurse. Fewer still would know that she aided Amish youth looking to leave their faith and go out into the world. Was accepting an unwanted baby part of her plan to help an unwed Amish girl escape into the *Englisch* life?

He didn't want to believe she would lie to him, but did he really know her? They hadn't spoken in years. People changed.

Maybe it wasn't a coincidence that Hannah had been left on Miriam's doorstep. If the mother knew Miriam, would she be able to stay away? He figured she would need to know how her little girl was doing. The sight of

Miriam with the child just might draw that woman out if she were still in the Hope Springs area. He wanted to be around when that happened. It would mean spending time, lots of time, in Miriam's company.

Could he keep his mind on his job when she was near? At the moment, all he wanted to do was run his fingers through her gorgeous hair. The early morning sun brought fiery highlights to life in her red-gold, shoulder-length mane as it moved like a dense curtain around her face and neck. It was the first time he'd seen her without the white bonnet the Amish called a prayer *kapp*. In his youth, he'd fantasized about what her hair would look like down. His imaginings paled in comparison to the beauty he beheld at the moment.

He realized he was staring when she scowled at him. Forcing his mind back to the task at hand, he asked, "Are you sure you can't think of anyone who might be Hannah's mother? Maybe you gave a ride to her or to her family recently and mentioned you were a nurse."

"No one stands out. Believe me, I've been racking my brain trying to think who she might be."

"I need to get back to the office and have our note and the hamper run for prints. Why don't you make up a list of the families who might know you're a nurse? We can go over them later. Something may click in the meantime. If it does, give me a call."

They returned to the house, covering the quarter mile in silence. When they reached his SUV, Miriam whistled for the dog. As Bella ambled up, she stopped to give Nick a parting lick on the hand. He patted her side. "She's a nice dog."

"Thank you."

"When did you rescue her from the pound?"

Miriam paused. "How did you know that?"

"It seems to be your MO."

"My what?"

"Your modus operandi, your mode of operation. Runaway teens, sick people, foundling babies—it just makes sense that your dog would be a rescue, too."

Her frown turned to a fierce scowl. "Don't think you know me, Nick Bradley, because you don't. You don't know me at all."

She turned on her heels and marched toward the house.

At the porch, she stopped and looked back. "My mother was right. This is Amish business. We will handle it ourselves. Have a great vacation."

Chapter 4

Miriam stopped short of slamming the door when she entered the house. Nick infuriated her. How dare that man presume to know anything about her? She didn't want him to know anything about her. She didn't want him to read her so easily.

She was scared of the way it made her feel. Like she could depend on him.

She balled her fingers into fists. She couldn't decide if she was angrier with him, or with herself. For a few minutes, she had forgotten what lay between. Somehow, after everything that happened, Nick still had the power to turn her inside out, as he'd done when she was eighteen and a naive country girl.

Well, she wasn't a teenager anymore. She wouldn't fall under his spell again. She had too much sense for that. There was too much that stood between them.

How could she have forgotten that even for a second?

She had gone months without running into him. Why now? How much more complicated could her life get? Perhaps in the back of her mind she knew this would happen. That Nick would use his charm to make her forget her anger and forgive him.

If she forgave Nick, she would have only herself left to blame for Mark's death. She was the one who had sent her brother on his panicked flight that night. The guilt still ate at her soul. If only she'd had the chance to beg Mark's forgiveness, perhaps she could learn to live with what she'd done.

When Mark's *Englisch* girlfriend, Natalie Perry, had come begging for a word with him, Miriam had been only too happy to inform her Mark wasn't home. When the tearful girl explained that her parents were making her leave town the following evening, Miriam had been relieved. It was God's will. Without this woman's influence, her brother would give up worldly things and be baptized into the faith. Miriam had given up Nick's love for her faith. She had passed that test. Mark would, too.

Natalie had scrawled a note and pressed it into Miriam's hand, pleading with her to give it to Mark as soon as possible. At the time, Miriam had no idea what the note contained, but she didn't give it to Mark until late the next day. Only afterward did she understand what harm she had caused.

Mark had flown out of the house, stolen a car and tried to reach his love before it was too late. Nick had stopped him, and Miriam never had the chance to beg her brother's forgiveness.

The front door opened, and Nick came in looking as if he expected a frying pan to come sailing at his head.

The idea of doing something so outrageous made her feel better. Slightly.

When he saw that he didn't need to defend himself, he said, "Ada, is there anything you need me to do before I leave? I can chop some kindling if you need it."

"*Nee,* I reckon we'll be fine."

He nodded. "You let me know if you hear anything from the baby's family."

Ada nodded toward the baby sleeping in the newly washed bassinet. "Do not worry, Nicolas. The mother, she will come for her babe."

"I pray you are right. Miriam, I'd appreciate knowing what the doctor has to say about Hannah."

He waited, as if he expected Miriam to say something. When she didn't, he nodded in her direction. "Okay, I've got to get back to town."

When the door closed behind him, Miriam took the first deep breath she managed to draw all morning. "I thought he would never leave."

"It was *goot* to see him again. I remember him as such a nice boy."

"It's too bad he turned out to be a murderer."

"Do not say such a thing, Miriam!" Her mother rounded on her with such intensity that Miriam was left speechless.

Ada shook her finger at her daughter. "You are not the only one who has suffered, but you are the only one who has not forgiven. The more you pick at a wound, the longer it takes to heal. I don't know why you refuse to see that. I'm tired of your selfish attitude. Maybe it is best that you go back to your *Englisch* home."

Dumbfounded, Miriam stared at her mother in shock.

Not once in her life had her mother raised her voice in such a manner.

Miriam struggled to muster her indignation. "That man caused the death of your only son. Have you really forgiven him for that?"

"It was *Gottes wille* that Mark died. I can't pretend to understand why such a thing had to happen, or why your father was taken before me, too. I can only try to live a good life and know that I will be with them when it is my time." Ada turned her back on her daughter and began to wash the coffee cups in the sink.

Miriam's anger slipped away. She wanted to punish Nick, but she'd wound up hurting her mother instead. "Do you really want me to leave?"

Her mother seemed to shrink before her eyes. Ada heaved a deep sigh. "I want what I cannot have. I'm tired. I'm going to lie down for a while. Can you watch the baby?"

"Of course." Miriam fetched her mother's cane from beside the table and watched her head toward the hallway. Ada moved slowly, leaning heavily on her cane for support.

Overcome with guilt, Miriam said, "I'm sorry if I upset you."

Her mother paused at the doorway and looked over her shoulder. "I forgave you the moment you spoke. We will talk no more about your stubborn, willful ways and the bitterness you carry. I leave it up to *Gott* to change your heart."

After her mother disappeared into her room Miriam sat down beside Hannah. Bella had staked out her new territory beneath the crib. She looked up at Miriam with soulful eyes and gave a halfhearted wag of her tail.

Miriam leaned down to pet her. "You love me no matter what I do or say. Thank you. That's why I have a dog."

The following morning, Miriam sat in the waiting room of the Hope Springs Medical clinic with Hannah in her borrowed car seat on the floor beside her. They were waiting to be seen for Hannah's first well-baby appointment.

Miriam was starting to wonder if she *was* a well baby. How soon did colic set in? If Hannah wasn't sick, she was certainly a fussy baby. It had been a long night for both of them. Miriam's eyes burned with lack of sleep. A headache nagged at the base of her neck. The baby had fallen asleep in the car on the way to the clinic, but she was starting to fidget now that the car ride was over.

"The doctor will be with you shortly. Would you like some tea or coffee while you wait?" Wilma Nolan, the elderly receptionist, asked with an encouraging smile.

Miriam shook her head. What she wanted was a few hours of uninterrupted sleep. The outside door opened. She looked over and saw Nick walk in.

He was out of uniform this morning. He'd traded his dark blues for worn, faded jeans, Western boots and a wool sweater in a soft taupe color that made his tan look even deeper. No one could deny he was a good-looking man. She struggled to ignore the sudden jump in her pulse.

The elderly receptionist behind the counter sat up straight and smiled. "Sheriff, how nice to see you. I'm afraid you will have quite a wait if you need to see the doctor this morning. Dr. White isn't feeling well, and Dr. Zook is the only one seeing patients."

"Not to worry, Wilma, I'm not sick. I just came to check on Ms. Kauffman and…the baby."

Wilma's eyebrows shot up a good two inches as she glanced between Miriam and Nick. "I see. Is this official business?"

Mortified by what she knew the receptionist was thinking, Miriam wanted to sink through the floor. Nick obviously came to the same conclusion because he quickly stuttered, "It's…it's personal business, Wilma."

"Oh, of course." A smug, knowing smile twitched on her thin lips as she blushed a bright shade of pink.

Nick took a seat beside Miriam. "Hi."

"What are you doing here?" she snapped under her breath, keeping a bland smile on her face for Wilma's benefit.

He leaned down to gaze at Hannah in her carrier. "I wanted to make sure she is okay. Amish babies have a higher incidence of birth defects, you know."

"Of course I know that. I thought you were going to wait for me to call you with an update."

"I wasn't sure you would call me."

He was right. She had no intention of involving him any more than she absolutely had to. "You didn't have to come in person. You know what Mrs. Nolan is thinking, don't you?"

"I'm not responsible for what people think."

"'It's personal business, Wilma.' Oh, you're *so* going to be responsible if word gets out that *we* are a couple with a new baby."

Nick shifted uncomfortably in his chair. "She's

known me for years. We go to the same church. Even if she thought it, she would never repeat it to anyone."

"Hannah Kauffman?" A young man with thick-rimmed black glasses stood at the entrance to the hallway. He had two pens in the top pocket of his lab coat and a manila folder in his hands.

"It's not Kauffman, Dr. Zook," Nick stated as he picked up Hannah's carrier and walked toward the young doctor.

Miriam took the carrier away from Nick. "It is for now."

The doctor turned and walked down the hall ahead of them. "Let us know what you put on the birth certificate and that will be her legal name."

"Legally, she's a Jane Doe." Nick stood close behind Miriam. The warmth of his breath on the back of her neck sent shivers rippling across her skin.

Dr. Zook stopped and looked at him in surprise. "She's a foundling?"

Miriam nodded. "Someone left her on my mother's doorstep two nights ago. I caught a glimpse of a buggy going down the lane. A note said her name was Hannah, but that's about all."

"I see now why you are involved, Sheriff. This is very odd."

Nick said, "I'm hoping you can help us."

Dr. Zook's eyes narrowed behind his glasses. "You do understand that I can't reveal any information about my patients."

"Even if you think you know who the mother might be?" Nick asked in a tone of voice that made Miriam glad she wasn't the one he was questioning.

Dr. Zook drew himself up to his full height, which

was a good four inches shorter than Nick's six feet. "Not even then."

Miriam expected this roadblock. "I'm a nurse, so I understand how it works. We won't ask for confidential information."

The young doctor relaxed. "Good. Let's take a look at this little girl and make sure she is healthy."

He held open the door to an exam room. Miriam walked in and set the carrier on the exam table. Carefully, she unlatched the harness and lifted the baby out. Hannah began fussing but soon settled back to sleep as Miriam soothed her with rocking and quiet words.

Nick took the carrier and put in on the floor, making room for Miriam to lay the baby on the exam table. She took a step to the side, but kept one hand on Hannah. Dr. Zook quietly and thoroughly went about his examination.

Miriam had met him a few times before. She preferred Dr. Harold White, but the older physician was well into his eighties. Dr. Zook had taken over a small part of Dr. White's practice, and his involvement had grown in the past year until he oversaw almost half of the patients.

Miriam had been impressed with his handling of her mother's health issues and had no qualms about letting him see Hannah. She said, "I've always meant to ask, are you related to our Bishop Zook?"

The young doctor smiled. "All Zooks are related in one way or another, but in the case of Bishop Zook and myself, it's not a close connection. My family comes from near Reading, Pennsylvania."

Nick spoke up. "Can you tell if Hannah has any birth defects associated with being Amish?"

"I can rule out dwarfism and Troyer Syndrome, which is a lethal microcephaly or small head, and several others diseases just by looking at her. Only blood tests or time will tell us if she suffers from any inherited metabolic defects such as glutaric aciduria, PKU, maple syrup urine disease or cystic fibrosis. I'll draw her newborn screening blood tests today. That will check for many of the things I've mentioned and more. Do you want me to draw blood for DNA matching, as well?"

Nodding, Nick said, "You read my mind. If someone shows up claiming to be her parent or grandparent, I want to make sure they are related before I release her."

Miriam said, "The mother's note did say she would be back for Hannah, but she also said it wasn't safe to have the baby with her. Can you think of anyone in a situation like that?"

The doctor rubbed the back of his neck. "I honestly can't."

Miriam laid a hand on his arm. "I know the Amish are reluctant to go to outsiders with their problems, Doctor. If you hear of anyone in a difficult situation, please let us know."

Dr. Zook stared at her hand. She withdrew it hoping she hadn't made a mistake.

He looked into her eyes and said, "I do understand the reluctance of the Amish to become involved with Social Services and the legal system in general. They have not always been treated fairly. I respect the way they take care of each other. I deeply admire their faith in God. I will let you know if I hear of anything like this."

Miriam blew out a sigh of relief. "Thank you, Doctor."

"Not at all." He was actually blushing.

Nick gave Miriam a funny look, then said, "Thanks, Doc."

"I'll draw some blood for those tests and I'll have Amber follow up with this little girl just as she would one of her home deliveries. If you have any questions, feel free to call me. Day or night."

He took a card from his pocket and scrawled a number on it. He handed it to Miriam. "This is my personal cell phone. Don't hesitate to use it."

She smiled at him. "I won't hesitate for a minute."

"Is there anything else?"

Miriam said, "She's very fussy, Doctor, especially after she eats. I'm wondering if I should switch her to a soy-based formula."

"You can certainly try that, but don't make an abrupt switch. Mix the two together a few times until you gradually have all soy in her bottles."

"All right. We'll try that."

"Fine. I'd like to see her again in two weeks. Sooner, if you have any concerns," he added.

When the appointment ended, Nick scooped up Hannah's carrier and held the door open for the doctor and Miriam to go out ahead of him. Outside the clinic, he handed the baby over to Miriam. She opened her rear car door and leaned in to secure the carrier.

He knew he shouldn't say anything, but as usual, his good sense went missing where Miriam was concerned. "Doctor Zook seems quite taken with you."

She popped up to gape at him. "What has that got to do with anything?"

"Nothing. It was a simple observation. I assume he isn't married?"

"No, he isn't, and I'm sure that is none of your business."

He liked the way her eyes snapped when she was angry. If only her anger wasn't always directed at him. He took a step back and raised his hands. "Don't get all huffy."

"I have every right to get huffy. What if I suggested Wilma had a crush on you?"

"Since she is old enough to be my grandmother, I'd say that would be weird."

"There's no talking to you. Now that you've been reassured Hannah is in good health, please go away. The less I see of you the better."

He hid how much her words hurt and gave her an offhand salute. "As you wish."

She rolled her eyes and turned her back on him to finish fastening Hannah's car seat. She struggled to get the last buckle fastened.

He didn't want to leave on a sour note, but he knew when he was butting his head against a brick wall where she was concerned. In spite of his best intentions, he couldn't help making one parting comment. "That chip on your shoulder isn't doing you any good, you know."

She backed out of the car with a growl of exasperation. He nudged her aside, leaned in and deftly secured the baby. Straightening, he looked at Miriam and calmly said, "It isn't going to do Hannah any good, either. We have a better chance of finding her mother if we work together."

"I thought you were leaving town for a fishing trip?"

He gazed at her intently. "The fish can wait. Hannah shouldn't have to."

He wanted Miriam's cooperation. He didn't believe

in coincidences, he still believed whoever left the baby with her knew she was a nurse. "Did you put together the list of families who know you're a nurse, the way I asked?"

"Yes." She dug into her purse and pulled out a hand-written sheet.

It was a short list. There were only seven names on it. It wouldn't take long to interview these families. He looked at her. "I appreciate your cooperation."

Miriam considered carefully before she spoke again. If Hannah's mother didn't come forward, there would be little she could do on her own to find her. Nick, on the other hand, had an entire crime-solving department at his beck and call. If he was willing to put some effort into finding the baby's mother, Miriam shouldn't be discouraging him. In the end, finding the young woman who needed her help took priority over her feelings for cooperating with Nick.

She said, "I have an idea how we can check lots of buggy tires in one place."

He looked at her sharply. "How?"

"The day after tomorrow, Sunday preaching services will be held at Bishop Zook's farm. Every family in his congregation will be there. Including all the people on that list. The younger men usually drive separately so they can escort their special girls home afterward. Why go farm to farm when there will be dozens of buggies in one place? It's a start."

"A good start. Still, his isn't the only Amish church in the area. I can think of at least five others. I can try to find out where the other congregations are meeting.

Tuesday is market day. That will be another opportunity for us if she hasn't come forward by then."

The thought of working with Nick should have left Miriam cold, but it didn't. Instead, a strange excitement quickened her pulse. What was she getting herself into?

"I'll see you Sunday," he said and walked away.

When he reached his vehicle, he glanced back. She was still standing by her car watching him. An odd look of yearning crossed his face. It was gone so quickly she wondered if she imagined it.

What was he thinking when he gazed at her like that? Was he remembering happier days? She licked her lips and tucked her hair into place behind her ear. Did he think she had changed much? Did he still find her attractive?

The absurdness of the thought startled her. Why should she care what he saw when he looked at her? Impressing him should be the last thing on her mind. She walked around her car, got in quickly and drove away.

But no matter how fast she drove, thoughts of Nick stuck in her mind. She couldn't outrun them.

Chapter 5

Sunday morning dawned bright and clear. Miriam knew that because her mother was clanging pots and pans around in the kitchen before any light crept through Miriam's window. The sounds echoed up the stairwell into her room because she had the door open to hear Hannah when she cried. She needn't have bothered. Each time the baby fussed, Bella was beside Miriam's bed five seconds later, nosing her mistress to get up.

Miriam's mother had put a cot in the kitchen to sleep beside the baby's crib, but Miriam had been the one to get up and feed the baby through the night. Her mother's intentions were good, but she needed her sleep, too. Tonight, Miriam would insist on taking the cot. That way she might get a little more sleep.

The soft sound of her mother humming reached Miriam's ears. Ada was delighted her daughter was taking her to the Sunday preaching. Her mother might say she accepted that Miriam had left the Amish faith for good, but for Ada, that door was always open. Any former Amish who sought forgiveness would be welcomed back into the Amish fold with great joy.

Her mother hollered up the stairs. "You should feed the horse, Miriam. She will have a long day."

Miriam groaned. Arriving at a church meeting in a car was unacceptable to Ada. Amish people walked or drove their buggies. End of discussion.

To keep her mother from trying to walk the six miles to Bishop Zook's farm, Miriam would have to feed, water and hitch up their horse. She might be out of practice at harnessing the mare, but she hadn't forgotten how to do it.

After dressing in work clothes, Miriam walked through the kitchen. At the front door, she waited for Bella to join her. "Come on, the baby's not going to wake up for another two hours. I just fed her. This might be your only chance to spend time with me today because you are not coming with us to church."

Bella reluctantly abandoned her post beneath the crib and trotted out the door Miriam held open. Her mother, looking brighter than Miriam had seen her in weeks, was mixing batter in a large bowl. "You'd best get a move on, child. I'll not be late to services at the bishop's home. Esther Zook would never let me live it down."

"I can't understand why such a sweet man married that sour-faced woman."

Ada chuckled, then struggled to keep a straight face. "It is not right to speak ill of others."

"The truth is not ill, *Mamm,* it is the truth. There is only one reason I can think of why he fell for her."

The two women looked at each other, and both said, "She must be a wondrous *goot* cook!"

Laughing, Ada turned back to the stove. "How many times did your father say those very words?"

"Every time he talked about his brother's wife, Aunt Mae."

"She was a homely woman, God rest her soul, but your *onkel* was a happy man married to her." Ada spooned the batter into a muffin tin.

Miriam's smile faded. "I miss Papa. He was a funny fellow."

"*Ja.* He often made me laugh. God gave him a fine wit. You had better hurry and get the horse fed or these muffins will be cold by the time you get back." Ada opened the oven door and slid the pan in.

Miriam walked outside into the cool air. Even after six months, she was still amazed by the stillness and freshness of a country morning. She scanned the lane for any sign of a returning buggy. It remained as empty as it had all night. She knew because she'd looked out her window often enough. Perhaps Hannah's mother wouldn't return. What would become of the baby then?

Had Nick had any luck lifting fingerprints from the note or hamper? Surely, he would have called if he had. She still found it hard to believe that he had agreed to leave the baby with them. Was he trying to make amends? Did he care that she hadn't forgiven him?

Annoyed with herself for thinking about Nick once again, she hurried across the yard to finish her chores. In the barn, she quickly measured grain for the horse and took an old coffee can full to the henhouse. Opening the screen door, she sprinkled the grain for the brown-and-white-speckled hens. They clucked and cackled with satisfaction. She didn't bother checking for eggs. She knew her mother had gathered them already.

By the time she returned to the house, hung up her jacket and washed up, her mother was dumping golden brown cornmeal muffins into a woven wooden basket lined with a white napkin. The smell of bacon filled the air and made Miriam's stomach growl. A few more years of eating like this and she would be having her own heart attack.

"What was your blood sugar this morning?" Miriam snatched a muffin and bit into the warm crumbly goodness.

"104."

Miriam fixed her mother with an unwavering stare. "Have you taken your medicine?"

"Ja."

"Checked your blood pressure?"

"Ja."

"What is your blood pressure this morning?"

Ada's eyes narrowed. "Before or after my daughter began badgering me?"

Miriam didn't blink. "Before."

Ada rolled her eyes. "110 over 66, satisfied?"

Smiling broadly, Miriam nodded. *"Ja, Mamm dat* is very *goot."*

"And we will be very late if you don't hurry up and eat." Her mother carried the empty muffin tin to the sink and then returned to the table. After bowing their heads in silent prayer, the woman began eating.

Ada asked, "Have you decided what to tell people about Hannah?"

"The truth is generally best. I will tell people she was left with us to care for until her mother returns."

The baby began to fuss. Miriam reached over to her cradle, patted her back and adjusted her position.

Ada smiled. "She is such a darling child. I dread to think we might never see her again when her mother does come for her."

Miriam remained silent, but the same concern had taken root in her mind, too. Hannah was quickly working her way into Miriam's heart and into her life. Letting go of her wasn't going to be easy.

Nick stopped his SUV near the end of the lane at the Zook farm. He knew the church members wouldn't appreciate his arrival in a modern vehicle on their day of worship. He wasn't here in an official capacity, so he wasn't wearing his uniform. It was almost noon, so he figured the service would be over and he would be in time for the meal.

Most Amish Sunday preaching lasted for three or four hours. The oratory workload was shared between the bishop and one or two ministers, none of whom had any formal training. They were, in fact, ordinary men whose names were among those suggested by the congregation for the position and then chosen by the drawing of lots. It was a lifelong assignment, one without pay or benefits of any kind.

Following the services that were held in homes or barns every other Sunday, the Amish women would feed everyone, clean up and spend much of the afternoon visiting with family and friends.

Approaching the large and rambling white house, Nick looked for Miriam among the women standing in groups outside of the bishop's home. Their conversations died down when they spotted him. It was unusual to have an outsider show up in such a fashion. Although many people knew he had Amish family members, he was still an outsider and regarded with suspicion by many.

He gave everyone a friendly wave and finally spotted Miriam sitting on a quilt beneath a tree with a half dozen other young women. Hannah lay sleeping on the blanket beside her. He caught Miriam's eye and tipped his head toward the house. He needed to pay his respects to Bishop Zook and the church elders before speaking with her. She nodded once in agreement and stayed put.

Inside the house, several walls had been removed to open the home up for the church meeting. The benches that had arrived that morning in a special wagon were now being rearranged to allow seating at makeshift tables. The bishop sat near the open door in one of the few armchairs in the room.

A small man with a long gray beard, he looked the part of a wise Amish elder. Nick knew him to be a fair and kind man. He rose to his feet when he saw Nick. Worry filled his eyes. "Sheriff, I hope you do not come among us with bad news."

More than once, Nick had been the one to tell an Amish family that their loved ones had been involved in a collision with a car or truck. He often asked the bishop to accompany him when he brought the news that the accident had been fatal.

"I don't bring bad news today, Bishop. I'm here to speak with Miriam Kauffman, and to give you greetings from my grandmother."

"Ah, that is a relief. How is Betsy? I have not seen her for many months."

"She's well and busy with lots of great-grandchildren, but not enough of them to keep her from trying to marry off the few of us who are still single."

Bishop Zook chuckled. "She always did fancy herself something of a matchmaker. I believe Miriam is outside with some of our young mothers. The case of this abandoned babe is very troubling. I cannot think any of our young women would do such a thing."

"I understand, but we have to ask."

"We have several families who would be pleased to take the child into their homes."

"Where the child is placed, if her mother doesn't return, will be up to Social Services."

"I feared as much. We would rather handle this ourselves. If the mother returns, the child will remain with her, *ja?*"

Nick didn't want a string of hopeful women showing up and claiming to be Hannah's mother. He needed to be very clear it wouldn't be that easy. "Once we have proof, by a blood test, that she is the mother, and we can see that she is in a position to take care of the child, then yes, it is likely that Social Services will agree to her keeping the child. If you do come across information about the mother, please get word to Miriam or myself."

"This is the Lord's working. We offer our prayers for this troubled woman and for her child."

"Thank you, Bishop."

Nick glanced again to where Miriam sat surrounded by young Amish mothers with their babies. Except for a slight difference in her dress, Miriam could have been one of them.

She had been one of them. It had taken a lot to drive her away. What would it take to make her return? If she found it in her heart to forgive him for Mark's death, would she return to the life she'd left behind?

The bishop said, "You will stay and eat with us this fine day, *ja?*"

Nick pulled his troubled gaze away from Miriam. "I would be honored, Bishop Zook. I hear your wife makes a fine peanut butter pie."

"She made a dozen different pies yesterday, and chased me away with a spoon when I tried to sample one."

"I hope for your sake there will be leftovers."

There was never a lack of food at an Amish gathering. The makeshift tables were laden with home-baked bread, different kinds of cheese and cold cuts. There was *schmierkase,* a creamy, cottage cheese-like spread, sliced pickles, pickled beets, pretzels and, Nick's favorite, a special peanut butter spread sweetened with molasses or marshmallow cream. He liked the marshmallow cream version the best. There were also a variety of cookies, brownies and other baked goods as well a rich black coffee to dunk them in.

A rumble deep in his stomach reminded Nick that breakfast had been hours ago. He had already visited two other church groups that morning and looked at dozens of buggy wheels. There was no way to keep his examinations quiet. The community would be abuzz with speculation, but it couldn't be helped.

Nick thanked the Bishop for his invitation to eat and walked toward the lawn where Miriam was sitting. She caught sight of him and rose to her feet. She spoke to Katie Sutter who was sitting beside her. At Katie's nod of agreement, Miriam left Hannah sleeping on the quilt.

Before he could say good morning, she said, "I expected you hours ago. Hannah got fussy so I took her out of the house during the service and I was able to check all the buggies that are parked beside the barn. I didn't get a chance to check those parked on the hillside."

He smiled. "Good morning, Miriam. How are you this fine morning? How is Hannah? Is she keeping you up at night? I hope your mother is feeling well."

Miriam planted her hands on her hips. "Do you really want to waste time on pleasantries?"

"It's never a waste of time to be civil."

"Fine. Good morning, Nicolas. Of course Hannah is keeping me up at night. She's a baby and she wakes up wanting to be fed every three hours. My mother is on cloud nine because I came to church with her, and Bella was pouting because she couldn't come along. Now can we go find the buggy I saw leaving Mom's place?"

"That's the plan." He started walking toward the pasture gate. Several dozen buggies and wagons were parked side by side on the grassy hill. The horses, all still in harness, were tied up along the fence dozing in the morning sun or munching on the green grass at their feet.

Miriam tipped her head toward Nick and asked quietly, "How are you going to do this without attracting attention?"

He glanced around and leaned closer. "Under the cover of bright sunshine, I'm going to stroll along the hillside with you, stopping beside every buggy. If anyone happens to look our way, I hope they think we're just having a Sunday stroll."

Her scowl vanished and she tried to hide a grin.

Glancing over her shoulder, she said, "News flash, Sheriff. *Everyone* is looking at us."

"I guess our cover is blown. Did you know your eyes sparkle when you smile?"

She blushed bright red, folded her arms over her chest and stared at her feet. He could have kicked himself for making such a foolish, but true statement.

He once again became all business. "If anyone asks, which they won't, I'll say it's official police business and that's all I'll say. It's my best line. I use it all the time. The Amish are so reluctant to involve themselves in outsider business that they will politely pretend they don't see anything out of the ordinary."

She nodded. "You're right. They won't ask you questions, but they will ask my mother questions."

"Ada can tell them I said it's police business."

They stopped at the first buggy on the hill. Nick did a quick check of the wheels. There were no marks similar to the one he'd seen on Miriam's lane. When he looked up, Miriam was studying the farmhouse.

She said, "If the mother is here and she sees us looking at buggies together, she may put two and two together and come forward."

"Or, she could put two and two together and redouble her efforts to keep hidden. Did anyone appear particularly interested in Hannah today?"

"Nothing more than the usually flurry of interest a new baby generates. There was a lot of disbelief when I said I found her on my doorstep."

"I imagine."

"I didn't notice any young woman deliberately avoiding me, either. If she saw the baby, she's really good at hiding her emotions."

"Aren't we all?" he said with a wry smile. He was hiding the fact that he was falling for her all over again.

Nick quickly moved from buggy to buggy without discovering the one he hoped to find. At the end of the line, he said, "It's not here. I don't know what else to do except try again on Tuesday when people go to market. The problem with that is I'm going to end up checking most of these same ones all over again. It's not like I have a way to tell them apart."

"Wait a minute." Miriam slipped her purse strap off her shoulder, reached in and withdrew a tube of lipstick. Looking around to make sure no one could see, she dabbed a spot in the lower corner of the orange triangle on the back.

From a few feet away, it didn't show, but when Nick moved closer he could see the mark because he was looking for it. "Nice. Now, if it just doesn't rain."

They made their way back along the line of buggies as Miriam unobtrusively added a dot of lipstick to each one. When they came out the pasture gate, he held out his hand. "Mind if I borrow that? I've got two other congregations to visit today."

She handed it over. He turned the tube to read the label. "Ambrosia Blush. I like that."

"It's not your color, Sheriff. It's a shade made for redheads."

He tucked the tube in his pocket. "I'll keep that in mind. Have you eaten yet?"

"No, we were waiting for the elders to finish, but I'm not hungry. Mom insists on making a breakfast fit for a farmhand."

By this time they had reached the quilt where Katie

Sutter sat holding a fussy Hannah. Miriam reached for the baby. "I'll take her."

Katie handed her over. Hannah quieted instantly. Katie smiled at Nick. "Hello, Nick, it's good to see you again."

"You, as well, Katie. Where is Elam?" He looked around for her husband.

Katie had gone out into the world and returned to the Amish several years ago. She was happily married now with two small children. She understood the challenges of both worlds.

"Elam is out in the barn with Jonathan talking horses. Jonathan was just saying the other day that he hadn't seen you in weeks. He was wondering if you'd forgotten where he lived."

Nick laughed aloud. Hannah, who had quieted in Miriam's arms, started crying again. He cupped her head softly. "I'm sorry, sweet one, did I scare you?"

The baby quieted briefly, then began protesting in earnest. Miriam said, "I think she's just getting hungry. Who is Jonathan?"

Nick recounted the story. "The Christmas before last, Jonathan Dressler was found, beaten and suffering from amnesia on Eli Imhoff's farm. I investigated the case and eventually solved it, but not until after Jonathan recovered his memory."

"And fell in love with Eli's daughter Karen," Katie added. "He is *Englisch,* but he will be baptized into our faith soon and then everyone expects a wedding will follow. Quickly."

"Not quick enough for Jonathan." Nick knew his friend was counting down the days until he could marry the woman who saved his life.

Miriam had taken a bottle of formula from her purse. Nick held out his hand. "Let me take it up to the house and see if the bishop's wife can warm it up for her."

"Thanks." She held it up for him.

Her fingers brushed against his as he took the bottle. Her touch sent a jolt through his body and sucked the air from his lungs.

Miriam gaze flew to Nick's face. She saw his eyes widen. Just as quickly, his jaw hardened and he looked away. He said, "I'll be back in a couple of minutes."

When Nick was out of sight, she drew a shaky breath. How was it possible that the chemistry still simmered between them?

The answer was simple. Because it had never died.

Katie said, "We like Nick Bradley. He is a good man. He cares about the Amish. His cousin Amber delivered both my babies. Are you going to her wedding?"

Miriam was delighted to talk about anything except Nick. "I didn't know she was getting married. When is it?"

"This coming Saturday. She is marrying Dr. White's grandson, Phillip. He is a doctor, too. When they first met, no one imagined they would end up together. He had the whole community in an uproar when he put a stop to Amber doing home deliveries."

Since the vast majority of Amish babies were born at home with the help of midwives, a doctor trying to stop home deliveries would not be popular. "If they are getting married, they must've come to terms somehow. Is she still delivering babies at home?"

"Oh, yes. I think it took a lot of soul-searching and compromising on both their parts. Isn't it wondrous how God sends love into our lives? Not when we are expecting it, even when we think we don't want it or deserve it. He has His own time for everything if only we open our hearts to His will."

Miriam had closed her heart to love after Mark died. She had filled her life with caring for others. In spite of the good works she did, and she knew they were good works, there was still a measure of emptiness inside her. Opening her heart to love would mean forgiving herself. Was she ready to do that? She studied the baby in her arms. It would be so easy to fall in love with this child. What if she opened her heart to love Hannah and had to give her away? Wasn't it better not to love than to feel the pain of another loss?

"Elam and I are going to Amber's wedding. You could come with us."

"I don't know."

Nick came walking back with a mug in one hand. The formula bottle sat warming in it. In his other hand he carried a bundled napkin. He sat down and placed the mug carefully between them. He held the napkin out to Miriam. "Your mother put together something for you to eat."

"I can't believe she thinks I need to be fed. I'm still stuffed from breakfast."

"Are you sure? Because if you're not hungry, I am."

"Help yourself. Is Hannah's bottle warm enough?"

Laying his lunch aside, he checked the milk. "I think it's good. Don't babies drink formula at room temperature? My sister never heated up her baby's bottle."

"I've tried, but Hannah seems to like it better if it's warm. Otherwise, she gets fussy and doesn't eat as much." Miriam positioned the baby in her arms and gave her the bottle. It was exactly what Hannah wanted. The only sounds she made were contented sucking noises.

Katie said, "I was just telling Miriam that she should come to your cousin's wedding. I know Amber would be delighted to see her there."

Miriam shook her head. "I would feel funny showing up without an invitation."

Nick took a bite of his sandwich and mumbled around his full mouth. "I've got you covered."

He leaned to the side and pulled an envelope out of his hip pocket and held it out to her.

Miriam's hands were full. "What is it?"

Grinning, he said, "Your invitation to the wedding. I asked Amber to invite you. There will be plenty of room in the church, and it's not like there's going to be any shortage of food at the dinner afterward. Half our family is Amish. Believe me, there will be food." He laid the envelope beside her and took another bite of his sandwich.

"See, now there is no reason not to come," Katie said with a bright smile.

Miriam still wasn't sure it would be a good idea. It was one thing to work with him as they tried to locate Hannah's mother. It was another thing to spend time with him at a social occasion. She opened her mouth to decline but ended up saying, "I'll think about it."

Katie got to her feet. "I see the elders have finished eating. I must go and help Elam feed the children. It was nice talking with you, Miriam. I will pray that Hannah's mother comes for her soon."

As Katie walked away, Nick said, "You know, she

may not be coming back The letter could have been a ruse. We may never learn who she is."

"I know that."

"Are you prepared to accept it?"

Miriam gazed at the baby in her arms. "I won't have any choice in the matter, will I?"

"I guess not, but you do have a choice to attend a fun-filled wedding or to stay home and mope about not having fun."

"What makes you think I would mope?"

The teasing grin left his face. His eyes grew serious. "It would mean a lot to Amber, and to me, if you come. Will you?"

"I said I'll think about it." It was the best that she could until she figured out how she felt about spending more time with Nick.

Chapter 6

Hannah was crying at the top of her lungs. The dog was whining and pawing at Miriam and the kettle was whistling madly. With only four hours of sleep out of the past twenty-four, Miriam reached the end of her rope at ten o'clock Monday morning. As she struggled to get an irate baby into a clean sleeper for the third time in as many feedings, she shouted at the dog, "Bella, stop it! Mother, will you *please* take the kettle off the fire."

Her mother had gone to her room to read and seemed oblivious to the pandemonium in the kitchen. Miriam finally got Hannah's flailing fist through the sleeve and quickly tied the front of the outfit closed. She lifted the baby to her shoulder to calm her. Nudging Bella aside with her knee, Miriam reached for clean burp rag. She threw it over her shoulder, but before she could switch

Hannah to that side she felt something warm and wet running down her back.

Miriam closed her eyes and gritted her teeth. "You did *not* just throw up on me."

From the doorway, a man's amused voice said, "Oh, yes, she did."

Great. Why did Nick have to show up when she was too tired to keep up her defenses? "Don't you knock?"

"I did. Several times."

He crossed the kitchen and pulled the kettle from the heat. The whistling died away, but Hannah was still crying at the top of her lungs, and Bella was still whining and dancing underfoot, upset that her baby was unhappy.

Nick returned to the door, held it open and said, "Bella, outside."

The dejected dog trotted out the door, and he closed it behind her. Then, he crossed the room to Miriam and lifted the baby away from her soggy shoulder. "Come here, sweet one, and tell me what's the matter."

It wasn't the first time in the past few days that Miriam felt inadequate as Hannah's caretaker, but it was the first time she'd had her shortcomings displayed to an audience.

Nick took the clean burp cloth from Miriam, tossed it over his shoulder and settled the baby with her face nuzzled into the side of his neck. She immediately stopped crying. Why she couldn't throw up on him was beyond knowing.

In the ensuing silence, Miriam dropped onto a chair and raked a hand through her hair. "Where were you eight hours ago?"

"Eight hours ago I was sleeping like a baby."

"Babies do not sleep. They fuss, they spit up, they make the dog crazy and they keep everyone else from sleeping, but they do not sleep."

Miriam didn't want to look at his face because she knew he would be smiling, amused at her expense. It was kind of funny now that she thought about it. She met his gaze and they both chuckled.

"Rough night?" he asked.

"Killer."

"Why don't you go change? I'll take care of her for a while."

"I had things under control, you know."

He smirked. "I saw that."

"What are you doing here, anyway?"

"I just wanted to check on the two of you. No sign of the mother I take it?"

Miriam stood up. The streak of warm formula down her back was quickly growing cold and sticky. "No sign of her or the father. At the moment, I'm beginning to think she was smarter than I gave her credit for."

"You don't mean that," Nick chided.

Miriam glanced at him and the little darling in a pink sleeper curled into a ball against his chest. The soft smile on his face as he looked down at the baby did funny things to Miriam's insides. There was something endearing about a man who held a baby so easily. "No, I don't mean it. I just need some sleep."

Ada walked into the room. "Nicolas, what a surprise. How nice to see you. Miriam, did the kettle boil? I didn't hear it. I'm afraid I fell asleep. A strong cup of tea will perk me up."

"Yes, mother, the kettle boiled. Nick just took it off the heat so it should be perfect for your tea. If you'll both excuse me, I'm going to go change my shirt, again. I hope this spitting up settles down when she is switched all the way over to soy formula."

Her mother said, "All babies spit up a little. You did. How your papa hollered when you spit up on his Sunday suit just as we got to the preaching. I tried so hard not to laugh at him. Is he home yet?"

Miriam exchanged a startled glance with Nick. She studied her mother closely. "Is who home yet?"

Ada's shoulders slumped. "That was silly. I know my William is gone. I must have been dreaming about the old days."

She turned and gave Nick a bright grin. "Would you like some tea?"

"Sounds great. Do you need any help?"

"*Nee,* you sit and hold our pretty baby. She's so *goot.* She barely made a peep last night. Miriam, would you like tea?"

Not a peep, but a whole lot of crying. Miriam was amazed her mother had slept through it. "No tea for me, *danki.*"

"That's right. You're a coffee drinker like your papa. Mark was the one who liked tea." She smiled sadly and turned back to the stove. "What was I going to do?"

"*Mamm,* are you okay?" Miriam stepped closer.

"I'm fine. I need another cup, that's what I was going to do." She pulled a second mug from the cabinet and placed a tea bag in it.

Miriam gave her mother one more worried look, then hurried upstairs. When she came downstairs five minutes later, Hannah was sound asleep in her crib. Bella was curled up on the rag rug beneath it. Her long tail thumped twice when she saw Miriam, but she didn't move. Ada and Nick were chatting over tea and oatmeal cookies at the kitchen table. Miriam joined them, but she couldn't stifle a yawn.

Her mother patted Miriam's hand. "Why don't you take a nap, dear. Nicolas and I will watch the baby."

"I'm sure the sheriff has other things to do besides babysit."

"I have a few errands to run, but I'm not in any hurry. I'll stay for a while. At least until the cookies run out." He bit into the one he was holding.

Ada grinned. "Miriam made them. They are sugar-free. She can be a *goot* cook when she sets her mind to it."

"Sugar-free doesn't mean calorie-free, so only two for you, *Mamm*," Miriam reminded her.

"How many can I have?" He slipped another one from the plate on to his napkin.

"None," she teased.

"You mean none after this one." He filched a fourth cookie and added it the stack in front of him.

Miriam shook her head. "Whatever."

Nick gave Ada a sympathetic look. "She's cranky today, isn't she?"

Ada glanced at the crib. "*Nee,* she is a sweet *boppli.* I wish she could stay with us forever."

He said, "I was talking about Miriam."

Ada glanced at Miriam and leaned closer to Nick. "She gets that way when she is tired."

Straightening in her chair, Ada gave Miriam a stern look. "Go lie down. We will be fine."

Miriam knew if she didn't get some rest she was going to fall down and sleep on the floor. "All right, but get me up if she gets fussy again."

"I will," Ada promised.

Miriam wondered if she would be the topic of conversation once she was out of the room. At this point, she really didn't care. She climbed the steps, walked into her bedroom and fell down on her bed fully dressed.

The next time she pried her eyes open, her watch told her she been asleep for four hours. She ran her fingers through her tangled hair and made her way back downstairs. The kitchen was empty. Hannah wasn't in her crib.

Frowning, Miriam was about to check the rest of the house when she heard a sound coming from the front porch. She walked to the window and looked out. Nick sat in her mother's white rocker. She couldn't see if he had Hannah, but she assumed he did because Bella sat quietly beside him watching him like a hawk.

Nick was singing softly in a beautiful baritone voice that sent chills up her spine. It was the old spiritual, "Michael Row the Boat Ashore." She stood listening for several stanzas, captured by the beauty of his voice and the healing words of the song. Death was not an end, merely a river to be crossed.

Mark and her father waiting for her on a shore she couldn't see yet, but someday she would. If only she could be sure she could gain their forgiveness.

How could she if she hadn't forgiven Nick? She pushed the screen door open and walked out onto the porch.

Nick looked over his shoulder as Miriam came out of the house. Her hair was tousled and her eyes were puffy, but she looked more rested than when he arrived. "Did you have a nice nap?"

"Better than you'll ever know. Where's my mother?" She paused to gaze lovingly at the baby.

"She went to take a nap shortly after you did."

"And she just left you with the baby all this time?"

"I didn't mind." He looked down at the baby nestled in the crook of his arm. She was so sweet and so innocent. In his line of work he often saw the seedy side of humanity. It did his soul good to realize how healing and calm holding a baby made him feel.

"I thought you had errands to run?" Miriam rubbed her hands up and down her arms as if she were cold.

It was warm on the porch. He knew it was his presence, not the temperature that made her uncomfortable. He wished it could be different. Would he ever be able to break through the barrier she had erected between them? He prayed to God that it was possible. They had been good friends once. He would settle for that again if were possible.

Miriam said, "I can take her now."

Reluctant to give Hannah up, he said, "I don't mind holding her. She's asleep. If I give her to you, she may wake up and start fussing."

Taking a seat in the other rocker on the porch, Miriam smothered another yawn. "I honestly don't know how new mothers do this."

"Beats me. I'm pretty much a wreck if I don't get eight hours."

He hesitated, then asked, "Has your mother been confused and forgetful before today, or is this something new?" Miriam had a lot on her plate at the moment. How well would she hold up under the strain?

"It's something new. I hope it's just the excitement of the past few days and not something serious."

"Don't take this the wrong way, but are you sure you're up to this?" He knew the moment the words left his mouth that he had made a mistake.

She scowled at him. "Exactly how should I take your inference that I can't take care of my mother and a newborn?"

"What I wanted to say was you have enough to worry about with your mother's health. It's understandable that you would have difficulty managing a new baby on top of that. Never mind. I can see by the look in your eyes that you don't want sympathy and you don't want help. No need to bite my head off. I'm sorry."

To his surprise, she took a deep breath and leaned back in her rocker. "I'm the one who is sorry. My mother is right. I get cranky when I don't get enough sleep. I may not want help, but I need it. You have no idea how much I needed this break. Thanks for sticking around today."

"You're welcome. Did you know your mother is talking about wanting to keep Hannah?"

"I do."

He could tell from the tone of her voice that she harbored the same wish. Nick looked down at the sleeping child in his arms. "It is easy to become attached to her. When she isn't spitting up or crying, she is adorable."

"Did she spit up again?" Quick concern flooded Miriam's face.

Nick smiled. Miriam was no different than his sisters or any other new mother. It was all about the baby. He raised the burp rag he had on his shoulder to reveal a damp stain. "It wasn't too much."

Miriam relaxed. "I was beginning to think it was just me. I'm happy to know she's willing to share."

He smiled at the baby and stroked her hair with the back of his fingers. "She seems to be an equal opportunity spitter, but she sure knows how to wrap a guy around her little finger."

"All babies can do that. You seem to have a knack for handling her."

"I've had lots of practice with a half dozen nieces and nephews. What can I say, I like babies."

"It shows." There was a softening in her tone that pleased him. He was glad now that he had stayed.

Miriam couldn't take her gaze off of Nick's face. There was such compassion and wonder in his eyes as he gazed at the baby.

Painting him as a heartless villain had been easy when she didn't have to see him. Face-to-face with him now, she didn't see a villain, just a man in awe of the new life he held.

Did it change anything? She wasn't sure.

He said, "I meant to tell you earlier that I drew a blank for fingerprints on the basket and note. It was a long shot at best. We recovered several prints but they were too smudged to be of any use. Which is rotten luck if she doesn't come back. It will leave us almost nothing to go on."

"I believe she'll come back for Hannah. I just wish we could locate her and find out what kind of trouble she is in."

"You're a practical woman. You have to know that women who leave their babies in a safe haven are unlikely to return for them. I don't know of a single case in Ohio where custody was returned to the biological mother."

"How many of those women were Amish?"

"No one knows. The point of the Safe Haven Law is to give mothers anonymity. Frankly, while the intention is good, I think the law has one big flaw."

"Fathers?"

"Exactly. Hannah's father has the same rights as her mother does. We don't know if he knew about this decision or not. I don't like the idea that a mother can give away her child without the father's consent."

"The world is full of deadbeat dads who couldn't care less what happens to their kids. Many of them can't be bothered to pay child support."

"There are many, many more men who would give anything to see that their children have good lives."

Nick would be one of those men, she decided. Mark would've been one if he had lived. Thinking about him made her sad but she didn't feel angry anymore. It was odd, because the anger had consumed her for so long. She felt empty without it. What would she find to replace it?

Nick said, "At least we know that Hannah will go to a loving family, even if her mother doesn't return. There are good people waiting to adopt a baby like her."

"I will be sorry to see her go."

"But you'll be able to get a decent night's sleep when she does," he said with a grin.

"There is that." She tipped her head to the side and stared at her dog. "Bella is the one who's going to be brokenhearted."

"You'll have to adopt a puppy for her."

"Ha! You do want to punish me, don't you? What makes you think a new puppy would be any less trouble than a baby? I could always adopt two and leave one on your doorstep."

"It wouldn't work."

"Why not? Don't tell me you'd take a helpless puppy back to the pound."

"No. However, among all my nieces, nephews and cousins, I wouldn't have any trouble finding a better home than my apartment."

Miriam knew that Nick was the oldest in his family. He had three younger sisters. She'd never met them, but he used to talk about them—make that complain about them—the way teenaged boys talked about their sisters. She was suddenly curious about his life. She asked, "What are the three terrors up to these days?"

Nick gave a bark of laughter that disturbed Hannah and made her whimper. He soothed her with a little bouncing, and she settled back to sleep. "I haven't heard them called that in years. They were the bane of my existence when I was growing up. Fortunately for me they didn't like the country or Amish living and refused to spend summers with Grandma Betsy. Summers were my great escape."

Miriam raised her foot to rest it on the rocker seat and wrapped her arms around her knee. She remembered waiting for him to return, eager to see him again and hear about everything he'd done in the strange *Englisch* world. "You never had much good to say about your sisters."

"True. Happily, I've learned to like them a lot better now that they have their own homes and aren't keeping me out of the only bathroom for hours on end. I never did understand why it takes a girl so long to get ready in the mornings. Multiply that by three, and you know I had like six seconds to get ready for school every day."

Miriam hesitated before asking her next question. Nick's home life had been difficult after his father's death. He had confided many things to her when they had been friends. Before she heaped all her anger and guilt on him. "How is your mother doing?"

"Better some days, worse other days. I know Dad loved her, I know she loved Dad, but they couldn't make it work. She wasn't cut out to be a big city cop's wife. She hated his job. After he was killed, she couldn't stand the guilt. She believed it was her punishment for leaving the Amish."

"I know you once said she was abusing prescription drugs. Is she still?"

"I don't think so, but I'm not there every day. My youngest sister lives close by. She seems to think Mom is doing okay. I know that having grandchildren has been good for her."

Miriam gazed at Hannah. "My mother would love grandchildren. That's why I'm worried she is getting too attached to Hannah. I don't want it to break her heart when the baby has to leave."

"As much as you love kids, I'm surprised you haven't married and had children."

She cocked her head at him. "Don't think it's because I haven't had offers. I just haven't found the right guy."

Hannah began fussing and squirming in his hold. He said, "I think she's getting hungry. It's been almost three hours since she last ate."

Miriam sprang to her feet. "I'll go get her bottle ready."

She entered the house with a sense of relief. Their

conversation had taken a personal turn that she wasn't quite ready for. It was one thing to have him talk about himself, it was another thing to expose her own life to his scrutiny.

Nick adjusted Hannah's position to his shoulder and patted her back gently. "Did you see how quickly she shot out of here when I started asking personal questions? Note to self—no matter how much I would like to know about Miriam's life, don't press, wait for her to volunteer that information."

At least she wasn't glaring daggers at him every chance she got. Something was different this afternoon. Her mood had softened. Perhaps having a baby in the house brought out her gentler side. Whatever was going on, he hoped it didn't change soon. He liked being able to spend time in her company without feeling like he was barely tolerated.

He glanced up as she came out of the house with a bottle in her hand. She self-consciously tucked her hair behind her ear and smiled slightly as she held out the formula.

The trouble with spending time with Miriam was that it made him wish for more. More of her time, more of her smiles, more of everything she cared to share.

"I can feed her if you want," she offered.

"That's okay, I'm already damp." He took the bottle from her hand and tried to shift the baby into a more upright position. Miriam bent down to help just as he leaned. Her face was inches from his. Close enough to kiss if he leaned forward a bit more. And he wanted to kiss her.

The timing was all wrong, the situation was all

wrong, but he wanted to kiss her. It took all of his self control to hand her the bottle, adjust the baby in his arms and lean back. He glanced at her to see if she had noticed his interest. Color bloomed in her cheeks. She gave him the bottle and took a step back.

Keep it casual. Don't blow it.

He could give himself good advice but he wasn't sure he could follow it. He cleared his throat. "I hope we have better luck finding our mystery buggy during the farmers market tomorrow."

Miriam took a seat in her chair and stared straight ahead. "I think we'll see a lot of the same ones. If I knew when the next singing was being held we could check out more of the young men's buggies."

"I know a lot of them like the open-topped buggies for courting. You saw a closed-top buggy."

"I'm sure what I saw was a standard variety, black, Ohio Amish buggy."

"It's too bad there isn't something to help us tell them apart."

"That's the point of all the Amish driving the same style. Uniformity, conformity, no one stands out above their neighbor."

"I understand that, but I can still wish for license tags."

"Well, unless the numbers had been three feet tall and could glow in the dark, I wouldn't have been able to see them, either. It was dark and the lane is a quarter mile long."

"I'm not faulting you for a lack of description. I'm frustrated by the fact that I can't do more."

"Are you sorry that we let you in on this?"

"Yes, and no. I know that Hannah is being well cared

for. I just wish I could bring the power of my office into the hunt. If I considered this a straight child abandonment, my office could offer a reward for information. We could have law enforcement officers going door to door. We could make it hard for this young woman to hide. While I've alerted the local hospitals and clinics to be on the lookout for a woman with postpartum complications and no baby, all I'm really left with is checking buggy wheels. It's not high-tech police work."

"You like your job, don't you?"

"I do, but it's not for everyone." Hannah had finished her bottle. Nick sat her up to burp her. She gave a hearty belch for such a tiny baby, but all of her formula stayed down.

Miriam got up and reached for her. Nick handed her over reluctantly. He had no more reasons to hang out on Miriam's front porch.

"I'm glad we let you in on this, and I'm glad you came by today. Thank you."

"You're welcome. Why don't I pick up you and your mother tomorrow? We can cruise the market together." He waited, hopeful that this new, softer Miriam would agree.

"That sounds fine." She hesitated, as if she wanted to say more, then simply nodded goodbye and walked into the house.

Nick walked out to his vehicle. He opened the door of his SUV but hesitated before getting in. He knew it was a selfish thought, but he hoped Hannah's mother stayed out of sight a little longer.

Without Hannah to bring them together he'd have no excuse to spend time with Miriam.

Chapter 7

A heavy morning shower didn't put a damper on the first market day of the spring. The small town of Hope Springs was bustling with wagons, buggies, produce buyers and tourists. Nick turned off Main Street onto Lake Street.

The regular weekly market had been held on Friday afternoons in a large grassy area next to the town's lumberyard. After a recent meeting of the town council, the day had been changed to Tuesday in an effort to draw in tourists from the other area markets held on the same day. The striped canopies of numerous tents were clearly visible, as were dozens of buggies lined up along the street.

Nick had been to the market numerous times. It was one way to meet and get to know the often reclusive Amish residents of his county. Today, he wouldn't be looking over homemade baked goods or cheeses. He'd be watching for anyone with a marked interest in Hannah as well as for their mystery buggy.

After he found a parking place, he got out of the vehicle and opened the door for Ada. She had been in good spirits on the ride to town, as was her daughter. Amish families looked forward eagerly to the weekly trip to town. Much of the day would be spent visiting and shopping with friends and family.

Ada said, "*Ach,* there is Faith Lapp with one of her alpacas. They are such cute animals. I must get some of her yarn to make Hannah a blanket."

Nick looked to see if her nephew Kyle was with her. He wanted speak to the boy and find out how he was adjusting to his new Amish family. Nick had had the unhappy duty of removing Kyle from his aunt's home when an overzealous and uninformed social worker insisted Faith's plain home was an unsafe environment. Fortunately, Judge Harbin, the family court judge, was familiar with the Amish and knew that Kyle would be raised with every care.

It took Nick several long moments to locate the boy. He was dressed in a wide-brimmed straw hat, dark pants and a white shirt beneath a dark vest. He was standing in a group of boys in almost identical clothing. They were laughing and patting the young black alpaca that Kyle had named Shadow. From the look on the young boy's face, Nick knew he was settling in well.

Miriam had Hannah out of her car seat and was settling her into a baby carrier that kept her snuggled against Miriam's chest. Nick said, "That's a nice little rig."

"She seems much more content when she is being held or carried upright. Amber brought it by yesterday after you left. It works wonders, and it lets me keep my hands free."

Nick surveyed the field. "Which end of the street do you want to start on?"

"First, I'd like to visit the tent where the quilts are being displayed."

Nick frowned at her. "There won't be any buggies in that area."

"I know, but I brought the quilt Hannah was wrapped in. I'm hoping someone will recognize it. I also wanted to say hello to Rebecca and Gideon Troyer. You know Rebecca's story, don't you?"

"Sure. I was one of the people bidding on her quilt last November when she was trying to raise enough money to have her eye surgery. Of course, Gideon outbid us all and ended up with a wife as well as a fine quilt. We are all thankful for God's mercy in restoring Rebecca's sight."

Ada said, "I think the bigger miracle was Gideon's return to the Plain life after being out in the world for so many years. It was a blessing to his family and our community."

Miriam couldn't get the strap of the snuggle harness to fit comfortably. Nick said, "Here, let me help you with that."

She turned her back to him. He swept aside her hair to see where the strap was twisted. Her hair whispered across his wrist and bunched like the softest silk in his hand. He paused, captivated by the sensation.

"Can you get it?" she asked.

"Yup. Just a second." He straightened the strap and let her hair slide through his fingers. If he lived to be an old, old man, he wouldn't forget the softness of it.

"Why don't we split up? Nick, you can take mother to buy yarn, and I'll go say hello to Rebecca and Gideon. We can meet back here and start checking buggy wheels."

"I think it would be better to stick together," he said.

Miriam gave him a funny look. "What difference does that make?"

"I want to be able to watch the people watching you and Hannah." He wanted to walk by her side and pretend they were friends again.

"Okay, alpaca yarn, quilts, once through the market and then buggy wheels?"

"Sounds fine. It's too bad it rained. Your lipstick marks will have been washed off all the slow-moving-vehicle signs. We'll end up rechecking dozens of the same ones."

Miriam giggled, a light, free sound that made his heart beat faster. "It's waterproof lipstick. It should still be there."

He shook his head. "Waterproof. A man learns something new every day."

Nick kept a close watch on Miriam as she moved through the crowds. There were a number of people who stopped to admire Hannah, but no one seemed overly interested, or out of the ordinary, except for a pair of Amish teenage boys who followed them but never approached her.

Nick said to Ada, "Do you know those boys?"

She looked to where he indicated the pair looking at hand-carved pipes. "Do you mean the Beachy twins?"

"Beachy? Which family do they belong to?" Since almost all Amish were descended from a small group of immigrants, there was very little diversity in their names. There were dozens of families with the same last name in his county.

"They are Levi Beachy's younger brothers. He is the carriage maker in Hope Springs. He rented the business from Sarah Wyse's husband shortly before he passed away."

"Yes, I remember that."

Nick said to Miriam, "I believe I'll have a word with the twins. Walk on and I'll catch up with you."

As Miriam and her mother made their way down the row of tents, Nick dropped back and approached the boys from behind, taking care to keep out of their line of sight until he was standing only a step away. "You two seem awfully interested in Miriam Kauffman's baby. Care to tell me why?"

The boy spun around, their eyes going wide at the sight of the sheriff towering over them. One stammered, "W-we don't know what you mean."

"I'm asking what is your interest in that baby? Is one of you the father?"

He doubted they could look more surprised if he'd suggested that they could fly. "*Nee*, we're no one's *daed*," they exclaimed together.

"Are you willing to take a DNA test to prove that?"

The boys looked at each other. One said, "We're not so good at taking tests. We'd rather not."

Nick folded his arms and clapped a hand over his face to hide his grin. "What are your names?"

The one on the right said, "I'm Moses, and this is my younger brother, Atlee."

Atlee elbowed him. "Younger by five minutes ain't hardly enough to mention."

Nick put a stop to what was clearly an old argument. "Why are you following Miriam?"

"Is that the baby that was left on the porch step?" Atlee asked.

"You answer my question first." Nick used his most intimidating tone.

"We were wondering what she would charge to drive us to Cincinnati," Moses said.

Atlee looked at him quickly, but then nodded. "Yeah, Cincinnati."

Nick considered their story. They looked to be about the right age to be on their *rumspringa,* the time following an Amish teenager's sixteenth birthday when they were allowed to experience the forbidden outside world prior to taking their vows of faith. Many learned to drive cars, but those who couldn't afford them would hire drivers to take them into the cities. "So why not just ask her?"

Moses looked at his feet. "She's so pretty."

Puppy love—that was all Nick needed. "Samson Carter will quote you a fair price on a trip that far."

The boys nodded. Atlee said, "But he ain't so pretty. Is that the baby that was left on the stoop?"

"It is. What do you boys know about it?"

"Only what we heard. Is the baby okay?" Atlee asked. Moses looked as if he'd rather be anywhere else.

Nick relaxed. "She's fine as far as we can tell. If you boys hear anything about a girl people thought might be pregnant but then didn't have a baby, I'd sure like to know about it. Now, beat it."

He didn't have to say it twice. The boys dashed away without a backward glance.

After coming up empty at the quilt tent and spending another fruitless hour of searching through the buggies, they called it quits. Nick, Miriam and Ada returned to his vehicle. With Hannah secured in her car seat, Nick started the vehicle and headed toward Miriam's house.

At the edge of town his radio crackled to life. He pulled over to listen. The dispatcher was asking for a unit in the Hope Springs area to respond to a domestic disturbance call. A neighbor had called in a report that a woman was being beaten. As each of his deputies replied, Nick realized he was the only one in the vicinity. The address the dispatch gave was only a few blocks away.

He glanced at Miriam. "I have to respond to this."

"What can I do to help?"

"Just stay in the car." He shared his intentions with his dispatcher, turned his SUV around and flipped on his lights and siren. In a matter of minutes, he was pulling up to a ramshackle house on the far edge of town.

The clapboard structure had been white once, but peeling paint and bare boards had turned it a dull gray. The yard was devoid of grass, but a tricycle and several toys leaned against the rusting chain-link fence. Several of the windows were covered with aluminum foil. Two others boasted broken shades but no curtains.

A young woman in jeans and a blood-spattered yellow T-shirt sat on the steps with a towel pressed to her face. There was no sign of her attacker. Nick handed the keys to Miriam. "If anything happens, if you feel unsafe at all, I want you to get out of here. There are deputies on the way for backup, so don't worry about me."

She grasped his arm. "I'm not leaving you here alone."

He opened the door and got out of the vehicle. Turning to her, he said, "Lock the doors and do as I say."

Miriam's first impulse was to assist the young woman. She couldn't sit by and do nothing when someone was so clearly in need of medical assistance. She took the keys from Nick. "I'm a nurse. I can help."

He shook his head. "Not until I know it's safe."

The words were no sooner out of his mouth than the screen door of the home banged open. A thin man with slicked-back hair started yelling at the woman. "Look what you've done now. You brought the cops down on us. How could you do this to me?"

The woman scrambled out of his way. Nick closed the vehicle door and approached the scene. "Stop right there, sir. I'm Sheriff Nick Bradley, and I just want to talk to you."

The man threw his hands up in disgust, spun around and reentered the house before Nick could stop him. The woman collapsed on the bottom step still weeping. Nick approached her and asked, "Are you all right?"

"Don't take him to jail. My husband is just upset because he's been out of work so long. He's been drinking today, but he almost never drinks. I'll be okay. Honest, I cut my head when I fell."

Nick didn't take his eyes off the door. "Does he have any weapons in the house? Does he have a gun?"

"We don't have anything like that. I'm sorry someone called you. I'm fine, really I am." She tried to stand, but her legs gave out and she plopped back. She tried a second time and succeeded, but she wobbled. Nick reached out to help steady her.

From along the corner of the house, Miriam saw the husband approaching with a long thick piece of wood in his hand. He was out of Nick's line of sight.

In that instant, she saw a terrifying scene beginning to unfold. The man rounded the corner of the house with the club raised over his head. Nick was in danger. Miriam pushed open the door and yelled, "Nick, watch out!"

Nick caught sight of the man an instant before it was too late. From his crouching position, he launched a sideways kick that landed square in the middle of the man's chest. His heavy boot connected with a sickening thud. The husband tumbled backward, the board dropping from his hand.

Seconds later, Nick straddled him using an arm lock to hold him down while he snapped on a pair of handcuffs.

Miriam's heart started beating again. Nick was safe. The emotions she'd kept bottled inside exploded into her mind. She pressed a hand to her mouth to keep from crying out. She cared about Nick. Deeply.

The wife started screaming hysterically for Nick to let her husband up. It was clear Nick had all he could handle. Miriam had to help. She jumped out of the car and rushed to the wife, placing herself between her and Nick. She grasped the woman's arms and held on.

"It's all right. He's going to be all right. Don't make things worse for him. Calm down."

Nick growled, "Miriam, get back in the car."

"Everyone take a deep breath. This doesn't have to end badly if everyone keeps their cool."

A movement at the window shade in the house drew Miriam's attention. The frightened faces of two small kids looked out on the scene. She forced the woman to focus on her. "You're scaring the children. You don't want that, do you?"

It was the first thing that seemed to get through to the distraught wife. "No, don't let them see this." She turned her face away from the house.

"Miriam, get back in the car, or so help me, I'll arrest you, too."

She ignored him. Concentrating on keeping the wife calm, Miriam spoke quietly to her. "The children have already seen this. They are going to need you to reassure them. You can't do that if you end up in jail for assaulting a police officer. Do you have someone you can call? Do you have a family member or a pastor who can come over and help take care of the children?"

The woman shook her head and started sobbing again. "Danny and the kids are all the family I have. Please don't arrest him."

Miriam glanced toward the car, where her mother was watching with wide worried eyes. Looking at the young mother, she asked, "What is your name?"

"Caroline. Caroline Hicks."

"Caroline, my mother is here. Is it all right if she goes inside and stays with the children for a little bit?"

Caroline nodded, but she couldn't take her eyes off her husband. Miriam motioned to her mother. When Ada reached her carrying Hannah, Miriam said, "*Mamm,* would you please go into the house and stay with the children. Caroline, what are their names?"

"Danny Jr. and Mary Beth."

Her mother nodded. "*Ja,* I will see to the *kinder.*"

"*Danki.* We won't be long."

Knowing that her mother would be able to soothe and calm the frightened children, Miriam focused her attention on Caroline. This woman wasn't much different than the confused and frightened teenagers who showed up at Mariam's door in the middle of the night.

Nick lifted Danny to his feet and led him to the steps, where he allowed him to sit and regain his breath. Danny looked up at his wife. "I'm sorry, Caroline. Please forgive me. I'll never do it again, I promise."

Caroline reached toward him. "I know you didn't mean it, Danny."

Miriam held back her opinion of men who hit women, and women who stayed with men who hit them. She knew the situation was never as black-and-white as it seemed. The best thing to do was to separate Caroline from Danny and get her to concentrate on what was best for her and for the children.

Taking her by the arm, Miriam led her down the block to a neighbor's vacant front porch. She stayed with Caroline until Nick's backup arrived. With a second and then a third officer on the scene, Miriam felt comfortable leaving Caroline in the hands of people who had been trained for exactly that type of situation. She walked toward the house and saw her mother putting Hannah's carrier in the SUV. Looking around, she asked, "Where is Nick?"

"In the house. He said we were to go home, and he would have someone bring him by to pick up the truck later."

Miriam glanced toward the house. She didn't feel right abandoning him. "All right. I'll let him know we are leaving now."

She walked up the steps and entered the shabby, rundown building. She spotted Nick sitting on the stairs and talking to Danny Jr. The boy looked to be about five years old. Both he and Nick had their hands clasped between their knees. Neither one noticed her. The little girl sat with a female deputy on the sofa.

Nick said, "This sure was a scary day, wasn't it?"

The little boy looked ready to burst into tears again. He nodded quickly.

Nick drew a deep breath and let it out slowly. "There is no way I can make it un-scary for you. Sometimes bad things happen and it's nobody's fault."

"It might be my fault," the boy whispered.

"I'm pretty sure it wasn't, but why don't you tell me why you think it might be."

It was a good response. Miriam waited to see how Nick was going to handle the child.

"I was making too much noise with my dump truck."

"I used to have a dump truck when I was a kid. Is yours yellow?"

Little Danny shook his head. "It's red."

"But the back tips up, right? So you can dump your load of blocks or dirt?"

"Yup. I was dumping rocks on the stairs."

"I've done that."

Danny slanted a questioning gaze at Nick as if he wasn't quite sure he couldn't believe him. "You have?"

"More than once. And sand, too. My mom wasn't very happy with me when I did. Can I see your truck?"

Danny nodded and tromped upstairs. He came down in a few moments with the red plastic truck in his arms. He sat on the floor near Nick's feet and began rolling the truck back and forth, picking up the gravel scattered across the floor. Nick said, "I imagine you could carry a ton of rocks in that thing."

"Yeah. I dumped my load on the stairs, but they rolled down and Dad stepped on one with his bare feet. He got real mad about it. Mom started yelling at him to leave me alone, and then…" His voice trailed away to nothing.

"And then something bad happened, didn't it?" Nick

waited patiently for the child to speak. He wasn't rushing the boy or trying to put words in his mouth.

Danny Jr. rolled his truck back and forth for a while, then he rolled it into the stair step. He looked up at Nick. "Dad pushed Mom. She fell and hit her head on the step. There was blood everywhere."

Nick laid a reassuring hand on the boy's small shoulder. "Your mother is okay, Danny. It wasn't a bad cut. Does your dad get mad often? Does he hit your mom?"

Danny Jr. shook his head. "No, so I know this is my fault. I wish he could get a job again. He was happier then."

"Has your dad hit you? Has he hit your sister?"

"No."

Nick nodded. "Danny, I'm going to tell you something that I want you to remember. It is never okay to hit someone, especially a woman or girl, or a boy like you. It doesn't fix things. It only makes things worse."

"Yeah, I kind of knew that."

"I could see you were a pretty smart kid as soon as I met you. Your dad is going to need some help. He needs help dealing with his anger. I'm going to see that he gets that help."

Miriam was impressed with Nick's compassionate handling of the situation. This was a new side to him, one she was glad she had a chance to see.

"Are you going to lock my dad up?" Danny Jr. asked.

"I'm afraid so. It's the only way we can get him the help he needs. Your mom is going to need you to be strong for her."

"She's going to jail, too?" He was close to tears once more.

"No. I don't want you to worry about that. A friend of mine who is a social worker will come and talk to your family about how to deal with being angry without hurting anyone. Now, your mom is pretty upset. She's going to be crying, but I want you to be brave for her and show her that you aren't scared. Can you do that?"

"Maybe." Uncertainty filled his voice again.

"If you don't feel brave, that's okay, too. There are lots of times when I don't feel brave."

"But you are a cop."

"Even cops get scared." Nick rose to his feet and held out his hand. Danny Jr. took it. They crossed the room to where Mary Beth was sitting holding a doll clutched to her chest. Danny Jr. offered his hand. She took it and jumped off the sofa. Nick led them outside.

Miriam held open the screen door for him. "Are you sure you don't want me to wait for you?"

He shook his head. "I'll have a lot of paperwork to do after this. It's best if you take your mother and the baby home."

"All right. I'll see you later." She started down the steps toward his SUV.

He handed the children over to their mother, who was waiting by the squad car. As Nick had predicted, she burst into tears and hugged them both tightly. Inside the squad car, her subdued husband fought back tears as he said goodbye to his family.

Nick followed Miriam to his SUV. He stood beside the door as she got in. "The next time I tell you to stay in the car, Miriam, you'd better do it."

His stern tone rankled. It wasn't as if she had been a liability. Maybe she had overstepped the bounds, but she hadn't been able to stand by and do nothing. She didn't want to respect Nick's authority or his abilities, but she couldn't deny how well he'd handled himself and the child just now. There was a maturity to him that was both calming and attractive. His compassion for the young boy touched her deeply. Nick had become the kind of man she could admire.

Alarm bells started going off in her head. There was no way she was going to fall for him again. She couldn't let that happen. It was easier to go back to being mad at him than it was to face the slew of new emotions churning in her brain. She scowled at him. "Fair enough, but the next time I see somebody about to swing a two-by-four at your head, I just might keep my mouth shut."

He pressed his lips into a thin line. "Okay, I owe you a debt of thanks for that one."

"Don't mention it," she snapped back.

Nick blew out a deep breath. "I'm sorry if I sound edgy. You may not want to believe this, but I still care about you. I don't know how I could have lived with myself if something had happened to you because I brought you here."

He was right—she didn't want to hear that he still cared about her.

When she didn't reply, he nodded in resignation. "Okay, thanks for your help and now get out of here so I can worry about my job without worrying about you and your mother's safety."

Miriam sketched a brief salute, started his truck and drove out of town. As he did, his words kept echoing in her mind. He still cared about her. What did that mean? Did it change anything? Oddly enough, it did. A small part of her smiled in satisfaction at the thought that Nick still had feelings for her.

They hadn't driven very far when Ada spoke. "There

is so much sorrow in the world. Will those children be okay?"

"It's hard to say. If the family accepts and benefits from the counseling, then yes, I think they'll be okay."

"Do you think Hannah could have come from such a home?"

"I hope not, Mother."

Chapter 8

Miriam didn't know if she was disappointed or relieved when Nick didn't come by the following day. Although he called several times to check on Hannah, Miriam was left to sort out her feelings about Nick without having to face him. No matter how she tried, she couldn't see a clear path ahead of her.

That she was still attracted to him was becoming increasingly clear. That she told herself she didn't want to revive those feelings didn't help. It was as if her body was waking up after a long sleep. She had been moving through life, but the texture had been missing. When Nick was near, she noticed everything, from the brilliant color of the sky to the deep timbre of his voice. She was becoming aware that her life was lonely.

After having destroyed her brother and Natalie's chance at happiness, she hadn't believed she had a right to reach for that same kind of happiness. So why was she suddenly thinking about what it would be like to love and be loved in return?

Miriam's emotions stayed in a state of turmoil over the following two days, but at least Hannah was doing better. Her episodes of fussiness and spitting up had passed. She began sleeping up to four hours at a stretch and woke up alert and eager to interact with anyone who would spend time talking to her. She was well and firmly on her way to embedding herself in Miriam's heart.

When Thursday evening rolled around, Miriam wasn't surprised when Nick's SUV pulled into the yard. Tonight was the night the note said Hannah's mother would return. Miriam knew Nick wanted to be here.

She was on her knees planting rows of black-eyed Susans along the front of the porch. Her mother was watering the rows she had finished on the other side of the steps. Miriam sat back on her heels.

Nick rolled down his window. "Can I park in the barn? I don't want my presence to scare anyone away."

"Go ahead. There should be room beside the buggy."

"Thanks." He strode to the wide barn doors, pulled them open and then drove his truck inside. After closing the door, he walked across the yard. He wasn't wearing his uniform.

Miriam's heart beat a quick pitter-patter when he smiled at her. She sternly reminded herself he was only being friendly and only here because of Hannah. She asked, "Do you think she will show?"

He stuffed his hands in the front pockets of his jeans. "Your guess is as good as mine. I've ferreted out the time and place of a local hoedown if she doesn't. It will give us a chance to ask around among the teenagers and check more buggy tires."

Hoedowns were gatherings of *rumspringa*-aged teenagers that involved loud modern music, dancing and sometimes drinking and even drug use. Amish parents often turned a blind eye to the goings-on, but their children were never far from their prayers. Until a child had a taste of the outside world, he or she could not understand what temptations they would have to give up to live orderly, devout Christian lives in their Plain community.

Ada said, "Supper is almost ready, Nicolas. I hope you like chicken with dumplings."

He patted his stomach. "It's one of my favorites, but you remembered that, didn't you?"

She grinned. "*Ja*, I remember that you and Mark could put away a whole chicken between the two of you and leave the rest of us nothing but dumplings."

Chuckling, she went into the house. Miriam rose to her feet and pulled off her gloves. Now that the time was finally here, she didn't know if she could let Hannah go.

Nick tipped his head to the side. "Another killer night?"

She shook her head and smiled. "No, the new formula is working wonders. She actually slept for five hours last night. I'm just worried, I guess."

"Worried her mother won't come, or worried that she will?"

"Both."

"I know what you mean."

She nodded toward the door. "Come in. I'll get washed up and we can eat. It may be a long night."

During supper, Ada happily reminisced with Nick

about the days when he had worked on their farm. Her mother's chatter was unusual. Most Amish meals passed in silence. Nick cast several worried glances at Miriam when her mother brought up Mark, but Miriam kept silent. For some reason, listening to talk of her brother no longer brought her the sharp pain it once had. She missed Mark dearly, but listening to her mother's and Nick's stories about Mark's life brought Miriam a measure of comfort. Mark was gone—he would never be forgotten. Not by Miriam and her mother and not by Nick.

When the meal was over and the table cleared, Ada went to bed leaving Nick and Miriam alone in the kitchen. He said, "It's a nice night, shall we sit outside for a while?"

Miriam glanced at the baby. "Sure. Hannah will make herself heard if she needs anything."

When they were both seated in the rockers on the front porch, silence descended between them. It was a comfortable silence broken only by the sounds of the night, the creaking of the windmill, insect chirpings and the distant lowing of cattle.

Nick said, "I'm sorry if Ada talking about Mark upset you."

"She needs her good memories. It's okay."

From inside the house, Hannah began making noises. Bella came to the door and barked. Miriam rose from her chair and moved past Nick, but he reached out and grasped her hand. "We all need to hold on to good memories," he said quietly.

Was he talking about Mark or about his memories of her? How would things have turned out between them if Mark had lived?

It was foolish to wonder such things, yet she did wonder.

His hand was warm and strong as he held her cold fingers. They quickly grew heated as a flush flooded her body. Bella barked again.

"Is there a chance we can be friends again?"

"I don't know," she answered quietly. She pulled her hand away and went inside, grateful that she had a few minutes to marshal her wild response to his touch. The simple contact of his hand had sent her reeling with a flood of memories. She remembered holding hands with him as they crossed the creek on the way to their favorite fishing hole. Once, he'd taken her in his arms to show her the way the *Englisch* teenagers slow danced together. Mark had been there, making fun of her awkward attempts to dance, laughing with them when Nick slipped and fell in the creek and his big fish got away.

They were good memories of a better time. Could she and Nick be friends again? She didn't see how. Too much stood between them, but seeing Nick every day was helping her heal—something she'd never thought would happen.

After feeding Hannah, Miriam retreated to the cot in the kitchen. She slept in snatches, waking at every creak or groan from the old house. Nick, if he slept at all, lay sprawled on the sofa in the living room. Twice Ada came into the kitchen to check on Hannah and to scan the lane but no buggy appeared. When dawn finally lit the sky, Nick came into the kitchen and began to stoke the coals in the stove. After that, he fixed a pot of coffee.

When he had it brewing he took a seat at the table.

Miriam pushed her hair out of her face and joined him. "Now what?"

"We are back where we started from."

As much as Miriam wanted to help Hannah's mother, she was secretly glad the woman hadn't shown up. She didn't want to give Hannah back. If only there was a way to keep her.

"Nick tells me you are coming to my wedding tomorrow. I'm so glad." Amber had arrived for Hannah's checkup on Friday afternoon. After she had weighed, measured and examined the baby, she turned her full attention to Miriam.

"I didn't say yes. I said I'd think about it. Mother hasn't been feeling well, and I don't like to leave her alone with the baby."

"Please come. I'll stop by the Wadler Inn and ask Naomi Wadler to come and keep your mother company. She mentioned wanting to drop in for a visit. Tomorrow would be the perfect time. If someone can stay with your mother will you come?"

"I really don't have anything to wear." Miriam still felt strange about her last-minute inclusion. She didn't know Amber that well, and she didn't know Dr. Philip White at all.

"That is absolutely the lamest excuse I've ever heard. You know that I have Plain relatives. My wedding is going to be far from fancy and as long as you don't come in a bathing suit, I'm okay with what you wear."

Miriam grinned. "I was just thinking how nice I would look in my teeny-weeny bikini."

"Is it yellow with polka dots?" Amber's eyes sparkled with mirth.

"How did you guess?"

"No, you can't wear that. I don't want Phillip's eyes on anyone but me. Nick, on the other hand, will be sorely disappointed when I tell him what you had in mind."

Miriam looked down at Hannah in her crib. "I'm sure that Sheriff Bradley couldn't care less about what I wear."

Amber tipped her head to the side. "I'm not so sure about that. Have the two of you overcome your differences? I had hoped that this situation would help. I pray that you can find it in your heart to forgive Nick for his part in your brother's death. I know Nick as well as anyone can. I know he would never willingly hurt someone."

Miriam wasn't ready to discuss her feelings for Nick. "Can we talk about something else?"

"I'm sorry. I was out of line, wasn't I? Phillip tells me I get carried away in my quests to right the wrongs of the world. Please don't let my foolish mouth keep you from coming to the wedding. You have to come, if for no other reason than to meet the most wonderful man in the world. I won't take no for an answer." Amber gave Miriam one of her endearing smiles.

"If you can find someone to stay with Mother and the baby, I'll come."

Amber squealed with delight and hugged her. Later that night, Amber called to tell Miriam that Naomi was thrilled to come and visit with Ada.

The following morning, Miriam picked through the clothes in her closet with disdain. She hadn't been lying yesterday. She didn't have a thing to wear that was wedding appropriate. A stay in an Amish household didn't lend itself to fancy attire.

Although she was sure the bride wouldn't notice what she had on, Miriam was afraid Nick would notice. He had a way of looking at her that made her sure he could see all the way through her.

After choosing a simple green skirt with a white blouse, Miriam slipped on her favorite high-heeled sandals and went downstairs. Her mother was rocking the baby and humming an Amish lullaby.

"Are you sure you will be okay while I'm gone?" Miriam asked.

"I'll be fine. Naomi Wadler will be here. She and I will have a nice visit. Do not worry your head about us."

"I won't be gone long." Miriam gathered her purse and car keys from the small table by the front door. Should she leave? She didn't want to disappoint Amber.

And Nick was going to be there.

The prospect didn't fill her with alarm the way it once had. Nick was a good man, not the monster she had tried to make him out to be.

"Are you leaving, or are you going to stand there staring off into nothing?"

Her mother's comment dispelled Miriam's sober thoughts. "I'm going. My cell phone will be right here on the table. Nick's number is in it. He will be at the wedding, too. If you need anything, he will get ahold of me."

"You know that I don't like that thing."

Miriam crossed the room and dropped a kiss on her mother forehead. "I know you don't like it, and I also know that you know how to use it. I'm not worried about you, I'm worried about Hannah."

The frown left Ada's face. "She hasn't been fussy in days. We will be fine."

"Maybe I should stay home. I don't know that Amber will miss me at her own wedding."

"You told her you would come so you must go. Hurry now, or you will be late. There will be a lot of buggies on the road. Amber is very well liked among our people and many will want to celebrate with her on this blessed day."

"Okay, I'll go, if only to see what her future husband looks like."

On her way out the lane, she met Naomi in her buggy coming in. That gave her one less worry. Her mother's prediction proved true. There were almost as many buggies lining the streets and in the church parking lot as there were automobiles. Inside the white clapboard structure of the Hope Springs Fellowship Church, she signed the guest book and took the arm the usher offered her. She allowed him to escort her to the bride's side of the aisle.

The church was nearly full. Many of the guests were wearing Amish dress and children were everywhere. Soft organ music filled the air. To her dismay, the usher stopped and indicated a seat next to Nick Bradley.

She looked around quickly, but there wasn't another empty spot close at hand. Unless she wanted to make a scene by cutting Nick directly, she would have to endure the ceremony seated beside him. Would he be able to tell the way her heart beat faster when he was close?

He scooted over slightly to make more room. There was no hope of finding a seat elsewhere. She graciously thanked the usher, sat down, gave Nick a friendly smile and proceeded to ignore him. What she couldn't ignore was the rapid rush of blood to her skin. She opened her collar slightly and fanned herself.

He leaned close. "Hot?"

His breath stirred the hairs on her temple and sent her temperature up another notch.

"A little. I had to rush to get here." *Please don't let him think it's because of his nearness.*

"I was afraid you wouldn't come. You look nice, by the way. Those are cute shoes."

Cute shoes? What man noticed a woman's shoes? She gave him a sidelong glance.

"Three sisters," he said in answer to her unspoken question.

He turned to speak to the person on the other side of him. It gave Miriam the chance to gather her composure and survey her surroundings.

It was her first time attending a service at the Hope Springs Fellowship Church. The inside of the church was simple and elegant with dark, rich wood paneling and brilliantly colored stained-glass windows. Off to one side of the altar, a young woman continued playing the organ. It felt good to be back in church. She had avoided going for fear of running into Nick. Now that her fear was no longer a factor, she was free to worship as she normally did. The soothing sounds of the beautiful melody began to ease the tension from Miriam's body. It was then she noticed the sound of muffled crying.

Looking across the aisle, she saw a woman in her late sixties crying softly into a lavender lace hanky that perfectly matched her lavender suit and hat.

Overcome with curiosity, Miriam whispered to Nick, "Who is the weeping woman?"

Nick leaned forward to look around her. He sat back with a grin on his face. "That is Gina Curtis. She is something of a town character. She is very attached to Dr. Phillip. When everyone else considered her a hypochondriac, he correctly diagnosed her fibromyalgia. I think she has been in love with him ever since, but she cries at everyone's wedding so it's hard to tell."

Miriam nodded, and then sat in awkward silence. *Please, Lord, let this be a quick ceremony.*

The organ music suddenly stopped as the minister and three men entered from a door behind the pulpit. As they arranged themselves at the front, the organist began the familiar strains of the "Wedding March."

The congregation rose and turned to see a pair of bridesmaids in plum dresses carrying small bouquets of pink roses. Amber, a vision in a simple A-line satin gown with lace cap sleeves and a short veil, started down the aisle on the arm of a short stout man that Miriam assumed was her father. As she approached the front of the church, Miriam saw she had eyes for only one person in the building—the tall man waiting for her beside the minister.

Phillip looked a great deal like his grandfather, Dr. Harold White, but where Dr. Harold looked distinguished with his high cheekbones and white hair, Dr. Phillip looked downright delicious. He was movie-star gorgeous with a deep tan, sun-streaked light brown hair that curled slightly above his collar and eyes so blue they looked like sapphires.

She glanced at Nick beside her. He was a good-looking man, too, but in a rugged way that she preferred to the young doctor's suave features. When the music stopped, Miriam listened to the preacher's sermon about the way love allows us to accept the faults of others and how that same love makes us strive to mend our own faults for them.

Amber and Phillip then faced each other for the exchange of vows. When it came time for Phillip to slip the ring on Amber's finger, he fumbled and dropped it. The ring went rolling across the floor. The minister stopped its flight by stepping on it.

He picked up the golden circle and held it aloft. "My grandmother used to say that something had to go wrong in the wedding or it will go wrong in the marriage. Not that I believe in such superstitions, but let's all be glad that Amber and Phillip are off to the best start possible."

The congregation laughed. The minister gave the ring back to Phillip and this time he placed it on Amber's hand without incident. Everyone applauded when he kissed his bride.

Miriam glanced at Nick. He was smiling—not at Amber, but at Miriam. She looked away quickly, but not before her heart did a funny little flip-flop in response. If things had been different, it could have been them standing together in front of their family and friends. Was he thinking the same thing?

After the wedding service, Miriam descended the steps of the church. Around her, families and friends were gathered in small groups, catching up on the latest news and events of the week. People surrounded Amber and Phillip. Words of congratulations and well-wishes flowed around them. Every one, including Miriam, was happy for them. It was clear they were very much in love.

Rather than join a group, she turned aside and walked

along the path that led behind the church to a small footbridge that spanned a brook at the edge of the church property. The source of the clear, small stream lay a short way uphill—the gurgling spring from which Hope Springs had derived its name.

When she reached the secluded bridge, she saw she wasn't the only one seeking solitude. Nick stood at the far end of the bridge staring upstream. His brow was furrowed in concentration. She started to turn away, loath to disturb him, but he spoke suddenly.

"Do you ever wonder where the water comes from? I mean, I know it comes out of the earth, but before it was trapped underground, it had to come from somewhere."

"I never thought about it."

"When I was a kid, I thought the gurgling of the water was laughter, delight at being out in the sun and the air again. It still sounds like that to me."

She leaned against the opposite railing and looked down at the water slipping over and around stones as it raced away downhill. "I think about where the water is going. It's just starting its journey. Imagine all the places and people it will pass on the way to the sea."

The silence lengthened between them. The sounds of the birds in the trees and the gurgling brook were soothing. It didn't surprise her that Nick was so introspective. He was someone who heard laughter in the sounds of a brook and truth in a little boy's worried words.

Silence was making her more aware of Nick's presence even though he stood a good six feet away and outside her line of sight. "It was a nice wedding," she said at last.

"All weddings are nice, aren't they? They mark the

beginning of what everyone hopes will be a blessed union. To bad it doesn't always work out that way."

"You sound like you're speaking from personal experience."

"I've never taken that plunge. I was thinking about my folks."

"I'm sorry."

"It was what it was. Mom couldn't reconcile herself to living the life of a cop's wife. One day, after one of their ugly fights, she told him she wished he would leave and never come back. After he was killed, she couldn't deal with the guilt she carried."

"I've been told guilt is a useless emotion." Useless but so hard to put away.

"It's also a very powerful emotion."

"Yes, it is." Reuniting Hannah with her mother would be Miriam's way of making up for the tragedy she had instigated so many years ago.

More than anything, Nick wanted to know what Miriam was thinking. He had hidden his surprise when she sought him out. He didn't want to break the tenuous thread that kept her from running away again. So instead of moving closer, he stayed put, allowing her to control the situation.

His heart ached to gather her in his arms and hold her close. He'd once dreamed of asking Miriam to marry him. Seeing the love and joy in Amber's and Phillip's eyes had driven home just how much he wanted to resurrect that sweet dream. Did he dare hope that Miriam was softening toward him? Didn't her presence here prove that? He prayed God would show him the way to heal Miriam's heart. His every instinct told him that if he moved one step closer she might flee.

"The sound of the water is soothing," Nick said, quietly.

"Yes, it is."

She didn't leave, but stood listening to the water with him. It gave him a reason to hope, a reason to believe they could repair the love they had once shared. He wanted that more than anything, because he was once more falling in love with Miriam Kauffman.

Chapter 9

Miriam gave Hannah a kiss on the top of her head before laying the baby in her crib late Monday morning. She had slept for five hours during the night and Miriam was feeling like a new woman after that much sleep. Ada, stirring a kettle of soup on the stove, said, "You are taken with her, aren't you?"

"Who wouldn't be? She's so precious."

"*Ja,* I feel it, too. The love for a child is a powerful thing."

"I know I said I wouldn't get too attached to her, but it's already too late." Hannah was firmly embedded in her heart. Giving her up was going to hurt terribly.

Ada came and wrapped one arm around Miriam. "She has crept into my heart, too."

"I think we made a mistake trying to keep her until her mother came back. All we did was set ourselves up for a big heartache."

"Heartaches are part of life, child. God brought this baby to us for a reason. We can only pray that He shows us His will."

Miriam's cell phone rang. She stepped outside on the porch to answer it to avoid her mother's disapproving glare. It was Dr. Zook on the other end.

"Miriam, I need you to bring Hannah into the office today."

A knot of worry formed in Miriam's stomach. "Why?"

"We need to repeat some of her blood tests. I'm afraid her MSUD screen has come back positive."

"MSUD? Hannah has Maple syrup urine disease?" Miriam sank onto the porch steps. Bella came from beneath the porch and sat beside her.

Dr. Zook said, "Let me stress that this may be a false positive. We need to double-check before we assume the worst."

"How often do you have a false positive?"

He hesitated, then said, "Not often but it does happen. I'm sorry to worry you but there is treatment now for this disorder if the test is correct."

"Treatment, but no cure."

"I'm afraid not. We'll repeat the test to be doubly sure, but in the meantime, you need to make a formula change right away. We have cans of a special powdered formula that you can start using today."

"I'll be there as soon as I can." Miriam closed her phone and stared at nothing. Her beautiful little baby might have a genetic disorder that in worst-case scenarios could lead to mental retardation and complete paralysis of her body, even death. The unfairness of it overwhelmed her.

Wasn't it enough that Hannah's mother had given her away? Why did God laid this burden on a helpless child? She wrapped her arms around Bella and burst into tears.

An hour later, she helped her mother out of the car and lifted Hannah from her car seat. As they approached the front door of the clinic, Nick's SUV spewed gravel as he turned into the parking lot and pulled up beside them.

He jumped out of his vehicle and slammed the door. His hair was still damp and he had one missed button on the front of the shirt. "Dr. Zook just called me. I could tell from his voice that this is serious, but how serious?"

"That's what we have to find out. There are variations of the disease. Some types are not as serious as others."

"Do we know what type she has?"

"They aren't sure she has it. That's why she needs further testing."

He pulled the clinic door open so that she could go in. Wilma rose from behind the desk and came forward to meet them. "Dr. White and Dr. Zook are waiting for you in Dr. White's office. I'll show you the way."

Miriam followed her down the hallway with growing dread. She prayed as she had never prayed before. *Please let this be a false alarm, Lord.*

When Wilma held open a door, Miriam froze, unable to move forward. She felt a comforting hand on her shoulder and turned to look at her mother but it was Nick who stood beside her. He said softly, "We can bear all things with God's help. He is with us always."

She nodded, drew a deep breath then walked in.

Dr. White was seated at his desk, his head of snow-white hair bent over a book laid open on his desk. Dr.

Zook stood beside him. As soon as he saw Nick was with them, he said, "I'm glad you could all make it. Miriam and Ada, please have a seat. I'll get another chair for you, Nick."

He shook his head. "I'd rather stand."

Dr. White closed his book and laced his fingers together. "I'm sure hearing that Hannah may have MSUD is very disturbing news."

Nick said, "You're going to have to use plain English, Doc. I don't know what your medical terms mean. I'm sure Ada doesn't, either."

"My apologies, Sheriff. MSUD, or maple syrup urine disease, is an inherited disorder. It's a rare disorder in the general population, only about one in every 185,000 births worldwide. Unfortunately, in the Amish and Old Order Mennonite communities the incidence is much higher. Almost 1 in every 380 Amish children will have some form of this disease."

"What type does Hannah have?" Nick asked.

"Let me stress that we aren't sure she does have it. However, in the most severe cases, a child's body is unable to properly process certain protein building blocks called amino acids. The three essential amino acids a child can't break down are leucine, isoleucine and valine. They are often referred to as the branched-chain amino acids or BCAAs. The condition actually gets its name from the distinctive sweet odor of affected infants' urine."

"I haven't noticed that," Miriam said quickly, hoping to prove their diagnosis was wrong.

Dr. Zook said, "Not all babies will show that symptom until they are in crisis. It used to be that babies with this condition showed poor feeding, frequent vomiting, a lack of energy and finally developmental delays before anyone knew what was wrong with them. Fortunately, in recent years all babies in the state of Ohio began being tested for this condition because if untreated, maple syrup urine disease can lead to seizures, coma, paralysis and death."

Nick looked from Dr. Zook to Dr. White. "If left untreated. That means there is treatment available, right?"

"Yes." Dr. White extended a pamphlet toward Nick and Miriam. "Treatment of MSUD involves a carefully controlled diet that strictly limits dietary protein in order to prevent the accumulation of BCAAs in the blood. The cornerstone of this diet is a special formula that does not contain any leucine, isoleucine or valine but is otherwise nutritionally complete. It contains all the necessary vitamins, minerals, calories and the other amino acids needed for normal growth."

"How soon do we start it?" Miriam asked. This shouldn't be happening. It wasn't fair, but then how often was life really fair? Without Hannah's family in the picture it would be up to Miriam to give the baby the best possible start in life.

Dr. Zook gave her a sympathetic smile. "Initially, Hannah will need the MSUD formula to be supplemented with carefully controlled amounts of the protein-based baby formula she is on now until we know for certain that the test is correct. It if is, I'm afraid Hannah is going to become a frequent flyer here. She will need frequent monitoring of her blood levels."

"Will she grow out of this?" Nick asked. He was grasping at straws. Miriam knew better.

Dr. White shook his head. "No. Lifelong therapy is essential. Typically, the MSUD diet excludes high protein foods such as meat, nuts, eggs and most dairy products."

Dr. Zook said, "Children can gradually learn to accept the responsibility for controlling their diets, however, there is no age at which diet treatment can be stopped."

Ada had remained silent until now. "What does this mean for her mother and father?"

Dr. Zook and Dr. White exchanged glances. Miriam said, "If the test is correct, it means they both carry the MSUD gene. If they have more children together, there is a strong possibility that those children will have the same disease."

A strange look came over Ada's face. "It is *Gottes wille* if their children are sick or if they are healthy. Perhaps that is why He brought the child to you, Miriam. So that your knowledge can help her."

It was the first time her mother had even come close to admitting that Miriam's education was a good thing.

Dr. White sat back in his chair. "What is really important is that we make sure we have correct test results. Let's not panic until we know for sure she has this thing. In the meantime, we don't allow Hannah to develop a BBCA crisis. High fever, vomiting or diarrhea, not eating, these can all trigger an elevated level of BBCA in her blood, and that can lead to brain damage. She is going to require close medical supervision."

Nick asked, "Should she be hospitalized now? What kind of further testing does she need?"

Dr. White rose to his feet and came around the desk. He perched on the corner and reached for Hannah. Miriam handed the baby over to him. He lifted her to his shoulder and bounced her gently. Looking at Nick, he said, "You are wondering if you made a mistake by allowing Amber and these women to talk you into keeping the baby out of child care services."

"Did I?"

"I don't believe so. There's no reason to hospitalize Hannah at this point. We can draw the additional blood we need for testing here."

Miriam saw the tension ease in Nick's shoulders. Dr. White continued, "No one has more respect for the Amish than I do, Sheriff. They welcome and lovingly accept children with any kind of disability as a gift from God. Fewer and fewer people in the general population feel the same way. If her mother doesn't return for her, I would hope that she can be adopted by an Amish couple here in this community."

Miriam stood and took the baby from Dr. White. "How can I get the formula that Hannah needs?"

Dr. Zook smiled at her. "We have some that we can give you. I will also give you the number of our formula supplier so that you can order all you need."

"Thank you."

Dr. Zook moved to open the door. "If you'll come with me, we can draw her blood. We should have the final test results back in about twenty-four to forty-eight hours. Hopefully, all this worry will be for nothing."

Nick stayed behind as the women left. Folding his arm over his chest, he spoke to Dr. White. "I wish I could compel you to reveal all you know about Hannah's mother."

"Sheriff, I wish I had something to reveal. Sadly, I don't know any more than you do."

"But you have seen this disorder in families around Hope Springs."

"I have. Too many times, as a matter of fact."

"I don't suppose you could give me a list of those families' names. I don't mind looking for a needle in haystack, but if I could have a smaller haystack to search, that would be better."

Dr. White chuckled. "I can imagine it would. I'm sorry I can't be more help. The baby is in good hands now, and that is what's important. I hear that you've been checking buggies all over the county."

"The buggy that left Hannah at Miriam's had a crack in the left rear wheel in the shape of a long Z. It's all we have to go on. I must have looked at over a hundred buggies, and I haven't been able to locate it."

"Levi Beachy is here waiting to get stitches taken out of his hand. He's the local buggy maker. It's possible he might know who owns a rig with a wheel like that. I'll tell him you'd like to speak to him."

"Thanks, Doc."

Nick left the office and saw Miriam waiting outside by the car. She looked tearful and worried. All he wanted was to hold her close and reassure her.

No, he wanted much more than that. He wanted to tell her that he loved the color of her hair. That he loved the way her eyes sparkled when she was happy. That he wanted to spend the rest of his life making her eyes sparkle.

A dozen ways to tell her how much he cared about her ran through his mind. None of them seemed like the right thing to say at the moment. Soon, he would find a way to tell her how he felt and pray that she might return his affection. Soon, but not now.

He didn't see Hannah or Ada as he left the clinic and stopped beside Miriam.

"At least it's a treatable disease," she said before he could say anything.

"That's right and she may not even have it. Where is your mother?"

"She's changing Hannah. I needed some fresh air." She pressed a hand to her mouth. Her eyes filled with unshed tears. "I'm so scared for her, Nick. Any illness she gets could result in permanent brain damage. A bad cold, the flu…"

Nick wrapped his arms around her and pulled her close. He pressed a kiss to her forehead. "I know you're scared. I'm scared, too."

Her arms crept around his shoulders. To his surprise, she returned his hug. "How is a teenage Amish mother going to handle this if I'm terrified and I'm a critical care nurse?"

"Maybe we should stop looking for her." Nick held his breath as he waited for Miriam's reply.

Softly, she said, "I've thought of that. Hannah is so easy to love. The longer she stays with me the harder it's going to be to give her up. Now that I know she may be sick, I can't bear to let her go."

Nick stepped back and held Miriam at arm's length. "There may be a way for you to keep her. Have you heard of being a treatment foster parent?"

"Of course I've heard of it. They are foster parents that provide medical care to children with emotional or serious medical problems."

"Right. There is an agency called The Children's Haven, Incorporated. They cover foster children in Ohio and Indiana. I might be wrong, but I would think a registered nurse, who's already a foster parent in Ohio, would have an easy time becoming one for them. If I were you, I'd start making phone calls."

"How do you know about this?"

"It's called the internet. Ten minutes with a search engine was all it took."

"And when did you do this search?"

"Last Monday after I left your place.

"We didn't know about Hannah's condition then."

"I've watched you with her. You looked at her the way other mothers look at their babies. I can see that you love her, even when she's throwing up on you. Since I knew you were already a foster parent, I wanted to see if there was a way for you to keep her. It seemed worth a shot to do some research."

"I'm stunned."

"The Children's Haven was one of the sites I ran across. Now that she may have this disorder, it makes me believe that God intends for you to take care of her."

Nick's revelation was a stunning one. Miriam wanted to believe she might be more than a temporary part of God's plan for Hannah. "Do you really think so, Nick?"

"He had some reason to lead Hannah's mother to your house."

The clinic door opened and a young Amish man came out. He wore dark trousers and a pale blue shirt and sported a straw hat on his head of curly brown hair. He was clean shaven. Only married Amish men wore beards. He had a thick dressing around his left hand.

He stopped in front of Nick, but wouldn't meet his eyes. It took him a moment to speak. "I'm Levi Beachy.

The doctor said...ya wanted to know about a buggy with a broken rim."

Miriam and Nick exchanged a quick glance. Nick said, "Yes."

"It was my buggy. I replaced the wheel rim two days ago." His face grew beet-red as he spoke.

"Did you visit Miriam Kauffman's farm a week ago on Thursday night?"

"*Nee,* I did not." The man looked up at last. Miriam realized he was painfully shy. He took a step back and tried to hurry away, but Nick called out, "Do you have twin brothers about sixteen years old?"

He stopped, but he didn't meet Nick's gaze. "I do."

"Could they have taken your buggy without you knowing it?"

"What night did you say that was?"

"It would have been a Thursday night."

Levi rubbed the back of his neck. "My best mare came up lame on Friday morning for no reason. I mentioned it to the boys, they didn't say anything, but I did wonder if they'd taken her out and driven her hard. I don't like to pry."

Nick said, "I need to talk to those boys."

"They're at home." Levi nodded to the Sheriff and walked away down the street.

Miriam said, "I should come with you."

"I can handle it."

She said, "I know you can handle it. I also know that I am less intimidating than you are. They might be more willing to confide in me."

He considered it for a moment and said, "All right, we'll go out there together, but let's take Hannah and your mother home first."

"What shall we tell Mom?"

"The truth. That we're checking a lead, but it could be a wild-goose chase."

Miriam agreed. After taking her mother and the baby back to the farm, Miriam climbed into Nick's SUV for the trip back.

"I had a feeling those two boys knew more than they were saying." Nick sped up to pass a wagon pulled by two large draft horses.

"When did you talk to them?"

"The day of the market, I saw them following you and I asked them what their interest was. They said they wanted to find out how much you would charge to drive them to Cincinnati. I don't think either one of them is the father. You should've seen their faces when I asked them point-blank if they were."

Miriam said, "I believe the buggy shop is on the east side of town."

"I know where it is. It used to belong to Sarah Wyse's husband before he died."

A few minutes later, they pulled into a lot with buggies ringing the perimeter. They were in all stages of construction and repair.

Miriam saw a young woman sweeping the front steps of the office. She stopped work, and waited until Nick and Miriam approached. "Good day. I'm Grace Beachy, how may I help you?"

Nick said, "You can tell us how to find Atlee and Moses."

"My brothers are chopping wood behind house. Shall I get them for you?"

Nick shook his head. "I'll find them."

Miriam remained silent and followed his lead. Behind the small house, the twins were splitting logs at such a rapid pace than Miriam knew it had to be a contest.

One of them, she couldn't tell them apart, caught sight of her and stopped swinging. A wary look crossed his face. He spoke to his brother who instantly stopped working as well.

Nick surveyed them closely. "Afternoon. Which one of you is winning?"

"I reckon we're about tied."

Nick pointed to the ground. "I want both of you to put your axes down and answer a few questions."

One rolled his eyes at his brother. "Told you that you didn't fool him, Moses."

"You should hush, Atlee." They both laid their axes aside.

Nick stepped closer and towered over the two of them. "No, I want you to keep talking. A week ago on Thursday night, a buggy with a cracked rim on the left rear wheel drove up to Ada Kauffman's place and left a baby on her doorstep. I don't think you know how much trouble you are in. You had better tell me everything I want to know."

Atlee looked at Miriam. "The baby was all right, wasn't it?"

"Where is her mother?" Nick demanded.

The two boys looked at each other. Atlee said, "I told you it was a bad idea."

"Like you wanted to bring it home and say, Levi, look what we found while we was over to Millersburg without you knowing it? We'd be chopping wood until Christmas."

Nick growled, "Anything your brother would do or

say will pale in comparison to spending time in jail. Where is the mother?"

Atlee spread his hands wide. "We don't know. We sneaked out after Levi went to bed and took the buggy into Sugarcreek. We left the buggy there and went to see a movie in Millersburg with some *Englisch* friends."

"Friends?" Nick arched one eyebrow.

Atlee said, "Girls we met a few weeks ago at a hoedown. One of them has a car."

Moses said, "After the movie we came straight back to the buggy and home."

"Well, we meant to come straight home," Atlee conceded.

"We didn't know the baby was in the buggy until we were almost to the Kauffman place."

Miriam held up one hand. "Wait a minute. Someone put the baby in your buggy while you were at the movies?"

The twins nodded. Miriam tried to wrap her brain around what they were saying. "You don't know who did it?"

"No, honest we don't," Atlee insisted.

"How did you boys know that I was a nurse?" She glanced between their faces.

They looked at each other and shook their heads. Moses said, "We didn't."

Nick stepped closer with a fierce scowl darkening his face. "I don't believe you."

Atlee's eyes widened in fear. "It's true. We left the buggy in the parking lot at the convenience store. On the way home, we stopped when we heard the baby crying. Who would give us a baby? We didn't know what to do. We couldn't take it home with us, 'cause then Levi would know we'd been sneaking away. Moses knew Ada Kauffman didn't have grandchildren. We thought she might like a baby, and her farm was the closest."

Nick turned away and ran a hand through his hair. "This is unbelievable."

"It's the truth." Atlee looked ready to cry.

Nick paced across the grass and came back. "Hannah's mother didn't choose a safe place for her. She stashed her in the back of a buggy in a parking lot. We're lucky she didn't pick a trash can instead. These two just dropped her at the closest farm. This is child abandonment and child endangerment with reckless disregard for the baby's safety. I've wasted more than a week of investigation time."

Miriam pressed her hands to her mouth. "Oh, that poor, poor woman. She must be dying inside since no one returned with her child. How terrible it must have been to wait for someone who never came, and now she has no idea where her baby is or even if she is safe."

Chapter 10

Nick struggled to rein in his anger and frustration. He had no one but himself to blame for the situation. He had allowed his feelings for Miriam to override his sense of duty and his better judgment.

Atlee Beachy and his brother Moses fidgeted as they waited for him to say something. He let them wait. All he had to show for a week of investigative work was a pair of scared sixteen-year-olds worried that they were going to jail or that their brother would be mad.

They had every right to worry. He did, too. They had all helped cover up a crime, but he was the one who should've known better.

"What do we do now?" Miriam asked.

He looked into her beautiful green eyes so filled with concern. Any second now, she was going to realize that Hannah had to go into protective custody. She was an abandoned child in need of care. The law was very clear on what he had to do.

He said, "We can't keep waiting for her Amish mother to reappear. Unless she reports her baby as missing, our hands are tied."

Her eyes widened and he knew the reality of the situation was sinking in. He would have to take Hannah away from her and her mother.

His heart ached for the pain he knew she was going through. The pain he was causing.

He laid a hand on her shoulder. "We don't know that Hannah's mother is even Amish. The note didn't say that. We only assumed it."

He had a crime scene that spread from one end of his county to the other. After so long, he could only pray he'd find some leads to follow.

"Are we in trouble?" Moses Beachy's voice cracked when he spoke.

"Yes!" Nick snapped as he spun back toward them. He was tempted to haul them down to the station just to make himself feel better, but it probably wouldn't help.

He said, "I am going to impound the buggy and have a forensic team go over it with a fine-tooth comb. Hopefully, there is still some evidence left. Are you sure you didn't see who left the baby?"

They shook their heads. "All we saw was a bad movie," Atlee said.

Glaring at the boys, Nick said, "I should take you both in for child endangerment. Did it even cross your minds that you should notify the authorities when you found her?"

"We did think about taking her to Bishop Zook," Atlee admitted.

Miriam laid a hand on Nick's arm. "It won't do any good to arrest them."

"It will make me feel better."

"But it won't get us any closer to finding Hannah's mother."

"The odds of us locating her now are next to nothing. Even if she came back, as she said she would, her baby wasn't there and she didn't report her as missing. Atlee, Moses, go tell your brother that someone from the sheriff's office will come to pick up the buggy. And tell him why."

They took off leaving him alone with Miriam. She said, "This is all my fault. I should've let you start an investigation right away."

"There is enough fault to go around." He headed toward his truck. She followed behind him. Opening the driver's-side door, he picked up his radio and started giving instructions to the dispatch desk. When he finished, he looked up to see Levi Beachy striding toward him with two chastened boys at his heels.

Levi stopped beside Nick. "My brothers have told me what they did. They wish to help in any way they can."

"I want them to separately write out what went on the entire time they were gone from home. One of my deputies will be out later to question them. If they think of anything else that might help, I want you to call me."

"*Ja,* it will be as you say." Levi spoke to his brothers in quick Pennsylvania Dutch. Nick didn't understand all the words but he recognized the tone. The twins were going to be chopping wood until long past Christmas.

When they left, Nick turned to Miriam. With a sinking feeling in his stomach, he said, "I need to go pick up Hannah."

"No. Isn't there something you can do? Some way she can stay with us?" Her eyes pleaded with him to agree. He was going to give her one more reason to hate him.

"I've got no choice in the matter, Miriam. I'm sorry."

Miriam could see that it would be useless to argue with Nick. She'd opened her heart to Hannah and now she was paying the price. Why had she done something so stupid when she knew how much it hurt to lose her?

Nick said, "Get in. I have to get rolling on this."

He was angry and he had every right to be upset. He loved Hannah, too. This couldn't be easy for him.

Miriam went around the SUV and climbed in. As soon as she clicked her seat belt, he sped out of the parking lot and onto the highway. He didn't slow down until he reached her mother's lane.

When he stopped in front of her house, she hesitated to get out. "Mother is going to be upset. She's become so attached to Hannah. That baby has become the grandchild she never had."

He bowed his head and closed his eyes. "I know. I don't want to do this."

"Is there a chance she could be returned to us?" Miriam was ready to grasp at straws.

He shifted in his seat to face her. "Now that we know her mother abandoned her, she won't be put up for adoption anytime soon. Efforts have to be made to locate family and see if there is anyone suitable to take her. Her placement will be up to Child Protective Services and Judge Harbin."

"I'm sorry, Nick."

He looked toward the house. "We should go in."

"I know." She didn't move.

Miriam sat beside him in silence for a few more minutes. He finally opened his door and put an end to their procrastination. Miriam followed him to the house with lagging steps.

Inside, Ada was rocking Hannah and singing a lullaby. She looked up with a happy grin. "She is such a charmer. She smiled at me. I don't believe she is sick. The doctors are wrong about that. They are wrong about things all the time."

Miriam crossed the kitchen and knelt beside her mother's chair. "*Mamm,* there is something we need to tell you."

Ada's grin faded. "What is it, Miriam? You look so serious."

Nick stepped up. "We went to see Levi Beachy, the buggy maker."

Ada held Hannah closer. "Does he know something about our baby's mother?"

Miriam nodded. "It was his buggy that left the mark on our lane. His brothers took the buggy without his knowledge."

"Boys will be boys. The twins are in their *rum-springa.* So why did they come here?"

Nick said, "They drove to Sugarcreek and met some friend who took them to see a movie. While they were there, someone left Hannah in their buggy. They don't know who it was. When they realized what had happened, they were near your lane and decided to leave Hannah with you."

Miriam laid a hand on her mother's arm. "Hannah's mother may not be Amish. She won't be coming for her. She doesn't know where she is."

"That is *goot*. Hannah can stay with us, *ja?*"

"No, *Mamm*. Hannah can't stay with us anymore. She has to go with Nick. She must go with the *Englisch*. It is the law. They will find a wonderful home for her with parents who will love and care for her."

"I can love and care for her." Ada pressed the baby against her chest so tightly that Hannah began to fuss.

Nick dropped to one knee beside the rocker. "I'm sorry, Ada. She must come with me. Please let me have her. Don't make this any harder."

"No. You can't take my boy away from me and then take this baby, too. It isn't right." She began to sob.

"It's all right, mother. It will be okay." Miriam gently took the baby from her mother's arms. She rose to her feet and carried the baby to her crib.

"Ada? Ada, what's wrong?"

Miriam turned around when she heard the panic in Nick's voice. Her mother was slumped in her chair holding her left arm across her chest. Her face was ashen colored, and twisted into a grimace of pain. Miriam hurried to her side. "*Mamm,* are you all right?"

"I can't…get my breath," Ada gasped.

Nick jerked his phone from his pocket. "I'm calling 9-1-1."

Miriam laid a hand on her mother's forehead. Her skin was cool and clammy. Grasping Ada's wrist, she felt a weak irregular pulse. It wasn't good. She looked up at Nick. "Tell them to hurry."

Miriam felt her mother's pockets until she located a small vial of pills. Pulling it out, she shook one into her palm. "Take one of your nitroglycerin. It will help with the pain."

When her mother had done as she asked, Miriam

jumped to her feet and raced into her mother's bedroom. She grabbed the oxygen canister and mask from closet and returned to the kitchen as quickly as she could. Turning on the oxygen, she placed the mask gently over her mother's face. "Try to take deep slow breaths."

Nick snapped his phone shut. "The ambulance is on its way. They should be here in twenty minutes."

This was her worst nightmare coming true. She was going to watch her mother struggling for breath and die waiting for an ambulance to reach their rural home.

Nick said, "It will be quicker if we take her and head toward them."

Without waiting for her to agree, he lifted Ada from her chair. Galvanized into action, Miriam grabbed the oxygen tank and followed behind him as he carried her mother to his SUV. Miriam opened the door to the backseat and climbed in. Nick gently laid her mother on the seat with her head pillow on Miriam's lap.

He said, "I'll get Hannah."

Miriam cupped her mother's face. "You're going to be fine, mother. We'll get you to the hospital in no time."

Ada tried to speak. Miriam had to pull the mask away from her face to hear what she was saying.

"I am in God's hands. His will be done. I love you, child."

"I love you, too."

A few minutes later, Nick raced out of the house with the baby in her carrier. As he opened the passenger's side front door, Miriam said, "She can't ride up front."

"She can in this vehicle. I can turn the passenger side airbag off. Don't worry, Miriam, I won't let anything happen to her."

He slammed the door, raced around and got in behind

the wheel. The engine roared to life as he sped out of the yard and down the lane with Bella running behind them barking madly.

Chapter 11

It was the longest ride of Miriam's life. Nick tore down the highway with lights and siren blazing. There was nothing she could do but hold her mother's head, keep the oxygen mask on her face, tell her that everything was going to be okay and pray that she wasn't lying.

Please, God, please let her be okay. She loves you so much, but please don't take her away from me.

They met the ambulance ten minutes after leaving the farmhouse. The paramedics were efficient, competent and sympathetic. The roadside transfer went smoothly. Miriam tried to summon her nursing expertise, but she couldn't. At the moment, she wasn't a critical care nurse, she was a terrified woman whose mother might be dying.

Once her mother was inside the ambulance, hooked up to an IV and on a heart monitor, Miriam was able to relax a little. She could read and analyze the information the equipment provided. Not knowing what was happening was the hardest part.

It wasn't until the ambulance crew started to close the doors that she realized Nick was standing outside with Hannah in his arms.

Tears sprang to Miriam's eyes. Was this the last time she would ever see the baby? She prayed, not for herself, but for the child she loved.

Please, Lord, if it is Your will that she go away from me, hold her in Your hand no matter where she goes in her life.

She met Nick's gaze. "Can you follow us to the hospital?"

"Of course." He nodded to the driver who closed the door blocking them from her sight.

The remainder of the trip to the hospital was a blur for Miriam as she concentrated on her mother's pale face, her ragged breathing and the green blip steadily crossing the surface of the portable monitor.

In the emergency room, her training started to kick in again. She shared her mother's recent cardiac history with the attending physician and was pleased when he immediately consulted her cardiologist. Her mother was transferred to the coronary care unit after her doctor arrived at the hospital. It wasn't until Ada was taken for a heart catheterization procedure that Miriam had time to think about Nick and Hannah.

She found them in the waiting room outside the intensive care unit. Nick was feeding the baby and didn't see Miriam. Her carrier sat on the floor at his feet. He was alone in the room except for the infant he held.

His monologue of baby talk had Hannah enthralled.

The baby couldn't take her eyes off him. Miriam smiled at his antics. He was so cute. Parenting seemed to come naturally to him.

He tipped Hannah's bottle to give her the last drops, then set it aside. Lifting her to his shoulder, he patted her back gently until a loud unladylike burp was heard.

"That's my girl," he cooed as he settled her in the crook of his arm and dabbed at her chin.

"I leave you alone for thirty minutes and already you've taught her to belch like a sailor." Miriam walked into the room and took a seat across from him. The minute she sat down she realized how tired she was.

"How's your mother?" Nick asked.

"She's stable for the moment, they've taken her downstairs for a heart catheterization. Her doctor suspects that one of the blood vessels in her heart has closed off. He's going to try to put a stent in to keep it open. I knew this might happen, I thought I was prepared for it, but I wasn't."

"You did everything you could."

Looking back, she realized it was true. She'd done everything she could under the circumstances. The outcome was up to God and Ada's doctors. Miriam held out her hands for Hannah. "May I?"

Nick gave the baby over. "She finished her bottle, but I haven't changed her yet."

"Leave the tough stuff for me, that's so like a guy."

"Hey, if you had shown up five minutes later, it would have all been done."

"Sure. Sure."

"That's my story, and I'm sticking to it." His teasing was just what she needed. He had a knack for reading her mood and finding a way to lighten it. She loved that about him.

The thought startled her. She gazed at him intently. He was focused on Hannah and didn't seem to notice her scrutiny. He had changed a lot from the young man she once knew. His eyes were bracketed with small crow's-feet, and laugh lines were carved into his cheeks. He smiled a lot. She loved that about him, too.

He had a small scar on his chin that was new, or at least she didn't remember it. His eyes were the same intense blue, but there was a weariness behind them that told her life wasn't always easy for him. How could it be for a law enforcement officer?

"You'd better take this." He held out the burp cloth.

She took it, kissed Hannah's head and settled the baby in her arms with the burp cloth under her chin just in case.

If only it could be like this forever, the two of them taking care of the most beautiful baby in the world. It couldn't be, but just for a moment, she could imagine what it would be like. Much as she wanted to, she couldn't keep reality at bay. "How soon do you have to notify Child Protective Services?"

"Soon."

"Can you wait until I know that Mother is going to be okay?"

"Yes. I'm so sorry, Miriam. I didn't realize she would take it so hard."

Miriam saw the regret in his eyes and heard it in his voice. He wasn't to blame for her mother's condition. Even if the stress of the situation had triggered this episode, none of it was his fault. He didn't need to carry that guilt.

"Nick, Mother could have had another attack at any time. I don't blame you for this, and you shouldn't blame yourself."

"I appreciate that."

There was so much she needed to tell him about Mark and about the days leading up to his death. Some of what she had to say would reflect poorly on her, but Nick needed to know the truth. Even if it changed what he thought of her.

"Nick, I need to talk to you."

"I have things I've been wanting to say to you, too."

She opened her mouth to speak just as his phone began ringing. He gave her an apologetic glance and pulled his cell phone from his pocket. "Sheriff Bradley."

As he listened, his expression hardened. "I'm already at the hospital. How soon will she be here?"

He glanced at his watch and then rose to his feet. "I'll meet you in the emergency room."

Nick snapped his phone shut and gave a deep sigh. "I'm sorry, Miriam. There are a lot of things I want to talk to you about, but they're going to have to wait."

"What's going on?"

"EMS is bringing in a suicide attempt. An eighteen-year-old girl has slashed her wrists. Apparently, her boyfriend is the one who found her. I need to interview both of them and sort out what happened."

"Eighteen. That is way too young to feel life has nothing to offer."

"Amen to that. I don't know how long I'll be."

"What about Hannah?"

"As far as I'm concerned, she's in the best possible hands."

She smiled in relief. At least she would have a chance to say goodbye. "Thank you."

"If you want, I'll make arrangements for someone to take you home in case I'm tied up later."

"I'm staying here until I know Mother is doing okay."

"All right, keep me informed. You have my cell phone number, right?"

"I do. Don't worry about us."

She could tell he was reluctant to leave. Suddenly, he crossed the room and bent to kiss her. She was so astonished that for a second she didn't respond. The firm pressure of his lips on hers sent her heart soaring. Then the warmth drew her in and she kissed him back as joy spread through her, making her ache to have his arms around her.

He drew back and said, "When this mess is over and your mother is better, we need to talk."

"Yes, we do," she muttered as she came down to earth with a thud.

He nodded and headed toward the door. She accepted that conversation needed to wait until they could have some uninterrupted time together, but she hoped it wouldn't be long before she could ask him exactly what the kiss meant.

When he was gone, she gazed at Hannah's face. It was amazing how a baby changed things. With God's help, Miriam had come to understand that forgiving Nick was her first step on the journey to forgiving herself. For the first time since Mark's death, she was able to believe in the possibility. And the possibility of a future with Nick.

Nick was waiting in the emergency room when the ambulance carrying the girl who had attempted suicide arrived. As they wheeled her past him, he thought how small, pale and alone she looked. Her eyes were open, but they were empty of emotion.

One of the nurses stopped a young man from following the gurney into the exam room. She directed him to the information desk and told him someone would be with him shortly. Nick had a chance to observe the man wondering if he was the boyfriend. He looked a lot older than eighteen. Nick would've pegged his age closer to thirty. He was unkempt with dirty clothes and greasy hair.

Nick saw his deputy's cruiser pull in behind ambulance. Lance Medford got out and came inside the building. When he caught sight of Nick he stopped. "I was surprised to hear you were already here. I hope everything's okay?"

"I was out at Ada Kauffman's place when she had a heart attack."

"That's a shame. How's she doing?"

"I'm not sure yet. They're still working on her. Is that the boyfriend?" Nick nodded toward the nervous man standing in front of the reception desk.

"That's him. Said he found her in the bathroom when he got home tonight. He claims the cuts were self-inflicted."

Nick gave Lance a sharp look. "You don't believe his story?"

"I do, but I'm running the name he gave us, anyway. I suspect it's an alias. He has conveniently misplaced his ID. Our crime scene tech was pulling some fingerprints from the apartment when I left. My guess is that we'll get a hit and it won't be on Kevin Smith."

Lance pulled out his notebook and opened it. "He

says she's eighteen years old. To me, she doesn't look older than sixteen. He's twenty-eight and claims he was just giving her a place to stay."

"Does he have an idea why she might have wanted to kill herself?"

"Yeah, he said she had a miscarriage a little over a week ago and she hasn't been the same since then."

Another woman who'd lost a baby. He couldn't help but think of Miriam waiting to have Hannah taken away from her. Life wasn't fair. "What about the girl's family?"

"He says she doesn't have any. She wouldn't talk to me at all. As far as I know, she hasn't said a word to anyone."

"All right, you sit with Mr. Smith until we can figure out if we need to hold him or cut him loose. I'll check with the doctor to see how soon I can talk to her."

After speaking to a nurse in the emergency room, Nick learned it would be at least two hours before he could interview the young woman. She was in serious condition and on her way to surgery to have her lacerations repaired.

He no longer had an excuse to put off making his call to Child Protective Services. With lagging steps, he went back inside the hospital to search out Miriam. He found her sitting beside her mother in the intensive care unit. Hannah was asleep in her carrier on a chair beside Miriam. When he entered the room, he met Miriam's eyes. She raised a finger to her lips, and came to the door to speak to him. By mutual and unspoken consent, they stepped outside of the room before speaking.

"How is she?" he asked.

"The procedure went well. They were able to get the

stent in place and increase the blood flow to her heart. The doctor is optimistic that she will make a good recovery."

He let out a breath of relief. "That's the best news I've heard all day."

"How is your suicide attempt doing?"

"She's in surgery. I'm still waiting to talk to her."

"I hope she's okay."

He cupped her cheek and stroked it softly with his thumb. "How are you doing?"

"I'm tired. I'm sad. I'm angry."

"At me?"

"At the universe. At God. Why bring Hannah to me only to tear her away? Why make my mother suffer with a bad heart? Hasn't she suffered enough already? Life is so unfair, it makes me want to scream."

"Come here." He pulled her close in a comforting hug. For a second she resisted, then she settled against him with a weary sigh.

"Thank you. I needed a hug."

"I will always have one for you if you need it." It was the least he could do after the grief he'd brought into her life.

Miriam pulled away and folded her arms over her chest. "Have you talked to Child Protective Services?"

He pulled out his cell phone. "I was just about to make the call."

She nodded, but there were tears in her eyes. He had no choice in what he was about to do, but it didn't make him feel any better. Miriam didn't deserve this. She deserved happiness and so much more. He noticed the sting of tears at the back of his own eyes and knew he wasn't doing any better than Miriam at letting go of the child they had both grown to love. He dialed the number of Child Protective Services and swallowed back his grief when a social worker came on the line.

When he explained the circumstances of Hannah's abandonment, he was surprised to find Hannah's new case worker was sympathetic. She was familiar with the Amish and understood the reluctance of the Kauffman family to report an abandoned child. She wasn't quite so understanding of Nick's part in the affair, but as the baby had received adequate care and medical attention, she didn't intend to make an issue of it.

At her direction, Hannah was to be admitted to the hospital for observation. Once they were certain her condition was stable, she would be placed in foster care. He arranged to meet the social worker shortly and turn the baby over to her.

He closed the phone and shoved his hands in his pockets to keep from reaching for Miriam again.

"Are they coming?" she asked.

"Yes. A case worker named Helen Benson is on her way here. I know her. She's a good woman. She wants Hannah admitted to the hospital until the pediatrician here is certain her condition is stable. After that, Hannah will go to foster care."

"They'll be good to her, won't they? I've heard so many horror stories about children in foster care."

"I'll keep an eye on her and her new family, whoever they are."

"Thank you, Nick. I know this is difficult for you, too."

"The social worker will be here soon. Do you want to come with me when I turn Hannah over to them?"

Miriam opened the door to glance into the room. She whispered, "I should be here in case Mother wakes up."

From the bed, Ada said, "You can stop whispering. I'm not asleep and I hear just fine."

Nick and Miriam reentered the room. He said, "I'm sorry for disturbing you, Ada. You gave me quite a scare earlier today."

She chuckled. "Could be it was well earned, but I imagine I should be sorry for upsetting everyone."

"I'm certainly sorry for upsetting you," he said as he leaned on the bed rail.

"Old women get foolish sometimes. We think of things we should have done differently and we wish for chance to do them over. The baby is not ours to keep. *Gott* will take care of her."

"She has to come with me now," he whispered. He could barely get the words past the lump in his throat.

"Let me give her one more kiss before you take her."

Miriam lifted the baby from her carrier and placed her in Ada's arms. She spoke to the child softly in Pennsylvania Dutch and then kissed her on each cheek. "All right, Nicolas, you may take her now."

He picked up the baby and glanced at Miriam. She said, "I already said my goodbyes."

After settling the baby in her carrier again, he left the room without another word.

Miriam willed herself not to cry. If she broke down it would only upset her mother.

Ada said, "I know it is a hard thing for you, but rely on God for strength and you will get through this."

"Is that how you did it when Mark died?"

"*Nee,* I railed against *Gotte* for taking my son. Grief

is a human thing. No mother should have to lose her child, but we must accept *Gottes wille* for we cannot change it."

"I'm not sure I can do that. I'm not sure I can accept that the sorrowful things in life are God's will."

"Understanding his ways are not possible for us. Our faith must be as the faith of a child."

"That is easier said than done."

"Don't you think it's time you told me what is really troubling you?"

Miriam's defenses shot up. She wasn't ready for this. "I don't know what you mean."

"Yes, you do. You know exactly why you ran away from your faith and your family. Whatever fear you carry in your heart, it is not a burden you must carry alone."

Ada grimaced and shifted in her bed. Miriam moved to help adjust her pillow. "You should rest now."

Ada closed her eyes and sighed deeply. "I think you're right."

Miriam thought her mother was asleep until a few moments later, when Ada said, "I saw your brother in a dream, earlier."

"That's nice." In Miriam's dreams she searched for Mark but could never find him. She smoothed a few strands of hair away from her mother's forehead.

"He loves you, and so do I." Ada's voice trailed off. Her mother's breathing grew regular and Miriam knew she was sleeping at last.

A nurse peeked into the room and asked quietly, "How is she doing?"

Glancing at the monitor over the bed, Miriam was satisfied with the numbers it displayed. Her mother's color was definitely better and her heart rhythm was normal. The heart cath and stent placement had done wonders. "She's resting comfortably."

"Sleep is the best thing for her. Let us know if she needs anything."

Miriam nodded. "I will."

The nurse left, closing the door softly behind her. One more crisis averted.

Miriam sat down and glanced at the empty chair where Hannah had been only a short time ago. The tears she tried so hard to hold back began to slide down her cheeks.

Chapter 12

Helen Benson was waiting for Nick when he arrived in the hospital lobby. A petite woman with a short bob of white-blond hair, she was wearing a business suit and carrying a large briefcase. Her smile when she saw him was warm and welcoming. It eased some of his fears.

He set Hannah's carrier on the floor between them. "This is the baby I was telling you about."

She squatted in front of Hannah and said, "You are a cute one."

"Careful, she'll steal your heart before you know it." Nick stuffed his hands in his front pockets.

Helen rose. "Don't worry, Sheriff, we will take good care of her."

"Will I, or the family who has been caring for her, be able to see her here in the hospital?"

"I'm afraid not. I will keep you updated on any

changes in her condition and let you know when she is ready for discharge. Other than that, don't expect to hear from me until we've found a placement for her. How is the investigation into finding her parents going?"

"At this point, there's little to go on. Just a blue-and-white patchwork quilt and a wooden laundry basket with green trim and a note saying she would be back. Since no one has reported a missing baby in the area, I have to wonder if it was a ruse to give her more time to get away."

"Placing the baby in an Amish buggy might indicate she wanted the child raised by Amish parents."

"Or, it might have been the first handy place she saw. I've already had the buggy impounded. We'll check it for prints and trace evidence. We'll be expanding the search tomorrow and focus on the store in Sugarcreek. I'm hoping they have a surveillance camera in their parking lot. Either way, we'll do door-to-door interviews in the area. Finding the woman who discarded this baby is going to be my top priority."

Helen picked up the carrier. "I understand. And making sure the baby is happy and well cared for is going to be mine. How are your friend and her mother doing?"

"Things are looking hopeful for Mrs. Kauffman. Miriam is coping with a lot right now, losing Hannah and having her mother so ill."

"I'd like to visit with her in the next day or two. I understand she has a foster care license in our state."

"Yes, but she fosters teens in Medina."

"It wouldn't take much for us to do a home study of her new residence."

"Are you saying it is possible she could keep Hannah?"

"Finding willing and skilled foster parents to take

children with medical issues is an ongoing problem for our agency. Encourage her to go ahead with her application. Who knows, it may be possible to place Hannah with her eventually. So much depends on finding the child's parents."

It was a small ray of hope, but it was better than nothing. Hannah had succeeded in bringing Miriam back into Nick's life. Her arrival had opened a door he thought was closed forever. He would always be grateful for that. "I'll relay your information to Miriam. Thank you."

"I'm sorry this didn't turn out as you had hoped."

"You and me, both. How are Danny Jr. and his sister doing?"

"The family has agreed to counseling. I'm hopeful that we won't need to intervene. Both parents realize it was an unhealthy situation, not only for them, but for the kids, too. The dad says he is willing to do whatever it takes to keep the family together, including anger management classes. I hope he follows through with it."

"I have a friend who works in construction. He's going to see about getting Mr. Hicks a part-time job. He understands the man's out on bail, but I think he'll get community service rather than jail time. It was his first offense."

"That would take a tremendous amount of strain off the family. Thank you."

Helen bid him goodbye and walked toward the admissions desk carrying Hannah. Nick watched her leave with a heavy heart. He missed the little girl already. What was life going to be like without her?

He made his way back to the emergency room and

found his deputy selecting a candy bar from the vending machine just outside the doorway of the waiting room. "Any word on the girl, Lance?"

Shaking his head, Lance pulled his selection from the bin. "We're still waiting for her to come out of surgery."

"Is the boyfriend talking?" Nick looked inside the room and saw Kevin Smith pacing back and forth by the windows.

"He hasn't said much, but he sure is nervous. I'm not sure how much longer he'll stick around."

"Do you want me to question him?"

"It's your call, Boss, but I'd really like to take another crack at the guy. Besides, I figure you'll do better with the girl."

As they spoke, a woman in blue scrubs came to the doorway. "Family of Mary Smith?"

Kevin came across the room. "Friend, not family. She doesn't…she doesn't have any family."

"I'm afraid I can only give information to family members. There is a form that Mary will have to sign before I can give you any information."

She turned to leave but Nick stopped her. "How soon can I speak to her?"

The nurse said, "She's being moved to her room now. If you officers will come with me, I'll have the doctor speak to you."

Kevin objected. "Hey, how come they get information and I can't?"

"Because they are officers of the law," she said and walked away.

Lance laid a hand on Kevin's shoulder. "As soon as we find out anything, I will let you know. These hospital rules and regulations are for the birds. Have a seat, I'll be back in a jiffy."

Nick and Lance followed the nurse down the hall and around the corner. They waited outside the recovery room doors until the doctor emerged until the doctor emerged.

Nick asked, "How is she?"

"She is stabilized but she is still in serious condition. She's already had two units of blood. We're going to give her another two. The lacerations were deep. She was serious about killing herself. We're giving her something for pain. She will recover from her injuries, but she's going to need counseling."

Nodding, Nick asked, "How soon can I interview her?"

"You can talk to her now, although she may be a bit groggy."

"Did she say why she tried to kill herself?"

"She hasn't said anything. I think we're dealing with a lot of factors, and one of them may be postpartum depression."

"The boyfriend mentioned a miscarriage." Lance frowned deeply

The surgeon shrugged. "She has certainly had a baby. If something happened to the infant, that might well have triggered the suicide attempt."

Nick held out his hand. "Thanks, Doc. I think we'd like to get a little more information from the boyfriend before we see her."

"Very well. She's not going anywhere."

Nick and Lance returned to the waiting area. Kevin Smith jumped to his feet. "How is she?"

Lance took the lead. "The doctor says she'll be okay but she's gonna be here for a while. Any idea what might've made her do this?"

"I guess it must've been the baby. She miscarried a while back."

"I'm sorry for your loss." The compassion in Lance's voice was real. Taking Kevin's arm, Lance led him to a sofa in the middle of the room.

"Yeah, well, I wasn't into being a dad, so I'm not exactly torn up about it."

Nick was pacing back and forth behind Kevin. "Dad? I thought she was just staying at your place. Now you're the father of her child. Which is it?"

Kevin craned his neck to see Nick behind him. "Um, both I guess."

"What doctor did your girlfriend see after her miscarriage?"

"Nobody, as far as I know."

Nick planted his hands on the back of the sofa on either side of Kevin neck. "Your girlfriend had a miscarriage, and you didn't take her to the hospital?"

"I was out of town for a couple of days. When I came back, she told me she'd lost the baby. She didn't seem broken up about it at the time."

"Was it a boy or girl?" Lance asked gently.

"I didn't ask. I mean what's the point?"

This guy was some piece of work. Nick hoped he could find a reason to haul him to jail since being a jerk wasn't against the law.

The man glanced between Nick and Lance. "Can I see her or what? 'Cause if I can't see her, then I have things to do."

The buzz of his cell phone caused Lance to pull the device from his pocket. He read the text, held it out so that Nick could read it and then tucked it back in his pocket.

He clamped a hand on the man's shoulder. "You're not going to see her just yet, Kevin Dunbar, wanted for check fraud over in Wayne County. First, we're going to take a ride downtown, and then you're going to see the inside of our lovely jail. Put your hands behind your back."

"There's been some kind of mistake."

"You'll get to tell it all to the judge."

Once Lance had him handcuffed, Nick walked out with them and waited until Lance had their prisoner secured in the backseat of the cruiser. He said, "Make sure you do a real thorough job of running a background check on this guy. Something tells me he's been doing more than writing hot checks."

"You got it, Boss. If I had my way, I'd lock him up and throw away the key. Didn't even ask if it was a boy or a girl. What kind of father is that?"

"The worst kind. I'm going to have a talk with the girlfriend now."

Lance walked around to the driver's side of his car "The poor kid. She's too young to be involved with a loser like him."

After Lance drove away, Nick went back into the hospital and learned that Mary Smith had been taken to a room on the fourth floor. He took the elevator to the ward and asked at the nurse's station to speak to the charge nurse. After a brief conversation with her, he was relieved to learn that Ms. Smith would have a sitter with her through the night.

When he entered her room, he saw a middle-aged woman sitting in a recliner with a book open on her lap. She looked up and asked, "Would you like me to step outside, Sheriff?"

"No, it's best if you stay."

He pulled a chair up to the side of the bed where Mary lay curled up beneath the covers. Sitting down, he leaned forward with his elbows propped on his knees. "My name is Sheriff Bradley, and I'm going to have to ask you some questions."

"Where's Kevin?" she asked in a tiny, hoarse voice. She didn't make eye contact but stared at the wall instead.

He decided it was best not to share the fact that Kevin was on his way to jail. He needed this girl's cooperation. "He's fine. You'll be able to see him later. I need you to tell me what happened tonight."

She sank farther beneath the covers. "You know."

"I'm not sure that I do. Why don't you tell me?"

Glaring at him, she raised her bandaged arm.

"You cut your own wrists? Are you sure that Kevin wasn't holding the knife? It's all right. You can tell me if he hurt you. I'll see that he never hurts you again."

"Go away."

"I'm only here to help, Mary. Why don't you tell me what happened."

She gingerly tucked her arm back under the sheet. "Go away."

She picked up her call light and pushed the button.

When a nurse answered, she said, "I need something for pain."

Nick could see he wasn't going to get anywhere with her, but he made one last try. "Was your baby a little boy or little girl?"

Tears filled her eyes. She rolled over and turned her back to him.

Discouraged, he left the room and stopped at the nurse's station. Speaking to the woman at the desk, he gave her his card with instructions to call him if anything changed with Mary Smith.

Dawn was breaking outside the hospital window as Miriam sat up and stretched sore muscles. A night spent in a hospital-grade recliner was a sure way to earn a stiff neck. Her mother's condition hadn't changed much through the night. She was on the mend, but her blood pressure had been all over the place.

Miriam rose and moved to the side of the bed. Ada's eyes snapped open. "It's about time you got up. It's been light for almost an hour. The horse will be wondering where her breakfast is."

"Good morning, *Mamm*. How are you feeling?"

"Better. Can I go home now?"

"I doubt your doctor will let you go home today, but it's good to see you are on the mend."

Ada moved to sit up in bed. "I'm hungry. Where is Hannah?"

The reminder brought a sharp pain to Miriam's chest. "Hannah is upstairs in the nursery."

"Oh, dear. I was hoping that part was a bad dream. She isn't coming back to us, is she?"

"I'm afraid not, *Mamm.*"

"You look tired, dear."

"I am."

There was a knock at the door and a young woman in blue scrubs looked in. "Mrs. Kauffman, are you ready for some breakfast and a bath?"

"I am. Miriam, why don't you go get something to eat while I get *redd-up.*"

The nurse's aid was setting a tray on the bedside table. She glanced at Ada. "What does *redd-up* mean?"

"To get ready or cleaned up," Ada said with a smile. She made shooing motions to Miriam. "Go get something to eat and find out how soon I can leave."

Miriam left the room and headed toward the elevators. As she passed the small waiting room beside them, she glanced in and saw Nick sprawled on one of the chairs. He was wearing the same clothes he'd had on yesterday. His cheeks bore a shadow of stubble, and his hair was sticking up on his head. She smiled as comfortable warmth filled her heart. She wanted to comb his hair and find out exactly how rough his cheeks would feel beneath her fingers.

He opened one eye. "What are you smiling at?"

"You look like I feel."

"How's that?" He sat up with a grimace.

"Like you've been pulled through a cornfield backward."

"That about sums it up. The social worker in charge of Hannah's case wants to meet with you later."

"I imagine I'll be here. She's welcome to stop in."

"She also said to go ahead and apply for a home study here. It's possible—now, I said possible, so don't hold your breath. It's possible that you could foster Hannah once you get the go-ahead from the state."

"Oh, Nick, really?" Miriam's heart surged with renewed hope. There was a chance Hannah could come back to her.

"Really, but try not to get your hopes up too much. It all still depends on finding her family. How's your mother?"

"Bossy."

"That's good to hear. How are you?"

"I'm tired and I'm hungry."

He rose to his feet. "The hungry part I can fix. Would you care to join me for breakfast?"

She did want to join him. He understood how much his news meant to her. "If you'll let me buy."

"Sorry, no can do. I invite, I pay."

"That is very old-fashioned of you."

"Yes or no? Breakfast with an old-fashioned man or go hungry?"

"I'm not likely to go hungry. I'm sure the cafeteria serves a great breakfast."

He glanced at his watch. "Not for another hour and ten minutes. However, there is a vending machine behind you."

She glanced over her shoulder and wrinkled her nose. "No, a candy bar or pretzels will not do it for me."

He shoved his hands in his pockets. "I know a place where you can get great scrambled eggs and bacon."

"All right, you win. Since I'm without a car, are you driving or are we walking?"

"I'll drive."

Miriam walked beside him as they left the hospital and climbed into his vehicle. Five minutes later, he pulled up in front of a duplex. He said, "It's not much to look at from the outside, but I promise you the food is good."

"It looks like an apartment." She frowned at the building.

"Actually, it is my apartment. But there are farm-fresh eggs in the fridge along with a new slab of bacon. I have bagels, English muffins or Texas Toast, and gourmet coffee just waiting to be brewed."

"Okay, you won me over at gourmet coffee. Lead on, let's see if you are all talk or if you can cook."

His eyebrows shot up and he slapped a hand to his chest. "I wasn't planning to cook. I thought you would."

"Are you serious?"

"Ha! Gotcha. Of course I can cook." He grinned as he unlocked the door and pushed it open.

Miriam stepped inside what was clearly a bachelor pad. An oversize TV took up most of the wall along one side of the living room. It was flanked by bookshelves filled with an assortment of movies and novels. Opposite the TV was a well-worn brown leather sofa and a low coffee table. Beyond the living room was a small dining room with a glass-top table and two café-style chairs.

Nick gestured to the table. "Have a seat, or you can freshen up if you want. The bathroom is down that hall, first door on the left."

Miriam decided she needed to freshen up more than she needed coffee. It wasn't as good as a shower, but she was able to wash off and run a comb through her hair. Nick's bathroom, like the rest of the house, was spotless. Was he that good a housekeeper, or did he have someone come in?

By the time she returned to the dining room, the smell of frying bacon filled the air. Her stomach rumbled, and she pressed her hand to her midsection to quiet it.

"It smells good," she said, feeling odd to be in his home. It was nothing like she had imagined. She wasn't sure what she thought it would be like, but not once had she pictured Nick cracking eggs in a bowl.

"How do you like your eggs?" he asked without looking up.

"Over hard, break the yolks. It's the only way my mother ever fixes them."

He chuckled. "I do remember that, now. I asked her for a sunny-side up egg the first morning I came to stay with you. She looked at me like I had asked for rat poison."

"I remember. We call them dippy-eggs."

She remembered a lot about that summer, and there were things she needed Nick to understand, but not now. For a little while, she wanted to enjoy his company and pretend her secret didn't exist.

Smiling too brightly, she asked, "Where is the coffee you promised me?"

He pointed over his shoulder with the spatula. "On the counter behind me."

She entered the small kitchen and brushed past him. "And the cups?"

"If you can't find a cup in a kitchen this size, you're not much of a detective."

"Ha! Ha! You've been wanting to say that for days, haven't you?"

She could feel his shoulders shaking with suppressed laughter behind her. *"Ja, Fräulein."*

"Your Amish accent is terrible." She got a cup and elbowed him in the ribs in the process.

He ignored her puny attempt to rile him. "You've managed to get rid of yours. Most of it, anyway."

"It took some work."

"Diction classes?"

"Yes. I didn't want to sound like a hick from the sticks when I applied for jobs. I encourage all the kids who stay with me to take the classes."

She filled a cup and returned to the table. She knew her cheeks were flushed. Would he think it was caused by the hot coffee, or did he realize it was because of his proximity? When they had been close years ago she had fantasized about what it would be like to be married to him, to wake up with him, to have breakfast, just the two of them, in his *Englisch* house. Her girlhood daydreams didn't do justice to the reality of sharing a meal with him. How could she know that the intimate setting of his kitchen would be every bit as alluring as dinner in a fine restaurant? She took a quick sip of her coffee and scalded her tongue.

"Is that how you think of the Amish? Hicks from the sticks?" He brought a plate of crispy bacon to the table and set it in front of her.

She blew on her cup. "It's not my opinion that counts. I know Amish kids are naive, unused to worldly things and curious, but they aren't stupid. They simply can't make informed decisions because they lack knowledge, not intelligence. People have learned to take advantage of that. By sounding less Amish, they have a better chance at fair treatment."

He returned to the table with his plate and her eggs on his spatula. He slid them on to her plate and sat down. He bowed his head and silently prayed. Miriam waited until he was finished to ask for the salt. Smiling, he pushed it toward her.

It was a simple meal, but it had an intimate feel to it. It was a feeling she wanted to cultivate and enjoy more often. The thought had barely crossed her mind when his phone rang.

He looked at the number and shook his head. "I knew it."

"Work?" she asked. Was this cozy interlude destined to end early?

"It's my deputy. He's investigating our suicide attempt. I have to take this." He rose from the table and walked into the other room.

"This had better be important, Rob," Nick growled into the phone. His morning had been going so well.

"Hi, boss. The crime scene people are wrapping up."

"You called to tell me that?" Nick frowned. Rob Craiger was one of his most experienced deputies. He normally let his written reports do the talking.

"No, I just finished interviewing the woman who lives in the trailer next door. She didn't get home from work until thirty minutes ago."

"Did she give us anything useful?"

"She didn't have anything good to say about the boyfriend, but here is the odd thing. She swears that she heard a baby crying over here two weeks ago on Thursday. She remembers the night because someone stole a laundry basket off her back porch and a quilt off her clothesline that same night. There's no sign of a baby inside the Smiths' trailer. No diapers, no baby bottles, no crib."

All the pieces came together with a snap in Nick's mind. Mary's baby hadn't died. She'd left it in a buggy two blocks away at the Shop and Save Grocery Mart.

He asked, "Was the quilt blue patchwork and the laundry basket wooden with green trim?"

He could hear Rob thumbing through the pages of his notebook until he found the one he wanted. He said in surprise, "Yeah. How did you know that?"

"Never mind. Come back to the station. I'll be over at the courthouse as soon as it opens."

"Why?"

"To get a court order for DNA testing. I think I know where the baby is."

Nick looked over his shoulder at Miriam buttering a piece of toast. There was no way he wanted to tell her that Hannah was once again out of her reach. Still, if things were to go as he hoped, she had to see how difficult his job could be.

When he walked back to the table, she looked up and her smile faded. "Nick, what's the matter?"

"We think we've found Hannah's parents."

"Oh." Her shoulders slumped.

"Her mother is the girl who tried to commit suicide and the man we think is the father is in jail for writing hot checks."

"Will Hannah be returned to someone like that?"

"They aren't the best parents, but I've seen the courts give children back to worse."

"What do we do?"

"Wait until we have DNA evidence to prove who they are. If the mother is up to a visit, I'd like to try and interview her again. She wouldn't talk to me last time. You've had a lot of experience with girls this age. Would you like to give it a try?"

"Sure. Have you got time to finish your breakfast? Your eggs are getting cold."

He sat down but had taken only two bites before Miriam's cell phone began ringing. She flipped it open but didn't immediately answer.

"Who is it?" he asked.

She looked at him with a new fear in her eyes. "It's the Hope Springs medical clinic."

Chapter 13

Miriam answered the phone. Dr. White's craggy voice boomed in her ear. "I won't keep you in suspense. Hannah's tests have come back negative."

"Negative?" Miriam could barely breathe the word as relief flooded her.

"All negative. She shows no signs of maple syrup urine disease. It was a simple lab error. It seems her report was mixed up with another baby with the same last name."

Miriam turned to Nick. "Hannah is fine. Her tests came back okay. She isn't sick."

Nick closed his eyes. "Thank you, God."

Miriam smiled through tears of joy. "You have no idea how much we needed some good news this morning, Dr. White. Thank you."

"My pleasure." He hung up before she could tell him that Hannah was no longer in her care.

Knowing that social services would take care of those details, Miriam put her cell phone back in her purse. "If you're finished, we should get back to the hospital. Let me wash these dishes and we can go."

"What are the odds that I'll get a second date if I make you wash dishes?"

"Slim, since I wouldn't call this a first date," she teased.

Some of the tension returned to his shoulders. "What would you call it?"

"I'd call it an interrupted meal."

He shrugged. "That is the lot of a county sheriff. I've had more interrupted meals than I can count."

"What you need to do is learn how to take your food with you." She took two pieces of bacon and rolled them in a piece of bread.

She handed the concoction to Nick, took his keys from where he'd set them on the counter and headed for the door. "I'll drive while you finish eating."

"Yes, boss." He gave her a quick salute.

Once he was in the truck, he ate and lapsed into silence. She glanced at him several times on the way to the hospital, but he simply stared out the window. He was deeply concerned by the thought of Hannah having such troubled parents.

She said, "Thanks for breakfast."

"Egg peppered with good and bad news. It could have been better."

"I'm a big girl, Nick. I understand that sometimes the job has to come first. It's the same in my profession."

He smiled a real smile. "I appreciate that. Let's check on how your mother is doing."

When they got back to her mother's room, they found her mother's doctor making his rounds. Miriam was glad she hadn't missed him. At least one good thing had come out of her rapid exit from Nick's place.

The doctor spent a few minutes going over Ada's X-rays and lab reports. Although he was generally pleased with her progress, he felt it was necessary to keep her a few more days. Ada disagreed, but he had an ally in Miriam.

She was concerned about her mother's poor blood pressure control. She didn't want her mother going home only to have to turn around and come back again. Or worse.

When the doctor left the room, Ada said, "I don't know why you had to agree with him. This is costing too much money."

Miriam knew her mother's church would help cover the costs of her medical care. "Don't worry about that. Concentrate on getting better."

"I'm better enough," Ada grumped, but she couldn't hold back a yawn.

Nick pushed the bed control to lower it. "A little nap will do wonders for you. Miriam and I have some errands to run, but we'll be back soon."

Once the bed was down, Ada pulled the covers up to her chin. "Seeing Hannah would do wonders for me."

Miriam tucked the covers around her mother's shoulders. "I know. It would do wonders for us, too."

Ada said, "I miss her. I pray the Lord finds a loving home for her."

"So do I," Miriam replied with a deep ache in her

heart as she met Nick's gaze. She didn't know how she would bear it if it turned out otherwise.

Nick had no trouble getting the court order he needed. Since both Hannah and Mary Smith already had blood in the hospital laboratory, the process of obtaining a DNA match was simplified to some degree, but it would still take at least forty-eight hours before he would know if they were mother and child.

Kevin Dunbar refused to allow a DNA swab, claiming he wasn't the father and he didn't want to be forced to pay child support for a kid who wasn't his. By noon, he made bail. As he jogged down the steps on his way out of the building, Nick stood with Miriam at the door to his offices. "I doubt he will stay in town long enough to visit Mary. He has the look of a man who is going to skip out on his bail."

"How can you tell?"

Nick gave her a wry grin. "I've seen enough small-time crooks to know how they behave."

He needed to concentrate on this case, but all he could think about was how natural it had seemed to fix breakfast for Miriam and how good it had been to see her smiling at him from across his table.

He wanted to see her again. Not just at his table, but in every aspect of his life. He'd fallen head over heels in love with her and he still had no idea how she felt about him.

"Excuse me, Sheriff."

Nick looked over his shoulder to see his secretary standing in the doorway. "Do you need something?"

"Just to deliver this file from Child Protective Services."

"Thanks. I'll take it." He held out his hand.

She left the file with him. He walked into his office with Miriam and closed his door. He sat in his chair and stared at the folder in his hand.

"You're going to have to call Ms. Benson and tell her what you suspect," Miriam reminded him gently.

He smiled at her. Perhaps she would be able to get through to Mary Smith and get the young woman to open up about what had happened to her baby and why she'd tried to kill herself.

"If Hannah isn't Mary's child, then I have another missing infant somewhere in Sugarcreek."

The thought made his blood run cold. After nearly two weeks, he wouldn't be looking for a live child.

If Mary would just admit she'd left the baby in the Beachys' buggy it would save him a lot of time and effort. He picked up the phone to call her doctor. He needed to know when he could interview the girl again.

When he had her psychiatrist on the line, he asked, "Has Mary Smith started talking to anyone?"

"No. I have her on a strong antidepressant medication, but it takes a while for it to build up in the body. It may be several days before we see improvement. All she has done is to ask for pain meds. Other than that, she hasn't said anything."

"I have some information you may find useful. We have a baby that was found abandoned around the same time that Kevin Dunbar says Mary's baby was stillborn. A neighbor reports hearing a baby crying at the Smith address a few hours before the abandoned infant was found. It's possible Mary got rid of her baby by placing it in an Amish buggy at a nearby parking lot."

"I see. That is disturbing news. This may be a case

of postpartum psychosis rather than depression. Mary may not even realize what happened to her child. Thank you for the information."

"I'd like to question her again and mention what I just told you. I'd like to see what kind of response I get."

"I don't think that's a good idea at this point, Sheriff. I have to be careful. She is very fragile. I don't want her to regress into a more serious state of mind."

"This is a police investigation into a missing child, Doctor. I hope you understand the seriousness of it."

"I do, but I have to keep the best interest of my clients in mind when making these kind of decisions. Until I think she is strong enough, I won't allow you to question her."

"I can get a court order to interview her."

"Fine. When you have one in hand, I'll comply with it. Until then, good day, Sheriff."

The line went dead in Nick's hand. He hung up in frustration.

"Well?" Miriam asked.

"He says I can't see her."

"Can you get a court order to do so?"

"I doubt it. I don't believe any of the local judges would go against the recommendation of a patient's doctor."

"So what now?"

"We're back to waiting." It was something he didn't do well.

Miriam convinced Nick to run her home so that she could collect a few of her mother's things and get her own car. She knew he was frustrated and impatient with waiting.

Bella was delighted to see them and practically knocked her down with affection. There was still food in Bella's dish and water in her bowl, so Miriam knew the dog hadn't suffered anything but loneliness while they'd been gone. Nick took care of the outside chores while Miriam took a shower and changed into fresh clothes.

When she came downstairs, she found Nick staring into Hannah's empty cradle. There was so much sadness in his eyes that she went into his arms without thinking. She whispered, "I miss her, too."

He sniffed and wiped at his eyes. "I should put this back in the attic."

"Not yet. Leave it down here a little longer."

"All right. What's next?"

"I'm not sure how long mother will be in the hospital. I want to let Bishop Zook know so that he can arrange for people to come and take care of the animals."

"I could take Bella back to my place," he offered.

"That would be great."

Bella jumped into Nick's backseat, happy to be going for a ride. Miriam waved goodbye as Nick headed back to work. The moment he was out of sight she began to miss him. When had he become the person she depended on? Perhaps he had always been that person, she just couldn't see it until now. Within a few minutes she was pulling into the Zook farm.

The bishop was working on his corn planter, hammering a bent blade back into shape. He looked up, wiped the sweat from his brow with the back of his sleeve and came to speak to her.

"Good day, Miriam Kauffman, what brings you here on this fine afternoon?"

"I came to let you know that my mother is in the hospital in Millersburg. She had another heart attack."

"We shall pray for her recovery and ask for God's mercy."

"Thank you, Bishop Zook."

"Do not be concerned about the farm," the bishop added. "It will be taken care of until you and your mother return."

Miriam smiled with gratitude. An Amish person never had to worry about what would happen if they were unable to continue their farm work or provide for their family. The entire community would pitch in at a moment's notice to see that everything was taken care of.

No one went hungry. No one was left alone. The Amish took care of each other. When her mother came home, there would be fresh chopped firewood, kindling in the stove and a table full of things to eat.

As she headed back toward the hospital, Miriam couldn't help thinking about Nick. Before their relationship went any further, she needed to tell him about the day Mark died. There might not be a relationship after her confession.

Nick had shouldered the blame alone for years when she could have eased his guilt by admitting her part. Would he forgive her when he learned the part she had played? She prayed that he would. She no longer blamed him for the accident that took her brother's life. Nick needed to hear her say that. She needed to tell him.

Back at the hospital, Miriam found her mother was once again having chest pain with a spike in her blood pressure. This time it was so high that Miriam feared she would have a stroke. When the staff was finally able to bring it under control, Miriam took a seat near the window.

"Miriam?" Her mother raised a hand as if seeking her.

"I'm here." Miriam moved her chair to the bedside and took her mother's hand between her own.

"We should go visit your brother."

Gently, Miriam said, "Mark is gone. We can't visit him."

"I meant visit his grave. I want to plant new flowers there. You can do that for me, can't you?" Ada drifted back to sleep saving Miriam from having to answer. She hadn't been back to Mark's grave since his funeral.

Ada slept through most of the day. Miriam catnapped in the chair, watched some senseless afternoon talk show on TV and waited for Nick to call. When he finally did, she couldn't stop the happy leap of her heart. "Hi, there. I was beginning to think you didn't want to talk to me."

"I'm sorry. I've been busy. Hopefully, things will be wrapped up soon and I can get back to the hospital. Maybe we could try for dinner together?"

"I'd like that," she answered, amazed at just how much she wanted to spend time alone with him.

"How's your mother?"

"She had a bad spell right after I got back. She was talking about going to see Mark's grave. It has me worried."

"She's always been such a strong woman. I'm sure she'll be fine." His assurance rang hollow. He was worried, too.

"How's Bella?"

"She's hiding out under my desk after stealing my secretary's lunch."

"My poor baby. This has been rough on her."

"You couldn't tell it by looking at her. She's eyeing my cheese-covered pretzel as we speak."

Miriam chuckled. "Call me later. There are things I need to say to you."

"Can't you tell me now?"

"No, not on the phone. When I see you in person."

"Now you have me worried."

"Don't be. I have a feeling that you may already know what I have to say."

Throughout the day, Miriam divided her time between caring for her mother and waiting to spend a few stolen minutes with Nick. His promise of dinner turned into a late-night burrito that he carried into her mother's room in a greasy, brown paper bag long after visiting hours. It was the best burrito Miriam had ever eaten. Unfortunately, he couldn't stay.

The next evening she had a short, to the point meeting with Hannah's social worker. Mostly, the woman wanted to know about Hannah's schedule, her feeding issues and any type of history Miriam could provide. It wasn't much, but it felt good to be doing something that might help Hannah.

The woman was leaving when Nick showed up. They spoke briefly, but the woman again said she couldn't share any information about Hannah.

Miriam turned to Nick after she was gone. "Come on. I need a lookout."

He followed her into the hall. "What are we doing?"

"We are taking matters into our own hands. I want to know how Hannah is doing."

Miriam entered the elevator and pushed the button for the maternity floor. They walked down the halls listening to the sound of infants crying. None of them were Hannah. Miriam was sure she'd recognize her cry. She stopped beside the viewing window that looked into the special care section of the nursery and tried to get a glimpse of Hannah.

There was only one baby in the nursery. It had to be Hannah. Nick would have been notified if she had been dismissed.

Miriam tapped on the window and then noticed a sign that said to go to the door and not to knock on the window. The young nurse inside looked over and smiled. She gestured toward the door.

Miriam looked at Nick. "Keep an eye out for anyone who might know me."

"Is this illegal?"

"Can I take the Fifth on that?"

"No." He scowled at her.

"Then it isn't illegal." She waited as the nurse opened the door.

The young nurse asked, "Are you a relative?"

Miriam smiled. "No, I'm a critical care nurse and I'd love to tour your unit. I've often thought about working in pediatrics."

It was the truth. She had considered changing fields more than once.

"Actually, there is an opening on the night shift, but it's only part-time. This really is a great place to work. You should consider taking the job. Our charge nurse has stepped out, but she'll be back in about ten minutes. She knows more about what goes on here. I've only worked here a few months."

Miriam smiled at Nick and walked inside. "You don't have a very high census. I only see one baby, is that right?"

"Normally we run between three and five occupied beds, but right now all we have is a baby that is a police hold."

"I thought only sick babies were admitted here."

"The child was in to rule out MSUD but that came back negative. The baby has been spitting up a lot. She didn't seem to care for our regular soy formula."

"Have you tried holding her upright and rocking her for thirty minutes after her feedings instead of laying her down afterward? I once knew a baby with spit-up problems and that worked wonders."

"Funny you should say that. The social worker on the case came in a few minutes ago with the same suggestion."

Miriam stepped forward enough to see Hannah was sleeping quietly. Her color was pink and she looked perfect. "Can I sneak a peek at her?"

"I'm afraid not. Hospital policy and all that."

Miriam took a step back. "Sure. Thanks for letting me look around your unit."

Miriam turned to leave. The young nurse quickly asked, "Don't you want to talk to the charge nurse?"

Miriam shook her head. "I need a full-time job, but I'm sure you'll find someone who likes to work with babies."

She went out the door, gestured to Nick to follow her. He said, "If you want to take up police work, I can get you a recommendation."

"No, I'm happy being a nurse. We should get back to Mother."

"I'm going to stop and check on Mary Smith. I want to find out if I can talk to her soon. I'll catch you later." To Miriam's delight, he pressed a kiss on her lips. The thrill was over all too quickly when he pulled away. She longed for more.

She took the elevator back to her mother's floor. When she walked into her mother's room, she found Ada trying to get out of bed. Miriam rushed to help her.

"Mom, you should call for help before you get up."

"I called and I called, but no one came."

"I'm sorry, I went to see Hannah for a few minutes."

Her mother gave her a puzzled look. "Who is Hannah?"

"The baby that was left on our doorstep."

"Mark's baby?"

Miriam's heart sank to her feet. How had her mother learned about Mark's child? "No, Mother, it wasn't Mark's child. His baby was never born. His *Englisch* mother didn't want him."

Ada sighed heavily. "Have you been to plant flowers on Mark's grave? I wish you would. I can't go home until that is done."

Before Miriam could reply, her mother's eyes rolled back in her head and she collapsed into Miriam's arms.

Yelling for help, Miriam lowered her mother to the floor. A quick check of her pulse showed she was still alive. Relief flooded Miriam, but it was quickly thrust aside as the room filled with people. Miriam repeated what had happened to five different people including the nurses, a new resident and finally her mother's doctor.

He reviewed Ada's chart and listened to her heart for

a long while before he turned to Miriam. "Her blood pressure is too low at the moment. I believe that's what caused her to faint. We're having so much trouble getting this medication regulated that I'm going to try her on something else. I know this is frustrating for you."

"*Scary* is the word I would use." Low blood pressure meant a sluggish flow of blood through the brain. That would account for her mother's confusion. Still, her mother's words haunted her. "I can't go home until that is done."

Had she meant home as in the farm, or home as in her heavenly home?

The thought chilled Miriam. It was time, long past time, for her to face her mistakes and admit them.

She left word with the nursing staff to call her if her mother's condition changed. In the hospital parking lot, she got in her car and headed toward the other side of town. It wasn't long before she was in the country she recognized from her childhood.

The highway wound through low hills and past pristine farms. Everywhere, signs of spring were turning the landscape green. In the pastures, tiny black-and-white calves frolicked together while their mothers grazed nearby.

After ten minutes, she reached the fork in the road that led to a small Amish cemetery.

She pulled her car to a stop beside the white-board fence that surrounded the property. For a long time she sat in the car not moving. It was the first time she had been back to visit Mark's grave since his funeral.

Opening the car door, she stepped out into the bright sunshine. The smell of new grass brought back memories from her childhood. With barely a thought, she kicked off her sneakers and stepped barefoot into a thick, cool green carpet.

Like all Amish children, she had spent her childhood barefoot. Not until frost hardened the ground each fall had she and Mark put on shoes. It felt right to visit him barefoot.

She made her way between the rows of nearly identical white headstones to his gravesite. When she came upon his name, tears welled up without warning as emotion choked her throat. With a moan, she sank to her knees and covered her face with her hands.

"I'm so sorry," she wailed as she rocked back and forth with grief. "I'd change it all if I could. I'm so sorry."

She had no idea how long she knelt there, but finally her sobs subsided. Weak and spent, she put her hand on the face of his marker. Would he forgive her? As she gazed at the stone, she brushed aside a small bit of moss growing on the edge of the stone. The clump fell to the grass and exposed something glittery. Reaching down, she picked up a silver star made of foil.

Instantly she knew where she had seen one before. Nick made one every time he put a piece of gum in his mouth.

Chapter 14

Miriam spread the thick grass aside and saw more silver stars. Dozens of them lay around Mark's tombstone. Some were bright and new, others were old and dull, still others were mere flakes, having disintegrated from their time out in the elements.

"I started leaving them when I made sheriff."

Startled, she twisted around to see Nick standing behind her. She hadn't heard him approach.

Stepping forward, he laid a new star on the headstone. The breeze quickly blew it into the grass. "I put one out every time I come to visit."

Miriam rubbed at her tearstained face. "You've been here a lot."

"I have." He thrust his hands into the front pockets of his jeans. His shoulders were rolled forward as if he was expecting a blow across his back.

Was he waiting for her to say something? What words could convey the depth of what she was feeling? She looked up at his face. His hat cast a shadow across his eyes.

So much heartache. So much pain. Where is it all to end, Lord?

She knew the answer. It had to end with her. It was time for her confession. It was time to start healing. It might not happen today, or even tomorrow, but unless she spoke now, true healing would never happen for her.

"I'm glad you've come to his grave. I never could." She placed the star she held in her hand on her brother's stone. The wind died away and the star remained in place.

Nick squatted on his heels beside her. "Why haven't you come, Miriam? You were closer to him than anyone."

Sighing, she gripped her hands together until they ached.

Now or never. It was now or never.

"Because it was my foolish jealousy that led to his death and to the death of his child."

Nick's hand closed over her arm in a viselike grip. "What do you mean? What child?"

She looked into Nick's eyes. "Did you know he was in love with an *Englisch* girl?"

"No."

"All my life I thought I knew what I wanted, Nick. I wanted to grow old as a member of the Amish community. I thought Mark wanted the same thing. From the time we were little we talked about the day we would be baptized into the faith. That all changed the day *she* came into his life."

"Who was she?" Nick asked. He eased his grip on her arm but didn't take his hand away.

"A girl who lived in Millersburg. Her name was Natalie Perry. I don't know how they met—he never told me that. He stopped telling me almost everything after they began going out. What he did talk about was leaving the faith."

"Miriam, it's not unusual for young Amish men and women to have their doubts."

She shook her head. "You don't understand, Nick. I don't think he had any doubts at all. I was so mad at them, both of them, for disrupting our lives."

"That's understandable."

She shrugged off his hand and rose to her feet. "Maybe, but what happened that last day was inexcusable."

Walking to the fence, she braced her hands on the white-painted boards, feeling the roughness of the planks against her skin. She couldn't face Nick or her brother's memory.

"I've already said I'm sorry a hundred times, Miriam. How many more ways can I say it?" The anguish in his broken voice made her turn around. He stared at her with regret and pain etched in every feature.

Closing her eyes, she blocked the vision of yet one more life she'd damaged. "I wasn't talking about you, Nick. I was talking about what I did that forced Mark to steal a car and drive to his death."

Nick wasn't sure that he had heard Miriam correctly. "I don't understand. Are you saying that it wasn't a joy ride?"

She shook her head. "He was desperately trying to save his child's life."

"You keep talking about a child. What child?"

"Mark's unborn child. I promise you that I wouldn't have interfered if I had known about the baby."

He wanted to grab her and shake the truth out of her. All these years, he'd wrestled with the reason for Mark's behavior. It had never made sense. His death had been so meaningless. Nick forced himself to remain calm. "Tell me what happened."

"I know now that he must've loved her deeply, but he loved our family, too. I argued with him over and over that it was a mistake to go out into the world with her. I threatened to tell our parents and the bishop about them if he continued seeing her. Mark knew our family would be shunned if he ran off. I made him see he would break our parents' hearts—my heart, too. I convinced him it was God's will that he stay away from her."

Nick had been close to the Kauffman twins when they were all teenagers, but he had stayed away when he realized his feelings for Miriam went beyond friendship. Maybe, if he had hidden his own feelings better, Mark might have confided in him.

"Mark didn't see her for several weeks. The day before he died, she came to the farm. Mark had gone to visit some family with our parents. I could see Natalie was distraught, but I didn't have any sympathy for her. She had come close to destroying our family."

Miriam folded her arms across her chest and shivered. "Natalie told me her family was leaving the next day. She scrawled a note for Mark and thrust it into my hands. She begged me to give it to him as soon as possible."

"And did you?"

Tears ran unchecked down Miriam's face. "If only I had."

"Do you know what was in the note?"

"I gave it to him the next evening after supper. His face turned white when he read it. The look in his eyes frightened me to death. He dropped the note and ran out of the house. That was the last time I saw him alive."

"You said he dropped the note. You read it, didn't you, Miriam? Tell me what it said."

"It said she had just found out that she was pregnant and she didn't want the baby. I think her exact words were, 'I can't go through this alone. If you love me, come for me. I'll be waiting at the train station until nine o'clock. If you don't come, I will know you have made your decision, and I will have made mine. I'm not going to have this baby without you.'"

Miriam covered her face with her hands. "She was going to get rid of Mark's baby. That's why he stole our neighbor's car and wouldn't stop when you came after him. He was desperate to reach Natalie before she left town. The terrible accident was all because of me."

Miriam pressed a hand to her mouth and moaned. Her legs folded and she sank toward the ground. Nick caught her and held her against his chest as she cried.

Nick led Miriam to a small bench beside the caretaker's shed and sat beside her, holding her close as he'd always dreamed of doing. When her crying slowed, he lifted her tear-streaked face with a finger beneath her chin.

"Miriam, you can't keep blaming yourself for a mistake, no matter how serious you believe it is. We are human. We all make mistakes. Some of those mistakes have terrible consequences, but you have to forgive yourself. I know you thought you were protecting your brother."

She nodded. "I stopped seeing you because of my faith. I thought Mark should be able to do the same. I was jealous that his love for her was stronger than mine for you."

Nick pulled her close again. "I believe that Mark forgave you. He had to know you'd never willingly harm him or anyone. He was your brother. He loved you."

"I believe he has forgiven me, too. But can you forgive me? I let you carry the blame when I was the cause of it all. I'm so sorry for the harsh things I said and for the way I treated you."

"Of course I forgive you. Now that I understand Mark's motives for trying to outrun me it all makes sense. I respect what he was trying to do."

She cupped his face with her hand. "I'm glad I have given you some peace."

He turned his face to kiss the palm of her hand. "You have given me much more than peace. You've given me back one of the best friends I ever had. You."

And now he was going to give back pain. Taking her hand, he held it between his palms. "Miriam, I have something I need to tell you. We got the DNA report back. I know who Hannah's mother is."

Her eyes widened. "Are you sure?"

"Yes, her mother is the young woman who tried to commit suicide. Her name is Mary Smith, but we think it's not her real name. The father has skipped town, but we're looking for him. There's a good possibility that he never knew Mary gave the baby away."

"But why would she do it?"

"The doctor feels she may be suffering from a case of postpartum psychosis. If so, she wasn't responsible for what she did. She may not even be aware of what she did. With treatment, she can recover and be a good mother."

Miriam's eyes softened. "I know that you love Hannah, too. I can only imagine how hard this must be for you."

"I appreciate that you understand. We can hope and pray for her, but little else."

"Life is so unfair."

"Amen to that."

She drew back a little. "How did you know where to find me?"

"I stopped by the hospital and your mother told me you'd come here."

"Mother told you? I never told her I was coming here."

"Then she made a good guess. Or maybe she knows you better than you think."

Worry creased Miriam's brows. "I need to tell her about Mark and his baby."

"It can wait until she is stronger."

"I guess you're right about that. Now that I've told you, it's as if the weight of the world has been taken off my shoulders." Her smile was bright and genuine.

"I'm glad." He wanted to know where he stood in her life now, but he sensed it wasn't the time for such questions. It was a time for healing. What Miriam needed was a supportive friend and he could be that.

He asked, "Are you okay to drive back to town?"

"I am. I don't want Mother to start worrying."

"She seemed fine when I was there. She was eating a piece of peanut butter toast."

"Are you kidding me? She passed out cold this morning and scared me out of three years of my life."

"Like I said, she's a strong woman. You are, too, by the way. I hope you know that." He loved her strength and so much more about her. He prayed he'd have the chance to tell her exactly how he felt one day soon.

Miriam stared into Nick's eyes. She read more than friendship in their blue depths, but was she fooling herself?

He rose to his feet and offered her a hand up. She took it, cherishing the warmth that flowed from his hand to hers. He was a very special man, and she was going to do her level best to make up for the pain she'd caused.

He held her hand a moment longer than he needed to. "I'll let you know if I find out anything else about Hannah's father."

"It's an open case? I thought you couldn't talk about those."

"You've been involved from the beginning. I'll make an exception for you."

"Thanks. I guess I should get back."

"I've got to leave. Why don't you stay a little longer and visit with your brother? I think you need that."

"I think you're right. I'll see you later."

"Count on it." He tipped his hat and walked away.

Miriam followed his suggestion and spent a little time sitting by Mark's grave, talking about her life and about Hannah. In a way, she felt connected to him again—something that had been missing for far too long in her life.

When she returned to the hospital, she found her

mother sitting up in a chair and professing to feel great. It was a relief to see the new medication was agreeing with her.

"*Mamm,* how did you know I went to visit Mark's grave?"

"I couldn't think of any place else you would go without telling me if you weren't with Nick. And you've been talking a lot about your brother, lately."

Miriam frowned. "You are the one who has been mentioning him."

"Have I? I don't recall. I think the medicine has made me *narrisch.*"

"You're not crazy, Mother. You've had some bad side effects, that's all."

"I wish I could go home. I'll get well much quicker there."

"If you do well on this new blood pressure medicine, I think you'll be home before you know it."

"How is Hannah? Have you heard anything about her?"

Miriam hesitated. Her mother looked so much better, but would the news of Hannah's situation cause a relapse? She chose to err on the side of caution. "Hannah is still here in the hospital and she is fine."

"I do miss that child. Who knew a person could fall in love with a baby so fast? I reckon Nick will have to carry the baby bed back up to the attic. At least it got used for a little while. Perhaps I should sell it."

"That's something we can talk about later. For now, you need your rest."

"You need some rest, too, child. You look all done in."

"It's been an emotional day. Even that recliner isn't going to keep me awake tonight."

Later that night, Miriam woke with a start in the darkness of her mother's room. She had been dreaming about Hannah. She sat up in the chair to check her mother. Ada was sleeping peacefully. The monitor displaying her vital signs showed they were all normal.

Miriam sat back and closed her eyes, but she couldn't get Hannah out of her mind. There was no use trying to sleep when seeing the baby was the only thing that would make her feel better.

Miriam softly closed her mother's door as she left the room. It was after 2:00 a.m. and the hospital corridors were quiet. She took the elevator down one floor and turned left toward the nursery. As she approached the viewing window, she saw a young woman wearing a hospital gown standing in front of the glass. Her hair hung in a long blond braid down her back. She was barefoot and barely looked old enough to be a mother.

When she noticed Miriam approaching, she turned away quickly. Something in her posture made Miriam take a closer look. This wasn't a new mother happily looking in the window at her baby. This was a girl hoping not to be noticed.

The girl glanced over her shoulder. When she saw Miriam was watching her, she began walking away.

Miriam followed her and called out, "Wait a minute."

The girl walked faster. Miriam was practically running by the time she caught up with her. Reaching out, Miriam grasped her arm. The girl jerked away with a hiss of pain. It was then Miriam noticed the bandages on each of her wrists.

"I'm so sorry. *Ist es vay?*" Miriam asked with deep concern. The words meant, does it hurt? She wanted to know if what she suspected was true.

Shaking her head, the girl whispered, "Only a little."

"So you are Amish. I thought so. You must be Mary Smith, although Smith is hardly an Amish name. Why don't you tell me your real one?"

The girl froze, a look of fear in her eyes. She was so young. Little more than a child herself.

"Don't be afraid. I'm Miriam Kauffman. I'm sorry if I hurt you."

Staring at the floor, Mary remained silent.

"I saw you looking in the nursery window. She's in there, you know."

Mary raised her face a fraction. "Who?"

"Hannah. She ended up on my doorstep. Of course, you couldn't know that."

"I don't know anyone named Hannah. I don't know what you're talking about." Mary began backing away. "I don't want to get in trouble. I have to go."

"I'm talking about your baby, Mary. I know you told your boyfriend your baby was stillborn and that's why people think you tried to commit suicide, but that's not true."

"It is true—she's better off without me." Mary's voice was little more than a harsh whisper.

"I understand if you wanted her to have a better life, but I don't understand why you thought those Miller boys would make good parents. Between the two of them, they don't have enough sense to come in out of the rain."

Mary remained silent, but she didn't move away. Miriam began to hope she was getting through to her. "The only bright thing the twins did was leave the baby on my porch. Luckily, we found her before she got too cold."

"She shouldn't have been cold. I wrapped her in a quilt."

Miriam smiled. "The workmanship is quite lovely. Did you make it?"

"I stole it." The girl looked ready to bolt.

"With good reason." Miriam laid a hand on her shoulder in an effort to comfort her. The girl shrugged it off.

"I have to get back." She turned away and started to open the stairwell door.

"Don't you want to see her?" Miriam asked. "She's just down the hall in the nursery."

Mary froze. After a long moment, she closed her eyes. "I don't want to see her."

"Because you know if you do, you'll never have the strength to leave her again."

Mary's chin quivered but she didn't speak.

Miriam tried once more to comfort her. She gently brushed a strand of hair behind Mary's ear. Mary flinched, but allowed the touch. "I feel the same way about her. I had no idea how quickly I could fall in love with that little girl. I had no intention of loving her, but she has a way of looking at you that goes straight to your heart."

Mary looked up with angry eyes to glare at Miriam. "What do you want?"

"A long time ago, there was another young woman who didn't want to face being pregnant alone. I stopped her baby's father from helping her. I was never able to tell them how sorry I was and ask their forgiveness. Helping you and Hannah may just make up for that mistake."

"You can't help me."

"Oh, but I can. I do it all the time. I help young Amish people just like you to go out into the world."

"I've been out in the world. It's a bad place."

"Yes, it can be. Are you hungry?" Miriam glanced at her watch.

Mary looked perplexed, as if she couldn't follow Miriam's reasoning. "A little."

"Good. I believe the cafeteria is open for another half hour."

"I'm not supposed to leave the floor where my room is."

"You already have. I say we eat before we're caught. Sometimes it's better to beg forgiveness than to ask permission. I also need to check on my mother before I go. She's a patient here, too."

"What's wrong with her?" Mary glanced back toward the nursery as Miriam led her away.

"She has heart trouble. Having to give up Hannah brought on an attack. She's better now."

"Why didn't they let you keep the baby?"

Miriam pushed the elevator button. "*Englisch* law is a funny thing. It is designed with the best interest of the child at heart. They think Hannah belongs with her mother."

"But I gave her away. Doesn't that prove I'm a bad mother?"

The doors opened and Miriam stepped inside. "I guess that would depend on why you left her in an Amish buggy."

Mary didn't say anything, but she did enter the elevator.

Miriam breathed a sigh of relief. One small step at a time.

When the doors opened on her mother's floor, Miriam led the way, giving Mary a chance to follow or leave as she chose. At her mother's room, she opened the door softly to peek inside. To her surprise, the lights were on and her mother was sitting up in bed with a black knit shawl around her shoulders and her hair done up beneath her crisp white *kapp*.

She smiled at Miriam. "Come in. I've been waiting for you to come back. Esther Zook hired Samson Carter to bring her for a visit while you were gone yesterday. She brought us a shoofly pie and I feel like having a piece. How about you?"

She leaned forward to see behind Miriam. "Would your friend like some?"

Chapter 15

Nick glanced from the tearstained face of the night nurse to the furious, red face of Dr. Palmer, the shrink in charge of Mary Smith, to the bulked-up security guard standing with his massive arms crossed. They were all trying to talk at once. Nick held up his hand to stop them. "You're saying she just walked out of this building and no one saw her leave?"

First he finds Hannah's mother and then he loses her again. This was starting out to be a bad day, and it was only four in the morning.

The nurse said quickly, "I can assure you, Sheriff, this has never happened before on our floor. The sitter staying with Mary Smith says she only nodded off for a few seconds. When she looked up, Mary was gone."

"She vanished from the entire hospital in seconds. I doubt that," Dr. Palmer grumbled.

"Either way, she's missing. What about Hannah?" Nick asked quickly.

The security officer said, "The nursery says she's fine. I called them first thing."

Relieved, Nick nodded. "I'll get an APB out on Mary Smith right away." He spoke into his radio and ordered the all points bulletin for a white female, approximately five foot tall with long blond hair, wearing a hospital gown when last seen.

There was little else he could do at the moment. He looked to Dr. Palmer. "Did you tell her that we have her baby?"

"I did."

"And what did she say?"

"Nothing. She still won't speak to me or to the staff."

"Any idea what would make her cut out? Was her boyfriend in to see her?"

The nurse shook her head. "No one has been to see her."

"That you know of," Dr. Palmer snipped.

Nick turned to the security officer. "Organize a search of the entire building, every broom closet and storage room. I want the security camera footage of the doors reviewed to see if she actually left."

"Will do." The burly man walked away, talking into his radio.

Nick said, "I'll be in the cardiac care unit if you need me." Miriam would want to know what had happened. She dealt with runaway teenagers all the time. Maybe she would have some insight that would be helpful in locating Mary Smith.

And maybe he just needed to see her again.

When he reached Ada's room, he paused outside the

door. He didn't want to wake her or frighten her. He eased the door open to see if he could catch Miriam's attention. Instead of a dark room, he saw all the lights were on and the sound of Amish chatter filled the air. He stepped inside.

Ada was propped up in bed and involved in telling a story. Mary Smith sat cross-legged at the end of Ada's bed, a bright smile on her face. Miriam sat in a chair beside her mother and a nurse's aide sat in the recliner with a piece of pie on a paper plate.

Mary Smith saw him first. Her eyes went wide with fright. Miriam, seeing her distress, turned around. She waved at him. "Hi, Nick. Care for some shoofly pie? We have one piece left, but I'm afraid it's a small one."

Miriam turned back to Mary. "Don't worry, he's one of the good guys."

"Flattering as it is to hear you admit that, Miriam, can I ask what's going on here? Do you know that I have every officer in the county on the lookout for Ms. Smith?"

"Don't be silly, Nick. How could we know that? We've been in here since two-thirty."

"Having a party?"

Mary slid off the bed and spoke to Miriam in Pennsylvania Dutch. Miriam shook her head. The nurse's aide finished her last bite of pie and said, "I've got to get going. Thanks for the pie. It was great."

She had a faint German accent and Nick took her to be another ex-Amish. He stepped aside so she could slip out the door with a sheepish look on her face. He flipped the switch on his radio and canceled the APB, then he took a seat in the recliner. "What have I missed?"

Miriam brought him a thin slice of pie and said,

"Mary Smith is really Mary Shetler, she's fifteen, not nineteen and Kevin isn't her husband or Hannah's father. Hannah's father is a married man in Canton. Hannah was working as a maid there and he seduced her. She ran away because she couldn't go back to her family. Her mother had passed away and her stepfather wasn't happy about having another mouth to feed. Mary hooked up with Kevin because he promised to take care of her, but he's into drugs and not a nice man. Mary thinks he's a drug runner. Each week he makes a trip to Canada."

Miriam paused to look over at Mary for confirmation. Mary nodded and fixed her gaze on her bare feet.

"That's a very interesting story. What I want to know is why Mary left her baby in the back of a buggy?"

Miriam scowled at him, but returned to her chair and waited for Mary to speak.

"Kevin wanted to sell the baby." Mary's voice trembled with fear.

"We told you he wasn't a nice man," Ada added. "That's all right, child. Tell your story."

Mary smiled at her and stood straighter. "He said we could get a lot of money for a baby like mine. I was scared he would go through with it and I wouldn't be able to stop him."

"He can't hurt either of you now," Ada assured her.

Mary nodded. "I took the baby and put her in the Amish buggy because I didn't want her to grow up in the *Englisch* world. I knew she would be safe with a good Amish family if I couldn't return. I left a note to tell them I'd be back for her. I needed time to get enough money to get away."

She fell silent and Nick said, "When they didn't re-turn with her the next week, what happened?"

"I... I tried to be strong, but I knew I'd never see her again. Not knowing where she was, if she was safe—I couldn't stand it."

"Did you slash your own wrists?" Miriam asked gently.

She nodded as tears ran down her cheeks.

Nick couldn't begin to understand what this girl had been through. He was only grateful that she had sur-vived. One thing was certain. He'd make it his business to see that Kevin was brought to justice. "Will you tes-tify to Kevin's intentions in a court of law? Can you give me the names of the people he was working with?"

Ada said, "We must forgive him. It is up to God to judge."

Miriam laid a hand on Mary's shoulder. "We do for-give, but we must also care for those who can't take care of themselves. Kevin may try to do this to another woman and her baby."

Mary looked at Nick and nodded. "I have names. I'll testify."

Miriam hugged her. "Now, you must grow strong because your baby is going to need you."

It took a long, hard week of police work, but Kevin Dunbar was finally behind bars in Nick's jail, and there wouldn't be any bail this time. It was with intense satis-faction that Nick closed and locked the cell door.

He returned to his office and started to pick up the phone. He hadn't seen Miriam since her mother was dismissed from the hospital the day after Mary Shetler told her story. It had been far too long as far as he was concerned.

His secretary came in. "Sheriff, I took a message from Helen Benson. She wanted you to know that Hannah has been returned to the temporary custody of her mother. Hannah's case will remain open and the mother has to continue with her counseling but Helen is hopeful that Mary Shetler will be granted full custody in the future."

"Thanks. That's good news." It was for Mary and Hannah, but not for Miriam and Ada. Instead of the phone, he picked up his car keys. He'd rather deliver this news and his other news in person.

It took him thirty minutes to reach the turnoff to the Kauffman place. When he did, he saw Bishop Zook coming down the lane in his black buggy. Nick pulled to the side of the lane and waited.

When the bishop drew alongside, Nick rolled down his window. "Afternoon, Bishop. I hope all is well at the Kauffman place."

"All is better than well, Nicolas, for a lost sheep has returned to the fold. I performed a baptism this day. There is nothing but rejoicing in our hearts when such an event is brought about by God's mercy. I can't remember the last time I saw Ada so happy. I must get going, Sheriff, for I have cows that need milking and I have good news to spread." He tipped his hat and slapped the reins on his horse's rump. The mare trotted away, leaving Nick staring after the bishop in shock.

Miriam had been baptized into the Amish faith? Perhaps he should have seen it coming, but he hadn't. Not now, not when he was so certain they had a chance to be together.

He drove slowly up to the house thinking of all the lost chances he'd had to tell her how much he loved her.

He spotted Miriam hanging laundry on the clothes-line beside the house. His heart turned over at the sight of her the way it always did and probably always would. He'd gained her forgiveness and opened the door for her to return to her Amish roots. He wanted to be happy for her, but he wasn't ready for that. The pain of loving her and losing her all over again was too new and two raw.

She waved when she spotted him and walked toward him with a laundry hamper balanced against one hip. She wore a dark blue dress with the long sleeves rolled up and an apron tied around her waist. A white kerchief covered her gorgeous hair. Her smile was bright and open, the way he remembered it when she was young. It was good to see her happy.

One of them deserved to be happy.

He got out of the car and waited with his hands thrust into the front pockets of his jeans.

"Nick, I was hoping to see you. I have so much to tell you that I hardly know where to begin." She stopped a few feet away. When he didn't respond, her smile faded, as if she was uncertain of her welcome.

He couldn't wish her happy when she was breaking his heart.

"I just stopped in to say goodbye and see how your mother is doing."

She frowned slightly. "What do you mean you stopped in to say goodbye?"

"There are some trout waiting patiently for me to toss my hand-tied flies close enough to bite." Maybe wading in the swirling waters might help him forget the way she felt in his arms. The way he wanted to kiss her, even now, when he knew it was wrong.

Relief filled her eyes. "I forgot, you have a vacation pending. You deserve some time off after all you have done for us."

"How is your mother?"

"The stent has helped enormously with her energy level and her new medication is working. She is happy as a lark and bossing everyone around again."

"I'm glad." He braced himself to say what he didn't want to say. "I'm glad, too, that you have found your heart's desire, Miriam. It means a lot to me to know that you are happy and at peace. I wish only the best for you."

"You sound so serious. Is something wrong?" Worry crept into her eyes once more.

Didn't she know how he felt? "Did you think this would be easy for me? I wish you had told me yourself instead of letting me hear it from the Bishop Zook."

"I thought you would be happy with my decision."

He took a deep breath and tried to disguise the hurt in his voice. "I will try to be happy for you, Miriam. Goodbye."

He turned back and started to open the car door. She dropped her laundry basket and stopped him by grabbing his wrist.

"Okay, I really didn't expect you would jump for joy, but I thought you'd be a little more enthusiastic. Tell me why you're unhappy about this?"

The warmth of her hand on his bare skin crumbled his defenses. "Do you really need to ask that?"

She stepped closer. "Apparently I do. Talk to me, Nick."

He closed his eyes. "I have loved you since I was

twenty years old. I have never stopped loving you. I kept silent back then because I knew how much your faith meant to you. I could not ask you to choose me over your relationship with God. After Mark's death, it was almost a relief to realize how much you hated me. It made it easier to stay away from you. I'm glad you have returned to the Amish life, Miriam, but it will never be easy for me to stay away from you."

He felt her hands cup his face. Years of pent-up longing broke free and tears squeezed out from beneath his lashes. "I love you so much, Miriam."

"And I love you, Nicolas Bradley. I don't know where you got the idea that I have returned to my Amish roots, but you are grossly mistaken. I have no plans to leave my *Englisch* life."

His eyes popped open and he focused on her face so close to his. "Bishop Zook said everyone, particularly your mother, is rejoicing because the lost lamb has been returned to the fold. I thought he was talking about you."

"He was not talking about me. He was talking about Mary Shetler. She is the one who has returned to the fold. Yes, my mother is happy because she has a new daughter and a new granddaughter to help rear. That's the news I wanted to tell you. Mary and Hannah have moved in with me and my mother."

Unable to contain his joy, Nick pulled Miriam against his chest in a crushing hug. "Oh, thank you, God, for taking pity on this man. Thank you, God."

Miriam pulled her arms free of his grip and then slipped them around his neck. "I thank God daily for bringing you back into my life. I have been so blessed."

Rising up on tiptoe, she kissed him as he had dreamed she would one day.

When she drew away, he saw love glowing in her eyes and his heart expanded until he thought it would break, not with sorrow, but with joy.

She smiled at him and he knew he would never tire of seeing that smile. "Nick, I have cared deeply for you since I was a teenager, but I never realized that I loved you until the day I found you rocking and singing to Hannah on the front porch."

He still couldn't believe he was holding her in his arms. "I love you. I don't care when you fell in love with me, only that you did."

"I didn't think I deserved to find love. Now I know God wants all his children to love and be loved in return. So maybe what I need is a little more practice at loving you." She lifted her face inviting his kiss. He was all too happy to comply.

As his lips closed over hers, the world narrowed to the softness of her skin and the taste of her lips, the way they fit his perfectly. His pulse hammered in his ears. He never wanted to lose her again.

When she finally broke away, he pulled her head forward and tucked it against his neck. "I think you're getting the hang of it."

Miriam smiled, breathing in the wonderful scent that was uniquely Nick's own. Resting in his arms, she was happier than she had ever been in her life. She loved him, and he loved her in return. God was indeed good.

She couldn't resist teasing Nick a little more. "You're lucky I'm something of a perfectionist. I'll keep trying until I get it right."

"Oh, you have it right, sweetheart. But if you want to keep practicing, I'm going to be available for the next seventy years."

She pulled back to look up at him. "Careful, Sheriff, that sounded surprisingly like a proposal."

He cleared his throat and held her at arm's length. "I've always believed that good communication is the key to any relationship. So let me be clear about this. Miriam Kauffman, will you do me the honor of becoming my wife?"

She stared at him in stunned surprise. "Nick, are you serious?"

"I've never been more serious in my life. We have wasted enough time."

"Two weeks ago I didn't even like you."

"If you've come this far in two weeks, I can only imagine how good things will be in two months or two years. I understand that this was rather sudden because, believe me, I didn't come here intending to propose. So if you want some time to think it over, I understand completely, but I couldn't stop myself from offering you my heart. I thought I'd lost you."

"Yes."

He eyed her intently. "Yes, you want some time to think it over? Or yes, you will marry me?"

"In an effort to improve the communication in our relationship, let me be perfectly clear. Yes, Nicolas Bradley, I will marry you."

"Are you sure?"

"Are you trying to make me change my mind?"

He pulled her close once more. "Not at all, darling. I just can't believe that I've attained my heart's desire."

She snuggled closer. "I'm good at helping people discover what it is that they really want."

He chuckled and she felt the sound reverberate in his chest beneath her ear. She would never grow tired of being held in his arms. He lifted her hand and placed a kiss on her palm. "When?"

"When what?" she asked with dreamy happiness.

"When can we get married?"

From behind Miriam, Mary said, "It looks like it had better be soon."

Miriam twisted in Nick's hold but she didn't move out of his embrace. "I think I would enjoy a long engagement. What do you think, Nick?" She gave him a saucy glance.

"I will wait for as long as it takes. As long as it doesn't take more than two months."

"Two months!" Ada had come out onto the porch with Hannah in her arms.

Nick said, "I can take her off your hands faster if you need me to, Ada."

"Bah, no one can get ready for a wedding in two months. We shall need at least six months."

"Is that what you want?" Nick whispered into her ear. His warm breath sent a chill of anticipation sweeping across her body.

"I want to stay here, wrapped in your arms for the rest of my life."

"My thoughts exactly." He pressed a kiss on her temple. It was nice, but she wanted more. She turned and raised her face. His lips found hers and she gave herself over to the magic of his touch.

Hannah began to fuss. Ada said, "Enough with the

kissy-kissy. The baby wants to be fed, and we have many plans to make. Come inside, everyone."

Nick stopped kissing Miriam long enough to say, "We'll be along in a little bit, Ada. Your daughter and I have a lot of lost time to make up for."

Mary laughed and shook her head. She took Hannah from Ada's arms. "Kids today, they never listen to their elders."

As she followed Ada back inside the house, Miriam gazed up at Nick. She would never grow tired of seeing the love shining in his eyes. "Before we get hitched, there is one thing you should know."

"Only one?"

"This is an important thing. I intend to adopt Mary. Both she and my mother are in favor of it. That way, if anything happens to my mother, or to me, Mary and Hannah will always have a place to live."

Nick raised one hand to rub his jaw. "You mean in addition to getting a bride, I'm also going to be getting a teenage daughter—with the baby."

"That's right, Grandpa."

He groaned. "Grandpa? I thought I'd have twenty-five or thirty years before I got stuck with that label."

"Well?"

"Well what?" he asked as he pulled her close and settled her against his hip.

"We come as a package deal. Take all of us or take none of us."

He kissed the tip of her nose. "You drive a hard bargain, Miriam Kauffman. I'll do it as long as you include Bella in the deal."

"Done." She smiled at him with all the love in her heart.

"What do you think Mark would say about this?" His question held an odd edge.

"I think Mark is glad. He loved both of us."

"How do you think your mother would feel about having an English grandchild?"

Miriam rolled her eyes. "You are getting a little ahead of yourself, Sheriff. You haven't walked down the aisle with me yet."

"I wasn't talking about us. I've been debating whether to tell you this or not, but I think I should. I did some digging, and I found Mark's girlfriend, Natalie Perry. She lives in St. Louis now, with her eight-year-old son."

Miriam blinked hard. Had she heard Nick right? "She kept Mark's baby?"

"Yes, she did."

"Nick, that is wonderful. Oh, my goodness, how I agonized over the thought that I was responsible for two deaths. I'm so glad."

"I knew you would be—that's why I came here today. I wanted to give you some good news, and to tell you Kevin Dunbar has been arrested. Will you tell your mother about Mark's child?"

"I have already told her about my part in Mark's death. I told her the reason he was on the road that night. She will be as thrilled as I am that Natalie kept the baby. Do you think there's any chance that we could meet her and see him? Do you know his name?"

"His name is Mark."

Tears welled up in her eyes as words failed her. Nick slipped a finger beneath her chin and tipped her face up. "Please, don't cry."

"They are happy tears, Nick. Come inside and give *Mamm* the news."

She started toward the door, but he caught her hand and pulled her back. "Not so fast. We have unfinished business."

She grinned at him. "What business would that be?"

"You haven't said *when* you will marry me. I'm not leaving this spot until I have an answer."

Miriam wrapped her arms around his neck. "In that case, we could be here all night."

"I'm in favor of that." He lowered his head. Miriam had a moment to thank God for His mercy and goodness before Nick's kiss made her forget everything but the wonder of his love.

* * * * *

We hope you enjoyed reading

Any Sunday

by *New York Times* bestselling author
DEBBIE MACOMBER
and

A Home for Hannah

by *USA TODAY* bestselling author
PATRICIA DAVIDS.

Both were originally Harlequin® series stories!

From passionate, suspenseful and dramatic
love stories to inspirational or historical,
Harlequin offers different lines to
satisfy every romance reader.

New books in each line are available every month.

LOVE INSPIRED
INSPIRATIONAL ROMANCE
Uplifting stories of faith, forgiveness and hope.

Harlequin.com

Get 4 FREE REWARDS!

We'll send you 2 FREE Books plus 2 FREE Mystery Gifts.

FREE Value Over $20

Both the **Romance** and **Suspense** collections feature compelling novels written by many of today's bestselling authors.

YES! Please send me 2 FREE novels from the Essential Romance or Essential Suspense Collection and my 2 FREE gifts (gifts are worth about $10 retail). After receiving them, if I don't wish to receive any more books, I can return the shipping statement marked "cancel." If I don't cancel, I will receive 4 brand-new novels every month and be billed just $7.24 each in the U.S. or $7.49 each in Canada. That's a savings of up to 28% off the cover price. It's quite a bargain! Shipping and handling is just 50¢ per book in the U.S. and $1.25 per book in Canada.* I understand that accepting the 2 free books and gifts places me under no obligation to buy anything. I can always return a shipment and cancel at any time. The free books and gifts are mine to keep no matter what I decide.

Choose one: ☐ **Essential Romance**
(194/394 MDN GQ6M)

☐ **Essential Suspense**
(191/391 MDN GQ6M)

Name (please print)

Address   Apt. #

City   State/Province   Zip/Postal Code

Email: Please check this box ☐ if you would like to receive newsletters and promotional emails from Harlequin Enterprises ULC and its affiliates. You can unsubscribe anytime.

Mail to the **Harlequin Reader Service:**
IN U.S.A.: P.O. Box 1341, Buffalo, NY 14240-8531
IN CANADA: P.O. Box 603, Fort Erie, Ontario L2A 5X3

Want to try 2 free books from another series? Call 1-800-873-8635 or visit www.ReaderService.com.

STRS22

Love Harlequin romance?

DISCOVER.

Be the first to find out about promotions, news and exclusive content!

Facebook.com/HarlequinBooks

Twitter.com/HarlequinBooks

Instagram.com/HarlequinBooks

Pinterest.com/HarlequinBooks

YouTube.com/HarlequinBooks

ReaderService.com

EXPLORE.

Sign up for the Harlequin e-newsletter and download a free book from any series at **TryHarlequin.com**

CONNECT.

Join our Harlequin community to share your thoughts and connect with other romance readers!
Facebook.com/groups/HarlequinConnection

HARLEQUIN

Heartfelt or thrilling, passionate or uplifting—Harlequin is more than just happily-ever-after.

With twelve different series to choose from and new books available every month, you are sure to find stories that will move you, uplift you, inspire and delight you.

SIGN UP FOR THE
HARLEQUIN NEWSLETTER
Be the first to hear about great new
reads and exciting offers!

Harlequin.com/newsletters